1305

MAY 03

DATE DUE

FEB 04 '06

DEC 07 '06

GAYLORD			PRINTED IN U.S.A.

LAKOTA DAWN

**Center Point
Large Print**

**This Large Print Book carries the
Seal of Approval of N.A.V.H.**

Lakota Dawn

Janelle Taylor

Center Point Publishing
Thorndike, Maine

Dedicated to:
Dawn Wren, who's like a sister to me;
and to three of my best friends and talented writers:
Bobbi Smith Walton, Constance "E.G." O'Banyon, and
Elaine Barbieri.

This Center Point Large Print edition
is published in the year 2003 by arrangement with
Kensington Publishing Corp.

Copyright © 1999 by Janelle Taylor.

All rights reserved.

The text of this Large Print edition is unabridged. In other
aspects, this book may vary from the original edition. Printed in
Thailand. Set in 16-point Times New Roman type by
Bill Coskrey and Gary Socquet.

ISBN 1-58547-261-1

Library of Congress Cataloging-in-Publication Data.

Taylor, Janelle.
 Lakota dawn / Janelle Taylor.--Center Point large print ed.
 p. cm.
 ISBN 1-58547-261-1 (lib. bdg. : alk. paper)
 1. Oglala Indians--Fiction. 2. Black Hills (S.D. and Wyo.)--Fiction.
 3. Large type books. I. Title.

PS3570.A934 L28 2003
813'.54--dc21

 2002073907

CHAPTER ONE

JULY, 1854

Chase Martin took a deep breath and slowly released it. He kept his rifle sheathed and his handgun holstered to indicate he was no threat to the approaching Red Shield warriors as he guided his horse from concealing trees. He was not surprised that the party's leader spotted him immediately and alerted his followers to a stranger's presence. Chase reined in and lifted his hands to signify he only wanted to parley with them. He wasn't afraid to die for a just cause, but his heart still pounded in suspense and blood sped through his veins in anticipation of what he would learn. He watched the warriors race forward and encircle him. He said to the young man who sat astride a mottled mount before him, "I've come to speak with Chief Rising Bear. Will you take me to his camp and tepee?"

As Chase saw the leader's keen gaze search the trees behind him, he added, "I've come alone to see your chief. This is no trick or challenge. Do you speak English and understand me?"

The warrior nodded, still on alert. "Why you seek my father?" he asked.

Chase eyed the speaker with great interest as he said, "My words are for the ears of Rising Bear alone. I come in peace, War Eagle."

"How you know my name, *wasicun?*"

Chase knew he appeared to be at least part Indian, even

if War Eagle had called him a white man, and in a near insulting tone. Considering the past and growing hostilities between the two races, he was lucky he hadn't been slain on sight. "At Fort Pierre, I was told Rising Bear has two sons: Wind Dancer and War Eagle. You are Rising Bear's second son?"

"It true. Why you ask men at trading post about my family? You Bluecoat come to scout our camp for attack?"

"No, War Eagle, I'm not a soldier or an enemy. I come from far away and had to ask questions at Pierre so I could find Rising Bear and his camp. You must take me to him, for the words within me are powerful medicine." *If they don't heal me, I don't know what will . . .*

"What big medicine words you bring to my father?"

"I must speak them to Rising Bear; only he can tell them to others if he so chooses." Chase observed as War Eagle scrutinized him intently and considered his bold request. He listened as the leader spoke with his hunting party, pleased that he understood the Oglala tongue he had not heard for many years.

War Eagle felt there was something oddly familiar about the intruder, but he could not determine what it might be. From somewhere deep within him, a voice—perhaps the Great Spirit's—advised him to take the evasive man to his father. "Give weapons to Swift Otter."

Without protest or delay, Chase surrendered his rifle, pistol, and knife to the warrior, who edged close to his mount and confiscated them.

"Come. I take you to my father. If you speak false words or seek to harm him, *wasicun,* you die by my hand before this sun sleeps."

"Trust me, War Eagle, for I speak the truth."

"I trust no white man, for truth does not live in their hearts or come from their mouths; they prove this on each rising sun. Come. We go."

Chase knew it was futile and a waste of valuable time to argue with War Eagle, so he remained silent. He rode behind the leader, with the other warriors positioned on either side of him and to his rear. *So far, so good,* he told himself.

They journeyed over the edge of the Great Plains where tight bunches and singular stalks of various grasses swayed in a constant wind, and traveled into foothills of fragrant pine and cedar and fully leafed hardwoods. Along the way, they encountered straggling buffaloes who were not members of the vast herds which spread across the rolling grassland like enormous dark blankets and unknowingly awaited the Indians' impending annual summer hunt. They also sighted small groups of antelope, several coyote, a few turkey, and many deer. Amidst flower-filled meadows with winding streams and creeks, they spooked grouse, other birds, and burrow-dwelling creatures. Beyond their current position were canyons and higher elevation of ebony or gray granite boulders, towering needles, spiky spires, and picturesque cliffs. Those rugged mountains with their jagged peaks and lofty pinnacles comprised the Black Hills, the sacred Paha Sapa.

From childhood recall and the maps he'd studied, Chase knew they were between Swift and Bear Gulch creeks, and north of a site called Cave Of The Winds, where powerful spirits allegedly dwelled. He realized he would soon reach the Red Shield camp to face Rising Bear and others. A multitude of contradictory feelings and thoughts filled him: tension and serenity, eagerness and dread, trust and doubt. The moment of truth would be at hand soon.

At long last, the village was in view. Numerous buffalo-hide tepees with lodgepoles jutting upward were situated on the relatively flat surface of a canyon floor, which was sheltered against the harsh winter forces by evergreen-tree-covered hills and large, dark rock formations. Most featured what he knew were colorful paintings of their warriors' skills and exploits. There was no circular pattern to the arrangement, as was the custom on the Great Plains for self-defense in the open. In the spaces between them, Chase saw racks with pelts and hides being dried and stretched for tanning. He saw campfires enclosed by rocks. Kettles were suspended above the fire from three-pronged stands over them and smoke and vapors rose from the simmering meals. Some horses were picketed near conical abodes, and others were grazing and drinking at the nearby river. Weapons were proudly displayed on trilegged stands as they soaked up the powers of the earth and sun. Women were busy with daily chores. Older children played on the camp fringe; younger ones and infants were tended near their homes by their grandparents or sisters. Men talked and worked on their tasks, mainly preparations for the impending annual buffalo hunt. It was all so familiar and yet alien to Chase. For a moment, he wondered if he had been wrong to come there, if he should have left the past dead and buried. Yet, even if he had made a grave mistake, it was too late to change his mind now.

Chase noted that many people halted their chores and headed toward them—whispering and pointing—as the riders entered the busy area and dismounted near their chief's tepee, their curious or narrowed gazes focused on him, a white man who arrived unbound. Several young boys took the horses away to be tended, including his own. He waited in silence as Wind Dancer and Rising Bear scrutinized him with keen dark eyes before looking quizzically at War Eagle for an explanation. The leader hurriedly related the news of Chase's "capture" and persistence in speaking with the chief.

Wind Dancer gave the man another quick study and had a strange feeling they had met before. He asked in English, which he had learned from his wife during the last few years, "Who are you and why do you come to see my father?"

So, like War Eagle, you don't recognize me, either. I guess the same is true for our father and everyone else here. "I want to speak with Rising Bear alone; my words are not for the ears of others unless he so chooses." Chase waited and listened as Wind Dancer translated those words into Lakota, and the older man responded to his eldest son.

"My father says you can speak your words before his family and people," Wind Dancer said. "But who are you? Why do you come to our camp?"

Chase had yearned to be remembered and for this initial meeting to take place in private. His hurt and displeasure sent forth a response in a near-surly tone as he frowned, "Does Mato Kikta not recognize the face and voice of Yutokeca Mahpiya, son of Rising Bear and Margaret Phillips, the white woman he called Omaste, Sunshine, for her golden hair? Is my father not happy I have found my way home after being stolen from him twelve summers

9

past? Has he forgotten his own flesh and blood?"

A shocked Wind Dancer glared at the scowling stranger and almost gritted out the angry charge, "You lie, *wasicun!* My brother is dead. You are foolish to come here and claim to be him. What evil trick is this?"

Chase leveled his gaze on the man whose height matched his own of six feet. "Do I look dead, Wind Dancer, my brother who is five winters older than I am? Do you not remember Cloud Chaser who followed in your shadow on most suns after he learned to walk? It isn't a trick or a lie. I have proof: the clothes and possessions I was wearing when I vanished long ago, they're in the saddlebag on my horse. In my medicine bundle is the feather you gave me from the first bird you killed with an arrow. Also there is the sacred red stone my father gave to me following my first vision and the golden lock of my mother's hair, and I wear the locket which holds her parents' image. If I'm not Cloud Chaser, how would I have and know such things?"

Wind Dancer eyed the stranger with astonishment. He and Cloud Chaser had been separated by evil forces when Wind Dancer was fifteen winters old and his half-brother was ten, and Cloud Chaser had been presumed dead or lost to them forever. Was this man speaking the truth? Was that what evoked such eerie feelings within him? If this was Cloud Chaser, he had changed from the almost black-haired and -eyed boy who had looked Indian to a man who appeared mostly *wasicun* with his medium brown eyes and hair with lighter streaks. His features were larger and different, but the passing of time could account for those changes. As a curious Rising Bear nudged his arm and questioned his reaction, Wind Dancer's muddled thoughts cleared. He translated the shocking words to his father, whose widened gaze jerked toward and stared at the stranger who oddly tugged at his emotions.

Two Feathers snarled in the Lakota tongue, "It is a trick! Cloud Chaser walks the Ghost Trail, not the face of Mother Earth! This man is a white man who has come to spy on us for our enemy! We must slay him where he stands. I will do the deed for our chief," he offered as he withdrew a weapon.

Wind Dancer told his irate first cousin in their language, "Hold your tongue and sheathe your knife, Two Feathers, and allow him to speak." In English, he asked, "Who are you, *wasicun*, and why do you come here?"

Chase ignored his hostile cousin as he avowed, "I told you such news should be revealed in private to my father. Our long-awaited reunion was not for the eyes and ears of others." When Rising Bear failed to smile, embrace, and welcome him home, disappointment and bitterness shot through Chase and provoked angry words, still in English. "Tell me, Father, would you have tried to find and recover me if I weren't half white or if I had been one of your other three children? Does it bring you shame and sadness to have me return and remind you of past dark days?"

Of necessity, Wind Dancer translated those words to their father.

"Do not speak such bad words and show such bad feelings to our chief or your tongue will be taken!" Two Feathers shouted in a threatening tone.

Chase disregarded his cousin, whose Lakota words he had understood. "If my father will not answer the questions which trouble my heart, then you tell me, my brother, how long and how hard did he search for me when I was stolen by the Whites? Why didn't he follow the cloud-covered wagons? They move slowly and he is a great warrior, so he could have easily overtaken them and rescued me. Was he glad to have me gone?"

"He and others searched many suns and moons, but Cloud Chaser could not be found," Wind Dancer rebuffed. "He followed the wagons but did not see him among the Whites, so it was foolish to attack them and call forth a war with the Bluecoats. He found Crow tracks near his last moccasin prints; he followed our enemy and recovered his pony, but all Crow were slain in that battle and there were no signs of him in their camp. He did not know where he was or what happened to him. If you are Cloud Chaser, why did you wait so long to return to us? Why do you return in this season?"

"I was wounded by the enemy," Chase began his explanation, "and thrown from my pony; my leg was broken. White settlers found me, tended me, and took me with them to a place far away called Oregon and named me Chase Martin. I was told my people were attacked and killed and that I must remain with them to recover and be safe. And I did not know the long path home. Before my white father died, he revealed the truth to me, but begged me to forgive him and to stay with the woman who raised me as her son to help her on the farm and to protect her. After her death, I returned here."

"Why did those who took you speak such lies?" Wind Dancer asked.

"Because they wanted a son badly and couldn't have children. They also believed I was a white captive being held and reared by the Indians. They said nobody came searching for me or claimed me, so they kept me."

After Wind Dancer translated those words for their father, Two Feathers snarled, "The Oglala blood he carried at birth has been slain by his many seasons with the Whites; he is more *wasicun* than Red Shield. He must be slain or sent away or he will cause much trouble for us."

Chase glared at his cousin and refuted, "The blood of Rising Bear lives strongest within me; that is why I have returned to him and the Oglalas."

"You speak our tongue?" Two Feathers asked in astonishment.

Chase replied again in Lakota, "I speak the tongue of my father and our people. I have forgotten little about my life here long ago." He realized he had to settle down or he would be sent riding before he gleaned the truth. "Give me time, Father, and I will earn your love, respect, and acceptance; but you must also earn mine and my forgiveness. I will—"

"You speak foolish and dangerous, half-breed!" Two Feathers shouted. "How do we know you are Cloud Chaser and not a *wasicun* who uses his thoughts and possessions to trick us?"

"I have not forgotten what I was taught as a child, but you have done so. You forget it is not the Oglala way to walk upon the words of another, son of my father's sister. Do you still hold a wicked grudge against me for the many times I beat you in foot races and in arrow practice? After so many years, do you still hate me and wish me dead?"

"Do you come to cause trouble and to shame our chief? Do you—"

"Be silent, Two Feathers, and let him speak what lives in

his heart and head," Wind Dancer interrupted his angry cousin. "Do you wish to speak in our tongue to my father or will I reveal your words to him?" he asked Chase.

"It has been a long time since the Lakota tongue has lived in my mouth, but I will speak it." He turned to the chief. "What of the Four Sacred Virtues, Father? You must show Courage and Generosity by allowing me to return and to prove myself. Where is the Wisdom in rejecting or slaying me? Where is your Fortitude, your strength of mind and body at this difficult and painful event? Are we not taught to be fiercely loyal to our family and people? I did not leave them by choice: I was stolen from both by the enemy. You did not refuse to take back your wife when she returned from our enemy's captivity, so why do you retreat from one who carries your blood and came from your man seeds? What Red Shield or Lakota law have I broken that says I must be banished? Give me until the first snow falls from the sky to prove I am more Lakota than White. If I fail to do so, you can slay me or order me to leave and I will obey; you have my word of honor as a man and as your son by blood."

Nahemana stepped forward. "Three summers past when we gathered near Fort Laramie for the Treaty of the Long Meadows," he said, "I had a dream and revealed it to Wind Dancer. The sacred dream said: 'The past is not wrapped in a blanket or buffalo hide and does not rest on a death scaffold. It hides in clouds and will be seen before many more seasons pass.' That message has come to be: Cloud Chaser is alive and has returned."

Chase remembered the shaman, father of Rising Bear's wife, and grandfather to Wind Dancer, War Eagle, and Hanmani—his half-brothers and half-sister. It was evident from everyone's expression and reaction that the elderly white-haired man with much weathered skin and stooped shoulders was loved and respected and was believed to know and speak great wisdom.

Nahemana continued. "The moon your adopted white mother died, an Indian maiden appeared to you in a dream and said it was time for you to return to this land and your father's people. Is that not true?"

Chase was amazed by that news. "How did you know about my dream?"

"The Great Spirit put that thought inside my head, for He knows and sees all things," Nahemana replied. "He has a purpose for calling you back to this land, but He has not revealed it to me."

Wind Dancer knew his grandfather's revelation about his dream long ago was true. Yet, even if this man was Cloud Chaser, the motive for his return might not be a good one. Perhaps evil forces were at work in Chase's life and heart, powers which could endanger his loved ones. Wind Dancer decided that until he was certain his half-brother was no threat to their father and people, this long-lost man must be watched closely.

"You must prove yourself worthy to rejoin our band, if that is the Great Spirit's will," Nahemana told Chase. "You must prove when the time comes—for surely it will do so during this hot season—you are more Oglala than White and you will side with us in all things and ways against our enemies, those who carry the same White blood as did your mother and the people who reared you far away. Can you turn your face from the Whites forever? Can you raise your weapons against them when they attack us?"

"I will do whatever I must, Wise One," Chase vowed to the shaman.

"Let him prove himself at the Sun Dance pole," Two Feathers scoffed.

"I will surrender myself to the Sun Dance to prove myself worthy to be a Red Shield and to give thanks to Wakantanka for bringing me home, but I will do so when the time is right, not by your challenge, my cousin."

"Are you afraid to—"

Rising Bear lifted his hand. "Enough, Two Feathers. Our shaman has spoken and so it will be until the Great Spirit tells him otherwise or our laws are broken." He said to Chase and his other two sons, "Come to my tepee; there are many words to speak between us."

As the four men headed for the chief's dwelling, Chase glanced to his left. His gaze widened and he missed a step as he stared at a young maiden not far away. If he didn't know she was real, he would swear it was the female spirit who had appeared to him in his beckoning dream months ago! She was the most beautiful and tempting woman he had ever seen. He saw her lower her gaze and turn to speak with a younger girl beside her, and he refocused his strayed attention on his retreating father and brothers. Even so, he experienced a strange and powerful pull toward her and knew he must discover her identity. As he glanced toward Two Feathers, he saw the warrior's sullen gaze flicker from him to the maiden and back to him. Judging from the scowl on Two Feathers' face, Chase concluded the other man was going to cause trouble for him as he had in the past, but he would ponder that problem later. For now, other matters were more important. He was eager to see how his father and brothers treated him in private, for they had shown no affection, joy, and acceptance in public, to his dismay.

As the crowd dispersed to return to their chores, the two young women walked into the forest to speak beyond the hearing of others.

Hanmani, cherished daughter of Rising Bear, told her best friend Macha, "I was only four winters old when he vanished, so I am not sure I remember him. After living so long as the half-white man he is, why would he want to return to a land filled with conflict and hatred between the two bloods he carries? How will he bring himself to side with one against the other? If he is not loyal to his mother's and adoptive parents' side, how can we trust him to be loyal to ours? Dawn, what do you think of him and his coming?"

Macha vividly remembered the boy called Cloud Chaser, though she had been only six when he disappeared. Even at that young age, she had loved him and used many pretenses to be around him. Now he was back, a grown man, a handsome and virile one with great courage, strength, intelligence, and boldness. "Perhaps the Great Spirit has summoned him here to help bring peace between our two peoples."

Hanmani shook her head. "Father and others say there can be no peace with the Whites who seek to destroy us and steal our lands. Already they have misused and broken the Long Meadows Treaty with us and other tribes. If a treaty born only three summers past has withered and died, what and who can give it new life, and how long will the second one last? It cannot be, my best friend, for our peoples and desires are too different."

"If there can be no peace as our leaders say, perhaps there

can be a better truce, for the Whites are here to stay, Han-mani. Even if all enemies who live or travel through our lands are slain, more will come, as will a bitter war if we attack them. Do not forget what we have learned: they have many powerful weapons and their numbers are larger than the buffalo herds which cover the grasslands. If we do not find an honorable way to live with them or a means to utterly defeat them, we, along with the buffalo, will vanish, and we will not be able to return as Cloud Chaser did. Perhaps the Great Spirit allowed his capture so he could learn the white man's ways, then return to teach them to us, or to help us use those ways against our enemy."

That speculation intrigued and excited Hanmani. She smiled and asked, "Do you really think so, my friend?"

Macha thought for a short span, then sighed and shrugged. She could not outright lie to her best friend, but she was not ready to expose her deepest feelings on the matter. "I do not know why he has come, but surely the Great Spirit will soon reveal it to our shaman."

"If he seeks to trick us, he will be slain by Wind Dancer or War Eagle."

"Could they truly slay their own brother?"

"If he is a threat to us, they will do what they must. I am sure they will watch him as keen-eyed hawks until they know he can be trusted. We must gather our firewood so we can hurry back to see what happens."

As they worked, Macha struggled to quell her fear at that possibility, and her elation and suspense at his sudden return. It was as if she had been dreaming and waiting for Cloud Chaser to reappear since the day he had vanished. Why, she did not know, as any kind of relationship with him was impossible. She had noticed Two Feathers' study of them when they had glanced at each other. The warrior had begun to crave her as his wife. Yet, she could think of little which would be more saddening or repulsive than mating with Hanmani's cousin. Macha sighed. She felt trapped in a powerful whirlwind that was blowing her in two directions at once: one toward the bond to her people and one toward the man who caused her body to warm and tingle, her heart to pound, and her mind to race with forbidden thoughts and desires.

As she did her daily task, several questions plagued Macha. What if his *wasicun* blood and years with the Whites had changed Cloud Chaser from the boy she remembered? What if his reason for returning was not a good one? What if he called down the wrath of their enemies upon them? Even if he had not become more White than Indian, what if he could not bring himself to choose sides when that awesome moment arrived? If he could not convince the others he was being truthful and sincere, would he be slain or simply sent away? She, too, must watch him for answers.

When their woodslings were filled and they headed back toward camp, Macha somehow knew that her parents, especially her father, would tell her to come home whenever Cloud Chaser visited his family and to avoid him completely. Could she—would she—obey that impending command? She could not decide how she would react if Cloud Chaser approached her, especially in private, or surmise how she was going to handle the imminent and repugnant joining offer from Two Feathers.

Help me, Great Spirit, for my heart and mind are caught

in traps and I do not know how to free myself.

CHAPTER TWO

Inside the chief's tepee, the four men sat cross-legged on oblong fuzzy hides, Chase facing Rising Bear and Wind Dancer facing War Eagle. It was as if each had assumed one of the four points on a compass, and leaving a space of three feet between him and the man opposite him. Since the Red Shield leader had implied he wanted privacy, all knew they would not be disturbed, even by his wife Winona or his daughter Hanmani.

Wind Dancer opened their talk by asking Chase to relate the news of his capture, life far away, and his journey back to them. More confident of his knowledge of English than of his alleged brother's grasp of the Indian tongue, he told Cloud Chaser to use the white man's language. Before reaching the tepee, he had whispered to his father that he and War Eagle would translate for their chief. He wanted Cloud Chaser to feel confident, comfortable. Perhaps then he might stumble more easily.

Chase focused his attention on Rising Bear, whose unreadable gaze was locked on him. "I was injured and captured because I disobeyed you, Father, and the teachings of the Great Spirit. There was much conflict between me and my cousin when we were boys, and from his behavior toward me today, that has not changed. After Two Feathers slayed the wolf who attacked your war horse and gave you its pelt, he boasted to me about his brave deed and teased me about being weak because I was half white. I yearned to give you a better gift and to show greater courage than he had. Such feelings were wrong, but I was blinded by love for you and anger toward him. I went after the ghost horse who roamed our lands and could not be caught, though you had told your sons not to do so, for it was dangerous. As I chased him, a Crow hunting party tried to capture me. I shot many arrows at them, wounding two. They were angered and sent an arrow into my arm," Chase disclosed, touching a spot just below his left shoulder.

"I was thrown from my pony when he stepped into a creature's burrow and stumbled. My leg was broken and my head was injured, and a great darkness came over me. When I awakened, many suns and moons had passed and I was traveling inside one of the settlers' cloud-covered wagons. When I told the white man and his wife I was from the Red Shield Oglalas and must be freed to return home or much danger would approach them, the man called Tom Martin said my people had been massacred by the Crow who had wounded me. He said I must remain with them to heal and to be safe from our enemies. When you did not come after me, I believed his claim that my family and people were dead. My heart was filled with more pain than my body suffered. My head was filled with anger and hatred toward the Crow and I hungered for revenge against them." Chase quelled his bitterness and disillusionment as his father showed absolutely no reaction to his tale.

"His wife, a gentle and generous woman named Lucy, tended my injuries. She called me Chase, for I had murmured part of my name while ensnared by the blackness. My blood mother had taught me much English, and I learned more from the Martins. I could not walk or ride with my leg in wooden bonds; I was weak in body and spirit and

I was in unfamiliar territory, and I was scared, for I was only a child of ten, and all I had known, loved, and was had been stolen from me. The Martins were kind to me and I believed my family and people were dead, so I stayed with them. I vowed to return and seek revenge on the Crow after I healed and learned my way home, but time escaped me as I waited to grow older and stronger and wiser before challenging such a powerful force."

Chase took a deep breath, but the others remained silent. "It is true I came to trust, love, and respect my adoptive parents. The land where they settled to make a farm was a wild and dangerous place. Many times I helped Tom Martin defend his home, wife, and land. I studied and learned all I could about their kind while I was with them, for I hoped one day to use such things for the good of my people—if any had survived. It is true they did not speak all of the truth to me, as they yearned for a son and they came to love me as their own flesh and blood. Just as my mother came to accept the Red Shields long ago. The one you called Omaste for her golden hair like the sun loved, obeyed, and respected you, your family, and your people. On his deathbed, my white father confessed he had spoken falsely to me long ago. He begged me to forgive him and to stay with his wife. Lucy was old and was always good to me, so I took care of her until her death. The night her last breaths were leaving her body, I dreamed of coming home, finding my family and people alive, and rejoining them."

He paused, but again no one asked any questions or made any remarks, so Chase continued his story. "I became a trapper for a fur company in order to work my way here and to learn the land which separated me from this one. I know the white man's tongue. I know his ways, his religion, his thoughts. I can read his words on paper. I know much of what has happened here while I was gone. I stayed at Fort Laramie and Fort Pierre for many days to gather news about the Red Shields and their allies and enemies. From my years among them and my travels here, I know there are many Whites and their weapons are powerful. I know they made a treaty with the Dakotas and other Indian nations and have not kept it. Many Whites are good people and do not desire war with us; yet, many seek our destruction. If you allow me to return home, I can be your eyes and ears against the enemy, for I can appear to be one of them. What do you say, my father and brothers?"

Chase saw Wind Dancer send their father a furtive message, and he had seen his older brother whisper to Rising Bear earlier outside. He suspected they did not trust him at this point and might try to dupe him.

Wind Dancer sought to select his words carefully and cleverly. "Our hearts and minds hunger to believe you and accept you among us, my brother," he finally said, "but you have lived among our white enemies for many seasons and it is hard and perhaps dangerous for us to do so."

Chase nodded. "I understand it might be hard to trust me, a near-stranger after our long separation, but why would it be perilous to do so?"

"If you lie or crave revenge from a bitter heart or cannot bring yourself to side with us during battles, you could endanger or betray us."

Chase noticed that his older brother was acting as the spokesman for their father. He knew that Wind Dancer was being groomed as the next chief, as it was the custom for leadership to pass from father to eldest son unless there was a specific reason not to do so, then another son had to earn that high rank. Yet, he was surprised and saddened that his own father didn't speak or show any favorable emotion toward him. "When your mother was taken captive by the Pawnee and forced to live among them for two years, she did not forget her identity or become a Pawnee or ever stop trying to escape and return home." Chase knew it was foolish to mention that it was during Winona's absence that Rising Bear had turned to his white captive one night for comfort and the result had been his birth. "After she returned from the enemy, she was welcomed home, and was still loved, respected, and accepted. Why is it different for me, my brother?"

"My mother did not carry the enemy's blood to pull her toward them," Wind Dancer answered. "She was a grown woman and her thoughts were clear. You were stolen as a child, Cloud Chaser, when your heart and mind could be swayed by others, by those who reared you as their son."

"My heart and mind have always remained Oglala, my brother. They could no more change me into a white man than you can change a doe into a buck. All I ask for is a chance to prove myself to my family and people. Surely you can use my help and knowledge during these hazardous times."

"The agent called Thomas Fitzpatrick who persuaded us to go to Fort Laramie three summers past to hear the words of the Long Meadows Treaty is dead," Wind Dancer divulged. "Broken Hand was the one white man who gave us respect and tried to do good. Life left his body almost five full moons ago, and much trouble has begun. Already our Lakota brothers ride against the Bluecoats and settlers, as do other bands and tribes."

"For them to break the treaty will cause trouble, Wind Dancer, trouble which will spill onto the lands and lives of those who still honor the truce," Chase cautioned. "The Red Shields must think long and hard before they ally and ride with other Lakotas against the Whites. It is perilous to break your word to them."

"My father did not sign the treaty," his half-brother replied. "The White leaders demanded we choose a head chief to speak and sign for all Lakotas: the man called Mitchell chose Brave Bear of the Brules and told all tribes to accept him as head chief. No other leader can speak or sign in our father's place, but we pretended to agree to give us time to grow stronger. Attacks by the Crow and a white man's sickness had stolen the lives of many of our warriors, and the lives of many in other tribes. The treaty"—Wind Dancer paused as he searched his memory for the English word used long ago—"des-ig-na-ted each tribe a separate territory and commanded all to live in peace. We hoped it would keep the enemy from hunting and raiding in our lands while we recovered from those past attacks. Our enemies the Crow, Shoshone, and Arapaho came and signed, but the Pawnee, Kiowa, and Comanche refused. The Gros Ventre, Assiniboin, Mandan, and Arickaree also came and signed, as did our allies the Cheyenne. The Bluecoats promised to protect any tribe from another's attack, but they have failed to do so. They make many new trails across our lands and they put up more forts; those are for the Whites', not the Indians', use and protection. They promised many goods in return for peace and for travel across our lands, but those goods are few and bad."

"What are the boundaries for the Lakota territory, my brother, and what goods did the treaty promise to deliver?"

"From where Cantewakpa ends its journey at Muddy Waters, travel the Mnisose to Skamakawakpa where Fort Pierre Trading Post stands, cross the grasslands and sand-hills to where Kampeskawakpa divides itself, take the branch toward the land where the sun goes to sleep and halt at Paha Luta. There, ride toward the land where winter is born and travel beyond the sacred Paha Sapa to where the Cante waters spring to life."

Chase's mind quickly translated those boundary sites and markers: along the Heart River to the Missouri, southward on it to the White River, overland to the Platte branch, west-ward along the North Platte fork to Red Butte, then north-ward west of the Black Hills to the Heart River mouth.

"We were to be given food, blankets, kettles, hatchets, knives, cloth, cows and horses, and tools to farm in Mother Earth. They did not bring such things to our camps; they told us to come to the fort and to . . . stand in line for them to be passed out amongst many people, as if we were . . . beggars. The Red Shields refused such demands; we accept no handouts from the Whites. To others, they give little and they take much. They slay the buffalo as a game or only for its hide. They slay females with calves and leave the young to die without a mother's nourishment and protection; that practice will prevent the renewal of herds. We find many carcasses rotting beneath the sun, the creature's life wasted. The stock they give out to others is weak and has little meat on its bones. The flour has tiny creatures in it. The blankets are thin and the cloth tears easily. They refused to give us weapons for hunting, for they feared we would use the fire-sticks to slay them. They enclose us in a territory where they destroy our food supply and demand we take so-called gifts from them to make us dependent upon them forever."

"If we make a claim on the farming tools promised in the treaty, my brother," Chase suggested, "I can teach our people how to plant seeds and grow food in Mother Earth before and after the great buffalo hunt each summer, for I was taught to farm by the Martins. Then, our people would have sufficient food and not become dependent on them. If they refuse, I can dress as a white man and buy tools and seeds at the trading post."

"We not farmers, Cloud Chaser; we hunters," War Eagle scoffed.

Chase looked at his younger half-brother when he spoke for the first time. There was a sharp edge to War Eagle's tone and a chilly glare of insult in his expression. "Can you still be a hunter when the buffalo are gone or there is not enough of them to feed our people during the winter, the cold season?" Chase reasoned in English, having noticed that both of his brothers now spoke the language with great skill. Yet, when one was speaking to him, the other was translating for their father, who sat erect and with an impassive but alert expression.

"If bad sun rises, we hunt and eat deer, antelope, elk, moose, bear, beaver, fish, and many birds. We gather berries, nuts, and plants. Great Spirit is good provider. Red Shields need nothing from White enemy."

"What of those creatures, War Eagle, when the white man traps them for their skins and many vanish from the streams, forests, and grasslands? Where will enough plants and berries and nuts grow when the white man clears lands for farms and ranches and homesteads? The Indian world has changed forever with the white man's coming, and you must change with it or perish, for they can never be driven from your land for all time. Though you yearn for the Old Ways, you must learn new ones. The sun will rise when you must trade with the Whites for things you need for survival. Pride will not feed your people in the years ahead, War Eagle. You cannot make enough weapons or fire enough arrows to slay all Whites who enter your lands or cross them, for more will take their places, and soldiers will come to attack you for such deeds. I can help our people learn these new ways, for they were taught to me while I was gone. I can read the Long Meadows Treaty and see where and how you were tricked; I can read a new treaty to be certain it does not happen again."

"We warriors, Cloud Chaser; we fear, slave to no enemy or force."

"Even a brave and skilled warrior must know when to fight, War Eagle, and when to make truce or retreat. If your warriors are slain, who will feed and protect your women, children, and old ones? Where is the wisdom in fighting a battle you cannot win?"

"Where honor in not fighting for what ours?" War Eagle argued. "Man cannot live without honor. Lakota must live proud, free."

"Even if keeping honor and pride means certain destruction?" When Chase realized War Eagle did not grasp his last word, he clarified it, "Even if keeping honor and pride means your death and loss of your land?"

Without hesitation, the young man vowed, "Good warrior

do, sacrifice what he must. We not become slaves to Whites. We be free or we die."

"If our father and people decide to fight, War Eagle, I will fight with them; and I will die with them if that is Wakan-tanka's will." He paused a moment before seeking an answer to a puzzling matter. "Tell me, how and when did my brothers learn the white man's tongue so well?"

"My wife speaks it and taught us," Wind Dancer said.

"You're married now? I mean, you have taken a mate?"

"I joined to a Brule woman from the White Shield band three seasons past when Mother Earth renewed her face; she is called Chumani. We have a son, Tokapa, who is two winters old."

So, he has a wife named Dewdrops and a son named Firstborn. A married man with a family should want peace for their survival . . . "That is good, my brother, and I am eager to meet them. What of you, War Eagle?"

"I have no mate. I live in this tepee. I am a Sacred Bow Carrier. My brother is a Strong Heart and Shirt Wearer."

Chase remembered the two warrior societies, and the Shirt Wearers who carried out the orders of their chief and council, the Big Bellies. He knew the Strong Hearts were comprised of elite and brave warriors who were first to respond to any threat and who took care of those in need. The Sacred Bow Carriers were band leaders during battles and must touch an enemy during each fight, and were last to leave a battlefield, as they were responsible for the safe return of their party members. He noted that his brothers had done exceedingly well for themselves and had earned important and high ranks, for their relationship to Rising Bear had given them no advantage.

Before Chase could ask more personal questions, Wind Dancer said, "You must camp nearby, but away from our tepees, while we learn more about you and test you. You must not enter our camp until you are summoned."

Chase looked directly at Rising Bear and asked, "Are you ashamed of me, Father? Sorry I was born? Sorry I have returned? Are you worried I will remind everyone of your one weakness long ago? If I was not meant to walk the face of Mother Earth and to return home, the Great Spirit would not have sent me to you twenty-two years ago and again today. I am as much a part of your Life-Circle as you are of mine. How can we deny or prevent what was meant to be before our births? How can we cut out a part of our Life-Circles and survive? Why do you look at me as a stranger when I am of your seed?"

As Rising Bear lowered his head, Wind Dancer grieved over his anguish. "Long ago, Father was forced to believe his eyes would never look upon your face again," he said. "Now you return amidst grave times and he does not know what to think or believe. You must be patient, Cloud Chaser, while his feelings and thoughts are unclear. It would be painful and reckless of him to take back a lost son who might prove himself to be a fierce enemy. We have only your claim your words are true; we must learn the whole truth for ourselves. Until that sun rises, Father cannot embrace and accept you before others. You must camp nearby and not leave that area without permission. Do you agree to obey those commands?"

Chase realized he had no choice except to concede, though this was far from the happy homecoming he had desired. He no longer knew who and what he was or where he belonged. "I agree. Guide me to my campsite so our father can relax and sort his thoughts."

Wind Dancer stood at the same time Chase did and said, "Come."

Chase took one final glance at his father, but his head was still lowered, as if the older man could not bear to look at him. Then he followed his brother outside, where many people halted their chores to study him again. He felt as if he were being inspected like an animal for sale, and that all were suspicious of his qualities. Would he be able to change their minds and feelings? So far it didn't appear promising. He was glad they didn't encounter Two Feathers, as he didn't want to quarrel with his cousin again today. But they did pass two females, an older one whom he recognized as Winona—whose name meant Firstborn Daughter, and who was the shaman's child—and a young one whom he assumed was his half-sister Hanmani, whose name meant To Walk in the Night. He realized Hanmani was the woman who had been standing with the enchanting beauty earlier, so he assumed they were friends, but the lovely female wasn't in sight now; and he found that fact oddly disappointing.

Chase noticed how both women glanced at him, then hurriedly averted their gazes, as if they had been ordered to ignore him. Just as his own mother had reared Wind Dancer during Winona's two-year captivity, Winona had tended him for a year following his mother's death from "winter in the chest." He had often—and still—wondered if his father's wife hated and resented him for being born of her husband's mating with their white slave, for the woman had never revealed or spoken of her feelings to him. It was apparent from the births of War Eagle and Hanmani after their reunion that Winona had not rejected Rising Bear for his one night of weakness.

They reached a grassy location near the river. It was shaded by trees and within sight of the village, one which would soon be dismantled so the band could head for the Plains for the buffalo hunt. In fact, if memory served him right, they should have left some time ago. "Why are you still in the winter camp, Wind Dancer?" he asked. "Why are you not on the grasslands?"

"Winter traveled far into the time for Mother Earth's rebirth season," he clarified. "The grass and buffalo returned late. We stayed here until She finished Her tasks before we can begin ours. We will leave after the next full moon."

Chase figured that span of time to be a little less than three weeks. "Maybe I'll be allowed to hunt with you. If summer's a short season this year, you could use another hunter to bring in the meat and hides required for next winter. I would enjoy us riding and working together again, like when we were boys. Do you think that's possible, my brother?"

Wind Dancer looked at Chase. "We will see what happens between this sun and the full moon. Now, remain here. I will send you food and wood, and water is nearby. Your horse will be kept with mine. Your other possessions will be brought to you for your use—all but your weapons."

"Can I at least have my knife returned in case I need it for protection? A wild animal or an enemy might attack during the night."

"I will send you the knife for protection. Do not leave

this place."

"I'll be right here, Wind Dancer, but don't forget about me," Chase joked, but his brother did not smile, only nodded before departing. He sat down on a fallen tree trunk and stared into the river's currents.

Why, Chase scolded himself, had he returned to face rejection and scorn? Hadn't he endured enough of those unpleasant feelings many years ago? The strange dream had irresistibly summoned him back to the land of his birth. No, he refuted, from the moment his adoptive father had confessed his deception, he had conjured up beautiful images of a loving and happy reunion with his Lakota family; and as time passed, those daydreams had come more frequently and had been light and happy. But he had deluded himself, and reality was grim and dark.

Chase thought about the Martins and his life with them. He had been accepted as their son and had been treated well by their neighbors and friends and others with whom they had come into contact at stores, church, and the small school he had attended. He had liked not being viewed as an outsider. He had liked being loved and accepted. He had called them Mama and Papa. He had hunted, fished, and worked the land with Tom Martin. He had gathered wood and water, laughed, sang, read, and talked with Lucy Martin. In all ways except one—blood—he had been their son for twelve years; and he had grieved over their deaths, despite the false story they had told him years ago. He understood why they had done it and he'd forgiven them. What his heart and mind yearned for now was his own father's love, respect, and acceptance. Would he ever earn them? He didn't know. Did he deserve them? Yes, because it wasn't his fault he had been born of mixed blood!

Yet, had he honestly expected them to welcome him back with open arms? Why shouldn't they have qualms about his loyalty during future conflicts, questions about his motives for returning, doubts about his identity? After all, he half represented the people and fate they feared and battled most. Perhaps they all needed time to get used to him and to get reacquainted with each other.

Chase sent his warring mind down a different trail. He knew the Nebraska Territory, of which this area was included, had been formed on May 30 and the sites of Omaha and Nebraska City had been founded. More Whites would soon come to this region. America was marking off this huge land of hers from coast to coast, and from Mexico to Canada. The Nebraska Territory was bounded by those of Washington, Oregon, Utah, New Mexico, Kansas, Minnesota, and Iowa, and the country of Canada. How soon, Chase wondered, would it be before this new territory was divided into states like those east and south of there? Each of those measures of "progress" and "expansion" would alter the Indian world forever, and he didn't know if the Red Shields could survive such actions if they refused to acknowledge and accede to them.

Now that he had lived on both sides of the conflict, he had learned a great deal about each. Oddly, both were alike in some ways: most wanted freedom, land, food, family, joy, respect, and a simple life. Both believed in one Creator of all things, a great flood which cleansed the Earth and gave rebirth to it, and that one should honor one's family, and obey their people's laws. Yet, the Indians and Whites had many differences, a major one being the nomadic nature of the Plains Indians in contrast with the Whites' desire to settle and stay in one place—often in the direct path of the Indians' wanderings and hunting grounds.

The Dream, Chase's roaming mind hinted again, the dream which had beckoned him there. It was still as vivid inside his head as the night it had come to him: the beautiful maiden in a white doeskin dress, her dark hair flowing around her shoulders, her deep brown eyes sparkling with love and mischief, her mouth parted in a smile, her arms outstretched, and her musical voice whispering, "Come home, Cloud Chaser. Come home to me and where you belong. You must obey or we will all die. Come, my love."

Had he been foolish to place so much importance on a mere dream? He was about as wanted here as the cholera plague which had struck three years ago! Rising Bear certainly didn't want to be reminded of his sin with Margaret Phillips! And neither did his wife and people, which had to include his half-brothers and half-sister. Probably everyone had been glad when his mother had died and when he had vanished, removing all White signs and tainting from their village and their beloved chief!

Don't do this, Chase! he scolded himself. *You came to make peace, to find yourself. Don't forget these people never mistreated your mother and they didn't capture her; she was a gift from a Cheyenne chief. Don't forget she loved your father, loved him as a man, something she kept hidden from everybody except you. And don't forget Wind Dancer said Father* did *search for you. But for how long and how hard did you look, my father? Or did you only pretend to search? Did you lie to others and not look at all? Or did you give up too soon and too easily out of relief to have me gone? Am I nothing more than a shameful deed to you, one you want to forget? One you hoped and prayed the Great Spirit had removed from your life forever? Or do you really love me but are afraid of what others will think if you accept me? Are you only afraid I'm not really your son, or that I'll betray you out of bitterness? How, when, and where can I find truthful answers to those tormenting questions?*

Chase sought to calm himself. He had to keep his head clear and his emotions under control to obtain his objective. Surely there was some important reason why he had been born here, had been taken away, and had been summoned back. But what was it? When would it be revealed to him? What would he be forced to endure before it was? So much had changed here in twelve years. So many Whites had intruded on Indian lands, resulting in so much hatred and violence, which no doubt would worsen as time passed and more settlers and soldiers came. The territory assigned to the Lakotas was a large one, but there were many bands— from the Seven Council Fires of the major tribes—to share it and to live off its offerings for as long as those life-sustaining needs were available. Once those necessities were depleted, the Lakotas would not—could not—hold to their treaty promise or be contained in this area.

From what he had learned, it was evident the Whites didn't comprehend the Indian way of life, and their demands were contradictory to those customs. The Dakota Nation had conquered the Northern Plains long ago and controlled it with the might of their great number and elite warrior skills. But the white man's encroachment—which had begun and increased with the fur trade, California gold-rush, and Far West settlement and all things which enabled those three realities to continue and expand—had thrust other large Indian Nations closer and into this vast domain; many of those tribes were fierce enemies of the Lakotas, such as the Crow and Pawnee.

The pressing in of such powerful and skilled opponents had led to generational animosities. Battles over hunting grounds, for coups, retribution, and defense had become a way of life for Indians. With peace demanded by the treaty, there were no coups and glory to be earned, no plunder to be taken, no challenges to be met, no high ranks to be won, no need for warrior societies, no way to prove courage and manhood. This was like telling the grizzly to lose his claws; the eagle, his talons; a warrior, his strength, and honor, and purpose for being. A Lakota male's existence centered around his family, band, tribe, Nation, the "Four Virtues," the land and sky, the seasons, the animals, the hunt, his freedom, independence, his enemies, his training and prowess, and his belief in and worship of the Great Spirit, Wakantanka.

The 1851 Laramie Treaty, called the Treaty of the Long Meadows by the Indians, was meant to change that lifestyle. Yet, two huge factors had been overlooked: not all Nations and tribes had agreed to the treaty and not all who had done so would honor their pledges. When only one band or tribe attacked another or Whites, all Indians would be blamed, for the white man saw all Indians as one group of people. Why couldn't the Whites realize the Dakota Nation was as different from the Crow and Pawnee Nations as the American Nation was from the British or French or Spanish? Why couldn't they remember how fiercely they had battled those forces for independence and freedom and for possession of this enormous country? Had they forgotten the Indians were here first? Did they really expect the Indians to allow them to just ride in and take over their ancestral lands, to wreak major changes in their lives, all for some scant and inferior annuities?

On the other hand, Chase reasoned, did his father and brothers understand the grave situation—and him—better than he himself did? Did they truly understand the serious and deadly extent of the risks they would be taking if they challenged the Whites? Knowing the Army's certain retaliation could mean extermination of his people, could he help kill Whites when that moment arrived if they resolved to fight rather than submit? Did he have doubts he could comply and that was what his father and brothers sensed? Did he—

War Eagle's approach halted Chase's line of thought when he and another man arrived with food, his bedroll, saddlebags, wood, and his knife.

"Wind Dancer send supplies and your possessions. This Swift Otter; he friend and Sacred Bow Carrier. You eat, stay here."

Chase nodded a greeting to Swift Otter, the man who had ridden with War Eagle this morning and had confiscated his weapons. The warrior simply looked at him in return. In English, he said, "You were eight years old when I vanished, War Eagle. Do you remember me?"

"I remember a little about my brother."

Chase noted War Eagle had chosen his reply carefully. "But you aren't sure I'm Cloud Chaser?"

"You speak many true words from suns long past. You know them or Cloud Chaser speak them to you?"

"I swear on my life and honor I am Cloud Chaser, your brother. I—" A sharp voice using Lakota cut off the rest of his sentence.

"Did your father say this white man can stay?"

War Eagle turned to face Two Feathers, who had left the trees nearby and joined them, his expression one of anger. "Yes, he camps here."

"He must be guarded, my cousin; he is a threat to us."

"That has not been proven, Two Feathers. Father speaks; we obey."

Also speaking Lakota, Chase told the seething man, "The rivalry between us took place when we were boys, Two Feathers. We are men now. We must put our conflict behind us, bury it forever, for the good of our people."

"There can be no peace between us until you prove yourself a worthy warrior and loyal only to us. You have not done so with words and will never do so with deeds."

"If not peace," Chase urged, "make a truce with me so—"

"You can trick your way back into our band and people's hearts? Do not ask for my help and acceptance, half-breed, for I will never give them."

"Why do you hate me, Two Feathers, when the same blood runs within our veins, the blood of our grandparents, Chief Ghost Warrior and Redbird? It is the Red Shield way to be loyal to our chief, our family, our band, and our great Dakota Nation. Brothers, sisters, and children of our leader are the most important members of our band; we are among that group, Two Feathers, so there should be no swinging hatchet between us."

"I carry only Indian blood; you carry the blood of our

enemy, so we are different; there is no bond between us."

"You speak and behave as a bad child, Two Feathers. There is a blood bond between us whether you accept it or not." Chase wished he hadn't allowed his cousin to provoke him to speak what was taken as a grave insult by the man. He saw Two Feathers' gaze narrow and chill even more and the warrior's body stiffen with rising fury.

"You seek to stain my honor, half-breed? Do you challenge me to a fight? Take up your knife and we will settle our conflict here and now."

War Eagle seized Two Feathers' arm before he fully extracted the knife at his waist. "You will not fight Cloud Chaser," he ordered. "He is here by Father's command. You break our law to fight a man protected by a chief."

Swift Otter shook his head and told the man in a firm tone, "*Iya, Wiyaka Nunpa; Ecunsni yo.*"

Chase knew that meant, "Go away, Two Feathers; do not do it." He waited, as did War Eagle and Swift Otter, for his cousin's next action.

"*Mni kte lo,*" Two Feathers told his friends, but added to Chase, "*Tka ecana nitin tke.*" He spit on the ground as a sign of contempt and left.

Chase did not respond to his cousin's parting words of "I will go. But you are going to die soon." He waited until Two Feathers stalked away before he thanked War Eagle's friend. Again, Swift Otter kept his expression stoic, uncertain how he was supposed to respond to his chief's less-than-welcomed son. Concerned about his beloved animal, which was his one remaining bond to the Martins, Chase asked War Eagle, "Can my horse camp here with me? He does not know this place and people and will not be calm

40

without me being nearby."

"Horse stay there. He be safe and tended. Cloud Chaser stay here."

Chase decided not to protest what he assumed was their precaution against his escape, and hoped Red would be all right where he was. He nodded and requested that War Eagle thank Wind Dancer for sending him food and his belongings. "I'll stay here until Father sends for me," he promised.

War Eagle nodded. He started to warn Cloud Chaser not to fight and especially not hurt Two Feathers if he approached him again, but rejected that idea. He would relate the matter to his father and brother and they would halt Two Feathers from picking a fight with his brother, for he was convinced this man was indeed Cloud Chaser. But could he, War Eagle worried, be trusted? Soon the truth would be revealed; then it would be decided if Cloud Chaser would live or die . . .

CHAPTER THREE

While War Eagle was with Chase, Wind Dancer was in the tepee of Rising Bear. "What are your feelings and thoughts, my father?" he asked.

The chief shook his head, and sighed deeply, before answering. "My second son has been lost to me for twelve circles of the seasons when this man comes to us and says he is Cloud Chaser. I yearn to believe he is my child and he has returned to me, but I fear to do so. If he lies and tricks us, he can bring much danger to our people. Even if he speaks the truth of who he is, he can cause much trouble here, and for certain if evil dwells within him. I am chief and must do what is best for my people, even if I must lose my son again to honor and fulfill my duty and rank."

Rising Bear sighed deeply again. "I was not a good father to him, Wind Dancer, for each time I gazed upon him, I was reminded of my weakness with his mother and saw him as a punishment for that wicked deed. I feared if I treated him as I did you and my other children, my beloved wife and people would think I loved his mother and that could cause resentment and anger toward me, and I would lose their respect and obedience. When Cloud Chaser was taken from me not long after Omaste's death, I believed it was the Great Spirit's way of forgiving me for that weakness and removing all signs of it from my life. I acted wrongly toward Cloud Chaser, my son, for he was not to blame for my bad deed and should not have suffered for it. I was selfish and blind, and did not practice the Four Virtues. But now that he has been blanketed by White ways for so long, he may be more *wasicun* than Oglala, if in truth he is my son."

Wind Dancer's heart was touched by his father's unexpected confession. Yet, all men made mistakes some time during their lives; only a great and good man learned and grew stronger from them, as his father had done. Perhaps, he reasoned, there was another lesson to be learned. "How could this man know the things he told us and come to possess such belongings if he is not Cloud Chaser?" he asked.

"What if he was a brother or friend to Cloud Chaser and he learned and took such things from him?" his father argued. "What if he only uses them as a means to sneak into our camp and spy on us? If we allow him to live among us, he can learn our secrets and those of our allies and reveal them to our enemies. If he is Cloud Chaser and his heart and mind remained loyal to us, why did he take so long to return? He has been a man for many seasons. Why would he stay with those who had betrayed him?"

"Perhaps his mind was clouded by feelings of duty to them," Wind Dancer reasoned. "Perhaps his heart is kind and generous, my father, and he felt he must repay them for their many good deeds. He was a child. He was injured. He believed us dead. He was taken far away from all he knew and loved. He came to love and trust them before he learned the dark truth of their false words."

"You speak in his favor, my firstborn son? You believe his claims?"

"I do not know yet if he can be trusted, but I believe he is my brother. I am to follow you as chief, my father. For that rank and duty, you and Grandfather have taught me to study any important matter from all sides. It is true it is dangerous to accept him if he is not Cloud Chaser or his heart is now evil. But it is wrong to reject him if he is a son and brother and he is good, for we do not know if he was summoned by Wakantanka or sent by an evil force."

"Your thoughts and words are wise, Wind Dancer; you have learned well from our teachings and the guidance of the Great Spirit. Still, the question remains: Do we accept him back into our lives and band?"

"For many suns to come, we must only watch and listen, and wait for the Great Spirit to guide us along the right and safe path," he advised his father. "Do you not agree, Grandfather?" Wind Dancer asked the shaman, who had remained silent during the serious talk between father and son.

Nahemana smiled. "You have learned well, my grandson; you are both wise and cunning. It must be as you say."

"Go to him, Wise One, and see what you can learn," the chief urged.

Nahemana looked at Rising Bear, nodded, and left the tepee.

Chase took a last swallow of water to finish washing down the roasted venison and bread which War Eagle had brought to him earlier. He screwed the top onto his canteen and put it aside as he watched the shaman heading toward him. He wondered if the old man was displeased or worried about his return and would speak against his remaining there. He knew how revered and trusted the shaman was. Nahemana had great influence over his people's thoughts and actions, and he had proven many times he was in communion with the Great Spirit. All things which had been revealed to him in dreams and visions had come to pass. So where and how did this powerful and mystical man fit into his destiny?

Chase greeted him and invited him to come and sit on the log and talk. "*Hau, Nahemana. U wo. Cankaga akan yanka. Ia.*" As the shaman sat down, he added, "*Tanyan yahi yelo. Ake iyuskinyan wancinyankelo,*" telling the elderly man he was glad he came and was glad to see him again.

After remarking that he spoke good Lakota, Nahemana asked, "*Taku ca yacin hwo? Takunocin yahipi?*"

He wasted no time getting to the point of what I want here, Chase thought and urged him not to be afraid of his return home. "*Kopegla sni yo; wakuyelo.*" He continued in their language. "Can you not see or feel what is in my heart, Wise One? You knew what came to me in my dream, so do

44

you not also know I speak the truth?"

"The Great Spirit put that thought inside my head and those words in my mouth, for I did not know them before they came forth not from my will but from His. He has not shown me what lives within you or the true reason why you have come to us. If you are not Yutokeca Mahpiya and your purpose here is a bad one, you will be punished by Him and the Red Shields."

"I am He Who Chases Clouds, Grandfather. But the only clouds I chase are those created by fleeing enemies or game I am pursuing. I do not and will not ride in the dust clouds kicked up by our enemies or an evil spirit."

"What help can you, one man, be to my people?"

"I do not know, Grandfather," Chase admitted, surprised the older man did not seem to take offense at the name he called him, the same one he had used so long ago as a child. "I hoped you could tell me, Wise One. Will you ask the Great Spirit to reveal such things to you?"

"My heart asked Him to do so as soon as you spoke your name to us. But He will not answer until He knows the time is right. When He sends His message, be gone if you spoke falsely, or prepare to die."

"I hear your warning, Grandfather, but it will not drive me away, for I spoke the truth. Only the Great Spirit and my father can send me away. I am Yutokeca Mahipya; I am Red Shield Oglala; this is where I belong. The only family I possess lives here, and it is where I yearn to remain. Tell me what must be done to prove myself, Wise One, and I will do it."

"That is a deed or task for the Great Mystery to decide and reveal. I go now," Nahemana said, rising slowly and with difficulty.

"Tanyan yahi yelo. Ake u wo." Chase told him once more he was glad he had come and to "come again."

Nahemana nodded and left, many thoughts filling his head.

Chase well remembered the old man and days long past. Whenever Nahemana had been left in charge of his grandchildren and told them stories or given them instructions, it was always Wind Dancer and War Eagle sitting on either side of him on a buffalo hide and Hanmani nestled in his lap. As if an outsider, he was left to take a place on the ground before them, separate and alone. Although they had not been related to him by blood and mostly seemed to ignore his presence, Nahemana and Little Turtle were the only grandparents he had ever known. He remembered Little Turtle giving Wind Dancer and War Eagle hair-stuffed leather ponies and Hanmani a grass-stuffed doll and miniature tepee one day. He had stood nearby empty-handed and heartbroken. It had been his half-brothers who had let him play with their toys, who had let him shadow them, who had included him in games and mock hunts. It had been Wind Dancer, not his father or other male relatives as was the custom, who had taught him to make his first bow and arrows and had taught him how to use them and how to fight and track and hunt. It had been Wind Dancer who had kept Two Feathers from mistreating him and excluding him from boyhood activities.

So why, Chase wondered, did his older brother now reject and mistrust him? Perhaps the only reason was because Wind Dancer was trapped between him and his family and people and his duty to them. If he could win over the future chief and such a high-ranking warrior, surely half his battle to return home would be won. He also needed to win over the shaman and his daughter, for they held much sway over his father. But how could he convince those three people of his sincerity?

At dusk, Hanmani arrived with a wooden bowl of stewed meat and wild vegetables, seasoned with local herbs. She also handed him three half-inch cuttings of *wakapapi wasna*—pemmican—from last summer's stores, for it would last for several years if made and wrapped properly.

Chase smiled at the reserved female with tea-colored eyes and hair, who was now sixteen by his figuring. "*Pilamaya, tanksi.*" He thanked her and called her his younger sister.

"Am I truly your sister? Are you Cloud Chaser or a false talker?"

Chase smiled again with hopes of relaxing and even charming her. Too, he was both amused and impressed by her boldness and courage. "Yes, I am Cloud Chaser, your brother. You were only four circles of the seasons when I was taken away, so you must not remember me. You have become a pretty young woman while I was gone. I am sure our father is proud of you."

"He is pleased with me, for I obey and respect him and love him."

Chase noticed a gleam of pleasure in her eyes at his compliments and how she seemed to struggle to continue to appear aloof. "As I do, Hanmani; and I will prove myself worthy of my rank as his son when I am given a chance. Will you sit and talk with me while I eat? There is much I long to learn about my family. I was told Wind Dancer has a wife and son. Is there a young brave who steals your heart and eye?"

Hanmani was filled with curiosity about the man, but had been told not to linger near him. She made an excuse which she suspected sounded like a lie, but was partly true. "The sun sleeps soon and I have more chores to do, so I must go now. I will return with more food when the sun appears in the sky again." She noted his disappointed expression, one which touched her tender heart, for he might be her brother.

"I understand you must leave," Chase said kindly. "I hope we can talk on another sun. Thank you for your kindness and the food, and thank your mother for me."

Hanmani started to leave, but hesitated, then turned to face him. "If you are my brother and you stay with us, we will talk many times. I thank you for your kind words about me. It is sad, but I do not think I remember my brother. If I am wrong, such things will return to me soon. Eat while your food is hot. Do you have enough wood for a fire if needed?"

"I have plenty, my sister, and thank you for having a good heart."

Hanmani could not resist exchanging smiles with him before leaving. She was glad she had spoken her final words to him, for they seemed to make him happy. Perhaps if they became friends, even false ones if he was a trickster, he would tell her things he might not tell the others.

As Chase lay on his bedroll and placed an arm across his full stomach, he told himself that maybe he should be careful of what he ate. Probably nothing would please Winona more than for him to be resting on a death scaffold instead of on the grass outside her husband's camp and within his visual range. *But why shouldn't she hate and resent the bastard child of her husband with another woman, a white woman, one of the enemy?* his troubled mind shouted.

Immediately he scolded himself for that wicked thought, as Winona had tended him for a year after his mother's death: she had made, washed, and repaired his clothes; she had fed him; she had tended him when he was sick; she had allowed him to play with her own children; and she had not forced Rising Bear to send him away. She had not even asked his father to do so, to his knowledge. However, his heart cried, she had never embraced him; she had never spoken unnecessary words to him; and she had not even tried to comfort him—a small child—following his mother's death.

Yet, perhaps Winona had feared him in some way, feared he would draw Rising Bear's attention and affection away from her children, feared his presence would always be a reminder to Rising Bear of the night he had shared on his mat with the beautiful Omaste and also be a reminder to their people of the chief's one display of weakness. To be fair to the woman, he must remember what she had endured during her captivity with the fierce Pawnee. The woman must have suffered unspeakable torment under enemy hands. Then, to return to her own home to discover a bastard child in her tepee and her own son adoring the white woman who had lived in her place for two years—that would be painful for any wife and mother. Chase told himself to be understanding, patient, and compassionate where Winona was concerned; but still he must be wary of her.

As he lay on his back, he gazed upward at an almost fully black moon and had only the glow of a small fire nearby to provide scant light for his solitary setting. He had been back for only one day and had made contact with each of his old family members except Winona. Perhaps he hadn't done badly with such a difficult task in such a short span of time. Then, again, he was certain he wasn't trusted, as he sensed eyes upon him and no doubt was being guarded. He felt vulnerable without his weapons, but he did have his knife within easy reach.

As he heard movement nearby, he thought surely Two Feathers would not attempt to kill him, even with the hope an enemy would be blamed. As was their custom for someone under the protection of their leader, his cousin would be risking much to harm or slay him. At least he didn't have to pass the night bound to a post or staked to the ground! When he sighted two deer approaching the river to drink, he knew what had made those sounds.

Stop jawing with your shadow and get to sleep, Chase! he scolded himself. *You need your rest and clear wits for what lies ahead. Close your eyes and think about something pleasant and maybe you'll have good dreams for a change.*

Soon, Chase—Cloud Chaser—Martin slumbered almost peacefully as he dreamed of a beautiful and desirable Indian maiden who danced and sang through a verdant and dense forest and summoned him onward with her smiles and finger motions while she stayed just out of his reach.

The following morning, Hanmani returned as promised to bring him food and to fetch the bowl from last night. *"Hau, tanksi. Anpetu waste."*

"*Han, anpetu waste. Ota wayata he?*" She agreed it was a good day and asked if he had enough to eat as she placed his meal atop the log.

"*Han, pilamaya,*" he thanked her, observing how she concealed her communication with him from others by keeping her back toward camp. He quickly asked, "Who is the female who does her chores with you? I saw you two together when I arrived and working together last night."

Hanmani was surprised that was the person he chose to ask about during their short time together, as Macha also was greatly interested in her alleged brother. She replied in a hurry as she pretended to reposition the new bowl atop the log to prevent it from falling off, "She is Dawn, my best friend. She was six when you vanished. She played with you as children. Do you not remember her?"

"Perhaps that is why she seems familiar to me," he cunningly muttered as if to himself. He deduced she was using her wits and daring behavior to extract clues from him, so "accidentally" revealing a "secret" to her might win her over; and he was convinced she wouldn't repeat it and expose her defiance. "I thought it was because she favored the Indian maiden in the strange and powerful dream which called me home."

As she collected the dirty bowl, Hanmani glanced over at him where he sat on the ground and asked, "You saw Dawn in your vision-dream?"

"I do not know if it truly was her, but it seems that way to me. That is strange, is it not, *tanksi,* to dream of a female and then to see her?"

For an inexplicable reason, Hanmani's heart raced with excitement to be entrusted with a sacred secret. She yearned to hear more. Yet, she could linger there no longer. "The Great Spirit often works in mysterious ways, *tiblo*. I must go now. I will bring you more wood and food later on this sun."

"*Ake wancinyankin ktelo.*" He told her good-bye and that he would see her again. After she departed, he grinned in delight, for she had called him her older brother and he had discovered the enchanting beauty's identity.

He assumed Macha had been born at dawn, for it was the custom to take a child's name after an occurrence or sighting at the time of delivery from a mother's womb or after something cherished in nature if nothing unusual took place at that awesome moment. His mother had given him an Indian name to make him acceptable to his father's people, though her generous and cunning attempt had obviously failed. He wondered if his childhood name would be changed when he had his next vision-quest, for he had not been here when that ritual age took place.

Chase closed his eyes, called forth the vivid image from memory, and compared the dream woman to Macha. There was no denying or ignoring the fact that he had not lied to his sister. The dream woman and Dawn were either the same female or matched in looks and smiles down to the smallest detail. But how could he dream about a stranger, for Macha only slightly favored the little girl who played with him as a child? Either it was an odd coincidence, an evil force playing a wicked trick on him, or a message from the Creator. But which was it and what did it mean? Was she a good or bad omen?

In the forest while gathering plants and scrub wood, Macha halted her task and stared at her best friend, who had just related a stunning revelation. "Your brother asked about me? Why? What did he say? You were told not to speak with him. You disobeyed. If others learn of your defiance, you will be punished and kept away from him."

Hanmani also glanced around to assure herself of privacy as Macha had done before her rush of words. "I was careful and swift, so no one saw me speak with him," she whispered. "He is lonely and uncertain and he seeks a friend, so he might tell me many secrets he would not share with others. Perhaps I will be the one to learn if he is good or bad, if he is to be a curse or a blessing to us. Surely there is some powerful reason why he was sent to us at this dangerous time for our people, be it by the Great Spirit or an Evil One. You are my best and most trusted friend, so you will not betray my actions." She repeated her talk with Cloud Chaser and watched Macha's gaze widen with the same astonishment which had filled her.

"How can a man dream about a woman far away?" Macha unknowingly almost echoed Chase's query to himself.

"I do not know, my friend, but I believe he spoke the truth."

"Why did he reveal such a secret to you? Perhaps it is a trick," Macha suggested, though she hoped that was not so, as such a falsehood would get him killed, or at least banished forever. From a place deep within her, she wanted him to stay. For some inexplicable and irresistible reason she was drawn to him, had been drawn to him even when they were children.

"Perhaps he trusts me fully, Dawn. Or perhaps his gnawing hunger to learn your name was too painful to resist," she added.

"You tease me, Hanmani; that is unlike you."

"I do not mean to act badly, my friend. I am just ensnared by this mystery. Is it not exciting to be part of a sacred vision-dream?"

"If that is what Cloud Chaser had," Macha replied with a frown.

"If it is true, my friend, what do you think it means?"

"I do not know, Hanmani, and that ignorance is frightening."

"Do not be afraid, my friend, for the Great Spirit will protect you. Do you not remember how He protected Dewdrops when Wastemna tried to either slay or force her to leave after she joined to my brother? Wastemna was exposed and banished and was fortunate she was not slain for her evil."

"She was caught because you and Wind Dancer guessed her evil and exposed it. Will you help protect me if evil strikes at me through Cloud Chaser or the man who claims to be him?"

"I will stay alert and will help you if danger comes, but I am sure if any evil strikes at you, it will not come from my brother who has returned to us. The man you must fear and avoid is my cousin. I do not know why, but I sense Two Feathers has a wicked and cruel streak. I am certain you have captured his eye as a good mate, and that worries me. He has made his hatred and rejection of Cloud Chaser clear to me and others. He challenged my brother to a death fight with knives before War Eagle and Swift Otter on the past sun. Father ordered him to stay away from my brother."

Panicked by that dark news, Macha asked in a quavering

voice, "Do you think Two Feathers will obey our chief's command?"

"He must, Dawn, or he will be punished, perhaps banished forever. That action would sadden my father, my cousin's parents, and my brothers. It would bring great shame and dishonor to my cousin and his family."

"Such risks did not halt Wastemna from trying to harm Dewdrops, and her cruel deceit almost succeeded. If our past war chief's daughter had obtained her dark victory, our people would have lost a great female warrior in Dewdrops, a true Vision Woman, one who rode with Wind Dancer on the sacred and dangerous Vision Journey which saved our people from much harm and gained us peace until the treaty was broken by all who signed it."

Hanmani nodded, but added, "Wastemna was daring and foolish, for she was blinded by love and desire for Wind Dancer."

"Is not Two Feathers blinded by hatred and fear of Cloud Chaser and a fierce desire to have him dead or gone?" Macha reasoned.

Hanmani frowned. "That is true, my friend, but I hope he clears his eyes and cleanses his mind and heart of such evil." She smiled and changed directions. "What if you are a new Vision Woman like Dewdrops was long ago? She came to Wind Dancer in a sacred vision and he rode to her camp to claim her. They were joined and they did many great tasks for the good of our people. What if Cloud Chaser's dream is a sacred one, you will join to him, and do greats deeds for us?" the young girl said on a flight of fancy.

"I am not a female warrior as Dewdrops was. What could I do to help our people? I cannot trick and fight our enemies

55

as she did."

"I have not forgotten how she doubted and resisted Wind Dancer's vision. It was proven to be a message from Wakantanka and she obeyed it. She and Wind Dancer share great love and happiness, and a son. She is honored and loved by our people. Perhaps that is Cloud Chaser's destiny."

"Or perhaps Cloud Chaser learned of that vision and claims he had a sacred dream to trick us," Macha refuted, but did not believe her words. It was both exhilarating and intimidating to even imagine such a destiny.

"No one knows of that vision except our people and Dewdrops', the White Shield Brules. Such a dream is powerful medicine, Dawn. It is a message from the Great Spirit; it cannot be disobeyed. If it is the Creator's will for your Life-Circle to be entwined with Cloud Chaser's, you must not resist traveling that path, though it may frighten you at times."

"We speak of things which might not be real, Hanmani, so we must silence our tongues for now. We must tell no one of his dream."

"Have you forgotten news of it was spoken by Cloud Chaser and my grandfather on the past sun when he entered our camp?"

"But my appearance in his dream was not revealed."

"That is true, so we will tell no one what we have learned about it. Do strange and new feelings for him fill your mind, heart, and body?"

"Yes, but I do not understand them and they disquiet me. I must push them away, for they are forbidden and hopeless."

"Only if Cloud Chaser is rejected by our people. What

if he is not?"

"But what if he is, Hanmani? Such feelings can only bring me pain and sadness. I must not yield to them until he is one of us, if that sun rises."

"Has that sun not already shown its face, my friend?"

"No, Hanmani. He is here now, but will he stay or be allowed to do so? Perhaps he will give up his struggle for acceptance and ride away. Perhaps he will be banished, for many mistrust him. Perhaps some evil force will drive him away so he cannot help us in the way Wakantanka desires."

"There is no power greater than the Creator's, my friend."

"If that is true, Hanmani, why do His people suffer and die at the hands of both White and Indian enemies? Why does He allow our lands and animals, His creations, to be destroyed and misused?"

"Evil does exist, my friend, and it is powerful, but the Great Spirit will conquer it. Has the Great One not always brought us through dark times?"

"Yes, and it is wicked of me to show such doubts and weakness. I do not know what causes my bad behavior on this sun."

"It is the confusing and wonderful news I revealed to you," Hanmani suggested, "and the perils Cloud Chaser faces before him. And your hunger for him plays a large part as well."

"How can I feel such things for him when we are strangers?"

"I do not know, Dawn, for love and desire are unknown to me."

Love and desire wafted across Macha's troubled mind as the summer wind blew across the Lakota Plains, bending grasses and wildflowers to its potent will as perhaps those feelings would bend her to the will of Cloud Chaser.

Chase sat cross-legged on his bedroll as he ate the food Hanmani had brought to him this morning. He had been camped there alone for a week, and only his half-sister had approached him to serve him meals and to bring him wood for his fire at night, one to provide light during the New Moon's dark span. He speculated that maybe his patience, determination, temperament, and obedience were being tested by this enforced seclusion. He certainly didn't want to do anything that would be judged as a flaw or sign of guilt, such as stalking into their camp and demanding to speak with his father or leaving his site without permission.

During the past seven days, he had enjoyed quick and secret words with Hanmani, who continued to conceal from others her communications with him. He had learned a little more about his family and recent events from her, but stolen moments didn't allow enough time for gleaning many facts. Yet, he was convinced she believed his claims and had come to like, respect, and accept him. If only, he fretted, others would do the same.

He had observed Macha furtively as she had done her daily chores, and the hunger to speak to her and get to know her had grown stronger each day. He could not explain or understand his powerful attraction to her, but it existed and heightened steadily. He had taken great pleasure in hearing her alluring voice, in watching her radiant and easy smile, in following her graceful movements, in seeing the sun almost glisten on her shiny black hair, in trailing his tawny gaze over her lovely features and supple body. He wondered what she would think and how she would feel about his romantic interest in her, if he ever revealed it, or if Hanmani had done so. Would she find it flattering and pleasing, or repulsive and unwanted? Could Macha ever be receptive to a half-breed, an outsider? Even if she returned his feelings for her one day, would her parents and their people permit a joining between them? He doubted it, and should not even be daydreaming along that line. Thoughts of romance, love, and marriage had not entered his mind before arriving there; and this absolutely was not the time for him to be distracted by such ideas.

One thing he should concentrate on instead was his cousin. He had seen Two Feathers halt several times during the week to glare at him, and he had merely stared back to show he wasn't being intimidated. He had watched his brothers and their small parties leave to go on hunting and scouting rides, and he had yearned to join them. He hoped his horse was being well tended. The band stayed busy with preparation tasks; soon they would depart for the Plains and their buffalo hunt, and he wondered if he would be allowed to go with them. Or, Chase mused, would he be ordered to leave the area or be slain?

He had tried to pass the time reading portions of James Fenimore Cooper's *The Deerslayer* and the Martins' family Bible, both of which he had packed in his saddlebag. But he was becoming edgy, frustrated, and vexed by his coerced seclusion.

As Wind Dancer retrieved his bow and quiver from his weapon's stand, Chumani asked, "What will happen on this sun, my husband?"

Wind Dancer gazed at his beloved Dewdrops, who held their child in her arms. "Only the Great Spirit knows, my wife," he said. As he tousled the dark hair on his two-year-old son's head, he disclosed, "I go to carry out Grandfather's cunning plan to uncover the truth. Before this sun passes, the decision could be made on whether Cloud Chaser lives or dies."

"This task is hard and painful for you," she remarked knowingly as she looked into his sad and worried gaze.

"It will be more difficult and tormenting to lose my brother for a second time than it was to do so the first time; for on this sun, it may be a final loss to death and a black mark of shame on my family."

"Your family should not be held to blame for his deceit and destiny," Chumani refuted in a gentle tone.

"He is from the bloodline of Ghost Warrior and Redbird, and from the blood and seed of Rising Bear; if he betrays and endangers the Red Shields, we will be responsible and dishonored, for it is his bond to us which lured him here. Do not forget, my beloved wife, a man is his family, and his family is him; all that happens with one member relates to all in his circle."

"I will pray that only good lives within and comes from him."

"As will I, Dewdrops. Guard yourself and our son well on this sun."

As Chase observed his older brother's approach and studied Wind Dancer's resolved expression, he asked himself if the waiting was finally over and a decision about his fate had been reached . . .

CHAPTER FOUR

As they mounted and left camp, Wind Dancer told Chase he was taking him along while he scouted the nearby grassland area and perhaps hunted a deer or antelope for their evening meal. In reality and at his grandfather's suggestion, this outing was a ploy to see if his brother attempted to escape, to abduct him for a hostage, or to slay him. He knew that braves, led by War Eagle, were trailing them in secret to recapture or thwart Cloud Chaser if he tried to flee or to harm him. The taste of this trick was bitter in Wind Dancer's mouth, but he had to obey his shaman and chief, and he had to know the truth for himself. With each step his well-trained and alert animal took, he prayed nothing bad would happen.

As they crossed a flower-scattered meadow and traveled close to a clear and winding stream, Chase said in the Lakota language, "Thank you, my brother, for it is good to be moving about and sitting upon my horse again. He seems well tended but in need of this ride as much as I am. It is strange and tiring to lie around for many days and do nothing."

Wind Dancer kept his keen gaze aimed ahead. "How do you still know Lakota so well when it has been so long since you spoke or heard it?"

Chase smiled and explained, "During my return home, I journeyed with fur traders. One knew Lakota well and helped me remember it."

"Did he ask why you wished to learn our tongue?"

"Yes, and I told him I planned to live and work in this area, so I should know how to speak with the people who dwelled here."

"Did he not think it strange you knew much of our tongue?"

Chase was glad he had been given an opportunity to refresh himself on the Lakota verbal and sign languages. He understood how interpreters could make translation errors so easily—or intentionally—during parleys, and hoped he didn't make serious mistakes during his talks with his family. "I told him I had lived here long ago and learned it in the past, but had forgotten many of the words and signs. It does not matter what I told him, for he fell from a mountain and was killed before we reached this area."

Following a lengthy silence, Chase asked, "Why was I left alone near camp for so many suns and moons? Was I being tested?"

"Is that not what you told us to do?"

Chase nodded. "Did I find victory or defeat?"

"Which do you think you earned?" Wind Dancer asked.

"I deserve victory, my brother. Did I earn it?"

"If you did not, would you be riding with me on this sun?"

Chase laughed and jested, "You answer each question with another question, my brother. I do not remember you doing so when we were boys." With hopes of reminding Wind Dancer of old times and feelings, he said, "As children, you spoke to me with clear words and a strong spirit. Do you remember when Grandmother gave you and War Eagle the leather ponies? You told me: 'Do not be sad, my brother, for you can play with mine. Grandmother lacked enough doeskin to make three.' When Grandfather placed my brothers beside him and my sister upon his legs and told us stories or taught us many things about the Ancient Ones and our customs, you said, 'Do not be sad, my brother, for you sit before him and can look into his face while he speaks.' When our cousin threw rocks at me and called me bad names, you tended my injuries and said to tell no one, for he was jealous of me and I would show great courage and generosity if I held silent. You helped me make my medicine pouch and gave me a feather from the first bird you slayed to go inside it for good luck. You gave me a red stone chipped from the sacred pipe Father was making and said it was a gift from him for my medicine pouch. I walked in your shadow on many suns. Long ago, you taught me many things and protected me from harm; now, you speak and walk in circles I do not understand and I cannot follow your lead."

Wind Dancer's heart was touched by those remembrances, for they were special things only his brother could know. But had Cloud Chaser mentioned them only to trick him? "I am a Strong Heart, Shirt-Wearer, and next chief. My greatest duty is to my people. I must say and do what is best for them. Once you have proven yourself to us, I will speak to you of what lives in my heart and mind."

"That is good, fair, and wise, my brother," *but you're being evasive and wary with me. Something's afoot, because you're looking and acting odd. I guess I'll know soon enough what you're up to today.* As they rode into the edge of the vast Plains, Chase sought to continue their talk. "The Whites know your name and prowess well, as they do our father's," he said. "You will be a great and powerful chief when our father walks the Ghost Trail."

Wind Dancer nodded gratitude as his keen gaze scanned the terrain before them. The landscape was a mixture of rolling hills, near-flat spans, scattered evergreen groves or singular trees and bushes, various grasses, and ample wild-flowers. Behind them were the forested foothills and black rock formations of the sprawling Paha Sapa, and War Eagle's trailing party. Wind Dancer did not head for totally open ground, which would not provide the group places to conceal themselves. He also made sure he did not raise his left arm for any reason, since that would signal his youngest brother to rush to his aid. "In the seasons yet to come, I will seek to make your words true, Cloud Chaser, if I and my people survive the white man's greed and encroachment."

"You and they will survive, Wind Dancer, if you do not break the treaty and you try to live in peace with the soldiers and settlers."

"The treaty has been broken, Cloud Chaser, but by the Whites, for their leaders have not honored their words to us and others."

"How do you know that is true, Wind Dancer, if you cannot read the white man's words upon the treaty papers?"

"I know, for their words at Long Meadows do not match their actions since that sun."

As they topped a rolling hill, Wind Dancer sighted three Crow braves riding at its base, who halted in a hurry and looked at him warily. Many courses of response flashed across his mind. He knew what he wanted to do: attack and defeat them for their many evil deeds against his and other Lakota bands. That was what he had been taught and trained to do since birth and what he and his beloved wife had done with glorious success three summers past; but things had changed with the treaty's warning of lethal retaliation by soldiers. He decided, as a high-ranking leader and future chief, he must not spark a war which could flame into a roaring and destructive wildfire and engulf his people.

Wind Dancer scowled in disappointment as he noted his enemies' despicable sneers. He headed toward them, with Cloud Chaser following to his rear. He reined in and asked in Crow, "Why do you encroach on Lakota land? It is forbidden by the Long Meadows Treaty, which your people signed. Do you seek to call down the Bluecoats on your tribe?"

The leader responded in his foe's language. "Long before Lakotas came from far beyond the big muddy waters, this was Apsaalooke land and will be Apsaalooke territory again one day. We ride to visit our allies the Pawnee beyond the Platte River. You forget, Wind Dancer of the Red Shields, the treaty says we can ride across and hunt on this land as we have done since before your people were born. It will not help you to make friends with a few white men, for Bluecoats and Whites hate Lakotas more than other Indians and will one day destroy them."

"I am Oglala by blood," Cloud Chaser refuted, glaring at the Bird Warrior who had glanced at him during his final words.

The Crow leader eyed him up and down with a visible show of scorn and scoffed, "You are a half-breed, lower than the turtle's belly and more foul than the scent of the *maka*. You are too low to even look at me."

Chase did not like being compared to a skunk and ridiculed for his mixed heritage. He realized he needed to get his hands on a copy of that treaty and soon, for its unknown words could cause mistakes and conflicts on his band's part, and be used by sly enemies to their advantage. As he observed the confrontation, he wished he had his weapons so he would be prepared to come to his brother's aid if the Crow charged him, as it would be a large coup for the enemy who took the life, scalplock, and possessions of such a great warrior. He was amazed and pleased by his brother's bravery, but he hoped Wind Dancer would not incite the Crow to attack since the odds were in the opponents' favor.

"Do we pass on, my longtime foe, or do we fight here? Do you forget the treaty said no Indian Nation gives up a claim to other lands and may ride, hunt, and fish in any territory covered by it?"

"*Dee, Apsaalooke.*"

As soon as Wind Dancer told them to leave, the Crow leader laughed in amusement at his enemy's coerced position, kneed his mount's sides, and galloped away amidst taunting yips.

"I am proud of you, my brother," Chase said, "for you showed great courage, patience, and wisdom. Did he speak the truth?"

Wind Dancer frowned. "The words he spoke are in the treaty."

Chase was confused. "Why would the White leaders divide these lands into separate territories and then give any man permission to encroach on others? It is foolish and dangerous to force enemy bands to share areas and order them not to fight when they come into contact with each other."

"That is only one of the many reasons why we could not sign. Lakotas cannot dwell in peace in the same territory

66

with the Crow and Pawnee. We cannot allow them to slay all of the game on our hunting grounds while their herds and other animals flourish. For when the season came and ours were gone, they would not allow us to encroach on their hunting grounds; they would break treaty to have us starve and freeze in winter."

Chase related his idea about obtaining a copy of the treaty to see what it truly said. "Many times there is no Indian word to match a white man's word, for words come from the lives we lead. I understand the white man's language and can translate the treaty words to see if they mean what the interpreter told you at Long Meadows."

"Where would you get such . . . papers? How?"

"I am sure the signed papers are with the President, the Great White Chief, far away. But matching papers may be kept at Fort Laramie, for its soldiers are responsible for honoring its terms. I can ride there to learn if they exist and who has them. I can sneak into his work tepee at night and take them. I will bring them to you and read them for you."

"It would not please others for you to leave and return."

"It is the only way to get the treaty, Wind Dancer. I must do this task alone, for I can dress, speak, and act as a white man. You must trust me, my brother, for our people's survival may depend upon its words."

"I will think on your plan and reveal it to Father, but I feel its risk is great. Come. We ride to camp. If we sight good game, we will halt to hunt it."

Chase saw the small party of warriors, led by his younger brother, return to camp not long after he and Wind Dancer had. It was obvious they had been trailed and observed.

Even if he had not sighted a man or two along the way, he had sensed their presence. He grinned to himself, concluding he had passed another test. But how many more, he mused, must he take and pass? His challenges couldn't last much longer with departure looming before them in ten days.

Nearing dusk, Chase walked into the woods to relieve himself, as he had been given permission to tend that necessity in privacy. He finished quickly and started to return to his campsite when he heard sounds. He halted and listened: it was Dawn's voice, singing softly as if to herself. He could not resist the urge to meet and speak with her.

"*Hau, Macha,*" Chase greeted her from behind after making certain no one was nearby. He noted how she whirled in surprise, her dark gaze widened. "You pick flowers late on this sun." She glanced around furtively before speaking to him; no doubt she had been ordered not to do so.

"Mother has need of *wayuco-onzinzintka,* and they bloom as the sun goes to sleep," she explained. "I must hurry, for darkness will come to our land soon."

"You no longer have the little girl's face I remember," Chase said, ignoring the hint she could not tarry. "You now have one of a beautiful young woman. It is good to see you again."

Macha was warmed by both his compliment and his nearness. He was taller and his chest was broader than she had remembered. And his looks were even more appealing. She tried not to stare or to stammer. "Your words are kind. You no longer have the boy's face of Cloud Chaser; you have

68

changed much during the many seasons you were gone from us. But you have not lost your stalking skills, for I did not hear or see you approach."

She was so enchanting that Chase had to order himself not to stare at her. Being with her was like having a wonderful dream come true. He felt his heart pounding with elation and excitement. "I did not mean to stalk or frighten you. As I walked nearby, I heard singing in a voice as sweet as the nightbird's and was compelled to see who made such lovely sounds." He knew their time was limited, so he decided to ask an important question: "Do you have a mate and children?"

Macha was surprised by that query and wondered why he asked it. "No. Do you have a mate and children far away?" She almost held her breath as she waited for him to answer, though doing so only took a short time.

"No. Perhaps it will soon be different, for I have reached twenty-two circles of the seasons. How many are behind you?"

"Eighteen. Will you come with us on the buffalo hunt? We leave soon."

Chase shrugged. "That is for my father to decide, and he has not done so to this sun, but I hope to go. Do others in our band speak against me?"

She lowered her gaze in shame. "That is not for me to say."

Chase eyed her bowed head and guessed the truth she didn't want to voice. "That means the answer is yes."

"Not all speak . . ." Macha started to explain, but she halted when their gazes met and she read hurt in his. "Do not put meanings to my words which might be wrong," she urged him.

Chase smiled. "You still possess a good heart and quick mind. I remember when you played with me and sneaked me treats when other children would not. It is good you have not changed in that way."

"The Great Spirit and our teachings say it is wrong to be cruel. I try to be kind to all people, though it is hard to do so with some."

"That is true," he murmured as his gaze roamed her features.

"Did the Whites treat you bad when you lived far away?" Macha asked softly.

"No. At least, most of them did not. I was accepted as the son of the white man and woman who found me injured and reared me."

"Hanmani said you did not return sooner because you thought your people had been slain by the enemy."

"That is true," he said, then told her the other reasons he had related to his family. "I do not know why I was taken far away or why I was called back here by the Great Spirit, but He will reveal such things later."

Macha turned her head slightly, and tensed. "My mother calls to me," she explained. "I must go. Remain here until I am gone."

"After I am accepted as a band member, can we talk again?"

She nodded. "But we must not do so until that sun rises."

"I understand. Go before we are seen together. Until another sun?"

Macha smiled and whispered, "Until another sun, Cloud Chaser."

70

Chase watched her hastily disappear, then took a deep breath. Her radiant smile could vanquish the blackness of a moonless night and warm the flesh on a freezing day! Her gentle nature and musical voice could calm the most troubled soul! She was good, kind, and generous—as his mother and adoptive mother had been. She was so beautiful it was easy to understand why he desired her so, but his feelings for her went beyond anything he'd ever felt for any other female.

Chase returned to his assigned location to find Two Feathers inspecting it. He would have preferred to turn in for the night with pleasant thoughts and feelings flowing through him, but he suppressed a frown and harsh tone to prevent provoking the man into another quarrel. "What do you want here, my cousin?" As Two Feathers turned to face him, Chase read sheer hatred and contempt in the man's expression, and sensed rage boiling within him. Why, he wondered again, did his cousin so detest him?

"Your camp was empty. Rising Bear said not to leave it."

"I am allowed to go empty my body in the forest as needed. Were you sent to find and guard me or to fetch me for my father?"

"You cannot be trusted, half-breed." Two Feathers almost snarled the words.

"To insult me insults my father, for I carry the blood of Rising Bear."

"Your White blood is strongest within you and it paints your looks."

"Do you say your chief and uncle has weak blood and seeds? Do you say they are so weak they cannot overcome those of a lowly white woman?"

Wind Dancer had approached as the two men challenged each other with words and glares. "Why are you here, my cousin?" he asked Two Feathers. "You were told to stay away from Cloud Chaser's camp. Why do you disobey?"

"He was gone. I came to find him. He—"

Chase interrupted and explained his absence, withholding only the part about visiting with Macha for a short time. "My cousin hopes I will flee or disobey so badly that he spies on me and insults me and Father."

Wind Dancer glanced at his cousin and asked, "Is this true?"

When Two Feathers did not respond fast enough and glowered at Chase as if to dare him to repeat what he had said, Chase related their exchange of words, some of which his brother must have overheard.

Wind Dancer lifted his hand to indicate silence as he thought about the offensive matter for a while, trying to decide how best to handle it. He did not want to speak of his father's past weakness with either man or to reveal their words to others, which could cause trouble in camp. "Go, my cousin, and do not return to Cloud Chaser's camp without Father's permission," Wind Dancer ordered. "If you disobey, I will reveal your bad words to him."

After Two Feathers left in a sullen mood, Chase asked Wind Dancer the question that had been tormenting him: "My cousin hated me as a child and he hates me as a man, my brother. Why?"

"He fears you will betray and shame his beloved chief and uncle and you will bring pain to his heart," Wind Dancer speculated.

Chase guessed that was just a partly accurate supposition,

but he was grateful to be answered. Although he sensed tension and wariness in Wind Dancer, at least and at last they were talking. "Is that also what you think, my brother?"

Wind Dancer locked his gaze with Cloud Chaser's and felt compelled to admit, "I do not know my true thoughts and feelings, but they will be clear to me soon." He wanted to say more, but this was not the best time. He had loved his brother and grieved over his loss, and he did not want anything bad to happen to force him to experience those feelings again. He wished this grim situation was different and simple, but it was not; and a mistake in trust and judgment could be fatal for his people, for his family.

"Did your doubts lead you to have War Eagle and his small band follow us this morning? What did you expect to happen?" he asked, and witnessed his older brother's astonishment.

"They trailed us to prevent trouble," Wind Dancer said in honesty.

"Was that by your order or by Father's?"

"It was Grandfather's, for he seeks to protect the next chief."

"Protect you from me? He fears I would harm my own brother?"

"To protect me from any and all harm; that is all I can tell you."

"Thank you for speaking the truth to me; it brings great joy to my heart and spirit. Is there a chance I will be accepted one day, or am I wasting my time here? Should I go or stay?"

"That is your choice to make, Cloud Chaser."

"No, my brother; it is our father's and people's choice."

"If your heart and purpose are good, wait for that sun to rise. Now I must go, for darkness is here and my family waits for my return."

Chase smiled. "I am eager to meet your wife and son, my brother, when you say the time is right."

"It is up to you to make that sun rise, Cloud Chaser. I go now."

An exhilarated Chase watched his brother leave. Surely he had not misunderstood Wind Dancer's subtle attempt at encouragement: "*Wait* for that sun to rise." At long last, maybe he had made progress toward his goal. Perhaps all he had to do was be patient, obedient, and stay out of trouble. *Wouldn't it be wonderful to live here and have a home and a family of my own?* he thought as he settled on his bedroll, then asked himself why he was thinking such optimistic thoughts. He concluded it was because of his meeting with Macha, as she was even more tempting up close than at a distance. And it also had to do with his past experiences. He had lived his early years as a near-outsider, as the half-Indian child of a white woman, a mother who had been taken from him when he was only nine. He had yearned for his father to look at him and treat him as Rising Bear did his other sons, and he had believed that would happen one day. Despite the Martins' love for him, he had never felt he really belonged on a farm or living amidst all Whites. He had felt set apart, different, a guest in their Oregon home. He had made a few friends with schoolmates and neighbors, but those had not been close relationships, such as he had experienced with Wind Dancer and War Eagle, who had been called *Tokapa* and *Icinunpa* before sacred vision-quests gave them their adult names. He had missed his father, two brothers, and sister. He had always believed this was where he belonged; this was where he would be fulfilled. Deep inside, he knew his destiny was here with the Red Shield Oglalas and on Lakota lands, and with Macha as his wife.

Icinunpa. Chase's mind echoed the name he should have been given, for he was Rising Bear's "Second" son, not War Eagle, though he bore no resentment toward his younger brother for possessing it for many years. Wind Dancer had deserved his name of "Firstborn," the same as his own son of two years. *A son . . . a child I can rear with love and pride. A child who will not be forced to endure rejection and anguish. But is that possible to do in a territory filled with animosities and conflicts? I don't know.*

The next morning, Hanmani arrived with his usual meal and a surprise for him. As she passed the small bundle to Chase, she whispered, "This is from Dawn; she cooked bread with dried nuts and berries. She told me of your talk in the forest. You must be careful not to go near her until you are a Red Shield again. If my cousin learns of your meeting, he will get you and her into trouble, for he will soon ask for her to join to him."

Chase was shocked and vexed by that news. "Does Dawn love Two Feathers? Will she become his wife?"

"No, my brother, she does not love him or wish to mate with him. He is also of my lost grandparents' bloodline, but I fear he is bad. He has made whisperings to me about approaching her, but I have tried to stop him. He is viewed as a brave and skilled warrior and carries the blood of a past chief, so her parents will believe him a good choice for her and will ask her to accept him. I cannot speak against my cousin before others, for it would cause much trouble. Dawn is afraid, for she does not know how she will reject him without insulting his honor and displeasing her parents."

"Why are you telling me such sad things, my sister?"

"Because of the sacred vision-dream and because she is my best friend and I do not want her mated to him."

"What can I do to prevent it, my sister?" Chase asked.

"I do not know, but you must try to save her."

Chase perceived how worried and desperate Hanmani was, and hated to imagine Macha's feelings. "How soon will Two Feathers speak for her?"

"After the buffalo hunt, unless he learns of your feelings for her. If he does so, he will speak fast and strong for her only to hurt and defeat you. I must go now, but think on my words, for she is your destiny."

Chase did not have a chance to reply to that astonishing assertion before Hanmani rushed away to tend her daily chores. He sat on his bedroll and began to eat, his thoughts and emotions in a quandary. He was convinced by now that his sister believed and accepted him fully, though she dared not tell or show such feelings to anyone other than Macha. Yet, how did she think he could step between Two Feathers and his objective while he was still secluded and being tested? Hanmani was accurate in one area: if their cousin even suspected Cloud Chaser desired the daughter of Leaning Tree and Ohute, he would go after her with full force in order to spite him.

As Chase savored the sly treat and stroked the soft fur of the rabbit pelt it had been wrapped in and had been held in her hands, he thought, *It will snow on the hottest day in summer before my cousin touches her!*

At midmorning of the following day, War Eagle and Swift Otter approached Chase's campsite. "Do you wish to ride and hunt with us?" War Eagle asked. "Your horse needs a good run."

Chase noted that his brother had spoken in Lakota, not English, and was scrutinizing him. He presumed he was about to face another test of some kind, but he was glad to have a diversion and exercise. He smiled and thanked War Eagle, and greeted the other warrior, a Sacred Bow Carrier like his brother.

As they walked to their horses, War Eagle wondered if Cloud Chaser suspected he was taking him along to see what he said and did, actions he was to report to his father, brother, and grandfather. Besides Swift Otter, three men were going with them: River's Edge, Broken Lance, and Two Feathers. His cousin Broken Lance often rode and hunted with him, but Two Feathers did not. He was being taken along at Wind Dancer's request, to see how their cousin behaved toward Cloud Chaser. Wind Dancer had confided the lingering conflict to him and wanted to learn if Two Feathers was obeying his warning. If there was going to be trouble between the two men, Wind Dancer, as a Shirt-Wearer who handled such problems, wanted to know before their journey to the Grasslands began soon.

As Chase saddled his mount, he said to War Eagle, "I will need my weapons for hunting. May I have them?"

"You cannot slay the Great Spirit's creatures with a fire-stick. To give up their lives to a white man's weapon would bring them great shame."

Chase halted his task and looked behind him, but already knew who was standing there and speaking to him in such a harsh tone. Just as he dreaded, Two Feathers was going with them, and no doubt would spoil the outing. "I would use a bow and arrows, my cousin, but I do not have any. It is hard to slay a creature from horseback with only the knife I wear."

"You can use our weapons?" Two Feathers scoffed with a glare.

"I am skilled with a bow and arrows, for I made and used them far away to keep in practice for my return home."

"If that is true, why did you not bring them with you?"

"I thought it unwise to travel in the territories of the Whites and other tribes with such weapons. I will make another bow and arrows soon."

War Eagle had come prepared for this possibility. He handed Chase his old bow and a plain quiver of four arrows. "Use these," he offered. "I will test my new bow and quiver and ready them for the great buffalo hunt."

"Thank you, my brother; they are still good weapons," Chase said as he examined them, then suspended them around his torso in Lakota fashion.

War Eagle nodded, then glanced to where the other three members of his hunting party were mounting to leave. "Come. We ride," he said, and swung himself atop his horse with fluid agility.

Two Feathers glared at the half-White man and said in a low voice, "If you try to flee, weakling dog, I will send my arrow into your back faster than you can travel across our land."

"Your quarrel with me is foolish and must halt, my

cousin," Chase retorted. "We are no longer boys; we are men now and must behave as such. I have offered you my hand in peace, but you have refused to grasp it and only seek to cut it off. I will not offer you a truce again, for it is useless."

War Eagle overheard that exchange and delayed his departure to warn, "Such words are not needed, my cousin. If you do not want to ride with him, you can hunt with others or with us on another sun. A Sacred Bow Carrier must practice the Four Virtues. Such words, feelings, and actions do not show Courage, Wisdom, Generosity, and Restraining Endurance."

Two Feathers scowled. "I ride with you this sun, War Eagle."

Chase mounted and followed behind the other four men, all led by his younger brother, who had earned his respect and gratitude for War Eagle's bold words to their now-sullen cousin. He was surprised that War Eagle had come to his defense and had reprimanded Two Feathers so force-fully, and with what appeared to be gleams of anger in his eyes. He hadn't known that Two Feathers was a Sacred Bow Carrier, a high rank that only four men held at a time. How had the rancorous male earned that lofty position? Obviously there was more to know about his cousin than he had witnessed so far.

Although War Eagle was only twenty, it was apparent to Chase that his younger brother was confidant, respected, and intelligent. His status of Sacred Bow Carrier proved that War Eagle also possessed enormous prowess as a sea-soned warrior. Pride over both brothers' accomplishments surged through Chase, and he yearned to become more like them. With their help and acceptance, he reasoned, he could achieve that new goal. As he envisioned the three of them galloping across the Plains side by side while laughing and talking and defending their territory and people, excitement swept over him like the powerful waves crashing over jagged rocks which he had once seen on the Oregon coast.

The Great Spirit and Mother Earth had created immense beauty and diversity across this vast land, Chase concluded, so it was understandable why both cultures and others from across the Big Waters desired to make it theirs. It was a shame that they couldn't live in peace. If only the Indian Nations—ally and enemy—could band together and make a truce, they could keep the Whites at bay for a long time; and the Nebraska Territory could become Indian Territory, and avoided by Whites for any and all reasons. After all, the Whites did have a large country from which to select settling places without stealing this one. He knew that to be a fact because he had traveled a large section of it and had seen maps of the rest. His father and the others were right: this part of the country should not be encroached by the enemy, for it belonged to the Indians.

After a meandering ride, which he spent in deep thought, Chase cleared his head and came to alert when War Eagle held up his hand to signal them to halt. His brother gathered them closer to whisper his instructions, and Chase—along with the others—nodded, as all were compelled to obey the orders of the party leader.

War Eagle had decided to go after either elk or moose today, animals which preferred to graze and take brief rests in either lush meadows near woods or in marshy wetlands near rivers and lakes. To stalk their prey from three directions, they were separated into pairs: Swift Otter with Two Feathers, War Eagle with Broken Lance, and River's Edge with Cloud Chaser.

They spread out to surround the chosen area before closing in on it and entrapping between them whatever creature grazed there. Chase was in a good mood. He had ridden and talked with his older brother, who had seemed to slyly give him encouragement about an impending reunion. He was hunting with his youngest brother, who had taken his side against a fellow society member and close relative, just as Wind Dancer had done in a smaller manner two days ago. Many things he had learned or been told about their customs and ways during childhood were returning to his mind at a swift and clear pace. It was as if he had suppressed such knowledge in Oregon to lessen or prevent the anguish of losing what it represented. Now that he was home, a flood of memories filled his head.

Chase stole a sideways glance at the brave with whom he rode. He wondered if River's Edge resented being paired with him. They hadn't spoken, but they had to maintain silence to avoid spooking birds or small creatures which might in turn alert their prey to intruders and danger.

At one point, River's Edge dismounted to study the ground for tracks. After finding fresh ones, he motioned for Cloud Chaser to hold his position and remain quiet. River's Edge crept a lengthy distance ahead of the other man and his own horse. As he knelt behind bushes to scan the area beyond him to see if he sighted his prey, he heard threatening snarls and hurried movements to his rear and whirled to see a badger coming toward him. As he did so, he lost his balance and fell backward to the ground, a lack of time preventing him from retrieving his bow and an arrow on his back. With haste, he reached for a sheathed knife at his waist. Wide-eyed, he saw the ferocious creature stumble when an arrow thudded into its enraged body. He watched Cloud Chaser race forward, seize the thrashing animal by its scruff, and quickly and mercifully end its suffering and life.

River's Edge looked past the other man as his startled horse danced about in panic and stepped into a hole, then collapsed to the earth. He bolted forward to the beloved beast to find him in great pain with a broken leg. As the other man joined him and knelt to examine the severe injury, he said, "Such breaks will not heal; he must be released from this life. He has been a good companion, so this deed is hard for me to do."

"I will do it for you, River's Edge, for it wounds the heart and mind to take the life of a friend, even when that task is needed."

River's Edge took a deep breath and stared at the horse in agony. "It will be a good deed if you take my place in this matter. Do it fast and kind, as with the badger." He glared at the hole where a stump had rotted, one which had become filled and concealed by leaves and twigs. He had dismounted from the other side and had not seen that peril.

Chase wiped his sharp and bloody blade on the grass, then looked at the tormented brave. "It is over. You can ride with me to join the others. Do you want me to skin the badger for you?"

"I will do so, but I thank you for your help, Cloud Chaser. It is good to be companions on this hard day, for our sisters are best friends."

Chase eyed the brave and realized why he looked

familiar, as Macha's tepee was not within view of his campsite and he had not seen this brave enter or depart from there. "You are Dawn's brother?"

"That is so. We were born at sunrise near a river's edge; that is how we were named. I came first and she followed. We do not match in looks, but we are alike in many ways. I have not taken my man name, for I have not done that vision-quest to this sun. You and I did not play together as boys, for you were older, but I am glad you ride with me on this hunt. I will tell your father and brothers of your brave and good deeds."

"Thank you, River's Edge; it is an honor to ride with one such as you."

"I must sing the death chant for my companion before he is left here to be claimed by the forces of nature. I will join you soon."

Chase grasped that River's Edge wanted privacy to mourn his loss, so he nodded and walked a lengthy distance away, taking his mount with him. With his back turned, he listened to the soulful sounds and muffled words coming from behind him. As he did so, he stroked his horse's neck and forehead, for they also had been companions for a long time—since his sixteenth birthday, or the day chosen to celebrate it by the Martins. He remembered how Tom had sold extra vegetables and firewood he had chopped and how Lucy had sold two quilts she had made to pay for the animal. He cherished the gift and their many acts of kindness. He had no doubts they had loved and treasured him. Yet, how could he adequately explain his feelings and sense of loyalty to his adoptive parents to his family and people here when they viewed all Whites as the enemy? Yes, their deception had pained him, even angered him for a time; then, he had come to understand and forgive it. If only—

"I am finished. We will ride to find the others."

Chase turned to face River's Edge. He had been so deep in thought that he hadn't heard the chanting stop or the badger being skinned, for the brave now carried its pelt across one arm. He nodded instead of speaking, his throat feeling oddly constricted by emotion. He mounted and extended his left hand so River's Edge could grasp his wrist and swing himself up behind him. He glanced toward the fallen horse to see its body mostly covered by scrub-limbs. He understood the brave's sorrowful mood, for he knew how he would be feeling if that were his companion lying dead.

Chase guided his horse in the assigned direction to rendezvous with the other hunters. Perhaps his good deed today would have a favorable effect upon Macha and her parents. Maybe that was a selfish thought, but surely it was only being human.

Just as Chase suspected, his rescue of River's Edge did not sit well with Two Feathers; nor did what soon occurred . . .

CHAPTER FIVE

Chase spotted a large male elk, one with many points to its rack, as it grazed beyond them. With the wind in their favor and with their silence and stealthy movements, the creature had not heard, seen, or smelled them. He got the attention of River's Edge and motioned to their prey.

After the two men cautiously dismounted, Chase let his

reins dangle to the ground. He knew his well-trained and loyal animal would remain quiet and still. He whispered for River's Edge to take the lead and told him, "You must shoot your arrow first, for it has been many suns since I held and used this weapon. I will release my shaft after yours leaves your bow."

River's Edge nodded and crept nearer to their target, his weapon at the ready. Using trees, bushes, and other vegetation to conceal their approach, he guided them as close as possible without being overconfident about his stalking skills or carelessly misjudging the creature's keen senses. When they were within victory range, he halted them and prepared to fire his first shot.

Chase nocked a shaft and awaited his turn to take action. He—along with River's Edge—knew one arrow would not bring down an animal of that size; and for certain the wounded beast would take flight as soon as he was struck. He realized their eventual success depended upon the accuracy of their initial strikes, but he also knew triumph hinged upon their stamina and running pace during the ensuing quest to complete their task before the elk escaped beyond their reach, as it could probably survive a single arrow wound, especially if it wasn't in a vital body area like a lung or the heart. His heart pounded with anticipation.

River's Edge aimed and fired, and grasped another arrow as Cloud Chaser released his first one in the blink of the eye behind his. Both shafts embedded themselves in the startled elk, one in a lung and one in the heart. Even so, the huge creature bolted with amazing speed and agility to get out of the vulnerable meadow and into the protective woods.

"Come. We chase him, my friend!" River's Edge shouted

in elation and took off in pursuit across the lush grass and various-colored wildflowers.

"Come, Red!" he called out in English, and his sorrel quickly obeyed as Chase ran forward to join the nimble brave. It felt good to be hunting with this particular man, to be out of seclusion, to be trusted to be alone with any Red Shield. He didn't know why he wasn't being watched today, as he sensed no other eyes upon him. Also, he didn't know why he had been paired with the next to the youngest member of the hunting party who didn't appear to be a seasoned warrior. Yet, the brave could have more prowess than he realized, for surely he was a bowman.

The two men darted around trees and bushes and leapt over fallen limbs as they followed in the elk's frantic wake. When the animal paused for a minute and turned its head to check its peril, both men sent second arrows into its hindquarters at almost the same time.

River's Edge laughed. "We think the same as hunters, my friend: to injure his legs will slow his pace. He will soon be ours."

"You are skilled with your bow and possess much prowess, River's Edge, and must provide your family with much game and many hides."

The brave grinned in pleasure while keeping his gaze locked on his prey and never missing a step in his rapid movements. "That is true, and I thank you for your good words, for they come from a skilled hunter."

The elk jerked and stumbled aside following those third and fourth hits, then took off running. While trying to elude his determined predators, one shaft was snapped off midway by a sturdy pine. Two others were shoved backward several times by trees or wriggled by thick bushes, embedded too deeply to be dislodged. Each time the arrows were assailed by something, the extent of the damage to flesh and organs and his pain increased, as did his bleeding.

Water splashed on Chase's pants and River's Edge's leggings and it soaked boots and moccasins as they crossed a wide but shallow stream, dodging rocks within it. They spooked small animals and flushed birds in passing with the noise they created. Soon both were breathing hard through dry throats and were sweating profusely. Their muscles protested the exertion and their hearts pounded from the summer heat.

For a while, their target remained in view; then it was engulfed by dense trees and other greenery and was lost from sight and hearing. Using the creature's tracks and blood drippings, they continued to search for him.

"He slows his pace," River's Edge deduced as he studied changes in depth and shape of its tracks. "We will find him soon."

The exhausted and weakened elk looked wobbly when they came upon him in a small clearing in the forest, and halted to avoid provoking it to bolt again. Both studied its depleted condition and concluded its flight was over. Blood saturated its rib cage and flowed down its foreleg and hindquarters. Hearing their approach, it lifted its head and tried to make threatening signals with its sharp-tipped rack and warning sounds from a throat obstructed by blood. With haste and mercy, it was slain by River's Edge.

A winded River's Edge looked at Chase and grinned before he removed three still usable arrows and the broken shaft. The stone tip was recoverable, and as he did so, he remarked, "He is large and was strong. He has many antler points and a good hide. He will supply many people with meat. We must thank him for his sacrifice to us and the Great Spirit for placing him in our path and giving us the skills to take him."

As soon as those words of gratitude were spoken in prayerful form, River's Edge said, "We must summon our companions." He faced each direction and called out in a loud voice. He listened, but did not hear a reply. "If they do not come when we finish our work, we will find them."

While they waited for the others, they strung up the elk to a strong branch, with the sorrel helping them lift the heavy burden before the rope was secured to that same tree. River's Edge passed his blade across the animal's neck to finish bleeding it. Then he began the skinning and gutting procedure, with Chase helping him as needed.

"You found great victory, my friend," a smiling War Eagle praised River's Edge as he and the others entered the small clearing.

River's Edge paused in his familiar task and grinned broadly. "That is true. We wounded, chased, and slayed him together. He ran far before taking his last breath. We took him down with two arrows each."

War Eagle noted the man's use of "we" and cast his brother a sideways glance. He was relieved there had been no trouble, and felt great pride in Cloud Chaser's behavior and participation in the kill. He had been told to give Cloud Chaser the opportunity to escape and, if he took it, he and Swift Otter were to trail him to his destination while the others returned to camp. Wind Dancer also had told him not to shadow their brother during the hunt, for he had detected their presence the last time and would not take action this day knowing he was being watched. He was glad his brother had not fled or endangered River's Edge, and was happy the brave's opinion of Cloud Chaser was so favorable.

"We join you empty-handed, my friend, for we crossed paths with no game we wanted on this sun," War Eagle said. "We found your marks and those of the bleeding elk's upon Mother Earth and followed them. Where is your horse? There were tracks of only one during your pursuit, those of Cloud Chaser's mount. We did not know what to think until we saw the prints of your moccasins and his tracks together. We followed them to this place."

Unwanted thoughts thundered across Chase's mind: *Were you afraid I had slain him, little brother, and was trying to escape? I doubt Two Feathers would have minded his loss if it meant my defeat! How did you feel when you realized he was still alive and with me? Glad or disappointed? Don't think crazy thoughts, Chase,* he reprimanded himself, *and read War Eagle wrong.*

River's Edge took a breath, his expression one of sadness. In a ragged tone, he related the episodes with the badger and his beloved animal. "Your brother did a great deed for me. Bad badgers can rip out a man's throat. Cloud Chaser saved me from harm and death. He took the life of my companion when it pained my heart to do so. He sent him to the Ghost Trail with swiftness and mercy."

As if to flee that tormenting thought, River's Edge hurried on to relate, "Cloud Chaser gave me the first arrow shot, for he has not used a bow in many suns, but he has not lost his skill with it. He injured and slowed the badger with one arrow and attacked him without fear. He is a good hunter."

War Eagle was impressed by the man's news and grateful for the glowing remarks about his brother. It seemed obvious that River's Edge did not resent being paired with him; if the brave had been insulted or riled at first, that feeling had been vanquished. He looked at Cloud Chaser and said, "I thank you for saving our friend. It was a large and good deed."

Chase nodded appreciation to his brother, assuming War Eagle dared not say more before the others. As he had spoken his kind words, he saw Two Feathers scowling in irritation. And perhaps . . . *jealousy?* He looked at his other cousin and read what he thought were esteem and amazement in Broken Lance's eyes. When he nodded and smiled, the youngest party member averted his gaze. *At least I'm winning a few people's respect and approval, even if they don't want to display it.*

"We have much work to do," War Eagle said, and gave his orders.

While the elk was being butchered, the rest of the hunting party gathered fallen limbs and constructed a pull-along for hauling the meat to camp. After it was loaded with the chunks, haunches, hide, rack, and badger pelt, the travois was attached to Broken Lance's horse to prevent overburdening any mount, for his size was the smallest and lightest.

"All is done here," War Eagle said. "We head for camp."

"You ride with me," Two Feathers told River's Edge.

"Thank you, my friend, but I will return to camp with my hunting companion for this sun," he replied, and leapt up behind Chase.

Dreading that that bold choice might cause another

quarrel, War Eagle quickly said, "We go. Come, my friends and brother."

Chase refused to even steal a peek at his cousin, for he could imagine the man's outrage, and his action might be taken as a taunt and be used as an excuse to verbally or even physically attack him. He was pleased by the kindness of River's Edge and hoped it didn't make trouble for the brave. He also hoped War Eagle's actions and words prior to leaving camp didn't cause problems for him with his family and people. If so, the two people, not including Hanmani and Macha, whom he was getting to the fastest, would make hasty retreats. Chase reasoned that maybe the best way to become a Red Shield member again was by worming his way into people's hearts one by one, inch by inch, and day by day.

They reached the edge of camp by midafternoon as weary, sweaty, dusty, and hungry men, but most were in elated spirits. After thanking him again, River's Edge slid off the back of Chase's horse to walk beside Broken Lance to where the travois would halt at his family's dwelling. Once there, River's Edge would choose the portion of the elk he desired as befitted the beast's slayer, and remove other items which belonged to him from the two kills. Afterward, War Eagle—as band leader—would be given second choice, and so forth until the haul was divided fairly amongst the hunters, except for Cloud Chaser.

As River's Edge headed homeward, the others continued onward to various dismounting areas, some near their tepees and others in the edge of the forest. After parting with Swift Otter and Two Feathers, War Eagle guided Chase to

Rising Bear's rope enclosure. Two young braves hurried forward and offered to tend their horses, as that was considered a generous deed.

Chase was glad his cousin's horse was picketed elsewhere, as he was more than ready to avoid the man's foul mood and hateful glares. He stroked his mount's neck and forehead after unsaddling him. He smiled at one timid boy and said in Lakota, "He is called Red, but you must say his name in English, for he does not understand it in your tongue, which is Luta. If you stroke him while I am nearby, he will become your friend and allow you to take him for a walk to cool off and to the river to drink."

The hesitant boy looked at War Eagle for permission to do that task. Visitors' horses were always tended with eagerness and great care, but he did not know what the rank and acceptance were for this strange man.

War Eagle nodded, then furtively observed the interaction between his brother and the horse and the young boy. He was amused by the child's attempts to speak the animal's name, as he had difficulty with the unfamiliar "R" sound. He grinned in affection when the boy succeeded and the horse seemed to nod its head in greeting and approval. Following a few strokes with his brother's hand almost touching the youth's, the horse readily accepted the boy's handling and went calmly with him to the river.

"He is a good horse. Has he been your companion for many seasons?"

"Yes, my brother, for the passings of six circles of them. I called him Red after the name of my people's band and for his color. I thank you for taking me on your hunt this sun and for trusting me alone with River's Edge. It was a good journey. Do I return to where I camp?"

War Eagle looked past Chase, whose back was to the camp, and saw Wind Dancer motioning in sign language. He was confused by the order he received in secret, but obeyed it. "Come to our father's tepee to speak."

Chase hoped the uses of "my brother" and "our father," the hunting event today, and now a visit with his father were promising signs. He would know soon, he told himself as they reached Rising Bear's tepee, an abode highly and colorfully decorated with the numerous coups of his father. He knew Broken Lance had come and gone with the travois when he saw Winona and Hanmani preparing War Eagle's portion of today's kill, but neither female looked at him. He found Wind Dancer already present inside the dwelling, so he assumed this meeting was preplanned for when—and perhaps if—he returned with the hunters. He took the same position as the one on his first visit. *"Hau, Ate; ake iyuskinyan wancinyankelo."* He watched Rising Bear only nod to his genial greeting and assertion he was glad to see him again. His attention drifted to Wind Dancer, who became the apparent spokesman again, as his own good mood began to dissipate. This time, all spoke in the Lakota tongue.

"As I passed the tepee of Leaning Tree, I heard River's Edge telling his father and mother about a badger attack and the slain elk. Tell us what happened," he coaxed his youngest brother.

War Eagle related in detail the stimulating events during their hunt, filling him with renewed elation and a strong sense of family pride. Later, in private, he would reveal to Wind Dancer the prior confrontation between his second brother and their cousin. He finished with, "Cloud Chaser is skilled and brave. He obeyed my orders on this hunt."

"That is what his two deeds tell us. You did not flee on this sun."

Chase eyed Wind Dancer as he attempted to ascertain the man's true meaning. "Why would I want to leave the only family I have or our people? I will do so only if I am slain, captured, or sent away by our father."

"Does the yearning to finish your testing still beat within your heart and fill your head?" Wind Dancer asked, sensing a troubled spirit nearby, and he could not fault his brother's anger if the man was not a trickster.

Chase looked at Rising Bear and his warring mind shouted, *Why won't you speak to me? I'm not a prisoner or an enemy or a stranger; I'm your son!* His bruised heart ached in anguish and his mind reeled in frustration and disappointment. *Let's see if I can provoke you into talking to me. But do it carefully, Chase,* he told himself, *or you'll spoil everything you've accomplished so far, which isn't much. Watch your tone and expressions. Don't be smart-mouthed or sullen.* He asked with all of the sincerity he could muster, "What must I say and do to earn the forgiveness of my father and people for being born half white and for being stolen as a boy and reared by Whites? I cannot change the past. I cannot change my looks or what I am, for the Great Spirit created me this way. For what purpose, I do not know. I will do any task or test you choose to become a Red Shield and son again. I will purify myself in the sweat lodge. I will go on a vision-quest. I will fight or race any warrior you choose. You can test my skills with weapons. I will surrender to the Sun Dance Ceremony, though I do not believe this is the time to do so. I will endure sun-staking." *Anything,* Chase vowed. *Just allow me to reenter the band. Only as a member can I truly prove myself to my family and save Dawn from Two Feathers.*

Wind Dancer was impressed by his brother's words, by what the boy had suffered and for what the man now endured. He wished no obstacle stood between them, wished his brother had never disappeared. Yet, Cloud Chaser had been reared by Whites and could be lying to obtain revenge or to seek to help their enemies defeat them. If only so much was not at stake and he was certain his brother was honest, he would welcome him back this very sun and convince everyone to agree! But he could not risk losing another wife—his precious Chumani—and his second son to enemies' blades. Tokapa had reached the same age as his first son when he was slain, so perhaps he should take that reality as a warning sign to move slowly and carefully. He also could not endanger his family, people, and lands. Or his honor. Because of the uncertainty, the future chief could only respond with evasion. "We do not practice the torture of sun-staking, Cloud Chaser," he said.

That's all you have to say to me after what I told you and after such a long silence? And you, Father, you have no words for me, nothing? Stay calm and clear-headed, Chase, he advised himself. *No accusations or challenges.* "I know it is not an Oglala custom, my brother, but I will yield to it if it will prove I speak the truth and am worthy to rejoin our family and band." *You must have doubts about me being dishonest and unworthy, Wind Dancer, or you wouldn't have hesitated so long in replying. Are you feeling just as trapped by this situation as I am?*

Wind Dancer knew it was just as difficult and painful—no, undeniably more so—for their father to remain silent and distant to Cloud Chaser as it was for he himself to do, but Rising Bear was caught in the same kind of snare of protective duty to his family and people. "Other things and ways will reveal the truth to us," he said. "We break camp on the next sun to journey to the grasslands; we will not wait six more for the full moon as planned. If you want to come with us, be ready to leave when we do. Return to your camp for the rest of this sun and my sister will bring you food."

So, Father, my little ploy failed and you stayed quiet. Your expression didn't change a bit during my pleas. But I guess you've had plenty of practice holding that stoic mask in place when you confronted enemies. I know you're a brave man because your tepee and shield paintings and the stories I heard about you when I was a child and those at the forts shout of your prowess. What are you proving by giving me a winter shoulder and deaf ear? Chase drew a deep breath. "I need a bath; I am sweaty and bloody from the hunt. Where is a good place to go? I cannot use the river while women do their chores there and nearby."

After Wind Dancer gave him directions, Chase asked, "Do I go there alone, or do you want to send a guard with me?"

"I send no one to watch you." *If you escape, that is your choice and the Great Spirit's plan. But it will be difficult to get far without your horse and weapons. And you cannot reach the enemy in time to endanger our camp here before we leave. But I hope you are not foolish and do not damage all the good you have done, my brother. I cannot tell you such things, for they might prevent you from acting as you would without hearing them.* "Hanmani will bring you food before you wash your body."

Chase glanced at his father, whose gaze was lowered, and at War Eagle, whose calm gaze was locked on him. He nodded to his younger brother who returned the gesture, and departed. He walked to his solitary campsite and sat down by the log, feeling tired and depressed. Or was it more? he wondered. Was he soul-weary and defeated? Was he wasting his time and energy there? Was he pursuing an unattainable goal, as he had with the ghost horse when he was ten years old? The objective of both events were the same: winning his father's approval. Maybe he should just admit to himself this was a mistake, stop punishing himself, get the tarnation out of this place, and go find himself and peace elsewhere. He sighed deeply. No, he couldn't leave, not now, not after meeting Macha. Even if a reunion with his family wasn't his destiny, surely Macha was a part of it. Maybe finding her was the only reason he had been summoned there.

When Hanmani came to bring Chase food, she had with her another treat from Macha and a gift from Macha's parents for saving their son from the badger's attack, as it was the custom to reward one for a good deed. "They could not approach you on this sun, so Leaning Tree and Root asked me to bring this shirt to you. She finished it this morning for her husband, but they believe it should be given to you, and your size matches that of Leaning Tree. They say both are good signs the shirt was meant for you and this brave and generous deed. The berry and nut bread is from Dawn."

Chase was surprised by the two gifts. He accepted the garment and noticed with pleasure its fine beading and dangling fringes from the sleeves and at the waist. But it was the leather-enclosed treat from Macha which thrilled him most. "I did not know River's Edge was Dawn's brother before I helped him," he said to Hanmani, "but I am happy one she loves is unharmed and alive because of me. Carry my thanks to Dawn and her parents for their gifts and kindness."

After Hanmani nodded and stole a glance behind her, she whispered, "I will give you time to eat and wash in the forest stream. Wait for Dawn to come. I will stand watch while you talk, for you must not be seen together."

"Does Dawn want to meet with me in the forest?"

"I have not asked her, but she will come to you after we speak."

Chase recalled his thoughts before Hanmani's arrival, and felt he could trust his sister. The facts that she would aid him and that Macha would take such a risk both elated and unsettled him. "How will you two sneak away from camp?" he asked her.

"We must gather more wood before darkness comes. I heard my first brother tell you to go wash your body. I will bring her nearby soon." She eyed him and asked, "Do you not wish to see her for a short time, for this will be the only time you can do so before we break camp? During our journey and stay on the grasslands, a secret visit will not be possible."

Chase realized she misunderstood his hesitation. "I wish to see her for any span of the sun I can steal, but I do not want to cause trouble for you or her. We must make certain we are not caught."

Hanmani understood her father and oldest brother's motivations from talk she had overheard, but she was certain her actions could not imperil her family and people. Even if she had misjudged Cloud Chaser, his interest in Macha would give Macha the courage and strength to reject or at least slow Two Feathers' pursuit. Although Hanmani was almost always obedient and honest, she was consumed by the fact she believed her best friend and brother were meant to be together. She feared if she did not quickly help them move closer, something or someone would step between them and would cause far-reaching harm to the Great Spirit's plan from the dream. Since this was the will of the Creator, what she was doing could not be wrong, though others would think so. "Eat and go," she told Chase. "I will keep my eyes on your camp to see when you leave it. Soon, we will join you near the stream."

Chase was filled with renewed vigor. "Thank you, my sister. You are my best, my only, friend here. You and Dawn," he added.

"The sun will rise when you have many more." She smiled and left.

Chase's spirits rose as he recalled what Lucy Martin had told him on many occasions when things moved too slowly to suit him: "Sometimes, to our way of thinking, the Good Lord moves at a snail's pace or sends us in a crazy direction, but it's for a special reason. Be patient and trusting and walk whatever path He sets before you and you won't be sorry."

Chase bathed and yanked on clean clothes as fast as possible, his spirits soaring with anticipation and his body quivering with suspense. He was glad he took after his father and the Indians in at least one way—he never had to shave his face and he had little hair on his arms and legs and none on his chest. As he paced near the stream's bank while waiting for Macha, he began to worry she would not come. Perhaps he'd gotten ready more quickly than his sister had expected. But if they didn't arrive soon, the visit would be over before it began.

At last, they came into view, and his heart leaped with excitement. His sister seemed very alert, frequently glancing around her. He couldn't stop staring at Macha as she came forward. He listened as Hanmani reminded her of the bird call she would send forth if anyone headed in their direction. He smiled and thanked his sister, who sent him a cheerful grin, her dark gaze and expression full of delightful mischief.

After Hanmani moved far enough away to give them privacy while she kept watch, Chase murmured, "I am happy you came, Dawn, but I do not want trouble to attack you for doing so. Thank you for the gifts you sent to me, for I enjoyed each bite. My heart filled with happiness at your generous deeds."

"I come to thank you for your generous and brave deed, Cloud Chaser. My family's hearts would be filled with sadness if my brother had been slain or injured. We are grateful you kept him in our Life-Circles."

Chase knew the warmth assailing his body wasn't totally due to the hot weather. Macha sparked flames of love within his heart and the heat of desire within his loins. How she had done so this quickly, he did not know. "It was good to hunt as your brother's companion. I did not know he shared your bloodline before I helped him and I would have done so even if he was not cherished by you, but it pleases me you are his sister and I was given a chance to catch your eye and warm your heart toward me."

Macha felt hot and quivery and weak inside just from being near him. He filled her head with dreamy thoughts and her body with fierce cravings. She had first come to love him as a child, and those feelings had increased since his return, as if she were being carried away in a whirlwind. "How could your deeds not warm my heart, for we were friends as children, Cloud Chaser, and we are friends on this sun?"

"Is it too soon to tell you I hunger for us to become more than friends one day?" When she stared at him wide-eyed, he asked, "Did I speak too soon or speak words you do not wish to hear?"

"I do not know what is best to say." How should she answer him? What was "more than friends" to him?

"I do not want to frighten or insult you, Dawn, but I must reveal what lives in my heart. We break camp on the next sun; we will not be able to speak alone after we begin our journey. If you do not want to answer me here, that is not wrong. I speak now to prevent Two Feathers from stealing you before I can do so."

Macha's heart beat faster. He had made his meaning as clear as the stream's water with his last words. She was too amazed and elated to respond to him, so she listened intently as he continued.

"My cousin made himself my enemy when we were boys and he does so again while we are men. If he learns of my strong feelings for you, he will seek you out if only to harm me. Do not join to him," Chase pleaded, "for he is unworthy of you. I have not proven I am worthy of you to this moon, but I will seek to do so on every sun which rises."

Macha looked into his golden-brown eyes and she was convinced he spoke the truth. "Do not fear, Cloud Chaser, for I grasp the wickedness which lives within Two Feathers. I have no love or desire for him. I will not join to him unless I am forced to do so. My parents and our people do not see his bad side, for he hides it with cunning. He is viewed as a great warrior, a man from a chief's bloodline. If he speaks for me, they will not understand if I reject and insult him."

As Chase listened and watched her, suddenly memories poured into his mind like water cascading over a towering rock. He remembered sitting behind bushes and rocks with her while whispering and playing, hiding their special friendship from other children, for opposite sexes rarely played together, and many boys considered him unworthy of attention. Long ago, she had slipped him little gifts and praised his boyish prowess and urged him to believe in himself and comforted him when other boys or his father wounded his pride or feelings. He recalled giving her a gray hare's pelt, white during the winter season, and how she had made a pouch with it and kept her small treasures inside. How could he have forgotten such important times? Why had those memories returned at this particular moment? Was it because she was bringing them to the surface?

"Why do you smile, Cloud Chaser, when I speak such bad news?"

He disclosed what he had been thinking and it coaxed a smile to her lips. "Do you remember such times and things we shared?"

"Yes, for they stayed as green as the pines even during winter. When you were taken from us, I suffered much from the loss of my best friend. I became the companion of your sister to be close to anything which carried a part of you within it. As the seasons passed, we became best friends. I believed you would be returned one sun, and it has come to pass."

Chase hadn't known he could be so happy. Yet, everything about this woman created joy within him. She had not scorned him in the past and was not doing so today. Surely it was possible to win her, unless . . . "What if I am rejected and sent away again?"

Macha frowned in dismay, then smiled. "Surely you will not, for the Great Spirit called you here for a purpose."

"What if that reason has already been fulfilled?"

"I do not understand. You are not yet a Red Shield again."

"What if that purpose was only to be reunited with you?"

Before she could reply, Macha heard Hanmani's bird call. "Hanmani calls me. I must go."

Chase cupped her warm face between his hands, leaned forward, and brushed his lips lightly over hers. "Think on me, Dawn, for you will enter my thoughts each time I breathe. Go quickly, Sunshine of my heart."

"I will think much on you, Cloud Chaser," she said, and left, only to discover that Hanmani had been overcautious. No one was coming. She wished she could have finished her talk with Cloud Chaser, but perhaps it was best not to risk exposure by being gone too long. Flushed with joy, she rapidly told her friend all that had happened.

Hanmani hugged her and laughed. "Did I not tell you

your Life-Circles would be entwined one sun, for it was revealed in the Creator's dream message to my brother? When the moon comes in the seasons far ahead, you will help me capture the man who steals my heart," she murmured mysteriously, then gave a romantic and dreamy sigh.

Chase waited for a short while, then headed back to his campsite to bed down for the night, hoping his dreams would be filled only with Macha. Tomorrow morning the Red Shields planned to leave for the annual buffalo hunt on the Plains. He was being allowed to go with them, but could never have guessed what was going to happen next . . .

CHAPTER SIX

In the middle of the night, Chase was awakened by rumblings of thunder. Flashes of lightning lit the sky and he felt a strong wind blowing over him. He felt and smelled heavy moisture in the air, could almost taste it when he opened his mouth and breathed. He knew it was not unusual during that time of the year for violent summer storms to come without warning, and strike with awesome power.

"A storm comes fast, Cloud Chaser; it will be large and long. Gather your possessions and come to my tepee for shelter and sleep."

Startled, Chase reflexively grabbed his knife as he whirled and looked up at his older brother as the man arrived without his knowing and spoke from behind him. With him on the ground and with Wind Dancer standing close by, his brother seemed taller and larger than he actually was. Clad only in a breechclout and moccasins, his brawny muscles and sleek coppery flesh were displayed. The light of the nearly three-quarter moon, which was not yet obscured by clouds, and flashes of brilliant lightning also illuminated the Sun Dance scars upon his broad chest, as well as a few other scars. Chase studied his brother. In any world, Wind Dancer would be considered handsome and virile. In face paint and his finest array, surely Wind Dancer would strike fear and hesitation into the heart—the very soul—of any enemy.

As he sheathed his knife, Chase pushed aside those thoughts and said, "Your heart is good, my brother, and I thank you." As he gathered his things and packed them with haste, he added, "Your skills and cunning are large as the mountain, for I did not hear or see your approach." He glanced at Wind Dancer, who only nodded his appreciation. He tossed his bedroll over one arm, retrieved his saddle-bags, and stood. "I am ready to go. We must tend the horses," he added, concerned about his beloved animal.

"I tended them before I came to you; they are safe."

"Thank you, my brother, for Red is my friend."

They hurried to a colorfully decorated and well-con-structed abode, and entered quietly to prevent disturbing Tokapa. Using the glow of a small fire, Wind Dancer motioned to where Chase should spread his mat and store his possessions, then took his place beside Chumani and near their son.

Before reclining to pass the remaining night dry and cozy, Chase glanced at his family and smiled with plea-sure. If only, he thought, good luck and the Creator would grant him a wife and child of his own, he would be the happiest man alive. He lay down, closed his eyes, and soon slumbered in peace.

Unsettled by the same worry as his older brother, War Eagle had left his buffalo mat and gone to peer out the open flap to study nature's menacing signs. Only after he'd sighted Wind Dancer guiding Cloud Chaser to his tepee not far away, had he relaxed. He sealed the entrance against an imminent deluge and returned to his former position. As he did so, he heard his mother whispering to his father.

"The storm will be bad, my husband; Cloud Chaser has no shelter."

Winona's concern for Omaste's intrusive son took War Eagle by surprise, but pleased him. He did not give Rising Bear time to consider a hard decision before he murmured, "He was taken to my brother's tepee as I looked out, Mother. He will be safe and dry from the storm."

"That is good, my second son," Winona replied. "Return to sleep."

Hanmani, with her back to her family, grinned as she pretended not to awaken during their whisperings. Surely, she reasoned, their concerns for Cloud Chaser were good signs, even if they must stay hidden for a while. She assumed her best friend was awake and worrying, too.

As time passed and nature's fury increased, brisk winds raged against Leaning Tree's tepee as if trying to topple it. Macha tossed on her buffalo mat and fretted over Cloud Chaser's safety and condition during the severe storm's assault. Rain beat down on the conical abode as if each drop was a hard stone which was flung with great strength. Thunder growled almost like a provoked bear, and she knew from hearing the noisy bolts that lightning streaked across the sky. She feared one of its fiery lances would strike her vulnerable beloved or hit the tree at his campsite and a heavy limb would fall upon him. She could not endure losing him again and forever! She yearned to race to his side, to cuddle with him, and to face such awesome peril in his arms so he would not be miserable and alone amidst it.

Why, she fumed, was it taking so long to make a decision about his fate? Could everyone not see he was speaking the truth and was worthy of rejoining their band? What was it going to take for him to be accepted? How could it be that only she and Hanmani believed him? Even in the face of so much rejection and distrust, surely the two of them could not be wrong. Perhaps others did want to befriend him—such as his brothers and hers—and were as entrapped by the current situation as she and Hanmani were.

Great Spirit, protect and guide Cloud Chaser along the path You have chosen for him to walk, she implored. *Soften our people's hearts toward him. Make him a Red Shield again. Send peace and safety to our people and land. Join our Life-Circles, for I love him and need him as my mate.*

Ignoring the fierce storm, a drenched and excited Two Feathers went to Rising Bear's tepee the next morning. After the flap was unlaced and he was invited inside, he gazed around and saw only four people present, which greatly pleased him. "Cloud Chaser has fled, my chief; he and his possessions are gone," he announced. "I searched the forest for him to see if he had taken cover there, but he had not. He must be pursued, captured, and punished before he brings enemies to our camp to attack us. We cannot wait for the storm to halt; I will lead the hunting party to find and return him."

War Eagle concealed his anger as he asked in a calm tone, "Did you look to see if his horse is missing?"

"It is still among yours. He must have stolen another's to ride. Surely he goes to betray and endanger us. We must not allow his victory."

War Eagle allowed his exasperation to show as he scolded, "Your bad feelings for him misguide and ensnare you, my cousin. Cloud Chaser escapes the powerful forces of nature inside the tepee of our brother." He observed Two Feathers' astonishment and disappointment before they were masked.

"He is with Wind Dancer?"

"That is true. Return to your tepee and look into your heart and head to find what causes such evil to stalk you, and destroy it before the next sun rises and we break camp." He watched Two Feathers nod and depart in a hurry, no doubt concerned about being thwarted before Rising Bear. He turned to his parents and sister, who had remained silent. "It is time I speak to you of my cousin's bad deeds," he said, then exposed the man's recent words and actions.

"Why does he seek so hard to defeat Cloud Chaser?" Winona asked.

"I do not know, Mother, for I have not seen or heard Cloud Chaser provoke or challenge him. Two Feathers does not want him here."

"That is for Father and the Great Spirit to choose," Hanmani said.

"Your words to him were wise, my second son," Rising Bear said. "We must pray to the Great Spirit to purify him of such bad feelings."

"If that does not happen soon, Father, he will cause trouble, for his hatred of my brother is large."

"Watch him with cunning eyes to see what you can learn. When his troubled spirit calms, speak to him of such bad feelings. Say nothing to his family and others about this matter, for soon it may be gone. If not, I will speak away from camp with the son of my sister."

War Eagle nodded obedience, but was doubtful his cousin's feelings would change. All he could do to help was to keep the men apart. "After we eat," he said, "I will go to my brother's tepee to see what I can learn there. I will speak of all I hear and see when I return, but my visit may be long."

"Come, sit, the food is ready," Winona told them.

As Chase ate the meal served to him by Chumani, he watched his nephew eating and talking in the space between Wind Dancer's thighs. "The food is good, Dewdrops, and I thank you," he told her.

Chumani half smiled at him as she sat down and took Tokapa from her husband so Wind Dancer could eat and she could assist their son.

Chase was calm, as he had slept fairly well for the remainder of the night while the storm assailed the tepee and surrounding area. It still raged outside, so the departure plan was postponed until the next day. He had not been asked to return to his campsite and would stay as long as Wind Dancer allowed him to do so, with hopes of worming his way into their affections and close-knit unit. He watched Tokapa eating.

"You have a fine son, my brother. Many things seize his eye and tempt his hand," Chase said of the inquisitive child who had been toddling around as his mother worked, and getting into mischief on occasion. Each time Chumani had retrieved and distracted him from an object of interest— once he had played with his saddlebags, another time he had tumbled on the strange bedroll, and yet another, wanting to see the rain, he tried to unlace the entry flap— the boy's actions had greatly amused Chase. At one point, the boy had climbed into his lap to grasp the locket he wore around his neck, one which had belonged to his mother and bore pictures of her parents, the only way he knew how his other grandparents looked, as they were long dead. He had opened the locket and shown the pictures to the boy, whose stubby forefinger had touched them several times. He had been relieved Tokapa had not cried and fought when Chumani explained he could not have the locket and must not yank on it and break the gold chain. He was enjoying their child and those peaceful surroundings, and was wishing for his own even more than in past days.

Wind Dancer nodded and smiled. "He learns much on every sun and keeps us racing after him in his busy quests. His legs are still slow like the turtle's, but his mind runs as swiftly as the deer. If there is something unknown within his reach, he seeks to learn its mystery. Each time Grandmother tends him, she is weary before the sun is high above us; and Grandfather's voice is weak from answering his many questions."

Chase noticed the loving looks which passed between the couple and knew their feelings for each other ran deep and strong. "The Great Spirit blessed you with a good wife and son," he said to Wind Dancer. "You and Dewdrops are well matched."

"Did you leave a woman behind in the land far away?" Chumani asked as she removed their wooden bowls and the buffalo horn cups embedded in sturdy pine blocks to keep them erect. While she rinsed and stored the eating items, she listened and furtively watched him as he responded.

"No white woman captured my eye and heart as you did my brother's. Perhaps in the seasons to come, Wakantanka will choose a special female for me to join and we will have a fine son like Tokapa."

War Eagle looked at Chase and nodded a greeting when he arrived to join them, having overheard their last few exchanges as he unlaced and relaced the entry flap. As he sat down near the two men, he was reminded of his love and acceptance of Cloud Chaser when they were children and wished he could show them again. But he had become a warrior during his second brother's absence and he hoped to become his people's future war chief when Blue Owl was too old to carry that dangerous and demanding rank. With his current duties as Sacred Bow Carrier and future band chief if Wind Dancer was slain, he could not allow himself to be swayed by those feelings and memories. He knew it was the same for their father: Rising Bear feared it would cast a stain upon his honor and cause dissension if Cloud Chaser failed to prove himself. Yet, he was eager to learn more about the man his second brother had become, just as this near-stranger needed to learn more about them. "Tell Cloud Chaser how you found Dewdrops and claimed her," War Eagle coaxed, "and the many deeds you two did to save our people."

While Chumani sat a short distance away to bead and their son played beside her, Wind Dancer told Chase how he and Chumani had each lost a mate and son to Crow raiders and how he had been given a vision to go to the chief of the White Shield Brule Lakotas and lay claim to her as his Wakantanka-chosen wife and vision-quest companion in a bold and dangerous attempt to defeat the Crow in many ways and locations. He related the adventures they had shared. His voice filled with reverence and his expression with lingering amazement as he spoke about a mystical wolf-dog and Old Woman who had helped them several times, and Chumani's hawk.

Chase was saddened by the losses of their first families and knew it must be agonizing to have a mate and a child slain by enemies; he realized how a hunger for revenge must have gnawed viciously at the two of them. He was astounded to hear how Chumani had raised the hawk Cetan from a young age for both, how that bird had assisted them with such intelligence, and how Cetan had found a mate and returned to the wild. As he glanced at the lovely and feminine woman of twenty-seven, he was astounded that she had become a skilled warrior and had ridden on such a dangerous mission at her husband's side. He knew there was no one better to be the wife of a future chief than the daughter of a chief and ally, a woman who could defend his home and family when he was away hunting or warring, a woman who clearly adored and respected him, and a woman who possessed his love and esteem. *You're one lucky man, my brother, and I hope I have the same good fortune with Dawn.*

"Do you remember the story Grandfather told us as boys

about the Old Woman Who Quills At The Edge Of The World and her companion?" War Eagle asked when his second brother remained quiet.

Chase only nodded from a sense of shared awe.

"We believe our helpers were the Old Woman and her wolf-dog," War Eagle disclosed, "for when they came and went, they left no moccasin or paw prints upon the face of Mother Earth."

Chase thought about all the adventures Wind Dancer and Chumani had shared and asked her, "Were you not afraid when you sneaked to a Crow camp to rescue my captive brother, and when you appeared to the large encampment of many Crow bands as White Buffalo Maiden, and when you walked inside the wooden poles at Fort Pierre Trading Post to trick them?"

"Fear squirmed within me as a snake trying to find a place to strike and slay me, but it was fear for the safety of my beloved husband and friends and a dread of failing in my sacred tasks. I believed the Great Spirit was guiding and protecting us and had sent others to help us. Perhaps in the dark suns ahead, He will send them to us again as helpers."

Chase remembered what the Whites would call myths or legends, but he believed life contained many inexplicable mysteries and powers. He had heard the story of the beautiful White Buffalo Maiden, Pte Skawin, who had come to the Dakotas long ago to give them their Seven Sacred Ceremonies and other rituals and the Prayer Pipe. He knew the story of their creation and the Great Flood which had cleansed the world of evil and then been repopulated by The Chosen Ones: a great chief and a brave maiden, which reminded him of the Biblical flood with Noah and the union of Adam and Eve. He had not forgotten the tale about the Old Woman who quilled daily on a buffalo hide, whose work was unraveled by her wolf-dog companion when she went to add wood to her fire and stir her soup; for if she ever completed her task, the Dakota World would end.

He looked forward to meeting the best friends who had ridden with them: Red Feather and Zitkala. "The Creator gave you many skills and much wisdom, Dewdrops, and you used them with great cunning and courage at my brother's side when you defeated the enemies. When I find a mate, I hope she possesses your many good traits." *And I'm sure Dawn does.*

"I thank you for your kind words, Cloud Chaser, but both enemies—the Crow and Whites—seek to strike at us again. Peace often is as short as the night flower's life. Yet, while it blooms, it gives much beauty and joy."

When his brother began speaking, Chase had to halt his mind from racing back in time to his first meeting with Macha, who had been gathering night-blooming flowers, so he could listen to Wind Dancer's words.

"My wife speaks with much truth. With the death of Broken Hand Fitzpatrick, more conflicts will arise with our White and Indian enemies. The new agent does not think and act like Broken Hand, for Thomas Twiss does not know us as Fitzpatrick did. Already Spotted Tail and Little Thunder and other Brule chiefs challenge the Bluecoats and settlers, and all Lakotas are held to blame. The treaty will not halt either side from taking or doing as they desire, for all desire the same land and its gifts."

War Eagle took over when Wind Dancer grew silent. "The Bluecoats put up many forts on Lakota hunting grounds and on those of our allies and our enemies. The settlers do the same with trading posts to supply their people and to buy furs from Indians. During the last hot season, those called Mormons chased Bridger from his trading post on the Green River for selling and trading powder and lead balls to Indians for hunting and raiding, for those strange Whites said Indians used those weapons to attack their people and other settlers. The largest and most powerful are called Fort Laramie and Fort Kearny. We were told our enemies the Pawnee sold the Whites land at the Platte River for Fort Kearny, but the Pawnee did not own that area; all land belongs to the Great Spirit for the use of His people and animals. The Bluecoats say forts are to protect peaceful tribes from enemy attacks and to protect the settlers who travel the path called the Oregon Trail. That is the path you journeyed?"

"That is true, my brother, but it is a long and dangerous one. Oregon is not like the Plains. It has many rivers, trees, and mountains. Its mouth touches great waters I could not see beyond. Many forts and trading posts sit along the trail to far away, but reaching the next one is long and hard, and many settlers cannot continue and many die or are injured. We saw markers where many were buried, dwellings where some halted and stayed, bones of their animals, and discarded possessions, for many wagons were too heavy to cross such high and steep mountains or animals became too weary to pull them, and some were slain for food. Evil white men and hostile Indians attacked and robbed some on the fringes. Strange illnesses assailed them, but Lucy Martin kept me safe. When supplies ran low, she made sure I was fed before she ate; and sometimes she went without food so

I could have hers to get strong enough to heal."

"Why did the settlers endure such hardships to find new land?"

"To be free, Dewdrops, and to have land to call their own, for Whites put up their abodes and live in one place in all seasons. There are many troubles between the Whites in the land where the sun rises. Many have nothing: few garments and little food. To live in the Sunrise Land is like . . ." Chase paused to come up with a way to explain the North/South conflict which many Americans felt would lead to a great war one day. "It is like being a slave to the Crow or Pawnee, and they seek to escape far away where they can be safe and happy. But some Whites go to the land where the Sun sleeps to . . ." *How do I explain, to get rich?* "To gather many coups and possessions, for they are greedy and selfish. They are bad even to their own kind, for their hearts are evil. Their lives and customs are different from ours, and I lack the words in our tongue to reveal such things to you, for if you have not experienced what I have, you will not understand."

"That is why we cannot live in peace together," War Eagle asserted, "for we are too different and we must be enemies."

"Not all Whites are evil, my brother," Chase refuted in a gentle tone. "The Martins were good people who only wanted freedom, joy, and a way to live off of the land. They taught me to farm, and gave me my horse Red." He told them how the Martins had earned and saved money until they had enough to purchase the animal as a gift to him, and explained how the Whites celebrated the day one was born each year. "Do you remember when your mother was stolen by the Pawnee and you believed she was lost to you forever?" he asked Wind Dancer, who nodded.

"My mother Omaste took care of you and loved you as if you were her son. You told me you came to love, trust, and accept her as a second mother until Winona's return. I felt the same about Lucy Martin. I became Chase Martin, her son in all ways but blood. But in my heart, I was sad and lonely for my father, brothers, and sister; it pained me to think my family and people were dead, lost to me forever, just as your heart and mind were attacked when you lost your first son. It was filled with happiness when I was told my people still lived, and I was eager to return to them. I was reared by Whites, my brothers, but I did not become one in heart and spirit. After Tom Martin died and I learned the truth, I could not leave unprotected the woman who had made me her son. Was it wrong to be kind, generous, and forgiving to an old one who loved and needed me? If so, I am guilty of those deeds and mistakes. I will do what you say to purify myself to regain my honor and place here."

"Only the Great Spirit can answer your question and make a path for your return to us," Wind Dancer said. "Wait to learn if He does so."

Chumani had observed the three men during their long talk and had come to like, respect, and trust Cloud Chaser, and to enjoy his company. Yet, his fate was not in her hands. Certain her husband could use a reprieve from the arduous meeting, she stood and smiled. "The storm has passed. I will go fetch water and wood and do other chores. Do not forget, my husband, you must go to speak with Red Feather. Cloud Chaser can return to his camping place until we leave on the new sun."

Wind Dancer told his cunning and thoughtful wife, "I will

take Tokapa with me while you do your tasks, for he is restless and needs to run about to calm himself before he rests." To War Eagle he said, "You must meet with the Sacred Bow Carriers to be certain all plans are made for our journey on the next sun, for many dangers may strike at us along the way." To Chase he said, "Go to your camping place and prepare yourself for our long ride. I will come for you at first light."

Chase comprehended he was being dismissed by the kind-hearted Chumani and did not resent her for rescuing her beloved husband from what she must sense was a difficult conversation. He smiled. "Dewdrops speaks wise; there is much to do before the Red Shields ride on the next sun. I will return to my camp while you tend your chores. My heart sings with gratitude and joy for this time we have shared."

"It is good to learn more about each other," Wind Dancer replied, "but that path cannot be walked too fast when so much is at stake."

As he returned to his old campsite, Chase couldn't help but wonder if anything had changed with their visit, and hoped it had, for the better. For certain, he would have his answer soon . . .

CHAPTER SEVEN

With his new solitary campsite ready for use, Chase gazed at the nearby meandering Cheyenne River—called "Water Good," Wakpawaste, by the Indians—and then toward where he knew the Badlands, Makosica—an enormous sunken area with picturesque and rugged rocky spires, gorges, steep cliffs, entrapping pathways, and secret water-holes—were located. It was known to the Lakotas as "the jumping-off place," for the lush grassland halted abruptly and a sheer dropoff appeared as if from nowhere, the contrast in terrains and colors as diverse as a verdant meadow to a barren desert and a dark night to a sunny day. Before the coming of the horse long ago, "the edge of the world" and other similar places had been used during annual hunts when buffalo were stampeded off such precipices by braves afoot, and their women waited in the canyons below to butcher the fallen carcasses and haul the meat and hides home using dog-pulled travois.

Chase remembered how he, too, had roamed the Badlands with his father and brothers before he had been taken to Oregon. Those few outings were still vivid within his mind. Also vivid was the recollection of the time Two Feathers had lured him into a section where he had gotten lost in a maze of narrow passages with sides too steep to climb and his spiteful cousin had brushed away his retreating tracks so the "little half-breed" could not find his way back to camp. Later, when he had been found and rescued by Wind Dancer, Two Feathers had sworn it had only been a game and he had become confused and could not locate him. Not wanting to be a tattler, Chase had not exposed his cousin's dark mischief. Perhaps he should have told the truth.

After traveling for over five days from the heavily forested Paha Sapa, the Red Shields were erecting their first summer village in the customary ever-widening circular pattern near the southern flow of the Cheyenne River and just northwest of the Badlands. Many trees and scrubs along

119

the riverbank would provide shade and ample water for people and animals as needed, and wood for campfires, along with dried buffalo chips. The location chosen by the Council was mainly flat, though rolling hills were located nearby in three directions, and was covered by thick and windswept grass, scattered wildflowers, occasional trees and bushes, and various forms of wildlife.

The journey had gone well, to Chase's relief. Yet, he scolded himself for several brief and selfish nibblings of disappointment that he hadn't been given a single chance to provide aid and display his prowess during times of danger. Along the way, he had camped near the fringe of the sprawling group. Only Hanmani had ventured close to him; and her visits were short while delivering his food, for nothing could be concealed in such openness. He knew others studied him with curiosity, but everyone took hints for their behavior toward him from their chief and stayed away.

It made him feel lonely to be so close in body to his family and people, but so far away in spirit and acceptance. Yet, he couldn't blame the Red Shields; even if most of them remembered him as a child, surely it was as if he were a stranger to them now, and a man whose White half and rearing could not be ignored.

As the people worked with familiar assignments and efficiency, Chase watched women put up tepees, unload their possessions and haul them inside, build rock-enclosed campfires, position three-legged stands over them for kettles, fetch fresh water, and put evening meals on to cook. He saw men tending horses and setting up their weapons stands, erecting their society meeting lodges, and gathering to make plans for tomorrow's first hunt. Older children assisted their parents; girls, the women; boys, the men. Young children played under the watchful eyes of older siblings or grandparents. Babies and toddlers either slept or were tended by family members while the mother was busy. The Shirt-Wearers and anyone finished with his or her own tasks aided the elders or disabled with theirs. Among them was Wind Dancer. Small groups of warriors from the Sacred Bow Carriers and Strong Hearts Society rode off to scout the area beyond their sight for enemies, other Lakota bands, and the life-sustaining buffalo herds.

Chase wished he would be asked to perform some duty to help pass the time. He yearned to catch even a glimpse of Macha. He still was disquieted by something Hanmani had whispered to him during one of her hasty trips to his isolated location: his sister had warned him that despite his rescue and kind deeds for River's Edge, Leaning Tree and Ohute would not give their permission or blessing for him to approach Macha any time soon—if ever—about a future joining.

"Be careful, my brother," Hanmani had urged, "for your eyes glow with love and desire when you look upon her or speak of her. You must learn to hide such feelings from all but Dawn, for they can cause much trouble before you are a Red Shield."

As those grim words wafted across his mind, Chase wondered again how it was possible to carry off such a hard pretense, when it was easier to halt breathing than to control wanting her every hour of every day and night. He yearned to hold her in his arms, to taste her sweet lips, to make slow and thrilling love to her, and to share his life with her. Now that he had found Macha and opened his heart to her, he must not lose her. She was the one person who loved and accepted him fully as he was. Whatever it took, Chase vowed, he must have her in his Life-Circle and forever, no matter what the consequences might be.

As he glanced toward the busy encampment once more, he was disappointed that neither his brothers, his father, nor River's Edge had visited him for even a short time during their journey. It was as if he had said and done nothing to alter the Red Shields' opinion and treatment of him. How much longer, he fretted, would this near-exile last and what more could he do to prove himself to them?

The next morning, Chase was pleased—even surprised—when Wind Dancer and War Eagle came to his campsite and said he could go with the Red Shield party chosen for today's first seasonal hunt. War Eagle loaned him his old bow again and a quiver of well-made arrows to use. Wind Dancer loaned him his second buffalo horse, as Chase's sorrel was not trained for such a task. He thanked his brothers for their thoughtfulness and generosity, and hoped he passed whatever test he was being given today.

As the group gathered at the fringe of the village, Chase mounted the buffalo horse and positioned his weapons around his torso. This would be his first time participating in a buffalo hunt and he was excited and a little tense. He was glad his brothers had given him instructions during their walk to the other hunters, who only glanced at him upon his arrival, their stoic expressions revealing nothing to him about their feelings. He was certain Two Feathers would be annoyed he had been included, but he didn't see his cousin amidst the men closest to him. Perhaps the vexing brave was off scouting for enemies or watching the herd's movements and would join them later; or perhaps his offensive cousin was on camp-guard duty and wasn't a member of this first party, which would suit Chase. He saw many women preparing to trail them with travois, as they would skin and butcher the fallen animals, and young braves would haul the hides and meat back to camp and return for the next load.

Chase also didn't see Macha among either the women or observers and was disappointed to be denied even a short glimpse of her. He assumed Hanmani knew he was going along on this quest and had told his love, so apparently Macha thought it too hazardous to witness their departure.

After the white-haired Nahemana, clad in his finest array and Elk Dreamer headdress as their shaman, evoked the Great Spirit's guidance and protection and thanked the Creator for supplying the main source of their existence, a shout went up from many warriors as they galloped off to begin their hunt. Kicking up clumps of grass and stirring up dust, the exhilarated band raced over the terrain toward where a large herd had been sighted by scouts.

From a space between several tepees where she was doing her chores, Macha furtively watched the large hunting party gather, prepare, and depart. She dared not get closer or appear too interested in Rising Bear's second son. When she had located him in that crowd, her heart had leapt with joy and love, and her body had warmed with desire. She prayed for the Great Spirit to guide and guard him during his challenge.

Shortly after sunrise, she grimaced when Two Feathers strolled past her family's tepee while she helped her mother prepare their early meal. She had not smiled in return when the intimidating male slowed his pace and roamed her with his gaze from her black hair to her moccasined feet. She was relieved he had not halted to speak with them, but her mother had noticed the man's overt behavior.

"He smiles at you and watches you on many suns, my daughter," Ohute had whispered following his departure. "Though he does so with cunning, I have seen his looks. He is a great warrior and springs from a high bloodline. He would be a good mate for you, for the season has come when you must think of joining. Perhaps he seeks to see if he can capture your eye and acceptance before he speaks of such matters. You must also be cunning, my daughter, and let him know his pursuit will be welcomed."

Dread consumed Macha at those words. She had feared this grim moment would arrive, but not this soon. "His skills and bloodline are impressive, my mother, but he does not catch my eye and warm my heart. I would not want him to approach me in such a way, for I would not want to injure his feelings and pride with a rejection."

Ohute stared at her. "Is there another Red Shield warrior who calls out to your feelings?"

Macha was relieved her mother had not said "another man," so she was able to respond honestly. "No member of our band has done so to this sun," for Cloud Chaser was not considered one of them yet.

"You must allow Two Feathers to share the talking blanket and a ride with you if he asks such things. If you refuse, you will show great dishonor to him and his family.

Do not forget, he is the son of our chief's sister. Pretty Meadow and Runs Fast will be offended by your refusal of their son when no other warrior stands between you two as a reason to refuse him, as will our chief and shaman. Hear me, my daughter: Two Feathers is a good choice. Your father and mother will be much pleased to have him as your husband. When Two Feathers comes to speak with you, and I am sure he will do so before this season passes, if you love, respect, and obey your parents, you must listen to his words and lean toward him."

Macha felt as if a rawhide rope was tied around her throat, ever tightening, choking and squeezing her to death. "Even if I do not love and desire Two Feathers, I must sacrifice myself to him to please him and others?"

"Such feelings will come after you join to him. You do not wish to be as Little Deer was—old, childless, and living with your family."

"Winona's sister did not take a mate because the Great Spirit told her in a dream to remain unmatched. She was happy in the tepee of their brother Strong Rock. I beg you, my mother, say and do nothing to encourage him or his parents about such a union, for it will trouble my heart deeply." Macha watched her mother frown.

"It will be as you wish, my daughter. But if he comes to you of his choice, do not be selfish and cold and dishonor him and your families by scorning him. That would not be wise, and might force your father to command you join to him."

"Do not worry," Hanmani coaxed Macha later as they fetched water and gathered wood and buffalo chips for cook

125

fires, "for the Great Spirit will not allow such a union when He has chosen Cloud Chaser as your mate. You must be strong and brave, and force my cousin to remain silent with your actions. I will whisper in his ear many times that it is too soon to approach you and it would be unwise to do so until you smile on him."

"What if our plan fails, Hanmani? What if Two Feathers approaches me or my family and Father says I must join him?"

"Trust me, my friend; we will defeat him. Before that sun rises, my second brother will be a Red Shield and worthy of you in all eyes." Hanmani smiled at Macha. "I am sure your Life-Circles are to become entwined. If a wicked force battles the Great Spirit's plan, we will find a way to challenge and defeat such evil. You love and desire Cloud Chaser very much; is that not true?"

"So much it frightens me at times, for I fear I will lose him forever."

"That will not happen, Dawn, for I will not allow it. If you become entrapped, I will find a way to rescue you; this I promise. But you must help me by being distant to Two Feathers while Cloud Chaser becomes one of us."

As Chase lay on his bedroll that night and stared at the full moon overhead, his thoughts ran in several directions. When Hanmani had brought him his evening meal, in a rush, she had given him a shocking revelation about what had happened between Macha and Two Feathers, Macha and her mother, and Macha and herself. Everything within him shouted for him to do something fast to prevent losing his beloved, but he didn't know what he could do at this time. Yet, he had told Hanmani to tell Macha not to worry and to follow her instructions until he came up with a solution to the impending problem.

So much, Chase realized, depended upon him becoming a Red Shield again, and soon. Each time he believed he was making progress toward that goal and advancing toward his target, it was as if he were shoved backward to his beginning mark again. The hunt had gone exceedingly well; he had slain many buffaloes, and no one had treated him badly. Even so, no brave had extended friendship toward him, either, just ignored him. Upon their return to camp, he had not been invited to eat with his family or any other band member, or even been asked to join the men to recount colorful tales of today's and past hunts. While he sat and ate alone, he saw others gathered after meals, and that knowledge pained him deeply, even angered him.

So much was at stake, more now than when he had arrived in his father's camp. Eventually, if the situation did not change in his favor, he had two important decisions to make: one, to leave forever; two, convince Macha to go with him. Would she give up everything and everyone there for him, for a strange life far away, a life amidst those she considered enemies?

Help me, Great Spirit, for You summoned me here. Tell me what I must do and say to become Rising Bear's honored son. Protect Dawn from my cousin's evil hunger, and help me to win her for my wife.

Three days later, Chase left on a second hunt with his two brothers and another large party. This time, Two Feathers rode with them. They had just begun the hunt when trouble struck. Almost simultaneously, Chase and the others heard ominous gunfire coming from over the next rolling hill and the buffaloes closest to them spooked at the noise and started running in the opposite direction, which fortunately was away from the workers and encampment.

One of the scouts came galloping toward Wind Dancer, who was near Chase, and War Eagle and others hurriedly joined them to assess the situation. All listened as the anxious brave told the next chief about six white men who were slaying the large beasts with "firesticks."

Two Feathers scowled in anger. "We go challenge them."

"Wait, my brother, do not ride in haste!" Chase shouted. "It could be a trick to lure you into danger."

"They are the foolish ones to intrude on our lands and to slay our creatures! See how they frighten away the herd."

"That is true," Chase said to appease his irate cousin, "but does the treaty not say Whites can travel across these lands in safety? Take me with you, my brother, to speak with them, to urge them to leave. If you slay them, it will call down the soldiers on your camp and people."

"Wind Dancer and War Eagle speak English. Your help is unneeded."

Chase glanced at Two Feathers as he said, "That is true, my cousin, but they must not reveal such a powerful secret to the enemy. They speak English, so they will know all the Whites say to me and I say to them. Perhaps they will speak more freely if they do not know others understand. For certain, it is dangerous to attack them first."

"It is a good plan," War Eagle concurred with Chase. "We have much to do this season; we cannot war and hunt at the same time. If we do not hunt while it is hot, when the cold season comes, we will be hungry and will lack hides for shelter and garments."

Wind Dancer eyed his half-brother and gave the matter a hasty study, realizing there was no way the man could deceive them, and his younger brother had made a good point. He glanced at Red Feather and his friend gave a slight nod. "We go, and you will speak for us, Cloud Chaser," Wind Dancer agreed.

Chase watched the bearded white men observe their approach with their own awesome weapons at the ready. He surmised they must be curious about a half-breed dressed as a white man and signaling for a parley and riding with five well-armed Indians. He reined in and drifted his tawny gaze over them and then over the dead animals, which two had been skinning. "Why are you hunting on Lakota lands when it'll bring trouble for both sides?" Chase saw one burly man take a few steps beyond his companions, so he deduced that was their leader and spokesman.

"Name's Jake Hardin. What's yourn, stranger?"

"Chase Martin. So what are you men doing here?"

"The treaty says we kin hunt in this area. We hafta go where them buffalo are agrazin'. We don't intend to take more 'an fifty or sixty today; that leaves aplenty for them Injuns. Why you aridin' with 'em?"

"I'm staying with them for a while. I think it's best if you men go hunt elsewhere. They're hunting here for the next few weeks, and the area isn't big enough to share with you. Staying around will only provoke them. No need to do that when you can hunt a day's ride from here."

"We done took down about twenty and they be ready to skin. We cain't go alosin' that much ball and powder and time. We'll be gone by sun-up."

"Like I said, Hardin, your gunfire is spooking the herd, so you need to move along before these Lakotas get riled."

"You sayin' them Injuns is gonna attack us if'n we don't leave?"

"They got here first, five days back, and you're intruding. It's much easier for you men to move your camp than for them to do so. There's no need to spark trouble when you can hunt elsewhere."

"Like I said, Martin, we done got started on our work, so we cain't be obligin' you today. If they attack us, they'll be in big trouble; soldiers will come and punish 'em good and hard. You tell 'em that for us. I'm takin' it they knows what the treaty says and they agreed to honor it. Them is Sioux with you, ain't they?"

"*Sioux* is a white man's word, Hardin, and it's an insult to them, so I'd drop it from my vocabulary if I were you. These are Lakota warriors; they're highly skilled and well trained, so I wouldn't go antagonizing them."

"Don't make no never mind to us who or what they be, 'cause we got a right to be here. You start trouble and the soldiers'll finish it."

"If you men don't ride out now, we'll have to capture you and take you to the fort to check out your claim that you have permission to be hunting here today. It's my guess, the soldiers don't want you causing trouble they'll have to resolve. Why don't we just pack up and ride in to check out your story? Of course, accidents do happen along the trail, so I hope we can make it there without any of you men getting injured or killed, if you catch my meaning." Chase saw the man and his companions eye the Indians closer, no doubt assessing the warriors' strengths and weaknesses.

"Tell me, Martin, why are you sidin' with them Injuns?"

"They're my friends, and I'm trying to prevent unnecessary trouble. I'm sure the soldiers will agree with my line of thinking."

Jake huddled and whispered to his companions, then turned and said, "We'll be agoin', but don't go acrossin' paths with us again. Might not be healthy for you or them, if you catch *my* meanin'."

"Fair enough," Chase scoffed at the implied threat. As the Whites galloped off, he again stressed to Wind Dancer, "We must get our hands on that treaty, my brother, to know all it contains."

"I will think on your plan," was all Wind Dancer could say at that time, though he thought it was a good idea.

"Why not have the women skin and butcher the slain buffalo since the kills and meat are fresh?" Chase suggested.

"No, for their iron balls taint the meat," Two Feathers snarled.

"Cut off the area where the iron ball entered the animal," Chase reasoned, "but use the rest of it. If the meat is prayed over and cooked well, surely that will purify it of any evil."

"If Whites watch us, they will think we frightened them away so we can take their kills. We do our own hunting. Is that not true, our leader?"

Wind Dancer felt compelled to agree with his cousin to prevent trouble, and he saw Two Feathers grin in victory. "We will let the coyotes, sky birds, and others feast on their carcasses. Come. We must hunt before the sun sleeps."

When they returned to camp at dusk, Rising Bear and a

large group of men were waiting for them to get a report on the day's events.

After the news was given, Winona's brother asked, "What will we do if the Whites return and bring more men and weapons with them and scare away the buffalo? Will we move to another place or will we fight them?"

"You must not attack them, Strong Rock," Chase urged, "or soldiers will come to punish the Red Shields. The White hunters said the treaty gave them permission to hunt here. Do you remember if that is true, Father?"

"I do not remember such things being told to us at Long Meadows."

Chase was pleased that his father had responded directly to his question. Before he could speak again, Strong Rock made an accusation.

"The White leaders tricked us and put in words you were not told."

"Perhaps that is true, Father," Chase agreed with the older man. "Let me ride to Fort Laramie and get the papers with the treaty words so we will know what they say. I can read the white man's marks for you."

Runs Fast, the father of Two Feathers and Broken Lance, said, "It is dangerous to steal the treaty words. The soldiers will follow you and attack our camp."

Chase glanced at Runs Fast and hoped the man did not possess his first son's irascible traits. "I will sneak into the fort and find where the papers are stored. I will write them on other paper, return the others to their place, and bring my words to you so we will know what they say. I will be careful and cunning."

"I say it is dangerous to let Cloud Chaser ride to the fort."

Chase's concern over the man increased. He knew others were observing them and feared the man would incite mistrust and dissension. "Why is it dangerous, Runs Fast?"

"You could betray us while you are there."

"I would not endanger my family and people. I want them to remain unharmed and alive. Things are changing swiftly in these lands and the Red Shields must learn other ways to survive. I will teach my people to farm and we can cut and sell wood to the trading posts and steamships to earn money to buy goods and we will not need to depend on Whites and their treaty trade goods. We can buy cattle to raise to prepare for the season when the buffalo and other game have been slain and there are not enough to clothe and feed our band. Perhaps that is why the Great Spirit summoned me here."

"The white man's animals are too skinny to feed us," Two Feathers argued. "We have seen those given to others; they have only hide and bones and little meat."

"We can fatten them on the Plains, my cousin, for there is much grass there, and we can grow corn and other grasses to give them during the cold season. In the hot season, we can fence in areas to protect them from roaming too far from our camp; and in the cold season, they can graze in canyons with one entry. They will provide much meat and hides."

"Animals are not to be trapped by wood and ropes," Two Feathers scoffed. "They must be free, as we must be free. We must enslave no creature."

"The Red Shields must prepare for dark days ahead when the buffalo are few, my cousin, or they will go hungry, naked, and without shelter. The cows we raise will supply the same things we get from the buffalo: hides, meat, horns, hooves, stomachs, sinew, bones, and such. The females give milk which is nourishing for the young and old."

"You try to make white men of us. Next, you will ask us to dress, look, speak, and live as they do. We will never do so, will we, my Lakota brothers? Your mind has been stolen by evil spirits and you speak foolish."

Chase realized Two Feathers was attempting to rile the people against him. He saw nods of agreement from others. *Think and talk fast and smart, or you'll lose another battle to that sorry snake.* "No, my cousin, I try to find ways to help my people survive the changes the white man brings with him. I speak from all I have seen and learned about them. Their numbers are great and their weapons are powerful; it will be hard to push them out of these lands, for they have a strong grip upon it. You must think of peace, my father and people, for many of the Whites are not very different from Indians."

Two Feathers laughed aloud. "How are our enemies like us?"

Chase tried to explain the similarities between the two cultures and that many settlers only wanted freedom and peace. "There are good and bad people on both sides," he clarified. "Do not forget how one tribe wars with another from a different nation, how hunting grounds are taken by the strongest, how some tribes enslave their enemies, and how they raid them for possessions; it is the same with the Whites. Even if real peace is not possible, trick the Whites and enemy tribes into believing it is for as long as you can; for with each passing sun and moon, our band grows stronger and larger for the day when such enemies must be challenged."

"If you truly want to become a Red Shield, yield to the Sun Dance and vision-quest to prove your words and feelings," Two Feathers said. "If you are strong and true, you will find victory at the cottonwood pole."

"I have told you, my cousin, this is not the time for me to do so. I believe the sun will rise when I must ride among the Whites and soldiers to learn their secrets. If I submit to the Sun Dance, I will have scars to expose who and what I am." Chase saw his cousin frown when the shaman lifted his hand for silence and started to speak to the group.

"I will seek a sacred vision soon and the Great Spirit will tell us what we must do," Nahemana said. "Until that sun, we must continue our work. When you talked with the encroachers, did you believe their words?" he asked Cloud Chaser.

"No, Wise One; I think they spoke with false tongues."

"Why did you not slay them and hide their bodies?" Nahemana asked.

"Others might know they are here or might be watching and would ride to summon the soldiers to attack us. All should learn English, so—"

"We become White except for our skins? Your words are—"

Nahemana sent Two Feathers a silencing stare. "Let him speak."

"No, my cousin, I do not wish to make Whiteskins of my people. I say learn their tongue, so when contact is made anyone can pick up potential deceit. I beg you, Father, let me go scout for you at the forts."

"If he meets with our enemies, he will reveal our secrets."

Chase stared at his tenacious first cousin. *What bloody "secrets" do you keep talking about? Obviously there's something I don't know . . .*

Rising Bear frowned at Two Feathers and said, "We will do nothing until after Nahemana's vision-quest."

"If the Great Spirit orders him slain or banished, will you do so?"

Rising Bear studied the persistent son of his only sister and realized Wind Dancer and War Eagle were right about the younger man's distrust and animosity toward Cloud Chaser, and was concerned and mystified by it. "You should know by now, I always obey the commands of the Creator. Go to your tepees, my people, to eat and rest for our tasks on the new sun."

Chase nodded and returned to his secluded site, worried about the way many of the men had looked at him during his talk. He feared the Red Shields were not ready or willing to accept the truth about the grim situation facing them. It seemed to him as if he had to do something soon, something daring . . .

CHAPTER EIGHT

On the third morning following their encounter with the white men, Nahemana met with Rising Bear and others to reveal, "The Great Spirit gave me a sacred dream on the past moon. I saw Cloud Chaser talking with Bluecoats and other Whites who hunger to destroy us. I could not hear their words, but next I saw many Bluecoats riding against the Lakotas."

"What does the dream mean, Wise One?" Rising Bear

asked without glancing at Chase, who stood nearby and listened as he waited to go hunting with his other two sons.

"I do not know; that is all I was shown," Nahemana replied.

Before allowing others time to speculate, Chase ventured, "Our shaman saw me tricking the soldiers and Whites to learn their intentions against us and our allies, for I believe that is why the Great Spirit summoned me here. I have asked many times to go and steal their treaty words and plans, but I am forbidden to do so, for I am not yet trusted or accepted among you. How can we stop attacks and prevent trouble if we do not know from where and when it will come? At the fort, I could learn such secrets, return, and reveal them to you, Father."

When Rising Bear remained silent and stoic, Nahemana said, "I will seek a vision on the next sun and pray for answers from the Creator. He will tell us what we must do during this dangerous season and those to come."

Two Feathers could no longer keep still. "He has given you answers, Wise One, but you do not wish to accept them, for Wakantanka speaks against the second son of our chief and it is hard for you to believe one from Rising Bear's blood and seed can be evil."

The worried shaman responded quickly to avert trouble, "Your words and feelings have not been proven, Two Feathers."

"They will be soon, Wise One. I say we slay him to protect our band, for we cannot banish him to ride to them and join their side."

Nahemana shook his head. "Cloud Chaser has done nothing to this sun to earn his death by our hands. Until the

Great Spirit speaks to me in my vision or he betrays us, Cloud Chaser will stay alive and with us."

"But he seeks to make white men of us."

"No, my cousin," Chase argued. "I seek to protect my people and to tell them ways to adjust in this new world which surrounds us. Who is to say if the Great Spirit did not create all peoples and make them different? Perhaps that is why many of the things I learned about the white man's beliefs match ours, for I have told you about their Great Flood and how their Creator used one chosen man and woman to replenish the Earth and their people. Perhaps He gave each a territory, but when the Whites' number grew large, they spread out into the lands of others."

"You speak evil words, for Wakantanka did not create our enemies; they are the work of Evil Spirits."

"How do you know that is true, my cousin? Can you see into the heart and mind of Wakantanka? Do you grasp all of His mysteries and deeds?"

"This is not the time to speak of such mysteries," Nahemana said. "Go to prepare yourselves for hunting, my friends, for we have much to do."

As the men dispersed to gather their weapons and horses, Chase realized that the time had come to take action.

When Hanmani came to bring Chase his evening meal, he told her, "It is as clear as the water nearby, my sister, I cannot prove myself here; and Two Feathers seeks harder each sun to turn others against me. I must leave to carry out the tasks which the Great Spirit puts within my heart and head, for only by doing them can I help my people and win their acceptance. I will leave while the moon rides the sky and go to Fort Laramie. There, I will get the treaty words and scout for my people. With that proof of my love and loyalty, I will return. Speak to Dawn for me of my love for her."

"No, my brother, you must take her with you," Hanmani whispered, "for Two Feathers will ask for her in joining on the next moon and she will be entrapped by him. She will go with you."

Chase's heart began to pound with a mixture of dread and excitement. "How do you know such things, my sister?"

"I heard my cousin telling his brother of his plan to do so. Perhaps he suspects your feelings for each other and seeks to hurt and defeat you. It will be useless for you to approach her parents, for they will not give her to one who is not a Red Shield; they will command her to join to him. You must call upon the Old Ways to win her: if you two sneak away and mate, when you return to our camp, you will be viewed as husband and wife."

"You say she will go with me?" he asked, almost holding his breath in suspense.

"I am sure, for her love for you is great and she believes your Life-Circles must be entwined, as do you, as do I. Save her from Two Feathers and walk the path Wakantanka shows you to prove yourself to our people."

"I thank the Great Spirit for warming your heart and opening your mind to me. Without your trust and help, I would be defeated here."

"We must not allow Evil to find victory over Good; that is why I act as I do. I believe your heart and words are true and you are my brother."

Chase knew he needed her assistance to carry out such a daring plan, but he was concerned about his sister's fate if her role was discovered. "What will Father and your mother do if they learn of your help? It would pain me to cause trouble and sadness for you."

Hanmani took a deep breath before replying, "I will not reveal what I have done; but if they learn of it and ask me, I will not speak falsely. I must do as the Great Spirit tells me."

"You are brave and smart, my sister, and I have much love for you. Surely the Great Spirit will protect you from all harm and will reward you."

"The safety and survival of our family and people is the reward I need."

"I will do all I can to obtain them, my sister," he vowed, then made plans for his secret departure with Macha for later that night . . .

Macha's heart thudded fast and hard within her chest as she sneaked toward where her family's horses were hobbled with the others to graze during the night. Her parted lips dried swiftly as she took short and shallow breaths in the hot summer air. Her hands—clutching a small bundle of her possessions and food—trembled, her legs felt weak and shaky, and her thoughts spun with all sorts of imaginary dangers and punishments. She had escaped her sleeping family's abode and had slipped from tepee to tepee without being discovered as she headed for her first destination. At the last conical dwelling, she waited to be sure no man was lurking near the animals, as the camp guards were supposed to be positioned farther away. Sighting and hearing no one, she crept to her horse, removed his leg bonds, grasped his neck thong, and guided him toward her second destination, where she was to meet her beloved and flee with him. She walked slowly and quietly, her head shifting from side to side and glancing backward to watch for intrusion. At the riverbank, she headed southward to join Cloud Chaser to begin a daring future with him, unaware she was being followed . . .

Hidden amongst many trees and with the light of a three-quarter moon, Chase saw Macha coming from a lengthy distance. He noticed and recognized the man who stealthily trailed her. He left his horse there and crept along the riverbank to flank him, using other trees and vegetation to conceal himself. When Two Feathers slipped behind a cottonwood nearby, Chase moved in soundlessly and rendered his target unconscious with a mild blow to the head with a small log. Using leather thongs he had brought with him, he secured his cousin's wrists and ankles, bound him to a large tree out of sight of the camp, and gagged him with a bandanna. Satisfied Two Feathers could not free himself to sound a warning, and certain the man would be found by women when they came to fetch water, bathe, and wash garments, he hurried to join his beloved, made aware once more that his weapons—rifle, pistol, and ammunition— were in his father's tepee; and he had only the borrowed bow, arrows, and his knife with which to protect them during their long journey to Fort Laramie.

Macha gave a sigh of relief and joy when Cloud Chaser joined her. She hugged him and whispered, "I feared trouble had struck at you."

Chase smiled reassuringly at her and told her about Two Feathers. He saw her dark gaze widen. "What if another saw me and comes to halt us?" she asked fearfully.

"I studied the camp well, so we are safe. Come, my love, we must go fast while darkness gives us time to get far away. What more troubles you?" he asked when he noticed her worried expression.

"You take me with you because you love me and I was chosen for you by the Great Spirit, not because you seek to defeat your cousin and his quest for me, is that not true?"

Chase realized she needed confirmation of his feelings and motive before she took such enormous risks for him. He caressed her warm cheek and looked deep into her eyes as he replied, "That is true, Sunshine of my heart, for I love you and need you in my Life-Circle; it is what I desire and believe is the Creator's will. This is not how I wish our joining to take place, but it is the only way we can be together. I will never betray you or speak falsely to you. I must go to walk the Great Spirit's path, but I could not leave you within the evil reach of my cousin."

"That is good, for my heart beats with much love for you."

"We will talk soon, but we must ride now. Do not be afraid, Dawn, for I will protect you with all the skills I possess and with my life if it must be."

"As I will do for you, He Who Chased Me and Captured My Heart."

They exchanged smiles and a brief kiss, which seemed to warm their very souls, before they departed to skirt the southern edge of the Black Hills and travel onward to Fort Laramie.

Almost simultaneously in the encampment the following

morning, Macha's mother was approaching Rising Bear's tepee to see if her daughter was with Hanmani, and Broken Lance was doing the same to see if his older brother was with War Eagle or in Wind Dancer's abode nearby when women discovered the bound and gagged Red Shield warrior at the river, as Chase had predicted.

As soon as he was freed, Two Feathers checked where Chase slept, grinned sardonically, ran to Rising Bear's tepee, and revealed in a loud voice, "Cloud Chaser has fled, my chief, and taken Dawn with him."

Many men, including the shaman and Wind Dancer, had seen the excited Two Feathers racing into camp and—suspecting trouble was afoot—hurried to where he joined Rising Bear outside his tepee and began shouting the news. All listened as the agitated man exposed the tale of how he saw Macha sneaking away from camp during the night, trailed her, and was attacked; he declared the unseen foe was Cloud Chaser, whose camp was deserted and whose possessions and horse were missing.

"We must pursue, capture, and punish them for this wicked deed. I will gather a war party to go after them."

"Why do you say Dawn escaped with him?" Ohute asked. "She would not do such a bad thing. If she is gone, she is his captive."

"I do not wish to pain your heart, Root, but she did so," Two Feathers told her. "She took her horse and carried a bundle with her. She sneaked to the river where Cloud Chaser was camped. They are gone. You must move our camp, my chief, before he brings Bluecoats here to attack us."

Rising Bear knew the time had arrived when he must

admit the truth to himself and others and speak from his heart. He could not allow Cloud Chaser to be hunted down and slain, or permit Two Feathers to rile the people against his son. "There is no need to move our camp," he said. "If soldiers come to seek us, they would only follow our tracks to where we go. We will keep guards posted to watch for trouble, but I do not believe my son will bring it. There is a purpose to his actions and he will tell it to us when he returns, for he will do so. When that sun rises, I will embrace him as I should have done when he first came. He carries two warring bloods because the Creator and his father gave them to him, but he has done all he can to prove his Lakota blood is strongest. It was wrong and cruel of me to turn my back to him and to influence my people to do so, even for this many suns. I will not do so again, for he is being used and guided by the Great Spirit. I beg you to accept him, my people."

"How can we, my chief, when he is evil and has fled to our enemies?"

"If Cloud Chaser is evil, Two Feathers, he would have slain you," Nahemana refuted, "for you have challenged him many times. I was coming to Rising Bear's tepee to tell him of another dream which came to me last night. I believe Cloud Chaser's return is important to our survival. I believe his words to us are true and wise. In my dream, I saw our chief standing with only two sons and watching our people's defeat. Next, I saw Rising Bear standing with three sons and watching our people find victory. It is a sacred message telling us to accept him as one of us. Perhaps this message was not sent to me sooner because our reluctance to trust him was meant to push him toward the path the

Great Spirit chose for him to walk. I believe he has gone to find a way to help us and to prove himself to us, not to betray us."

Rising Bear nodded gratitude to the shaman for his generosity and wisdom. "Nahemana speaks the words which also fill my heart and mind. I believe the Great Spirit took away my second son, taught him many things about our enemy, and sent him back to us for a good purpose. I have much love, pride, and respect for him; he has been patient, brave, strong, and wise while we tested him. I say he is a Red Shield. Who speaks otherwise?"

"If that is true, my chief, why did he steal the woman I was to join?"

"You have not spoken for her," War Eagle refuted Two Feathers. "Is that not true, Root?" He watched Dawn's baffled mother nod agreement to his question.

"I was to do so on this very sun, my cousin. He took her to injure my heart and honor and to punish me for speaking against him many times."

"How can that be so, Two Feathers, when he cannot see into your thoughts to know your plans?" Wind Dancer reasoned, as elated as War Eagle appeared to be by this astonishing turn in events. "He is my brother, son of my father; to speak badly against him, speaks badly against us. Why do you seek to injure and destroy him?" He noted a strange but brief gleam in Two Feathers' eyes before his cousin concealed it, and when the man answered, Wind Dancer was convinced it was not the truth, or all of it.

"I do not believe as your family and our shaman do; I believe he is evil and will call down great dangers upon us. It is my duty to challenge him."

"If you challenge my son upon his return, you must also challenge me, Two Feathers," Rising Bear said.

"And challenge me," Wind Dancer added.

"And challenge me," War Eagle echoed his older brother's words.

Two Feathers looked at the three men and scowled. "There should be no conflict in our family circle, my chief and cousins."

"There is conflict only if you cause it," Rising Bear replied. "We have much to do, for our hunting time is short this season. If no other man wishes to speak against my second son, we must seek the buffalo."

When there was silence, Hanmani asked, "May I speak, Father?"

Rising Bear looked questioningly at his daughter and nodded.

"I am good friends with my second brother, for I have served him and talked with him many times since he came to us. Many moons past in our old camp, he told me of the sacred dream which called him back to us. He spoke of a part to me and Dawn which he did not reveal to others, but it is time to do so." After she related that information and explained why she had kept it a secret, she said, "As it was with Wind Dancer's sacred vision about Dewdrops, the Great Spirit chose Dawn for Cloud Chaser." Hanmani knew she must not further antagonize Two Feathers by mentioning Macha's distaste for him. "On the past sun, Cloud Chaser told me he must leave to prove himself and must take Dawn with him, for she possesses his heart. By now, they are joined in the Old Way. They were secret friends as children and love each other deeply. After I came to know him, I believed he was good and true, and the Great Spirit spoke to my heart to help him. If I was wrong to do so, I will accept my punishment."

Rising Bear smiled at her, relieved to learn Cloud Chaser had found kindness in their camp and family. "It was a good deed, my daughter; my heart feels great love and pride for you. There is no punishment."

"He will return, Father, and will do great deeds for us as did Wind Dancer and Dewdrops." To Macha's mother, Hanmani said, "Do not fear, Root, for they share great love and a glorious destiny together. He saved your son from the badger's attack and he will protect and make Dawn happy. He will be a great warrior among our people, for the blood of our chief and many past chiefs runs within him. Be proud he has joined your family."

Ohute smiled. "You speak wise for one so young, Hanmani. It is good my daughter has you as her friend. We will accept our new son."

"That is good, Mother," River's Edge said from beside her. "When he returns, we will ride again as friends, and as brothers."

Far away that night, Macha cuddled in Chase's arms upon his bedroll and shared tender kisses with him. They were tired from riding almost all of the past night and day, for they'd only made short stops to rest the horses and allow them to graze and drink. Both had been on constant guard against pursuers and that fierce concentration, added to their physical exertions, had nearly drained them of all energy. Yet, they felt enlivened for a time as they kissed and caressed and whispered words of love and endearment to each other. Kisses which had begun gently and playfully soon waxed slow, long, deep, and ardent.

"Do you know how much I love you and how much joy you bring to my heart and life?" Chase murmured near her ear as his lips nibbled her lobe.

"If your feelings match mine, your love is as large as the sky and your joy as broad as the grasslands. I quiver with great need for you."

"As I do for you, Sunshine of my heart."

Their mouths fused again in a soul-stirring kiss as they entwined their soaring spirits forever. Each explored the other's body with eager caresses that teased and tantalized. One kiss melded into another and another until they were breathless.

Chase tried to think of other things to distract himself from his enormous carnal urges, for Macha would soon tempt him beyond a point of retreat. He wanted them to be married at the fort before they surrendered to such passions. He leaned back, gazed into her eyes, and cautioned in a ragged voice, "We must stop these actions, my love, before we are consumed by them. We cannot join our bodies here, for an enemy or Red Shield party could intrude. We must not have our union spoiled by the encroachment of others or rush such a special event. Soon, we will become as one when we are safe and can think only of each other."

Macha looked at him and smiled. She took several deep breaths to help her gain control over her rampant emotions. She knew he was right, but it was difficult to cease such exquisite delights. He was the only man who made her feel this way, but she cherished him for his thoughtful restraint. "You are wise and strong, my love, for I am weak and dazed by you."

Chase smiled. "My body also is weak and my head is clouded with great love and desire for you; that is why we must leave this dangerous path and walk another one for now. We will speak of other things to cool our bodies and change our thoughts."

"That is wise, but hard, my love. What will we speak of to help us?"

"Do you know what large secrets my cousin feared I would learn and reveal to our enemies?" he asked.

Macha did not hesitate. "He feared you would tell Whites about the shiny yellow rocks they hunger for and will slay to possess, for there are as many in our sacred mountains as stars which fill the night sky. The two Whites who found them were slain and their bodies hidden forever so they could not tell others about them."

That revelation stunned and worried Chase, as gold could be an obstacle to lasting peace and hazardous to the Lakotas' survival. As he sat up and removed the locket from around his neck, he said, "That was wise, Sunshine of my heart, for many Whiteskins will do anything to have those yellow rocks. They are called *gold* and have great value to the Whites. This *wanapin* is made of gold; it belonged to my mother and holds the images of her parents. It was given to me when she died. I want you to have it and wear it as a show of my love for you and commitment to you. Turn your back and lift your hair and I will put it on for you."

The happy Macha obeyed, murmuring, "I thank you for this gift and will wear and protect it forever."

As Chase fastened the locket's chain around her neck, he explained, "Gold was found in the land far away in the direction where the sun goes to sleep; that is why many Whites cross this territory, to reach that area and search for yellow rocks. If news spread of gold being in our sacred mountains, Whites would flood them as a dry wash following a long and hard rain. Much trouble would come to our land and people. It is good that secret was buried, and I understand why Two Feathers would fear its discovery."

"He also feared you would tell the Bluecoats about the Big War Council to be held after the great buffalo hunt when all Oglala bands and other Lakota tribes meet to trade and talk as we do before each cold season."

That news distressed Chase more than hearing about the presence of gold in the Black Hills. He remembered the large trading fairs which took place at the end of summer when many of the bands of the Oglala branch and some of the other six Lakota tribes met to trade, talk, visit with friends and relatives, and discuss any important event looming ahead. "They are to speak about a possible war or to vote upon starting one?" he asked in dread.

"I do not know, for that is all Hanmani overheard. News of the council came from Spotted Tail and Little Thunder; they are both Brule chiefs who hate and fear the white man. Brave Bear of another Brule band is to speak for peace, for he was chosen as Head Chief of all Lakotas at the Long Meadows Treaty Council; he says all bands must honor the truce words or all Lakota tribes will be punished."

"Two Feathers is right to worry about such news filling the soldiers' ears at Fort Laramie. If the Army learned what was going to be talked about at the big meeting, they would be consumed by fear and would attack the encampment before a vote could be taken and warriors could prepare to ride against them and the settlers. Our people and other bands do not understand how powerful the Whites are, and how resolved they are to retaining a grip on this territory. They have weapons which can shoot hard balls at a swift and deadly pace and at a long distance, while warriors must make arrows and can carry only a few in their quivers and must be close to their targets to strike them. There are many soldiers at other forts who could be summoned here, while many tribes and bands refuse to fight together under one chief as one mighty force. The Army has many supplies to feed its soldiers and wagons to carry them in on the trail, while warriors can carry little on their horses and must halt to hunt and cook to keep their strength. A war so great would be bad for both sides."

"That is true, my love," Macha agreed, "but they are the enemy and they challenge us by stealing our land and animals; we have become as captives to them and must follow their orders or be punished or slain. There is no honor in such an existence, but there is honor in dying for what is right."

Chase caressed her cheek and smiled. "You are wise and cunning, Sunshine of my heart. What you say is true, but it will demand much. At the fort, I will listen and watch to learn all I can about our enemy. I must teach you their tongue so you can do the same."

Macha grinned and said in English, "Dawn know little English. Hanmani teach."

Chase chuckled and praised her effort in Lakota. "That is good, Dawn, and I will teach you more during our journey. There are words you must speak at the fort when we join in the white man's way." When she looked surprised and confused, he explained, "A joining ceremony, called a marriage, will give us a good reason for being at the fort so I can do my work there. And, if trouble comes to this land, you will be protected under their laws as my wife, since I was reared by Whites and am viewed by them as a white man. Now we must sleep, for soon we must ride again."

As they traveled for days toward their distant destination, it became increasingly difficult to restrain their desire for each other. Nights were the hardest to endure as they shared a bedroll since it had been impossible to bring hers along. They were awakened several times every night as their closeness aroused their passions even during slumber. Their constant longings and lack of sleep made them edgy, but excited with anticipation of what lay before them when they could surrender to great passion.

The journey had been made longer as they were compelled to skirt camps, working groups, and scouting parties of other tribes or Lakota bands who were hunting buffalo on the extensive grasslands in that territory. Often they were forced to veer eastward for miles to elude human obstacles in their path before heading southwestward again. Staying on constant alert for perils that might be just ahead cost them extra time and energy. But they could not afford to be stopped and questioned by Lakotas or white men.

Whenever they halted to rest or sleep, they talked about their pasts, eager to share all with each other. Macha filled him in on the events which had occurred during his lengthy absence; and Chase taught her more English, including the words she would need to use during their marriage ceremony, as well as his signals for her to speak them. Although he had done all he could to conceal their trail, they were surprised and baffled by the fact no Red Shield search party had come after them. If a hunt was on, given the tracking skills of his brothers and other warriors, they reasoned they should have been overtaken by now; and they gave thanks to the Great Spirit for continued freedom to complete their crucial tasks.

On the eighth day after they fled the Red Shield camp, despite all of their precautions and hopes to avoid it, trouble struck . . .

CHAPTER NINE

The route Chase and Macha were compelled to use while evading other Indian bands took them southward toward the North Platte River and its valley where eroded grayish bluffs, verdant forests, and a lengthy escarpment were located amidst thick grass and scattered scrubs. At the higher elevations, they saw ponderosa pine and juniper trees; and in the lower regions there were mainly box elders and sacred cottonwoods, with willows growing in ravines and other vegetation along the riverbank. At long last, such a combination of nature's beauty provided ample concealment for their movements which vast expanses of grasslands had denied.

Once they reached the river, they planned to take a trail so heavily traveled by countless emigrants and the Army, it was almost like a well-worn dirt road. Visible were the ruts of many wagons from settlers journeying on what had come to be called the Oregon-California-Mormon Trail and led to its next major landmark at Scotts Bluff. Added to those were ruts from Army wagons hauling supplies and stages taking mail and passengers to Fort Laramie and beyond.

Chase had viewed such scars on the earth long ago when he was taken away from this territory and again recently when he returned to it. He couldn't help but think if the Red Shields had not been camping and hunting in this area twelve years ago, his fate might have been different. To appease his anguish and to prevent anger and resentment, he had to believe there was a crucial purpose for those trying episodes in his life, and his existence and destiny were being planned and guided by the Great Spirit, Whom he believed was the same Deity as God. He mentally packed away those thoughts and refocused on the matter at hand.

As the cautious couple weaved their way past bluffs, hills, and trees, heading for the river and road, they heard ominous sounds, and halted.

"Firesticks," Macha murmured as her startled heart thudded in panic and her frantic thoughts whirled in dismay. "Whites are nearby. Do they hunt buffalo or do they attack a camp of Lakotas?"

Chase knew she was voicing aloud her fears, not asking him a question to which he could not know the answer. "We must sneak closer and see what is happening. Be ready to ride fast if we are sighted and pursued," he commanded gently. "Take no risks, Sunshine of my heart, for I could not bear to lose you."

Macha nodded and followed his lead as he guided her, using nature's creations to conceal their approach. She kept silent not to distract Chase from his intense concentration, praying for their safety and survival, and for those of the enemy's victims, as she was certain there would be some when the scene unfolded ahead. She knew something painful had disturbed him earlier, as she had glimpsed an array of various telltale emotions as they flickered across his handsome face. She surmised that he was thinking about the past, for it was near this place where she had first lost him, and must never do so again. She had given up a lot to be here with him now, but he was worth any sacrifice she would be called upon to make to share a Life-Circle with him. She did not know where they would go or what they would do if they could not return to their people. Yet, what must be, must be, for surely this was Wakantanka's will for them.

When the sounds were loud enough to indicate the trouble was nearby, Chase halted them behind a series of large sandstone formations and dismounted. He whispered for her to stay on her horse and be ready to flee at a moment's notice. When she nodded, he smiled, grateful she was so smart and brave. Taking his fieldglasses, he crept to the edge of a huge rock where scrubs grew, knelt behind them, and peered through their tangled limbs at a grisly sight ahead at the road. He used the glasses to be sure of what he saw.

His sienna gaze narrowed and his body stiffened as he witnessed the malicious aftermath of the slaughter. Even if he were well armed, it was too late to help the victims. All he could do was watch and wait until the attackers departed.

After they left, Chase joined Macha and related what he had observed: "White men dressed as Indians attacked five Bluecoats and killed them; they stole a travois filled with firesticks and hard balls for them. After the Bluecoats were slain, they shot arrows into their bodies and took scalplocks from them."

As Macha listened to the grim news, her gaze widened and her lips parted. "Why did they do such a wicked thing to their own kind?" she asked.

"To cause trouble between Bluecoats and Indians when Indians are blamed and punished for what happened, and out of greed for those weapons," Chase sadly explained. "Stay here while I go undo what I can of their evil. After I have done so, we will follow the white men to see where they go and to learn their names. On another sun, I will make certain they are exposed and punished." He wished he could report the slayings so their bodies could be recovered and buried, but he couldn't risk possible incrimination. Besides, he reasoned, soldiers probably wouldn't believe his charges against white men, and the evidence he needed as proof might be gone before he could return with troops. Shaking his head at the senselessness of it all, Cloud Chaser set about completing his gruesome task. When he had finished, he rejoined Macha, and used water from his canteen to wash the soldiers' blood from the recovered arrow tips, then placed the shafts inside his quiver. "It is done. We go now," he told her.

Using great prudence, Chase and Macha trailed the wagon and men to a farm many miles away. By that time dusk had arrived. There would be scant moonlight to guide them after dark.

Chase left Macha with the horses where she would be safe for a short time while he sneaked closer to see what he could observe. The man who appeared to be the gang's leader guided the wagon into a barn and the others dismounted and followed him. Keeping his guard up, Chase crept to the large wooden structure and listened to them planning their next mission—an attack on a stagecoach. He had to find a way to stop them.

Chase peered around the side frame of an open window and saw the men hiding the stolen items in a cellar, then covering the trapdoor with bales of last year's hay. Yet, even knowing where the evidence was stored, he couldn't be sure the crates and barrels would remain there long enough for him to ride to Fort Laramie, convince the Army of his claims, and return with troops to show them. He absolutely would not leave Macha behind to watch the barn and men for the shipment's removal, and she could not follow the villains if the gang transported the weapons elsewhere during his absence. He could only hope to bring their deeds to light as soon as he could do so without endangering his beloved.

Chase returned to an anxious Macha with just enough time to put a safe distance between them and the farmhouse before dark. As they sat close together on his bedroll and consumed the last of the food Macha had brought along and Hanmani had sneaked to him during his last meal back in camp, Chase related what he had learned and what he hoped to do later.

Macha was excited. "It is a good plan, my love, for they must be punished; and it is best for it to come from their own kind."

"That is true. At least we know part of the reason why they

did such an evil thing: if their plan had found victory, the Army would have blamed and punished Little Thunder and Spotted Tail's bands. With the Brules gone or their forces weakened, the man who owns this land could make his farm larger and other Whites could come to farm here. It is good dirt and has much water for growing food and special grasses for their animals. I will try to trick the Bluecoats into entrapping them soon so they can cause no more trouble."

"If our people allow us to return to them, when war comes between the Whites and Lakotas, will you fight our enemy to the death if it must be?"

"When I first returned, I hoped and believed peace or at least a truce was possible, but the more I learn about the troubles and bad feelings between and within the two sides, I know war will come one sun. When it rises, I will ride with my family and people if I am allowed to do so. I do not wish to slay those like my mother and adoptive parents, but I fear I will be forced to battle their kind for our safety and survival."

Chase was positive a horrific and bloody clash would result when the secret of the Black Hills was exposed and prospectors flooded them. There was no doubt in his mind that all seven tribes of the Lakotas would attack "yellow rock" seekers and sacred site encroachers with a vengeance, and soldiers would be sent to rescue and protect imperiled white men. During his travels, he had met and seen men ensnared by "gold fever" and knew what a dreadful and dangerous disease it was. He kept his worries to himself, as he didn't want to frighten his beloved.

"We must sleep now, Dawn, for we must ride at first light."

"Will it be safe for you to hold me and kiss me, for I need to draw courage and comfort from your arms and lips?"

Chase pulled her into his embrace and kissed her. He, too, needed to draw solace and encouragement from her love. One hand slipped into her hair and fingered its sleek strands. The other roamed her back, then cuddled her closer to his aroused body. She was so precious to him, and he yearned to possess her fully. But he wanted that unique moment to be special. By tomorrow night, if nothing else obstructed their path, she would be his wife and belong to him in all ways.

Macha adored the way he touched her. He was such a tempting mixture of strength and gentleness. She loved him with all of her being, and desired him with every part of herself. He warmed her as no roaring fire or scorching summer sun could ever do. She could hardly wait until she could discover the delights of bonding their bodies as one, to experience the sheer joy of having him completely. Soon, she vowed, soon.

Chase separated himself from her, took a deep breath, and said with reluctance, "We must sleep now, for on the next moon, we will get little rest after we are joined."

Macha smiled. "That good news pleases me greatly, my love, for I can no longer resist my craving for you."

"It is the same for me." *Tomorrow night* . . . his mind vowed.

Before they approached Fort Laramie on the sixth of August, Chase concealed the bow and quiver of arrows which War Eagle had loaned to him weeks ago, along with the shafts which had been embedded in the soldiers miles away. He knew it wouldn't be wise to ride up armed only with Indian weapons. He smiled at Macha, seeking to reassure her, as they neared the fort.

The military post was strategically positioned atop a lofty bluff overlooking the Laramie River, eastward of the Laramie Mountains and vast stretch of the Rockies. The wisely chosen site provided well for the troops and passing emigrants: they had easy access to fresh water from the river, food for their stock from the grasslands, and a road connected the area to forts and trading posts in both directions. There was no stockade encompassing its structures and cannons, as if the Army didn't fear an Indian attack. The compound included barracks, stables, a bakery, sutler's store, smithy, lumber shed, saddlery, magazine, guardhouse, supply storages, and officers' quarters. Most of the buildings were two stories high, with many windows, railed porches, and high-pitched roofs with multiple chimneys jutting from them. They were situated around an enormous parade ground with a tall staff, from which the American flag danced about in a strong wind. Fort John, a large adobe building which had first served this area and now belonged to the American Fur Company for trading with trappers and Indians, was set close to the river bluff. Unlike the new fort, John had two guard towers and an adobe-enclosed yard for protection against "hostiles," as well as two brass cannons and weapons within the workers' easy reach.

On a grassy area below one section of the extensive bluff, Chase glimpsed a few homes, other structures he didn't know the reasons for, and a cluster of Indian tepees where "loafers" camped and often lived year long. All of what he viewed, he tried to convey and explain to Macha as they approached, though so much of it was unfamiliar to her, it was confusing. He promised he would clarify such things to her at a later time.

The only reason Macha was not terrified of this new experience was because she was close to her beloved and had such confidence in him. She knew he did not fault her for not understanding all he was trying to tell her, for he knew her language lacked translations for everything they saw. But she was smart and eager, and he was a good teacher.

Chase glanced toward the office and dwelling of his target—Lieutenant Hugh Fleming, Fort Laramie's commander—for that was where any copy of the treaty and any enlightening letters from deceased Indian agent Thomas Fitzpatrick and the current agent Thomas Twiss would be kept. He had been told in May by a talkative soldier that Fleming had initiated an assault last year on the Minneconjous—one of the tribal members of the Seven Council Fires of the Lakotas. He hoped that didn't mean Fleming was an Indian-hater and troublemaker.

He knew his way around the site from a visit there in May before he traveled to the trading post called Fort Pierre and then made contact in early July with his family and people. As they got closer, he smelled bread being prepared in the bakery structure, and that indescribable scent which only Plains grass and the summer air seemingly possessed. He saw men unloading supply wagons which probably had arrived late the previous day, soldiers checking or repairing their gear, men tending the stock, a few standing guard, and the brilliant sun reflecting off windows and the river's surface. He heard the American flag flapping in a strong breeze, the smithy's hammer as he shod army horses, and the prairie wind whistling past his ears. He felt calm yet apprehensive, both ready for and dreading the hazardous challenge ahead.

Macha, too, felt very alert and on her guard. She did not fear as much for her safety and survival as she did for his. She could guess the enormous risks he would be taking when he crept into the commander's abode for the papers he insisted were so important to them. She did not want to even imagine what his fate would be if he was captured. It was as if she had waited her entire life for Cloud Chaser to grow to manhood, return home, and to join with her. Now, she could lose him again in the blink of an eye, and this time, to death, forever. What would she do if he were slain and her family and people rejected her when she returned?

Macha took a deep breath. Even if she were scorned and banished, she admitted, that would never be as bad as losing the only man she had ever loved. As she stole a glance at him, her heart raced. *Protect him for me, Great Spirit, for he is my destiny.*

Chase entered the sutler's large store, and Macha waited near the open door as he had instructed earlier. He was relieved only a few people were inside, and those men only glanced at her for a moment as if they were accustomed to seeing "squaws" with white men and such a female did not deserve their attention for more than an instant. "Do you have a dress and pair of shoes or boots I can buy for her?" he asked the owner.

"I got a few new ones and some I bought from women emigrants down on their luck. They're over there in that corner," he said, motioning to the back one on the left. "The new ones are four dollars each and the worn ones, two dollars; the shoes are three dollars a pair."

"Thanks, I'll go look them over. It sure would be nice for her to have a change of clothes so she can wash those ripe buckskins," Chase said and chuckled. He selected the loveliest new dress available and used a paper which he had outlined her foot size on with a piece of charcoal from a past fire to pick a pair of shoes for her. He chose a rifle and requested ammunition for it, and gathered other needed supplies, piling them on the counter as he did so. He told the sutler he had traded his old rifle, which didn't work well, for the woman with him because he needed help and a man's comforts at his cabin come winter time.

"Looks to me as if you made a good deal; she's a pretty one."

"Yep, and real obedient and respectful. Smart and hard-working, too."

"I know plenty of trappers who took Indian wives. It's hard on a man to live alone in the wilderness all winter and to do all the work himself."

"Yep, that's what I learned last season. I was lucky I came upon a camp of friendlies on my way here, and one of them needed to rid himself of a daughter. The unfortunate cuss had four of them, so his small tepee was overcrowded and his band didn't have enough young bucks to go around." Chase chuckled. "Good thing I got out of his area before her papa could learn that old rifle won't be much use to him."

The sutler laughed. "Most Indians aren't too smart about our weapons—and a lot of other things about us. And I doubt anybody would sell him ammunition for it anyways."

Chase paid for his purchases with money he had received from selling the Martins' farm, stock, and other possessions in Oregon. He made certain he chatted, joked genially with the store owner. He told the man he was there to buy those items and to rest for a day or two before heading out to find a better site to use that coming winter, since his last one was all trapped out. "Is it all right if she changes clothes in your storeroom? I'd be more relaxed if she's wearing white woman's garb so people won't be staring at her."

Since Chase had shopped there months ago and spent a lot of money with him today and perhaps would do so again in the future, the sutler said it would be fine, if she hurried and didn't touch anything.

Chase thanked him and told Macha what to do, knowing she could manage the buttons and shoe lacings alone following his lessons en route. He waited while she changed, and smiled when she returned with every task performed to perfection, her hair secured behind her nape with the ribbon he had purchased, and her garments and moccasins secured in a bundle. He thanked the sutler again, and they went outside to load their possessions and supplies on their horses.

Then they headed for their next challenge.

Chase was delighted when the preacher—who had built a small cabin nearby and who held Sunday services in his yard for soldiers, local settlers, and emigrants passing through the area—agreed to marry them under White law. When the man queried her identity, Macha replied, "My name is Dawn, sir," just as Chase had taught her to do when his thumb stroked the side of her hand which he was holding.

"I surely am much obliged, sir," Chase said, "because I don't want my children to be born bastards and I want the Good Lord's blessing on our union. These folks are lucky to have you in these parts."

The elderly man smiled. "Let's get started, because I'm having supper with some friends." He opened his Bible and read appropriate scriptures from it. "As Ruth said," he added, " 'for whither thou goest, I will go; and where thou lodgest, I will lodge: thy people shall be my people, and thy God my God.' Do you agree to those Holy Charges?"

"I do, sir," Chase responded.

"Do you agree to those Holy Charges, Miss Dawn?"

As Chase lightly squeezed her hand, she replied, "I do, sir."

After the preacher asked Chase if he took "this woman to be his lawful wife, to love, honor, and protect her in all times and ways," Chase said, "I do, sir."

After he asked Macha, "Do you take this man to be your lawful husband, to love, honor, and obey him in all things and times," she smiled at Chase and said, as he had taught her, "I do, sir."

Then the preacher said, "I now pronounce you man and wife. 'What therefore God hath joined together, let not man put asunder.' That's it, son, she's your dutiful wife now. Go in peace and love, Mr. and Mrs. Martin."

Chase's heart swelled with happiness and victory, for the woman he loved above all earthly things was now his beloved wife. If only, his mind whispered, the rest of his challenges would be this easy.

In a secluded and lovely area miles away, Chase and Macha

made camp near the river and amidst a cluster of tall trees. They tended their horses, ate their meal, and spread out his bedroll just as the sun kissed the distant horizon. Joy and blissful expectation filled them. Probably anyone traveling in the area would be camped by now. Just to make certain, he studied their surroundings with his fieldglasses. They didn't want to waste a single moment, for when daylight was gone, it would be dark beneath the new moon sky.

They stood beside the beckoning bedroll and gazed at each other for a few minutes, doing nothing more than savoring each other's presence. Love seemed to flow within and around them like a tranquil river of warm and relaxing water. They had no regrets or reservations about what they had done, and they vowed to do whatever was necessary to remain together.

Slowly, Chase's quivering fingers unfastened the buttons of her cotton dress. She raised her arms so he could lift it over her head. He dropped it to the grass as his breath caught in his throat at the first sight of her naked beauty and the tender glow in her brown eyes. He had no doubt she loved him completely and wanted this union as much as he did. He smiled when she unbuttoned his blue shirt and peeled it off his shoulders, then trailed her fingertips ever so lightly over his bare skin. As his tawny gaze settled on the gold locket around her neck, he wondered if his mother could see them from her tepee in the sky. If so, Margaret Omaste Phillips surely knew he had done well with his choosing.

Macha noticed he had no hair on his broad, well-muscled chest. He was tall, so the top of her head only reached the middle of his throat. There were only a couple of scars on his torso, and none marred his enormous appeal. She slipped her arms around his waist and leaned against him, their bare flesh making joyous contact. When his head lowered, she kissed him, reveling in the blissful sensations he created within her.

As Chase's lips drifted across her face and close to her ear, he paused there to murmur, *"Waste cedake, micante. Kopegla sni yelo. Ni-ye mitawa."*

Macha responded with similar words. "I love you, my heart; and I am not afraid. I am yours, as you are mine."

"I must not rush as I walk this new path, but it is hard not to do so."

"Winyeya manke." She told him she was ready. "We walk it as one."

They kissed many times as their questing hands roamed each other's bodies as if exploring and mapping unknown territory. Their breathing became ragged with excitement and they trembled with rising passion. Soon, she was the one who separated them so she could untie and discard her doeskin breechclout; and he removed his boots, pants, and undergarment.

Chase took her hand and guided her down to the bedroll. As they faced each other on their knees and with their hands clasped, he said, "See us, Great Spirit, for we ask you to join us as husband and wife in Your way. Guide us and protect us in our union."

Macha hugged him before they lay down side by side and resumed their lovemaking. It was not long before he moved atop her and possessed her with great gentleness and caution, and Macha sighed deep within her throat and pulled him more tightly against her as her legs banded his hips.

This was what they had craved and anticipated for a long time, this total joining of hearts, bodies, and spirits. Their control was strained from weeks of anticipation, and all too soon their passion peaked and crested, leaving them holding each other tightly as they rode out the wave as one.

Then they made love again, savoring each moment, before they slept cuddled together.

Early the next afternoon, Chase could hardly believe his enormous good fortune when he found a back window opened slightly in Lieutenant Hugh Fleming's quarters. He had assumed he would have to sit around his camp nearby and wait for the new moon cycle to end to give him suffi- cient light after dark to carry out his objective. He didn't know, and dared not ask, why so many of the seventy-one- man garrisoned fort were absent from the post or were laboring elsewhere, but he thanked the Creator for aiding his task. From his observation, the few troops present were working below the bluff with the stock; and the "loafers" were lazing around their tepees on mats. There was no wagon train passing by or supply wagons arriving and he was able to raise the window and climb inside without being seen.

Despite those propitious conditions, Chase did not lower his guard. He sneaked to the front window and peered out to be sure no one had headed in his direction while he was distracted making his stealthy entry. He found it almost graveyard quiet and still deserted outside. He hurried to a wooden cabinet which had been left unlocked and began to go through the stacks of papers he found stored there. He was elated when he not only discovered a copy of the treaty but also letters from Fitzpatrick and Twiss. Deciding he did not have time to copy them there and probably wouldn't have another chance to return them later, he stuffed the papers inside his shirt and asked forgiveness for his necessary theft. With luck or divine intervention still on his side, he escaped in the same manner in which he had come.

A short distance away, Chase saw three wagons heading to the fort with loads of freshly cut hay and wood. A group of soldiers surrounded them as if the wagons were more valuable than the post which had been left so vulnerable to attack. He reasoned that the commander or whoever had been left in charge during Fleming's absence was taking a huge risk in his assumption the Indians would not assault the fort and fur company. He could not understand why the Army didn't have more troops assigned there and the post didn't have protective walls when it was in the midst of several very large and powerful Indian nations who mostly despised and distrusted Whites. He hoped that one day a lot of innocent people would not pay with their lives for such reckless pride.

When her husband reached their temporary camp and dismounted, Macha raced into his arms and hugged him tightly, then covered his face and neck with kisses before burying her damp cheek against his chest. "My fear was great for your safety and survival, my love," she murmured. "My life would be hard and sad without you in it."

Chase lifted her chin and gazed into her brown eyes. He noted the tears of relief and happiness shining in them and upon her lashes and cheeks. "Do not fear or worry, my beloved wife," he comforted her, "for I am unharmed and my task was victorious."

With her arms still laced around his body, she asked, "What did you do at the Bluecoat camp? You were away so long."

As he stroked her hair, Chase related his adventure there. His words brought a smile of pride and joy to her face.

"The Great Spirit guides and protects you, for He has chosen you to do great tasks for His people. My fear and weakness shames me, for I must not doubt His power and purpose for even a short time."

"I believe He rides with us, Sunshine of my heart, but fear also sneaked within me at the fort, for I knew capture meant death and a loss of you and the lives and lands of our people. I remember Father telling Wind Dancer when we were boys: 'It is wise to have good fear, my son, for it gives sharp wits and tells a warrior to be careful and alert.' That is true."

Macha touched the area around his waist where she had felt something strange and bulky and asked, "What is here?"

Chase grinned. "The Long Meadows Treaty and the words of the past Indian agent and the new one. We will soon know their secrets."

Macha watched as he removed the papers, then sat before him in silence on the sleeping mat as his gaze traveled them. While she waited for him to absorb and relate their contents, her thirsty eyes drank in the sight of him. Whether or not Rising Bear ever accepted him, Cloud Chaser favored his father, and resembled his two brothers in small ways. All three sons were handsome and virile men; they were strong, brave, and skilled. If they ever rode together against their enemies, they would make a formidable force. She was blessed he had chosen her to love, for he made her happier and more complete than anything or anyone she had ever known. It would be wonderful to be accepted as mates in their band, to have their own tepee, to have children, to be safe and free. Would the Great Spirit, she mused, reward them with such things? She did not know, for His will was a mystery.

Chase read the two-page 1851 Fort Laramie Treaty and the third page of names of the signers, both Indian and White. He was grateful the Martins had sent him to school and worked with him at home to teach him this skill, and he was glad the Creator had sent him to such good people and to obtain such knowledge. "It does not say what the buffalo hunters claimed. It does not give white men permission to hunt on Indian lands." He read Article 2: "It says, 'The aforesaid nations do hereby recognize the right of the United States Government to establish roads, military and other posts, within their respective territories.' That means the Army, the soldiers, can make trails, forts, and posts in Indian territories."

Chase went to the second page and read part of Article 5: "It says, 'The aforesaid Indian nations do not hereby abandon or prejudice any rights or claims they may have to other lands; and further, that they do not surrender the priv- ilege of hunting, fishing, or passing over any of the tracts of country heretofore described.' That means, ally and enemy can hunt, fish, and travel the lands of others if they have done such things on them on past suns; that is what the Crow told Wind Dancer when we came upon them while we were riding and hunting together in the old camp. It is signed by the chosen Head Chiefs of the eight nations who met at Long Meadows and agreed to the treaty, and the White leaders and others who witnessed it."

"You say the White hunters spoke with false tongues, but the Bird Warriors did not?" she asked to make certain she understood him.

"That is true, but it is a foolish and dangerous demand of the treaty and White leaders. The next time White hunters encroach, we can capture them and take them to the soldiers for punishment. With our Indian enemies it must be different: Lakota chiefs must go to the White leaders and tell them enemy tribes cannot ride and hunt in the same lands if the peace they crave is to last for many circles of the seasons."

"Will they change the treaty words if our chiefs ask them to do so?"

"I do not know, but it would be wise of them to listen and obey."

"The one who would have ears for us is dead; the agent who sits in his tepee does not possess the same kind of heart and interest in us."

"Perhaps Thomas Twiss is entrapped by White laws or controlled by other leaders with more power and he cannot do as we believe he must for peace to live among us. Now, wife, prepare our food while I look upon their words," he requested in a gentle tone, "for another task lies ahead for us."

"What must we do before night comes and we sleep?"

Chase grinned, patted the bedroll, and murmured in a seductive tone, "It will be a good task."

Macha also grinned as she caught his tantalizing hint,

aroused by his voice and intention. "I will hurry so we can eat soon."

As she busied herself with their evening meal, Chase began reading old letters, or rather copies of most of them. He soon discovered that Thomas Fitzpatrick had brought about another treaty last year at Fort Atkinson with the southern tribes who had refused to attend the 1851 peace talks at Fort Laramie, along with a few minor treaties with smaller tribes and considered less important. He learned something the Indians didn't know about the man they had respected and trusted: it was clear to him that Fitzpatrick had been doubtful years ago that parleys with the Indians were useful or any treaty would be honored by them until the Indians had been taught the awesome power of the American Government and had been subjugated. The one they had called Broken Hand had warned, "It must certainly appear evident that something must be done to keep those Indians quiet and nothing short of an efficient military force stationed in their country will do this." Fitzpatrick had related he was certain the forts were garrisoned too low and were constructed too far apart to protect emigrants and settlers—or the troops themselves—or to prevent enemy tribes from warring with each other, which usually overflowed onto Whites. Yet, Fitzpatrick also believed the Indians should be praised and rewarded for allowing White encroachment, and their territories should not be entered without their permission.

As soon as Chase was about to change his mind about the deceased man, he read that Fitzpatrick thought it would be smartest and cheapest and safest if annuities were used to make the Indians become dependent upon the Whites for their survival, how they could be "civilized" and taught the White customs and farming; that way, when the buffalo was gone, tribal wars would not break out and settlers would not be attacked for subsistence.

Chase was disturbed when he read a letter—dated years ago—to the fort's past commander. After the treaty council, Fitzpatrick had taken eleven of the so-called Head Chiefs to Washington with him to let them observe the strength and number of White Power. One of those chiefs had been so alarmed and depressed by what he saw and heard that he took his own life, something which rarely happened in the Indian culture.

Chase was astonished to learn something he was certain his father and brothers did not know: the United States Senate had altered some of the treaty terms: the amount of the annuity and length of time it would be awarded. Fitzpatrick had been upset with those changes and, only last year, had convinced a few of the Head Chiefs to concur with them, while others refused. The agent had then written to the government telling them the Indians were "in abject want of food half the year . . . Their women are pinched with want, and their children are constantly crying with hunger."

Which tribes, Chase wondered, had the man been referring to, for he had not witnessed such a desperate need? Had Fitzpatrick mistaken the "loafers" as representative of the Indian plight? Had some of the tribes duped him in order to obtain more rations? Or duped him so he would believe they were weakened and subjugated when in reality they were growing stronger and hoped to crush the White force invading their land? Or were there bands somewhere—ally or enemy—in such dire need?

Chase realized these letters must be returned so they would be on record for the current and perhaps future commanders to read, and the treaty, for reference, so its terms could be checked and honored. He must copy the treaty and any important letters, then find a way to replace them. How, he didn't know, but surely the Great Spirit would show him a cunning path . . .

CHAPTER TEN

Chase was relieved Macha didn't ask him about the letters, as he did not want to discuss depressing news, at least not at that special moment when they were about to make love for the third time since their marriage. He noticed she had washed her long hair during his absence today and the summer heat had dried it before his return, making it shiny and sleek, as if the midnight black strands possessed an inner glow. He enjoyed burying his fingers in its depths and feeling its texture against his flesh.

He watched her for a while, reveling in her beauty. Her dark-brown eyes were large and expressive, her lashes long and thick. High cheekbones and a perfectly curved jawline added to her charm, as did her full lips. Her teeth were white and healthy; and her breath was sweet, as she often chewed on a fragrant herb or grass which she kept in a pouch suspended from a beaded belt. He could stare at her forever and never tire of her.

Macha was always stimulated and enslaved when Chase looked at her as he was doing now with his sienna-colored gaze so tender and adoring. She could almost feel the powerful emotions flowing from him and engulfing her warmth. She had no doubt he loved and desired her, that he was happy they were together, were mates. Every time she realized they were truly joined forever, her love for him increased, though she wondered how it was possible for her to love him more than she already did. "I love you, Cloud Chaser, and will never leave your side," she said with deep emotion. "Each sun and moon, I thank the Great Spirit for returning you to me."

"As do I, my cherished wife. No matter where we must settle later, we will be together and happy."

"That is true, my love," she murmured before they kissed.

As slowly as they could, they let their passion build, each enjoying the anticipation of what lay ahead. The sounds and scents of the coming night filled their senses as they lost themselves in the giving and receiving of love. A gentle wind wafted over them, but its summer heat did not chill their fiery, naked bodies.

Their desires grew and grew until they could wait no longer. With a soft groan, Chase joined with his beloved bride, surrendering to her sweet, welcoming heat until he had brought them both to blissful release.

As they lay entwined under the darkening sky, Chase told her, "When we have more time and privacy, my wife, I will give you more pleasure than I can do here so close to the Bluecoats and settlers. When I touch you in this way, my wits become clouded. I must not allow myself such joyous distraction for too long in enemy territory." Nor did he want them to be discovered while naked and vulnerable.

Macha laughed softly and jested, "How can there be more pleasure than I receive each time you possess me? If it were any larger, my body would melt into Mother Earth as the snow does beneath a hot sun."

Chase embraced her with a proud and possessive hug. "That is true, but I do not like to rush such a wonderful journey."

Macha wished she could view his expression—but it was now too dark—when she asked merrily, "Is such a ride more enjoyable if a slow pace is used?"

Since he was the first man to join with her, Chase surmised there were certain things she did not know. "No, but different paces offer us different adventures," he half explained. "A slower one will give us time to do other special things during our journey."

Macha had overheard women with husbands whispering during their chores and mothers giving daughters enlightening talks before their joining days, so she understood some of what he was trying to say, and found herself eager to make those discoveries. "When a safe moon rises, we will take a slow journey, for I hunger to learn all such things with you as my scout and teacher."

After a pleased Chase vowed they would do so, they nestled together until slumber overtook them.

Macha paced their camp for what seemed to be an alarming amount of time during her husband's absence the next day. As instructed, she stayed ready to leap on her horse and escape from any danger which threatened her while he was gone. Just in case she had to flee, they had chosen a place where they were to meet afterward. She had bathed in the river, put on clean garments, washed the dirty ones, and hung them across bushes to dry while he marked upon what he called "paper." Then she had packed their possessions, kissed him farewell, and watched him leave.

Her worries threatened to distract her. She could also not stop thinking about her family and Hanmani. She could not help but wonder what they were doing, if they were safe, what their reaction had been about her behavior, and what—if any—action had been taken about it. Surely if a search party had been sent after them, they would have been found and captured by now. That led her to believe their escape had been ignored, and she could not imagine why. She was certain that Two Feathers had said and done all he could to persuade Rising Bear and the council to send braves after them and to have them punished. Perhaps, she speculated, something or someone—probably the Great Spirit—had halted them from coming to prevent intruding with the Creator's plans. What would happen when they returned to the Red Shield camp, she could not imagine.

At long last, Macha saw Cloud Chaser coming and her heart pounded with elation and relief. When he reached her, she asked, "Did you find another victory, my cunning love?"

Chase grinned and joked, "It was an easy one with the Great Spirit's help. I went to the dwelling of the leader to speak with him, but he was gone. Another man, one called John Grattan, has taken his place until the leader returns soon. I told him I had come to ask if he knew of trouble in the area where I planned to ride. Before he could speak, another Bluecoat summoned him outside. While he was gone, I returned the words I had taken." He went on to tell her what Lieutenant Grattan said following his return, that the Indians were being quiet for now while they hunted buffalo. He also had checked the schedule for the stage from Fort Kearny along the North Platte Road. After he completed his revelations, he said, "We must ride to the place where the man lives who killed the Bluecoats and stole their weapons. We must entrap them so they cannot do this wicked deed again."

"You have already conceived a plan?" she asked.

"Yes, my clever wife, and I will speak of it while we ride."

"We will eat and go, for there is much sunlight left."

Following their quick and light meal, Macha retrieved her garments from the bushes, mounted her horse, and left beside Chase as they headed toward the farmhouse.

The next day, as Chase scouted out the farmhouse, he saw men gathering there. He was convinced the stage robbery would take place as their leader had planned. All he had to do now was gallop to Fort Laramie and entice Grattan to the site the villains were going to use tomorrow, west of Prayer Circle Bluffs. He had learned from a talkative soldier at the fort that Grattan was seen as cocky and eager to make a name for himself. Hopefully, his ambition would make him useful to Chase.

Chase was worried about endangering his wife if he left her near the farm and she was discovered, but he could not take her with him to dupe Grattan. Nor could he sneak her to the post and leave her there, as she might panic if he was gone too long. Besides, she was too beautiful and tempting to leave unprotected amidst so many Whites and soldiers. Too, the "loafers" might become suspicious of her if she lingered around their area. "I must go, Dawn, to reach the fort and return with Bluecoats before their next attack. You must ride with me for a distance and hide in the place we chose where you will be safe."

Later at that location, Chase leaned over to stroke her cheek and kiss her. "Hide yourself and your horse in the trees and rocks," he instructed. "Do not make a fire when it is dark, for others may see its flames and smoke. Stay alert, and flee to the other place we have chosen if danger approaches you. If you are not here when I return, I will come there."

Macha trailed her fingers across his cheek. "I will obey you, Cloud Chaser. Do not worry or fear for me."

"I will do so, as you will for me," he refuted with a broad smile.

"*Wakantanka nici un. Waste cedake, mihigna.*"

"May the Great Spirit go with you and guide you, also. I love you, my wife."

At dusk in his quarters at the fort, John Grattan looked at him and said, "We met yesterday. Chase Martin, isn't it?"

"Yes, sir; I was checking out any possible Indian troubles in the area before I headed out," he reminded him. "I returned today to speak with Lieutenant Fleming, but I was told he isn't back yet and you're still in charge."

"That's right; Lieutenant Fleming went to the American Fur Company downriver to check on the Indians' annuity goods before visiting Fort Kearny. He's expected back in a few days. Is it important?"

"Yes, sir, mighty important. It can't wait." Chase told him how he had come upon a small band of Indians who were planning to attack the stage from Fort Kearny tomorrow just east of Prayer Council Bluffs.

"How did you know what they were saying?"

"I speak a little Lakota, enough to understand them."

"How many were there?"

"Seven. All seasoned warriors from their looks."

"You think they're expecting others to join them?"

"No, sir, it didn't sound that way to me. Renegades is my guess."

"Why did you take a chance sneaking up on their camp?"

"It just seemed to me they were up to no good, sir. Indians don't paint their faces and horses and go prancing and chanting around a campfire if they aren't up to something. There's a lot of settlers and travelers and soldiers in these parts, so I figured I should creep up and see what I could learn, and the terrain offered me plenty of cover. Probably renegades from a tribe around here and working on their own. Since we know where and when they plan to attack, I figure we can set a trap for them. Since Fleming's gone and you're in charge, I guess it's your duty, sir. Might even be a stroke of good luck for you."

"What do you mean?"

"I'd think any officer would be eager to put down Indian trouble and show the Government and Army he's more than just doing his job. And it surely would liven up things for a while in this quiet place."

"How did you learn the Indian language?"

Chase had expected him to be suspicious, so he had answers prepared. "I've trapped in their territory north of here for three winters, ever since they signed that treaty and made it safe to work their waters. 'Course the beaver and other creatures are playing out, so I'll be moving on soon. While I was trapping, I did some trading and talking with the Lakotas. It don't take long to pick up their simple tongue and signs. I even did some translating for the boys at Fort Pierre Trading Post."

"Why did you come to this area? It's a long way from Pierre."

"Not too far over easy terrain like them grasslands. I was hoping to hook up with a wagon train and travel northwest with them to find new trapping grounds. I figured it would be safer than riding alone. A man by himself with money in his pocket, supplies, a good horse and saddle, and a fine rifle could disappear out there, if you catch my meaning. And accidents do happen along the trail. Might even be a young and pretty widow who needs a hand with her wagon and chores in exchange for meals and washing my clothes. Since I didn't see any wagons here, I was heading to Kearny to see if any were coming soon. If not, I can't hang around and get stranded here during winter. Would cost me too much time and money. That's how I happened up on those Indians camped miles away. So I turned around and headed back here since it was closer to their target."

"I'll get my men ready to leave at first light," Grattan said, satisfied with Chase's explanation. "We should reach that area in plenty of time to lay a trap for them. No need to go racing out there tonight when there's hardly a crescent moon showing herself. Why don't you bed down at the stables? You are riding with us, right?"

"Yes, sir; you might need a translator along; and I can ride on to Kearny afterward. I'm much obliged for the use of the stable. See you at dawn, sir," Chase said before he left to spend what he knew would be a restless and long night with his beloved wife so far away and alone.

Macha pressed her body against the rock formation and prayed no snakes or other perilous creatures would invade her space. At least a tiny part of the moon was showing, so she was not engulfed by blackness. The only times in her life when she had been so alone had been recently during Cloud Chaser's absences. She did not like feeling so vulnerable and helpless. She had a knife, but that weapon did not offer much comfort. Even so, she was skilled in self-defense, thanks to her brother's teachings and practices; and she would not hesitate to slay for survival.

Macha wished she were more like Dewdrops, for Wind Dancer's wife was a skilled warrior who had ridden into the face of danger alone and at his side many times in seasons past and showed great courage, and prowess. She would feel more worthy of being Cloud Chaser's wife and helper. But all she could do was wait and worry and question Wakantanka's will for her part in this quest.

She felt weary, but not sleepy, and doubted she would close her eyes all night. But if she did, surely her horse would alert her to any threat, and he was standing nearby, which provided a little comfort. *Watch over us, Great Spirit, for I am weak and afraid, and Cloud Chaser will soon face much peril amidst our enemies and many challenges amongst our people.*

By midday, Chase, Grattan, and twenty soldiers were concealed west of Prayer Council Bluffs and awaiting the arrival of the raiders and stage, which was due to appear on the road within the hour. The trap was set, and all that remained to be seen was if it could be sprung with success.

As they watched and tarried, Chase remembered one of the orders given by Grattan about shooting to kill so none of the seven warriors would escape. He wondered what Grattan would think when he learned the truth about his prey.

When the culprits—dressed like Indians on the warpath—came into view and hid themselves behind trees, bushes, and rocks, Chase felt calm and ready for what was to come. To avoid jeopardizing the lives of the driver, guard, and passengers, the soldiers were to strike as soon as the "Indians" made their move against the stage.

Soon, it rumbled and jostled into view. After the stage passed the villains, the action began when seven riders took off after it, whooping and shooting. As the first shots were fired, Grattan told his men to charge, and to pursue any warrior who tried to flee the scene.

As they galloped toward the action, firing as they went, the raiders tried to escape. Grattan and the soldiers pursued them with haste and resolve. As much as he despised their quarry, Chase didn't want to be one of their killers and made sure his shots didn't hit any of the villains; he would leave justice in the hands of the Army.

It was not long before all seven men had been slain. Only one soldier was slightly wounded. As Chase joined Grattan near the bodies, he observed the officer's reaction as he inspected them.

"These aren't hostiles. They're white men dressed and painted as Indians and wearing full head scalps. Did you know about this?"

"Yes, sir, but I figured if I told you the truth, you wouldn't believe me." Grattan didn't respond to him, but the lieutenant's expression told Chase that assumption had probably been right. "I knew if the Indians were blamed and their camps were attacked, they would retaliate and a war would break out. This was my way of preventing something which would get a lot of innocent people killed on both sides."

A lower ranking officer told Chase, "We have some real Indians doing raiding and robbing and we'll have to go after them as soon as we can learn which ones are involved. We'll have help by fall because more troops are expected by then. If you ask me, it's going to come to war. I hate to see that happen, but the Indians won't honor their word."

"What about our people's broken promises to them?" Chase responded as calmly as he could. "I hear some of the stock and rations are so bad even vultures wouldn't touch them. Some Whites are taking advantage of the treaty and settling in areas they shouldn't. And troublemakers like these men are pretending to be Indians to trick the Army into killing or running them out of the area. You've got Whites slaying buffalo for nothing more than their hides and sometimes their tongues. Maybe you haven't been here long enough to learn the Indians take great offense to that, because they use every part of a slain buffalo. It riles them to find meat rotting on the Plains, and to realize our hunters are destroying the main source of their survival. You've got enemy tribes being ordered to share hunting grounds. You're confining men who've roamed, hunted, and lived free and proud to one territory and they've been ordered not to fight each other, which goes against all they are, know, and have been for generations. You're talking about mixing tribes as different in customs and languages as the English are to the French and Spanish."

The soldier shrugged. "We had to drive them out of our country and may have to do the same with the Indians if they don't settle down."

"They might settle down if the Army and Government would listen to their protests and grievances and do something about them."

"That isn't for us to decide; we just follow orders. Right, Lieutenant?"

As Grattan nodded, Chase realized it was a futile waste of energy and time trying to reason with the soldiers. He wanted to finish his part in this matter and return to his wife. He related how he had stumbled onto the culprits after they attacked an army supply wagon heading to Laramie.

"We were expecting that supply wagon last week," Grattan said almost to himself after Chase finished relating the whole story. "We thought it was just late. Fleming's checking on it while he's gone."

"Well, now you know what happened to it and you've already gotten the men responsible. All this should look good on your record, Lieutenant Grattan. Since I've done my duty, I'll be riding on. But I'll give you one more piece of advice—if you hear about any more attacks by Indians, make sure they're truly to blame. I surely would hate to hear about this area becoming a bloody battlefield because of a foolish mistake. Just remember, the Indians can be pushed so far before they'll retaliate. If it comes to war, you'll discover their warriors are far more skilled and cunning than you realize, and they're superior fighters on this kind of terrain. Good luck, Lieutenant; I have a strange feeling you and Fleming are going to need it before summer's over."

As Macha cuddled in Chase's arms in the Wildcat Hills that night, he told her, "We must go share our findings with my father and our people. They must be told about the treaty words and warned about white men's tricks, so they will not fall prey to them."

Macha leaned her head back, stared at him with widened eyes, and asked in dread, "What if they doubt you and slay you or banish you?"

"We must take that risk, Sunshine of my heart. If we are banished, we will find a place to live where we will be free and happy. We cannot seek a new life together far away and leave them in danger."

She noticed he did not respond to her that he might be slain; she must have faith it would not be so. "That is true, my husband. Why did the white men seek to blame Lakotas for their evil deeds? The Pawnee live across the river and their number is larger in this area."

"The Pawnee offer the Whites no threat, but the Brules and Oglalas in this area resist White encroachment and stir up trouble at times. It would please the settlers and soldiers for all Lakotas to be far away from here."

"Will that sun rise, my husband?" she asked with trepidation.

As he caressed her cheek, he said, "I do not know," *but I fear it will in the years ahead.* To calm her anxiety, he lowered his mouth to hers and she responded with eagerness to his first kiss. When his lips left hers for a moment, he whispered, "We will think only of good things on this moon."

"That pleases me, my husband," she agreed, and kissed

him again, eager to let their unclad bodies speak for them now.

As their kisses deepened, Chase's left hand cupped and fondled her right breast, savoring the feel of that firm mound within his gentle grasp. He trailed kisses down her smooth throat, letting his lips then tease her taut, aching peaks. Macha gasped her pleasure and soon he was lost in the wonder of their love and smoldering passion. His fingers drifted over her bare flesh and gradually moved lower and lower until they reached the moist silken heat of her womanhood.

Macha squirmed in delight and increasing arousal as he pleasured her with his skilled hands and lips. Eager to share her joy, she sought and found his manhood and also tantalized him to writhing need. Knowing that ecstasy awaited her, she did not hesitate to head toward it.

They kissed and labored lovingly and generously until they could wait no longer. And as they joined together and moved as one, neither let thoughts of what lay ahead distract them from this magic they had found.

On a beautiful and tranquil Lakota dawn with a woman of that name beside him, Chase said it was time to head for the Red Shield camp. They packed their possessions, embraced and kissed, and mounted their horses. They gazed at each other for a minute, exchanged smiles, and rode away to face their destiny . . .

CHAPTER ELEVEN

Miles south of the Badlands on the White River, many days

later, Chase and Macha had halted to rest and water their horses and refresh themselves amidst concealment by an obliging landscape. Before their departure, he used his fieldglasses to study the terrain ahead and sighted riders in the distance. From years long past and what he'd learned since his return, he recognized the three men as Pawnee warriors. But it was the small and frightened burden clutched before one of them which astonished and angered him. His narrowed gaze scrutinized the situation as his mind sought a cunning and safe plan for rescue.

Chase hurried to where his smiling wife awaited him. She questioned his dark scowl. "Three Pawnee ride toward the river not far away," he explained. "Tokapa is with them. I must free my brother's son."

Macha stared at him in shock, then asked, "How will you do so, my husband? What trick will you use to get close to them? What will happen when Tokapa shows he knows you and they attack?" She did not doubt his prowess, but could he, she fretted, defeat three armed and strong foes? Yet, she knew he must try to do so.

"Surely they will halt to rest and water their horses at the river," Chase reasoned. "When they do so, I will circle behind them and lure them away from him. Then, you will sneak to that place, seize him, and ride swiftly to safety. After I fire upon them and challenge them, they will leave a small child behind to pursue me, for they cannot fight while holding him."

"What if I lure at least one or two from where they halt? If all do not pursue you, I cannot battle those who stay there. If one or two are provoked to chase me, you can sneak up, defeat he who stays behind, and rescue the boy. After he is safe, you can save me from the others."

"It is a perilous risk, my wife, for you are a great tempta-
tion. If my fight is long, you could be injured or slain before
I reach you."

"That is a challenge we must face, my husband, and pray
the Great Spirit travels with us. We must free Tokapa before
he is harmed or lost. Do not fear, for I am a good rider and
my horse is swift and skilled."

Chase admitted to himself that her plan was clever, but
was worried as Pawnee did not hesitate to slay even a
female of an enemy tribe. He wondered how they had captured Wind Dancer's only child and why he had sighted no
rescue party galloping behind them, but he lacked time to
ponder the mystery. "Your plan is cunning and brave, but
more risky to you than mine. I cannot risk sacrificing your
life to save Tokapa's. If we fail here, we will trail them and
find another trick to use." If necessary, he would fetch
Grattan to the Pawnee camp beyond the Platte River to
demand his nephew's release, as the treaty ordered no hostilities and raids against other tribes; and surely the Army
would want to avoid a war breaking out between enemy
nations. Too, Grattan was in his debt.

After all preparations and strategies were finalized, Chase
mounted and headed in a northwesterly direction to flank
his targets, the rolling surface masking his presence until he
could position himself to initiate his part of their daring
ruse. As he departed, Macha used the fieldglasses as she had
been taught in the past to observe the unfolding event, ready
to act when the melee began and praying for victory for
both of them.

By the time Chase topped the last knoll, he knew what he

would say to provoke them: *It is a bad day, Pawnee. You are going to die soon. Do not be afraid. Come! It is time to fight.* He stared at the Pawnee who had dismounted at the river and shouted to them in Lakota, *"Anpetu sica, Palani. Ecana nitin tke. Kopegla sni yo. U wo! Kiza iyehantu."*

As he rode closer and halted midway between his three objectives and the hill, Chase saw the startled warriors leap to their feet, face him, and shield their eyes from the brilliant sun, as they stared in disbelief. He motioned them onward with his left hand, sent forth insulting laughter, and shouted for them to hurry up and come on. *"Inankni yo! Hiyu wo!"* When they continued to stare at him as if he were crazy and to whisper amongst themselves, he told them to get out of there if they were too cowardly to accept his challenge. *"Tu we canwanka, letan kigla yo!"*

Chase saw them scan their surroundings, no doubt to see if he was a decoy for a trap. "Are you old women or warriors?" he shouted. "Do you fear to battle me? Do you fear dishonor and death at my hands? Run away, Pawnee; flee this area, for you stain the ground and air with your weakness."

Two of the warriors bounded upon their horses and came charging at him, whooping in anger and bravado and shaking bows clutched in their hands. "We fight atop the hill so the Creator can see who lives and dies," Chase yelled, and then galloped back to the one he had crested a short time ago, for the high and sloping ground gave him an advantage. Once there, he dismounted and fired a shot, taking down one opponent to even the odds, then cast the rifle aside and jerked out his knife to let the other Pawnee know theirs was going to be a hand-to-hand fight.

The warrior, who had slowed his pursuit when his companion was slain, fox-yipped in rage and rode toward him. With one agile movement, his foe was off his horse, then cast aside his bow and also drew his knife.

"Come, Pawnee dog, and fight me to the death if you have the skills and courage," Chase sneered with the intent of unsettling his opponent. He prayed he could defeat his enemy and fast, because the third man was still with Tokapa. He knew Dawn would attempt to save the boy, even by jeopardizing her own safety and survival. If he was slain or badly injured, he agonized, that would leave her and the boy at the men's mercy.

As soon as Chase showed himself atop the hill and captured the men's attention, Macha began to make a stealthy approach toward Tokapa. When only two of the men departed, she pulled her knife from its sheath and prepared herself to attack the third enemy. She knew her only hope of success—and survival—rested in catching him by surprise and striking a severe and disabling blow, a lethal one if she was lucky.

As she crept closer, the warrior—who had been sneaking wary glances to all four sides—focused his full attention on the slaying of one companion and the hilltop struggle of the other. She dared not even peek in that direction, as her love's peril would distract her. It seemed to her as if the nearby target was tempted to join his remaining friend and was struggling hard not to intrude on another's battle. She used great caution, fearing the little boy would see her and give away her presence.

Poised to do her task, she prayed for the Great Spirit's

protection and help. *Give me skills and courage like those of Dewdrops if only for a short time so I can save her son as a gift for all she did for our people.*

Just as Macha was about to take her last steps toward the enemy, the agitated warrior headed for his horse—she assumed—to aid his friend. She knew her beloved's chance for survival would lessen when faced with two opponents, so she raced forward to overtake him and plunged her knife between his shoulder blades. The stunned warrior arched backward, gave forth a shriek of pain and surprise, and whirled to confront his attacker. As he did so, Macha reached out, stole his knife, gripped its elk-horn handle with two hands, and lifted it above her head. The instant he faced her, she lunged the weapon downward with all the force she could muster and buried the second blade in the center of his chest.

The Pawnee's hands grasped her throat and squeezed as tightly as he could in his wounded state. Their gazes were locked, as if their minds did mute combat. Macha used both hands to shove and twist the knife several times to inflict more damage and to embed it deeper, hopefully within his evil heart before she lost consciousness.

She saw the man's hate-filled eyes slowly glaze with the grim reality of his fate. When his grip weakened, she gasped for air to calm her spinning wits and ease her throbbing head. She watched him collapse to the ground and remain motionless. Her body trembled from her exertions and with relief. It was only then that she realized Tokapa was tugging on the bottom of her dress and begging to be lifted into her arms. Feeling weak and shaky, she sank to the grass and gathered the frightened child into her embrace and tried to soothe him with gentle hugs and soft words. As he nestled against her chest, her gaze traveled to the hilltop, but only the horses were in sight. She deduced the two men were battling on the other side on the knoll, out of her sight.

Macha was hopeful that her husband would win that struggle. She was tempted to go to his aid, but had promised to retrieve the child and to flee, in the grim event he was defeated and the last Pawnee returned to the river. She felt it was her duty to obey him, so she returned to her horse, placed the child on its back, swung up behind him, and rode for the place where she prayed Cloud Chaser would join them. Her husband was convinced that if the Pawnee won their fight and discovered Tokapa missing, the warrior would not track her toward the place from which he had been stolen and perhaps encounter a larger search party of vengeful Lakotas. If her beloved did not come within a set time, she was to head for the Red Shield camp.

Chase fought his enemy with every ounce of strength and every skill he possessed. With great difficulty, he pushed aside worries about his wife and nephew so he could focus fully on the hazard nearby. Only by finding victory in that battle could he survive and remain unharmed to go to their aid soon. They had danced around each other, landed blows with unarmed hands, delivered kicks with nimble feet, and slashed out with sharp blades. So far, only the Pawnee had received cuts, and those were minor ones; yet, blood flowed freely from them.

Chase perceived that the man was becoming more agitated with each successful strike on his body and stain on his honor. He tried to stay calm and alert. The Pawnee lowered his right shoulder and charged toward him, a movement Chase evaded. While doing so, Chase swiped his blade across his rival's stomach and opened up a wide and deep gash.

The Pawnee whirled to confront him again, one hand pressed against the gushing wound. Chase faked a lunge at his left shoulder, sidestepped at the last moment to duck around his right, and slid his knife across the warrior's right thigh, creating another grave injury. While the man was slowed, he hurried up the knoll and looked toward the river. Tokapa and Macha were gone; the third Pawnee lay still on the ground.

Chase turned and watched the man stagger up the incline toward him. He saw his opponent's gaze narrow and chill, and sensed desperation was settling in on him. "Mother Earth does not want to drink Pawnee blood on Lakota land," Chase declared. "I have what I came after. The boy you stole—son of my brother Wind Dancer—has been rescued. If you halt your battle now, you can ride away. The choice is yours."

The warrior looked toward the river where his last companion lay dead beside his horse and noted the captive was gone. His gaze returned to his challenger's. "I choose to live or die fighting you, half-breed."

"So be it," Chase conceded; then their struggle was renewed.

Within five minutes, the warrior lay dead from his own decision.

Chase lifted his head, closed his eyes, and thanked the Great Spirit for his victory and for saving the lives of Macha and Tokapa. As soon as he arranged this grisly scene to make it appear as if the Pawnee had quarreled and fought and slain each other, he could join his wife. Before that occurred, he had to make certain that any soldier or Pawnee or Crow passing by would be misled by his cunning ploy so no trouble would result from his actions.

First he retrieved the bodies using the Indian's horse, since he didn't want shod tracks found in that area, then he arranged the fallen warriors to match it and shoved an arrow into the one bullet hole. He left their possessions and horses, as anything missing would imply an attack and ruse, and he knew the animals could graze and drink until they wandered off to freedom.

After his task was done, a weary but pleased Chase washed off their blood in the river and returned to his horse a good distance away. He pulled on his boots, having removed them to also prevent leaving their prints on the ground behind, mounted, and headed for the happy rendezvous spot.

When Chase joined them where the White River flowed between two sections of the Badlands, Macha and Tokapa were thrilled to see him. As he embraced his wife and kissed her, the boy she was holding wriggled into his arms and patted him on his cheeks with pudgy hands, laughing as he did so.

Chase chuckled. "It is good to see you, Tokapa."

Macha's fingers teased along his back as she said, "As it is good to see you, my beloved and victorious husband. You were brave to challenge the Pawnee."

Chase grinned and jostled the boy as he related the news of his battle and his subsequent ruse. "Tell me of yours," he coaxed as the child squirmed to get down and toddle about the area.

As they walked behind the energetic boy and watched him, Macha told Chase how she had sneaked up on her target, slain him, and escaped with the child. "The Great Spirit rewarded us with large gifts this sun," she concluded, joy shining in her eyes.

Chase looked at her throat where small bruises were forming from the Pawnee's strong fingers. He was lucky she was alive and unharmed; yet, a jolt of fear shot through him as he realized how close he had come to losing her forever, and at his doing. "Yes, He did, and I have thanked Him many times during my ride for helping us. You showed great courage and cunning, and I thank the Creator for saving your life, for mine would be empty of joy without you."

"As mine would be without you. Do we camp here?"

"It is best to travel until darkness nears to get far away from the trouble left behind," Chase explained. "Tokapa can journey with me if he so desires."

The boy wanted to sit with Chase, and grasped the saddle horn eagerly. Chase realized Tokapa remembered him and seemed to feel at ease in his presence. Having ridden with his father, Tokapa appeared to enjoy being on horseback. With one arm resting across the boy's waist to prevent a fall, Chase nudged the sorrel's sides and they departed.

At sunrise, Chase was watching his wife and the child sleep, for Tokapa had claimed the space he had created between them on the bedroll. A soft and warm feeling wafted over him as he imagined their first child doing the same thing one day. When Macha opened her eyes and met his gaze, they exchanged smiles, sure their thoughts and feelings matched.

"We must go, for my brother's heart is filled with fear over his loss," Chase surmised accurately. "Wind Dancer's eyes must gaze upon Tokapa and his arms must hold him soon to halt his pain and worry."

Macha nodded and gently awakened the boy, who arose in a happy and obedient mood, which delighted her. She prepared their meal while Chase saddled his horse and packed their possessions.

After they had eaten and mounted—Tokapa riding with Chase again—they headed toward the site they had left many weeks ago. As they journeyed on a pleasant day, the suspenseful couple wondered what kind of greeting they would encounter there.

At midmorning, the alert Chase saw riders coming at a fast pace. He fetched his fieldglasses from his saddlebag and scanned them. He could not decide if their identities should relieve or unsettle him. He related his findings to Macha, whose expression told him she had the same worry: *Should we put Tokapa down to wait alone and us escape, or should we continue and meet them soon?* "We ride onward," Chase suggested, and she nodded.

When the distance between them was almost closed, Chase and Macha halted for the five men to join them: Wind Dancer, War Eagle, Red Feather, Swift Otter, and River's Edge. The warriors slowed their swift approach and finished walking their winded horses toward them, the gazes of all five wide with astonishment.

Chase and Macha noticed that none brandished a weapon, and they were not encircled or threatened in any manner. In fact, the men's expressions implied friendliness, as if they were glad to see them, and not only because they had the boy with them . . . Yet, neither wanted to discard their wariness or trust their unproved perceptions too soon.

As Tokapa squealed with delight at seeing his father and other uncle, Chase said, "He is safe and returned to you, my brother." He lifted the boy and passed him to Wind Dancer whose eyes, Chase noted, were shiny with moisture and tenderness. Chase watched him hug his son and kiss his forehead, then close his eyes as if saying a silent prayer of gratitude to the Creator.

Wind Dancer looked at him and coaxed, "Speak, my brother, of how you came to rescue him from our cunning enemies."

Chase revealed his confrontation with two Pawnee and Macha's with a third man before she fled to safety with the child. He saw the men's gazes travel to her bruised throat. All looked angry enough to kill. Afterward, he divulged, "I did not take their possessions or scalplocks to bring to you." He explained his deception, and saw Wind Dancer nod in concurrence with his precautions. "How did Tokapa come to be with them?" Chase wondered. "Was our camp attacked by a larger band?"

Macha nodded and smiled to her brother who was watching them with curiosity, awe, and what she knew from experience was great pride. Yet, she did not interrupt the serious talk by speaking to River's Edge, though she was anxious to hear news of their parents.

Wind Dancer cuddled his son as he related, "Grandmother was tending him while I hunted on the grasslands and Dewdrops skinned and cut up buffalo to be hauled to camp. We had left camp only a short time before he was stolen soon after the sun rose. Grandmother was struck on the head and hidden in bushes. It was almost dark before we found her."

"Does Little Turtle live?" Macha could not help but ask.

"Yes, but she was injured badly from the Pawnee's strike and appeared to be lost to us; that is why the Pawnee did not slide his knife into her heart or across her throat. We waited until the sun returned to pursue them, for we could not see their tracks in the darkness and they sought to hide them from us. Surely the Great Spirit guided you to their path to save my son."

"That is what I believe," Chase concurred. "When we sighted them before they saw us, we were returning to camp to tell Father and our people of all we experienced and learned," he reminded them.

"Where did you go, my brother?" War Eagle asked. "Why did you sneak away? Why did you bind our cousin's hands and mouth? Did Dawn go with you because she is the dream-vision woman our sister revealed to us?"

After Chase answered the first two questions in full detail, he said, "The treaty words do not say what the White hunters told us, but the words of the Crow to Wind Dancer are true. It is a foolish and dangerous demand on the White leaders' part to force enemy tribes to share the hunting and crossing of their territories, and all chiefs must seek to have it changed. If all speak against it and say it imperils peace, perhaps they will listen and change it, for war between tribes will also imperil Whites."

Chase saw them nod agreement but look skeptical of Army compliance before he disclosed news of the second treaty last year with southern tribes, as the Pawnee—also the Kiowa and Comanche—had refused to attend the 1851 Long Meadows peace council with their longtime and fierce enemies, the Lakotas and Cheyenne. "The Pawnee broke their treaty promise not to raid others; if we report them to the soldiers, they will be punished, or perhaps only warned not to do so again. I have learned more Bluecoats will come to the forts at Laramie and Kearny before the cold season, for some Lakota bands stir up trouble in that area. That is not a good sign, so our people must stay prepared for self-defense."

"Do the Bluecoats plan to attack all tribes?"

"I do not know, Swift Otter, but signs pointing to a battle on the suns ahead are bad. Our warriors must be ready to fight when it rises, but we must not provoke conflict before its time." He reached out and grasped Macha's hand, smiled at her, and finished with, "Dawn rode with me, for much love lives in our hearts and minds for each other and we wished to be joined." Assuming a clever Hanmani had disclosed the full dream to them, he repeated its contents and said, "I could not leave her behind while I did as the Great Spirit commanded me, for Two Feathers desired her and was to seek her hand in joining on the next sun. The Great Spirit guided us toward each other and crossed our Life-Circles. Following the Lakota custom, we left camp in secret, bonded ourselves in the forest beneath His gaze, and now return to reveal our union to our people. She is my wife in all ways."

"That is good, my brother," Wind Dancer said, "for Dawn

was chosen for you by Wakantanka as Dewdrops was chosen for me. The Creator guides you to do great things for our people as He once guided me and my wife."

Considering his past treatment, Chase was delighted, though baffled, by their warm reception. "Thank you for your kind words, my brother. Do I return to camp to speak with our people or do we part here forever?"

Wind Dancer told Chase and Macha what had been said after their stealthy departure, which greatly pleased the couple. "That is why we did not come after you. There will be no punishments."

"I am accepted back into our band?" he asked for clarification. "I am Red Shield again?"

Wind Dancer smiled. "That is true, Cloud Chaser. We are shamed for doubting you, for testing you, for rejecting you after your return to us. Father accepts you as his son and awaits your return, for he was certain it would be soon. I am proud and happy to call you brother, friend, and Red Shield. We are family."

Chase looked at Macha, and they exchanged smiles. "My heart swells with joy and love to be family and Red Shield again. It is good."

"It is good," War Eagle echoed, a broad smile on his face.

Red Feather and Swift Otter grinned and nodded agreement.

"My heart beats with great love and pride, my sister," River's Edge said, "for your brave deeds and return; your family is much honored by them." He looked at Chase, extended his arm, and said as Wind Dancer had done, "I am proud to call you brother, friend, and Red Shield."

Chase grasped wrists with him, smiled, and nodded.

As Tokapa squirmed and made it known he was hungry, the others laughed in amusement and harmony.

Wind Dancer suggested they dismount and consume their food quickly before heading home. "We must ride fast, for Dewdrops fears for our son's survival, and I must end her suffering soon. Our camp is in another place, near this river, far ahead, for that is where the great herd roams."

As the party of eight rode into camp, their people—who had been alerted by scouts to their approach—ceased their chores, crowded around their horses, and rejoiced at the safe return of Wind Dancer's child, son of their next chief, grandson of their current chief, and the future leader himself of the Red Shields. Whoops of elation and shouts of victory over their foes filled the summer air. Though all were eager to hear why Cloud Chaser and Dawn were with the warriors, almost all present focused on the heady triumph.

Chumani took her child in her arms, hugged him, and kissed him as she smiled and laughed with happiness. The boy squealed with gladness to see his mother again. Chumani half turned him in her embrace so Winona and Little Turtle—whose bandaged head bore witness to her recent attack—could stroke his cheek and hair and kiss his forehead. "You have saved our son from the torment, sadness, and shame of captivity to our enemies, and spared his family and people of his loss," she said to her husband. "I have great love and pride for you."

"I did not do so, Dewdrops," Wind Dancer refuted in a gentle tone. "Your words are for another. Hear me, my family and people," he said in a loud voice. "Our son was rescued by my brother Cloud Chaser and his wife Dawn;

they fought and slayed the three Pawnee who injured Grandmother and stole Tokapa. They risked their lives and freedom to save him and return him to us. While they were gone from our camp, they did many brave deeds for us and they joined in the sight of the Great Spirit and return to us as mates. I will honor my brother with the gift of two horses and two buffalo hides. War Eagle does so with the gift of a new bow, quiver, and arrows."

As that news settled in, Winona smiled at Chase before she announced, "Our women must prepare a tepee for them and place it near his father's. We will do so on the next sun. On this moon, Cloud Chaser and Dawn will eat and rest with us." She rubbed the back of Chase's right hand and said, "I thank you for the life of my grandson," then did the same with Macha.

Before they dismounted, the couple smiled at her for that display of sentiment and acceptance and for her kind words and invitation.

While still on horseback where he could be seen and heard better, River's Edge proclaimed, "I will give Cloud Chaser leggings and moccasins to go with the shirt he now wears as a gift to him long ago from my family for saving my life from the badger attack. He is now my brother and friend."

Ohute and Leaning Tree worked their way to the front of the crowd to embrace their daughter and to welcome Cloud Chaser, their chief's son and future chief's brother, into their family. Ohute touched the marks on Macha's neck in alarm.

"The Pawnee's injuries will heal, Mother, so do not worry over them. I am sorry I could not tell you of our departure, but we had to obey the Great Spirit's command to us, for it was given in a sacred dream."

"Do not worry, my daughter, for your union is a good one."

Macha embraced her mother again and sighed with relief.

"I have no gifts to give Root and Leaning Tree for their daughter's hand in joining," Chase told Macha's parents, "but I will do so before the cold season comes. I will hunt and supply hides and meat for your tepee."

"The gifts of Tokapa and our daughter's return to us are enough to fill that duty," her father said. "We will share you with Rising Bear as a son."

"I thank you, Leaning Tree, and I will seek to be a good one."

Nahemana stepped forward and locked their gazes. "It is good you have returned, Cloud Chaser, for it is the will of the Great Spirit."

"Thank you, Grandfather; that is what I believe and seek to honor."

Little Turtle removed a *wanapin* from her neck and placed it around Chase's. "You have brought joy and honor back to me and our people, for I failed to protect Tokapa from great danger and suffering."

"You must not feel shame, Grandmother, for being used by the Great Spirit for the good of our people," Chase said after thanking her, "for He controlled our deeds on past suns. You must be proud you served His purpose, for often He leads us down mysterious and dangerous paths. Your mark reveals the sacrifice you made to fulfill His plan." He lifted and looked at the necklace: it was an arrowhead made of sacred redstone with the sign for *love* etched on its surface, suspended on a thong with pipe beads. As many other

Red Shields touched his hand or clasped his wrist or spoke words of gratitude for the rescue and praised his prowess— from the corners of his eyes, Chase saw Two Feathers staring and sulking not far away. He didn't want this long-awaited moment to be spoiled, so he dismissed his acrimonious cousin from his thoughts and sight.

"I must speak alone with my three sons," Rising Bear announced. "We will have a feast this moon to honor his return and chant his coups."

"My friends will speak to our warriors and reveal my brother's deeds and what he has learned while gone from us," Wind Dancer added.

Red Feather, River's Edge, and Swift Otter summoned the men to another location to relate Chase's exploits and discoveries. An eager and proud Broken Lance hurried behind the group to listen to his cousin's feats. Even Two Feathers tagged along to see what he could learn.

Chumani went to her tepee to share special moments with her son. Red Feather's wife, Zitkala, joined her. Zitkala knew her best friend needed comfort and assistance, as Chumani had slept and eaten little since her child's abduction. She carried along her daughter Cikala, of the same age, to play with Tokapa while Chumani shared her emotions to one she knew listened with a loving attentiveness.

As Winona and Ohute gathered with other women to talk about the stirring events and to make plans for the couple's new dwelling, Macha and Hanmani slipped away to Leaning Tree's tepee to share their news.

As Chase sat down with his father and brothers, this time in closer proximity, he was aware of how different this meeting was than the last two. He couldn't help but hope he had finally achieved his initial goal for returning. Yet, he pondered then how such changes would affect his and his wife's future . . .

CHAPTER TWELVE

Chase's heart thudded as he listened to his father's words.

"I have been wrong and cruel to you, my second son, long ago and since your return. When you were born, I was ashamed for mating with your mother, for it was not right to do so. Omaste was obedient and trusted me. She loved me, my family, and my people. In my heart, I believed my beloved Winona was not lost to me forever, and I felt I had betrayed her by taking another woman to the mat I had shared with her and she would return to one day with the Great Spirit's help. But in a moment of anguish, doubt, and weakness, I turned to her for comfort, and she gave it to me. I was ashamed I abused Omaste's love, trust, and obedience. I wished I could free her, but a chief does not give away a gift from another chief and ally, and Omaste had no family or home in another place. She was happy living among us and was not mistreated except for that one time, though she said I was gentle with her. After I lay with Omaste, I purified myself in the sweat lodge, made sacrifices to Wakantanka at Mato Sapa, and prayed for His forgiveness. Your mother forgave me, for she was happy to bear a son, to have her own child. Winona forgave me upon her return, for she understood my anguish and one weakness. But I never forgave myself and never asked you to forgive me. Each time I gazed upon you, I was reminded of my wicked deed. I feared I would be shamed before my people if I treated you as I did my other children, for you were not born of a mated pair whose union was blessed by the Great Spirit."

Rising Bear paused in his painful confession to take a few deep breaths to calm himself. "When Omaste was taken from us by death, I thought it was the Great Spirit's way of removing a stain against my honor. When you were lost to me and I could not find you, for I searched for many suns and moons and suffered much, the same thought entered my head. Both were wrong; both were only misguided ways of dealing with my two losses and my shame. When you returned, I feared to believe you were my lost son; I feared trouble would come if your heart and purpose were not good; I feared it would remind my people of my past weakness and if I accepted a half-White man among us during such grave times, it would cause conflict between me and my people. I ask you to understand my confusion and to forgive me for causing you to suffer. There is much love and pride in me for you, Cloud Chaser, and gratitude for saving Tokapa. I believe the Creator gave you to me long ago, took you away, and returned you this season. Stay with us, my second son, and be a Red Shield as you were born. I will never turn my eyes or heart from you again; this I swear on my life."

Before Chase could speak, Wind Dancer and War Eagle told him of the things which had filled their hearts since his return; they, too, asked for understanding and forgiveness.

Chase smiled. "The Great Spirit often works in strange ways. We do not know His purpose for such deeds, but He plans and guides them. I love you, my father and brothers, and there is peace among us. We will store the troubled past in a ghost pouch and never open it again. All is good between us now, and we must seek to help our people together."

"It is good." All three said the agreement vow simultaneously.

"Tell me all you have seen and done since you left our other camp and rode into the white man's world," Rising Bear coaxed.

Two hours passed as Chase complied while their family, closest friends, and people prepared for the impending celebration.

During the feast, Chase was positioned on a buffalo hide mat beside his father, with Macha sitting on his other side. Nearby were the rest of his family and hers, all in places of honor for this special occasion. The happy couple watched their brothers dance around a center campfire while singing and chanting the coups they had earned during their absence, their agile movements made to the accompaniment of a kettle drum and eight drum beaters.

Earlier, they had eaten food served to them by their people, who also were filled with joy, excitement, and appreciation for those cunning and brave deeds. After the sun had set, small ones with full stomachs and heavy lids had been lain on sleeping mats in their dwellings, to be watched by older siblings or grandmothers or mothers. The White River encampment was being guarded by braves who were posted around its fringes to prevent a surprise attack during the band's merry distraction, though they wished they could participate in or witness the splendid celebration.

A near-full moon had risen during the entertainment; it, along with the huge fire, brightened the area. The evening breeze was warm and steady, with the scents of grass and wildflowers and smoke traveling across the land with it. The roaring flames before them also seemed to dance with glee; the wood crackled and popped and sent an occasional and brief burst of colorful sparks into the night air. The drumming continued. People talked and laughed in low voices. Some nodded their heads or moved their torsos in time to the kettle drum's beat.

A proud and beaming Hanmani watched older girls and unattached young women eye her three handsome brothers, especially the remaining single one—War Eagle. She was thrilled for Macha and her half-brother, and felt they were well matched. She did not know how that union would alter her close relationship with her friend, but she was not worried. With her best friend now joined and so happy, she was eager for a romance of her own, but she was only sixteen and no one had captured her heart and eye, at least not from her band, or even from her tribe.

Macha and Chase exchanged smiles, their eyes meeting as they glanced around to view the wonderful and unexpected episode. Each sensed what the other must be experiencing. Now that their union had been blessed by their families and people, they could hardly wait to be alone, truly and safely alone for the first time since their lives and bodies became as one. At last, everything seemed perfect and surely nothing could go wrong to cause problems for them.

On the sly, Wind Dancer studied his first cousin several

times during the feast, and worry nibbled at him. He hoped and prayed his perceptions were wrong. To him, Two Feathers appeared to be watching the couple with a treacherous gleam in his eyes. The disgruntled man needed close observation in the suns ahead, he decided.

By dusk the following day, the Red Shield women—under the direction of Winona and Ohute—had constructed Chase and Macha their own tepee, their first home. Poles to form its shape had been cut, hauled, and prepared by skilled and eager hands; hides to cover them had been donated by many women from their stores. Many had sat in a circle to stitch them together while laughing and talking, then helped wrap them around the tall conical frame. Chumani and Zitkala had made the dewcloth to hang inside against those tanned skins for diverting rain, cold air, and smoke outside; for adding beauty to the home with the colorful designs upon its smooth surface; and for using its leather rope upon which to suspend possessions out of the way on limited floor space. Countless people had gifted them with items they would need for supplying it: sleeping hides, blankets for winter, sitting mats, willow and rush backrests, cooking and working tools, various storage pouches. Hanmani and Little Turtle had arranged those generous and thoughtful gifts in their proper places. Wind Dancer and Red Feather had painted Chase's first coups upon its exterior. War Eagle had completed a new set of weapons just in time to mount them on the three-legged stand made for them by Swift Otter and River's Edge.

While the people had worked, many in different shifts because of duties to their own families and the chores demanded by the annual hunting and tanning season, Chase had chatted and visited with the men honoring him while Macha had done the same with the women honoring her with their tasks. The couple had thanked people time and time again for their presents and assistance, only to be told they were much deserved and given with loving hearts and hands.

After everything was done, their parents, siblings, and grandparents guided the beaming couple to the abode and halted at its entrance. The shaman walked around the tepee while shaking a smoking cluster of special herbs and grasses to bless the dwelling, then wafted the gray haze over the people who would inhabit it. Following embraces and good wishes, Macha and Chase ducked and entered their first home to view its interior and contents while the others returned to theirs.

They strolled around hand-in-hand admiring the workmanship, beauty, and kindness of their people. At one spot and knowing they could not be seen since the flap faced the side of Wind Dancer's tepee, they shared a joyful hug and a long and tender kiss.

Each was aware that their first real privacy loomed before them, and their bodies warmed to that reality. Yet, they knew that before they could surrender to the desires chewing at them, they must eat and await cooling night air when they could seal the flap.

When that long-awaited moment arrived, no fire was built in the rock circle which Hanmani had placed in the center of the tepee. They needed no light other than that of an obliging full moon which flowed down the wide span created by the ventilation gap. As if the Great Spirit was helping them, fresh air swept downward in gentle gusts and swirled around the interior, keeping them cool and comfortable. Others were inside their abodes at that hour; the shelter hides were thick and muffled sound well; and night had blanketed the land, so it was almost silent.

They stood near the tepee's center and beside a sleeping mat where the romantic glow of nature's light washed over them. For a short while, they simply looked into each other's eyes. Then Chase's mouth covered hers with a tender kiss, which Macha returned. Afterward, he kissed her forehead and the tip of her nose. Her palms flattened against his chest while his hands cupped her face and his thumbs stroked the soft skin near her parted lips. Macha sent her fingers to delve into hair as tawny as a doe hide which curled under at his nape, and he slid his into her long tresses and drew her head toward his.

His lips brushed over her mouth as he said, "You have captured my heart, Dawn, and enslaved me forever. If I did not know the truth, I would vow I am only dreaming about you as I did far away and long ago."

"As would I, Cloud Chaser, but we are awake. Each time I am near you or think of you, I feel as if I have waited and yearned for you since you vanished so long ago. I somehow knew you would return to me."

He looked at her radiant face and into her luminous gaze, moved deeply by her soul-thrilling words. "I love you, my cherished wife; and I am a whole man at last because of you."

Macha unlaced his shirt ties and peeled the garment over his head. She waited in anticipation as he removed her fringed dress and let it slip from his fingers. He undid the side thongs of her breechclout and dropped it, and steadied her balance as she wriggled her feet to discard her moccasins.

Chase shucked his remaining garments and moccasins and pulled her into his arms as Macha looped hers around his neck. Their mouths united in a budding kiss which swiftly flowered into full-blown passion. They pressed together and shared numerous kisses as their naked bodies made blissful contact from head to feet.

Macha quivered like a blade of grass in a strong Lakota wind. She felt ignited to a roaring blaze by pleasure and suspense. Surely nothing and no one could make her happier than he did.

Time seemed to stand still and any reality beyond that tepee seemed to vanish as they explored each other's bodies and hearts. Their kisses soon became hungry and greedy, as did their caresses.

Chase was almost staggered by the enthralling way she clung to him. He told himself he must move slow and gentle as he'd promised near Fort Laramie, but she was making self-control difficult with her ardent responses. He trailed kisses over her face. His mouth journeyed down her throat as she leaned back her head to give him access to her sweet flesh. He was elated and enflamed that he could so arouse her to heady desire for him. He nestled his face against her hair and relished the feel of it against his cheek. He drifted his hands up and down her back, and felt her ebony hair tease over his fingers during each trip upward.

Macha slipped her hands beneath his arms to rove his broad back, and felt the strength which dwelled there. His body was taut and well muscled and she enjoyed every inch of her explorations.

She groaned in pleasure as Chase's hands wandered to her breasts and tantalized their already taut peaks to firmer points. When she grasped his manhood and stroked its full length, his embrace tightened and a low moan of intense emotion and need escaped his throat. They sank to the sleeping mat together.

Macha was awed by how delicious it felt to have him touching her breasts, kneading and stroking them. Her pleasure heightened when his tongue lavished hot moisture and teasing strokes there. The sensations he created were enormously arousing and she closed her eyes to absorb them. She had imagined their joining would be better with real privacy, but not as sensuously thrilling as it was proving to be.

Chase's right hand ventured over her bare skin as far as he could reach without dislodging his mouth from her breast. She was beautiful and alluring. She had a firm and agile body, and every inch was an enchanting enticement. His hand drifted over her rib cage and stomach, caressing its way down to the warm moist flesh between her thighs, which he aroused with light and slow strokes at first, then with firmer and faster ones as her hips began to squirm and soft moans escaped her mouth.

Macha's fingers played in her husband's hair as he feasted at her breasts and drove her wild with his hand. A ravenous hunger gnawed at her, though she tried to relax and slow her pace, eager to experience all her beloved would show her.

Chase's mouth traveled slowly back up to her lips as he moved atop her. He knew she was as eager to continue their journey as he was. With great care, he guided his manhood into her, then paused while he struggled to maintain self-control as her fingers pressed hard against his shoulder blades and she arched toward him. After he appeared to have mastered his surge of weakness, he thrust himself deeper within her, kissing and caressing her all the while. When her ankles overlapped his calves and she seemed to open and offer herself more to him, he penetrated her deeper and began a steady pattern of rocking to and fro.

Every movement he made seemed to increase Macha's yearnings. Each time he moved within her, it was ecstasy. It was beautiful and special and natural to have their bodies joined as one, to have such powerful feelings racing through both of them, to discover such joy and unity. To her, it was a total sharing of themselves.

Their hearts pounded in joyful unison as they mentally and physically pledged themselves to each other as mates for life. Upward they climbed a sensual slope, urging their spirits skyward.

"Do I travel too fast, my love?" a near-breathless Chase asked.

Macha whispered for him to continue as she reached her precipice and toppled over it shortly before an enraptured Chase did the same.

Afterward they cuddled and shared light kisses as their bodies cooled and their pounding hearts slowed.

"I love you, Dawn, and you always please me greatly."

Macha nestled into his embrace and rested her head on his shoulder. She sensed he was happy, calm, and connected to her, and she thrilled to each of those perceptions. "As I love you, my husband, for you please me in all ways, more than words can speak."

Chase stroked her hair and warm flesh, both damp from their lovemaking and the summer heat. He savored the feel of her bare body against his, the way her arm rested over his chest and a knee over his thighs, the way she cuddled up to him, and her occasional dreamy sigh. He had no doubt she loved and desired him, only him, and forever. No man could be luckier or more blessed than he was on this glorious day. Now, all that loomed before him as awesome challenges were honoring his sacrificial vow to the Great Spirit and risky pledge to his family and people.

At sunrise, Chase stood at the edge of camp and stared at the sturdy and sacred cottonwood pole which had been embedded in the grassy heart of Mother Earth on the day before his arrival. Although it had been selected and cut down by women chosen by the shaman for that honorary task and prepared for two other braves for their sacrificial ritual today, it was as if the Great Spirit had timed his return so he could be a part of it as he had vowed many weeks ago. It was usually done at the end of summer and the seasonal buffalo hunt, but Nahemana and those braves had said it must be carried out on the day of the full moon as instructed in his visions and their dreams.

Chase recalled from boyhood observations how hazardous and painful—and often lethal—the ritual was. He could not help but feel apprehensive of that peril and torment; yet, he also was exhilarated and proud that his time to endure it had come.

He knew the ceremonial dancers had been chosen and had practiced their movements to prevent any errors and each had been assigned a special pattern and colors with which to paint their bodies for their roles. The preparatory Buffalo Dance had been done during his welcome feast two nights ago. He had not eaten or drunk anything this morning, as he must fast today. He knew his wife was worried about his participation in the Sun Dance ritual, for she also was aware of the dangers involved in it. Yet, Macha realized it was a crucial path he must walk, and without her beside him. Even so, before he left their tepee, she had clung to him, kissed him many times, and begged him with her eyes not to take such enormous risks. He had comforted her as best he could with words and embraces, but knew he had failed to assuage her fears. As he stood there, he prayed for the strength to obtain his new objective, and for the Great Spirit to guard his wife if he did not survive it.

Chase was joined by his brothers, who would share the purification rite and walk along with him and blow whistles for encouragement during the Sun Dance ritual. Soon, the other two partakers arrived. Together, the five men went to the sweat lodge nearby to take the second step along their spiritual journey, as the fast was considered to be the first. The shaman and two warriors waited there to assist with needed tasks. The five ducked and entered a hut shaped like a turtle's shell; it was constructed of bowed willow branches and covered with thick buffalo hides.

The five men took their places on sitting mats which were arranged around a shallow pit. Heated rocks were brought inside and dumped in the depression; water was poured over them to create steam, mist believed to be the breath of Wakantanka, mist to cleanse their bodies of any evil and weakness. The hut was dark after the flap was sealed, and light entered only when it was pulled aside on occasion to add more hot rocks and water.

As a summer sun beat down on the snug shelter, it did not take long before sweltering heat and humidity filled it. As the men chanted, prayed, and sweated, they rubbed their wet skin with bunches of sage and sweet grasses. They did not speak to each other. It soon became difficult to breathe from a lack of fresh air, the water they had been denied, and from the energy-draining loss of body fluids.

The purification rite continued until midday when the shaman said it was time to take the third step along their sacred journey.

After Chase left the stuffy hut, the late August weather seemed cool when compared to that of the interior of the sweat lodge. At least there was a strong and constant wind outside to provide fresh air. As the others had, he dried his body with a pelt which had been smoked over a fire of special herbs and grasses and cottonwood branches. Clad only in a breechclout and moccasins, he awaited his turn to be painted. He had decided to use signs of the sky powers: lightning, stars, moon, sun, and clouds. The two helpers who were skilled at that task first painted all exposed skin from head to feet blue like a clear sky. By the time they finished their work, yellow lightning bolts zigzagged down each side of his chest from collarbone to waist, down each arm from shoulder to wrist, and down each leg from groin to ankle. A full moon was painted on his left cheek and a sun on his right, both in yellow. Across his forehead and on his chin were white stars. On his broad back were clusters of white clouds. To show honor to their brother, Wind Dancer and War Eagle were body-painted in the same way.

As the men left the ceremonial lodge at midafternoon, the signal was given for the Red Shield band members to gather beyond the fringe of their camp at the chosen site. The three participants approached the shaman, halted before him, and each revealed the kind of ritual he would endure. The three had given careful consideration to their choices before making them. One could choose to dance and chant around the pole for as long as he could stand and move and speak; allow small pieces of flesh to be removed and placed at the pole's base; have one's chest pierced and secured to the pole while he danced around it until he could pull free; or to have his chest pierced, his muscles secured by thongs, and be lifted off his feet to swing and sway until the fleshy bindings were rent and he fell free to the ground. Some braves picked the lowest or second task and later worked themselves up to one of the most dangerous and difficult. The ceremony lasted until all men either pulled free, yielded defeat, or died trying. If one lost consciousness, when he roused, he either had to continue or halt. None wanted death, but most preferred it over a show of weakness and dishonor.

Standing before the three men, Nahemana lifted a white sun-bleached skull of a buffalo bull which was painted with the symbols of the sky forces: rain, hail, thunder, lightning, and wind. Its openings were stuffed with buffalo and sweet grasses and with special herbs. As he held up the sacred object, he said a prayer to summon the gazes of the Creator and Good Spirits to witness the impending scene. He lit his Prayer Pipe and blew puffs of smoke into each man's face. As he did so, each inhaled deeply to capture it with his nose and used his hands to waft some over his head and chest, for it was believed to represent the breath of the Great Spirit.

Chase heard the soft beating of a large kettle drum by eight men, old and wise and respected members of the Red Shield Band and the Big Belly Society. He saw people sitting on the grass or on rush mats or standing, their number forming a dense human enclosure around the awesome scene. He heard and felt the incessant Plains wind which swept over his body and played in his hair. He felt the heat of the sun beaming down on him. He tasted the unpleasant flavor of a dry mouth, for he'd been denied water since last night. His eyes squinted against the bright sunlight and dry wind. His skin felt strange with the paints covering it. He pushed aside his discomfort as the ceremony began, a fourth step to be taken.

Ceremonial dancers came forth to perform their part of the exciting event. While keeping perfect time to the drumming, they moved around the pole doing intricate footsteps and graceful whirls and chanting to the Spirits. They were clad in their ritual attire, including feathered bussels and headdresses and heavily beaded garments and moccasins. After they finished, they resumed their places on sitting mats in a group.

Broken Lance, Chase's seventeen-year-old cousin, chose to have small pieces of flesh cut from his arms and placed as an offering at the base of the pole. After that was done, the young brave, who had endured the pain in silence, went to sit with his parents Runs Fast and Pretty Meadow, sister of Rising Bear, and with his brother Two Feathers, who had subjected himself to the highest level of the Sun Dance last summer.

Bent Bow, son of their war chief Blue Owl, chose chest

piercing. He looked reluctant and afraid to perform the deed, and was no doubt coerced by his father and other male relatives into doing so. During his preparation, Bent Bow writhed and grunted in agony. Afterward, he stayed seated with his head down.

Before Chase was asked to announce his choice, he stole a glance at the war chief and saw Blue Owl shake his head and scowl at his son's display of weakness. Chase told Nahemana, "As my father and brothers did in seasons past, I do this for myself and my people to seek the Great Spirit's blessing, guidance, and protection during the dark suns ahead. I do this to thank the Great Spirit for all He has given to me. Let it begin, Grandfather. I choose the piercing on foot."

Before he lay on a buffalo hide, Chase looked at Macha, read the fear and love in her eyes, and smiled encouragement. He looked at his father, and they exchanged nods of affection and resignation. He took his place, made his body rigid, and clenched his jaw to keep silent and still during what was sure to be a painful preparation.

Nahemana used a ceremonial knife to make two small cuts on Chase's left breast above his nipple. Blood instantly came forth and rolled downward toward his side. The shaman forced a sharp talon of an eagle's claw through the sensitive underflesh, pulled to separate and lift the severed section, and worked a lengthy thong beneath it. He did the same on Chase's right breast, and noticed the man did not flinch or grimace. He told Chase to stand, and after he obeyed, Nahemana secured those thongs to rawhide ropes which were attached to the cottonwood pole. He placed a peyote button in a small pouch suspended from Chase's beaded belt, a gift from Winona on the past sun for saving Tokapa's life. He previously had told the young man when he should chew and devour the "medicine stone" to evoke a vision. He told Rising Bear's second son to begin his ordeal when he was ready, then told Bent Bow the same thing.

Chase locked his gaze to sacred markings on the cottonwood pole to summon his strength and willpower to begin the agonizing task. There was no retreat now; it was onward to victory or death. He took a deep breath, backstepped until the ropes were taut, and leaned away from the pole to test the result of that action, one which must be repeated countless times to break free of those bonds. As astonishment thundered across his mind, pain shot through his chest and radiated from his arms and legs to his fingers and toes. He had known the attempt would hurt badly, but now he realized how terrible it was going to be. He heard the steady beat of the kettle drum and the chanting and praying of many people. As he began to dance sideways, halting often to yank backward in search of freedom, he blew on an eaglebone whistle from his father; and his brothers blew on theirs as they kept in step with his movements.

Chase's torment increased with the passing of each hour, and it was a constant struggle to endure and continue the self-inflicted ordeal. Despite intense concentration on his own challenge, he could not help but notice that Bent Bow would slacken his ropes and slow his pace to rest and to seek relief for a time, as Chase frequently encountered and passed the other man during his own circling movements. Chase also noted that Bent Bow already looked exhausted and frightened, but there was little damage to the man's chest because he was not yanking hard enough for release. Chase, himself was giving each jerk as much effort as he could muster because he wanted to end this suffering as quickly as possible. Even so, his flesh was being stubborn, and the thongs and ropes were strong. Those severed sections had loosened and separated from his body, but both sides refused to tear apart and release their grips.

After sunset, torches jabbed into the earth and a full moon illuminated the area. Only women with infants and young children and the most elderly people went to their tepees; all others remained to witness the culmination of this awesome event, to see who lived and succeeded, who had to halt, and who might have perished while trying to achieve victory.

It was not long before a bleeding, frightened, and pain-riddled Bent Bow conceded defeat and was cut free by Nahemana. The weakened brave was taken home by a displeased and embarrassed father, against whom he was leaning; he promised he would make another attempt during the next summer's season.

Chase pretended he did not notice the commotion, but he was aware not only of the other participant's difficult decision and departure, but of Two Feathers' intense observation of him. He was certain his hostile cousin was praying he would yield to defeat or would die from this ordeal. He must not disappoint the Great Spirit, himself, his wife, his family, and his people.

Before the bright moon was overhead, ignoring the agony and calling upon all of his strength, Chase pulled free of one imprisoning thong, sighing with relief when he did so. He refused to wipe away the sweat his arduous efforts, the summer heat, and tension had caused to form; some ran into his eyes and stung them, though that sensation was nothing compared to the salty drops which flowed into his protesting wounds and tortured them. Chase felt as if the second bond persisted in its stubborn grip more strongly now that it was alone, as if it was determined to hold fast and bring on his defeat. He had thought the work would become easier at that point; that wasn't true and it worried him, as it became ever more apparent that his body was weakening by the hour.

Macha watched her beloved's struggles and prayed for his release soon. She ignored her hunger and thirst, her aching muscles and exhaustion, as she must not leave for any reason. Would he—she fretted in panic—live or die tonight?

CHAPTER THIRTEEN

Rising Bear observed the ritual with pride, love, and empathy filling his heart and mind, as he knew from experience what his son was enduring. He savored his son's stamina, courage, and fortitude, and scolded himself for ever doubting and for hurting him. He and his people were blessed that the Great Spirit had returned him to them. Never again, he vowed, would he distrust or be ashamed of his second son.

More time passed as Chase's travail heightened. His legs felt trembly and weak, and he feared he might not be able to take another step soon. He feared his parched and aching throat could not send forth many more blows of the eaglebone whistle. His head spun round and round and he feared he would black out at any moment. Blood flowed down his chest, over his ribs, and soaked into his breechclout. He stumbled on a dislodged clump of grass, but recovered his balance before falling and prayed for renewed strength. He refused to halt his quest for victory, forcing himself onward step by step. He was thankful his brothers were nearby to keep him moving and conscious.

Chase retrieved the mescal button with quivering fingers and chewed it, but his dry throat was hard pressed to swallow the tiny pieces. Shortly after he managed to do so, he began seeing colorful spots dance before his line of blurred vision, as if they also were keeping time to the drum's beat. He saw Broken Lance extend blood-splotched arms and come forward to dance and chant with them, to offer added encouragement. Then, with the peyote's help, visions began to flash before his mind's eye.

As the sun rose on a beautiful Lakota dawn, Chase felt revitalized by its warmth and touch, and freed himself of his second and last confinement. His chest ached and he was exhausted, but he also felt exhilarated, relieved, and proud to have accomplished his goal. His gaze darted to his beloved wife and he smiled at her to let her know he was all right. He sank to his knees, leaned his head back, closed his eyes, and thanked the Great Spirit for his triumph and survival. He opened his eyes and stood on wobbly legs, his gaze fusing with the shaman's who joined him. He became aware just then that the drumming had ceased and most of the band members had returned to observe him.

"What did the Creator reveal to you during your vision?"

the shaman asked.

Chase divulged to the man all that had been told him: "I must not change my name, as it was given to me for a purpose. I am to hide behind my cloud of white looks to dupe our foes. I am to help rid our land of ominous storm clouds in the shapes of white men and Bluecoats. There can be no real and lasting peace with them in the seasons ahead; only one powerful force can live in and control this territory: that force must be the Lakotas or they will perish forever under the white man's grip. Trouble has already come to our land and will be revealed to us soon; after that sun, we must decide to break or honor the treaty. I choose to side with my father and our people the Oglalas. I will say and do what I must for victory."

"He speaks wise and true, my people," Nahemana said, "for the signs upon his body tell us such things. See how the stars, moon, and sun painted on his flesh now appear as clouds, as he was named. The lightning on his arms, legs, and chest now appear as long and sharp arrows to strike at our enemies. He has been sent to us to do great deeds for us. So it shall be."

Those who had remained nearby all night and those who had returned since sunrise listened, watched, and nodded or murmured concurrence.

Macha felt as if her pounding heart would burst from the abundance of happiness, love, and pride which filled it when Chase had broken free and looked at her; those feelings had increased when he had spoken, and their people had agreed. She felt Hanmani grasp her hand and squeeze it gently, clearly experiencing those same emotions. They exchanged joyful smiles before Macha refocused her tear-filled gaze on her husband.

With misty eyes and in a ragged voice, Rising Bear clasped both wrists with Chase's, gazed into his eyes, and smiled. "You have shown great courage and endurance, my second son," he said. "My heart beats with love and pride. As it does for my other sons who were your companions during this quest. Nahemana will tend your coup wounds with strong medicine. Then you must drink, bathe, eat, and sleep to regain your strength."

Chase nodded, his throat too dry from a lack of water and too constricted by emotion to respond verbally. He lay on the buffalo hide for Nahemana to cleanse the injuries of blood and dust and to cover them with a salve made from healing herbs. The shaman gently pressed the jagged flesh into its proper place, smeared more herbal balm over both swollen areas, and wrapped a wide band around his torso to hold the torn sections in place until they healed.

Winona and Hanmani brought revitalizing soup and water to Chase, which he consumed with difficulty, his throat abused for hours by thirst, chanting, and whistle blowing. Hanmani whispered to him that Macha would await him in their tepee, as she needed privacy to release her long pent-up emotions.

Wind Dancer and War Eagle helped him to the river where he washed sweat, salt, dust, and paint from his body. Afterward, they assisted him to his tepee where Nahemana gave him medicine-laced chokecherry wine to promote healing, prevent shock and fever, and to lessen his pain.

Chase thanked his brothers again, clasped wrists with each in turn, and told them their support during the ritual had helped him succeed. Then he entered his abode and, with Macha's aid, lay on his buffalo mat to get needed sleep, which came quickly in his depleted state.

Macha sat beside him for a while, looking at him, cherishing him, praising his prowess in her heart, and stroking his damp hair and handsome face. She lightly trailed one fingertip along his jawline and over his prominent cheekbones. She traced his thick and dark brows, and teased her finger over his full lips and strong chin, with its tiny depression in the middle. Her gaze roamed to his bound chest, and she winced thinking of what he had endured; then she thanked the Great Spirit for sparing his life on this sun.

She stroked her husband's cheek once more, kissed his forehead, then left to do her chores in a cheerful mood.

As Macha and Hanmani washed garments at the river that afternoon, Two Feathers approached them and hunkered down nearby.

"Why do you not hunt or scout, my cousin?" Hanmani asked.

"We hunt again on the next sun, and scouting is not my duty on this one. I come and speak with a heavy heart to both of you. There are things I do not understand. Why did you turn your eye and heart away from me and give them to Cloud Chaser?" he asked Macha.

Macha had not expected that brazen question, so she stared at him for a moment in confusion. "My heart and eye never roamed your way, Two Feathers. I have loved and wanted Cloud Chaser as my mate since we were children. I believed he would return to us, and I waited for that sun to rise. It is the will of the Great Spirit for us to be mates."

"Is it, Dawn? Or does your large desire for him trick you?

He has used you to harm me, for he has no love and respect for me and knew I desired you. He is cunning like the fox, bold like the bear, and fierce like the wolf. He uses you and Hanmani to help trick and betray our people."

"That is not true," both women protested simultaneously.

"It is true, and soon all will know it. When he betrays us to our enemies and is slain or banished, you will ask me to forgive you for doubting me. When he is here no more, Dawn, you will turn to me again."

"No, Two Feathers, I will not, for I do not love or desire you. It is wrong and cruel to speak badly of my husband and Hanmani's brother, our chief's son. You must fast and purify yourself in the sweat lodge and pray for forgiveness from the Creator, for He guides and protects Cloud Chaser."

"Before this season passes, you will not believe such things."

After Two Feathers left, Macha asked with a worried expression, "Why does he hate Cloud Chaser so much?"

"I do not know, my friend, but it frightens me."

"Do you think he will try to slay my husband?"

"He would not dare to do so, for my brother is Red Shield now, an honored and accepted son of our chief. But I believe he will seek to find cunning ways to hurt Cloud Chaser. Perhaps Two Feathers will seek to trick others into doubting him again, or find sly ways to make my brother appear evil. You must warn him to be wary of our cousin."

On the next day, Two Feathers stunned and baffled Macha, Hanmani, and a few others by joining to Sisoka, oldest daughter of Masleca, a Strong Heart Society member like Wind Dancer.

Inside the tepee where Cloud Chaser was still resting and recovering at the insistence of his father and their shaman, the two women sat close to him and related the shocking news in whispers. It struck him the same way it had affected them, as they had told him about their talk with his cousin yesterday.

"We saw it with our eyes and heard it with our ears, my husband: Two Feathers approached the tepee of Coyote and presented him with three horses, five buffalo hides, a beaded armband, and a new bow. He asked to make Robin his mate. Coyote and his wife were willing, as was Robin. I do not understand why she agreed, for she has many good looks and skills, and three other braves sought to join to her. She has shared rides and blanket talks with the others and listened to their flute playing; we have not seen her do so with Two Feathers. This matter is very strange."

"Perhaps she chose him because he, too, has many good looks and is a high-ranking warrior, and comes from a bloodline of chiefs, and is in the larger family of our chief. He is skilled, so he will be a good provider and protector."

"That is so, my husband, but he has not pursued her before our eyes and ears. If he had done so at other times, we would know, for Robin boasts of having many braves desire her. She is often scolded for her big pride, for she knows of her many good skills and looks."

"Perhaps he moved fast because he thought his loss of you stained his honor and face. Perhaps he wishes to trick others into thinking your loss does not wound him. I say it is good he turns his back to a fiery desire for my wife. If he did not do so, I would be forced to challenge him to keep away from you."

Macha sent Chase a playful scowl. "Your heart is too kind and pure, my husband, and your thoughts and words are too generous in his direction. Besides, a man cannot lose what he does not and can never possess. Do not trust him, for he seeks to trick all with this cunning match. He does not love Robin and he will not make her happy. She will be sad she chose him."

"Perhaps the Great Spirit will soften their hearts toward each other. It would be good for us if Two Feathers could find happiness, for such feelings might sway him from his hatred of me and hunger for you."

"Yes, love is a powerful force," Macha murmured. "But," she added in a grave tone, "will it remove the evil in his heart and head?"

"Soon, my wife, we will learn that truth for ourselves."

"When my cousin and Robin return from their mating journey, I will watch him with eagle eyes to see if I can learn the reason for his action on this sun," Hanmani told them. "I believe as my friend does: Two Feathers cannot be trusted, and this joining is a sly trick."

On the fifth day after Chase began his spiritual journey in the sweat lodge, he stood at the river stroking and talking to Red as the sorrel drank and grazed on lush grass growing near its banks. He was surprised and pleased by how fast he had regained his strength and by how quickly the Sun Dance injuries were healing. The shaman had visited him each morning to put more medicine on the wounds and to change the bandage around his torso. He and Macha had eaten with his father, Winona, his sister, two brothers, Chumani, and Tokapa two nights ago. They had talked for hours about past experiences, the successful hunt so far, and the tasks which loomed ahead until they returned to their winter campsite. Yesterday, he had enjoyed visits with River's Edge, Broken Lance, War Eagle, Swift Otter, Wind Dancer, and Red Feather. They had made plans to hunt together the following day, as he felt he was strong enough to do so.

Chase was glad his cousin was gone, but knew Two Feathers would return soon. This was the third day since his joining, and their new tepee awaited them between those of his and her parents. As when he and Macha wed, the women had constructed the dwelling as a gift to the couple. With all of his might, he hoped marriage would change his cousin, but he doubted it would, and wondered what the man's next aggressive act would be.

The annual buffalo hunt had continued with everyone staying busy with their seasonal and daily chores. As if luck was with them or Divine Intervention controlled the area and its events, no enemy had approached the camp and no White hunters had been encountered again. If the latter happened, at least Chase was now armed with a copy of the treaty terms.

After the excitement of the Sun Dance rite and the unexpected union between Two Feathers and Sisoka subsided, calm settled over the summer village. Even so, after what he had glimpsed in his vision, Chase worried it was only a quiet lull before a loud storm.

As if that thought summoned the first strike of trouble, Chase sighted Two Feathers returning to camp with a lovely young woman trailing behind him on her horse. He didn't want to spoil his sunny mood, so he turned toward his horse and stroked him.

Two Feathers used his skills to sneak up on his cousin from behind. "Why does a Red Shield warrior who heals and grows strong fast stay in camp with women, children, and old ones while others hunt and scout?" He saw Chase whirl in surprise at his voice, and grinned at catching him off guard. He was about to boast of his cunning and his cousin's lack of caution, but Chase responded before he could speak.

"I do as I am commanded by our chief and shaman. I hunt on the next sun with my brothers and our friends. You took a wife while I was upon my mat. May the Great Spirit bless you with happiness and children. It will be good for all if we can become friends now."

Two Feathers scowled at him and shook his head. "My largest joy will come when others view you as I do. In the suns ahead, Cloud Chaser, you will make a big mistake and all will see you as the worthless half-breed and evil trickster you are. After it rises and you are here no more, Dawn will become my second wife and will be happy to do so." He smiled as Rising Bear's bastard son glared at him in anger.

"Why do you hate me with such a force, my cousin? No ears will hear your words but mine. Speak from your heart if you have the courage."

Two Feathers matched Cloud Chaser's glare as his mind scoffed, *Reveal to you that, as a child, I wanted to be our chief's son and the next Red Shield chief? Reveal to you that my love and respect for Rising Bear have lately turned to hate and shame? A warrior who mates with a white woman*

and plants his seed in her body is not worthy to be our chief;
he is not worthy of breath. You are the outcome of that dark
mating and a sign forever of his weakness and shame. If the
Creator is all-knowing and all-wise, He will slay you both;
and He will slay the other two seeds of my mother's brother.
Then I am next in the bloodline of my grandfather Ghost
Warrior and will become chief. I will lead my people
against all enemies and defeat them.

"From your fierce look, my cousin, your head speaks to you as loud as the thunder and as hot as a roaring fire, but your mouth stays silent and cold. Why must there be conflict between us? Why do you refuse to take my hand in friendship? There is great peril ahead for our people and we must battle it as one powerful force; that cannot be if we are fighting each other."

"I am Oglala; you are White. We are enemies; we will not fight as one."

"I am only Oglala now, Two Feathers, for I have emptied myself of my White blood at the Sun Dance pole and purified myself of their touch in the sweat lodge. We are cousins; we are family; we are Red Shields. We must have a truce between us for the good of our people."

"You do not love and honor such things. You trick all into believing and accepting your false words and feelings. No truce. Never friends."

"If that is so, Two Feathers, it is of your doing alone, not mine. I—"

Their talk was interrupted when a shout went up in camp that riders were approaching.

"Our words are finished, half-breed. My duty as a warrior and Sacred Bow Carrier summon me to see what is wrong.

I go now, but my eyes and ears will stay on you."

After the chief, shaman, war chief, council, and warriors gathered in ever-widening circles on the grassland beyond camp, the three weary Brule visitors—who had been given water and food with which to refresh themselves—began their revelations; and all Red Shield men listened as they told of the horrible event which had occurred seven suns past and on the same day Cloud Chaser had returned to the Red Shield camp.

"We come from Spotted Tail to bring his words to our ally the Red Shields. We have entered many camps of other Oglala allies to speak with them during our long journey. Brave Bear, Head Chief of all Lakotas for the Long Meadows Treaty, is dead; he was slain by the Bluecoat called Grattan. Many iron balls from their firesticks entered his body and stole his life."

"Why did they slay a man of peace, a great chief?" Rising Bear asked.

"One of the white man's animals entered his camp. High Forehead of the Minneconjous was visiting with family and friends there. He killed the animal. Many Bluecoats soon came and asked for the animal's return. When Grattan was told it was slain and eaten, he said he must punish the man who killed it and all who had shared its meat. High Forehead and his friends would not surrender to them for such a foolish reason and prepared to fight. Spotted Tail, cousin of Brave Bear, also prepared to fight, for the Bluecoats had two giant thundersticks and many smaller firesticks. The man Grattan brought with him to translate the words of both sides was bad; he was feverish on the white man's firewater; he spoke many insults and made many demands. The Minneconjous, Brules, and Oglalas were filled with anger."

When the Brule paused to catch his breath, Nahemana asked, "Who struck the first blow and brought forth the first blood?"

"They talked much, but no man would yield because each saw the matter with different eyes and hearts. A Bluecoat brought his weapon to life first. Many warriors sent forth arrows in return; and more Bluecoats used their firesticks against them. The Bluecoat leader used his big weapon to send forth the sound of thunder and bring death. Brave Bear was slain. Fierce fighting began. All Bluecoats were killed during the battle."

Chase was angered by Grattan's recklessness and arrogance, as it could precipitate a full-scale war on the Great Plains. It was ironic that the first battle of a possible war had taken place so near where Fitzpatrick and Mitchell had negotiated the peace treaty and Brave Bear had served as Head Chief of the Lakotas. He recalled that Chumani was Brule and wondered if her band was involved in those ill-fated slayings. If so, Wind Dancer had to be deeply concerned over his wife's people, as her father was their chief.

"All Bluecoats at Fort Laramie are dead?" Wind Dancer asked as he imagined the repercussions of what would surely be viewed as a massacre. He could not help but be glad Chumani's people were not in that area.

"No, for all did not ride to Brave Bear's camp," the second Brule answered. "Spotted Tail spoke in favor of attacking the fort while it was weak, but the council would not allow it. They said the fight in camp was to defend ourselves, but to attack the fort would be viewed as a challenge for war."

"The council was wise," Nahemana said, "for if women, traders, and good Bluecoats were slain, much bloodshed would come to our land."

"That is true, our shaman, but the words and deeds of Spotted Tail also speak of the truth," Two Feathers said. "He said a man of honor cannot allow himself and his people to be attacked without fighting back. Is it not best to challenge and punish a powerful enemy or to drive an encroacher from our land when he is weakest, as Spotted Tail says? The White Chiefs will not believe the Bluecoats attacked first, and all Lakotas will be blamed and challenged for Grattan's evil deed. Is it wise to do nothing while our enemy summons more forces and weapons? Is it wise to let him grow larger and stronger to attack us for a deed we did not do? What did others do after the victory over the Bluecoats who hate us and enslave us and say we cannot even fight our enemies or defend our hunting grounds as we have done from father to son for more circles of the seasons than any here can remember?"

Before the Brule could reply, some Red Shield warriors who had existed for three years without the glory, excitement, and coups of battle nodded or murmured agreement with Two Feathers' conclusions.

Chase worried over his cousin's sly attempt to arouse their men against the Whites. He had knowledge of the white man's large number and awesome weapons, things he did not want his family and band to confront unless absolutely necessary. He had no doubt war would come eventually, but it was best to postpone it as long as possible. Somehow and some way, he had to convince them not to fight.

"Warriors took horses from the Bluecoat's travois and from the fort," the Brule said. "Others raided the American Fur lodge and took away the treaty trade goods promised to them, for the Whites there had refused to give them out on the chosen sun. Others raided Bordeau's Trading Post, but Little Thunder, chief of another Brule band, would not allow Bordeau and his friends to be slain. The camps were moved to another place before more Bluecoats could come to attack. Scouts told us Bluecoats and traders came and took the bodies to Fort Laramie. One among us who speaks their tongue said the Bluecoat leader Fleming is angry and afraid; he has sent for more Bluecoats and weapons. Spotted Tail says a big war will come soon and all Lakotas must fight or die. He calls for a war council on the next full moon. If the Red Shields wish to come to speak and vote, we will gather where the White River halts her flow," he disclosed and pointed southwestward.

"Come, my companions," the third Brule said, "we have shared our words and must ride for the camp of another ally."

"You must stay here this moon to eat and rest and sleep."

"We cannot, Rising Bear, for others must be warned and told of the war council. We thank you for the food and water and parley. We go now."

After the three men departed, an awed Nahemana said, "It is as Cloud Chaser saw in his Sun Dance vision: 'Trouble has already come to our land and will be revealed to us soon; after that sun, we must decide to break or honor the treaty.' It is true as the vision warned. Soon, we must choose between peace or war."

"When that sun nears, we must ride to the gathering place of our allies to see how they speak," Blue Owl said. "If they vote against war, it would be dangerous for Red Shields to challenge the Bluecoats alone. If they vote for war, we must do the same and fight with them, for all Lakotas will be blamed and attacked after more White blood is spilled from their bodies."

"Our war chief's words are wise and true, Father," Chase said. "Before our council rides to speak and vote at the gathering of allies, I must go to Fort Laramie to scout the Bluecoats' number and plans. It is twenty-four suns until that time and they are sure to challenge Lakotas for this deed. We must not walk in darkness of the mind before the war council meets while events take place which will affect our survival."

Nahemana nodded concurrence and urged, "Send him, Rising Bear, for this is why he was returned to us. We must learn such things and soon."

"It smells of great peril, my son, for the Bluecoats will be seeking trouble in all directions. If they learn of your true name, you will be killed."

"Even if they watch for tricksters, Father," Chase reasoned, "I can walk among them with my eyes and ears open, for my looks and the ways I learned from Whites will deceive them. I have visited there on past suns, so I am known to them and will not be doubted. It must be done, for we must know their plans and numbers to defeat them. You can share such things with our allies at the war council."

"My brother can do it, Father," Wind Dancer coaxed. "If we learn their secrets, we can fight them in sly ways. Do not forget how Dewdrops and Bird scouted for us long ago at

Pierre Trading Post during the sacred vision-quest journey. This is the path Cloud Chaser must walk as we did long ago to defeat our enemies, the Crow and the Whites."

"What does the council say?" Rising Bear asked the band leaders.

The group leaned close together and talked for a while before one of the oldest and a past great warrior said, "We vote he goes to scout for us."

A reluctant Rising Bear nodded and conceded to their decision.

"I will take Bent Bow with me. After I spy on the Bluecoats and see the changes at Fort Laramie, the son of our war chief can return to camp to bring you my message while I stay behind to learn more things."

"Why do you choose Bent Bow?" Two Feathers questioned, as all knew he had shown weakness and fear at the Sun Dance pole.

"Bent Bow has a brother to hunt with his father, or to hunt for Blue Owl if he is injured. All others have families to hunt for and protect. I say this task will teach Bent Bow courage, cunning, and strength. His heart and head are good; he will do what is best for his people. I trust him."

Bent Bow wriggled forward from another circle and vowed, "I will not fail you again, my father, chief, and people. I am honored to be chosen by Cloud Chaser. Such a task will remove the stain on my face. I will go."

"It is a generous deed for Cloud Chaser to pick one who has a great need to fill," Nahemana said. "I say, send Bent Bow with him."

"What does the council say?" Rising Bear asked the

leaders again.

After another short talk, each of those men nodded agreement.

"When will you ride, my son?" Rising Bear asked in dread.

"We will prepare ourselves to leave on the next dawn."

"So be it, my son. May the Great Spirit guide you and protect you."

"He will do so, Father, for we follow the path He marks for us."

In Chase's tepee a short time later, his wife stared at him in astonishment as he related the grim news of Grattan's defeat and the other raids and his impending departure to spy at Fort Laramie.

Macha almost flung herself into his arms and nestled her face against his chest as she hugged him and pleaded, "You must not go, my husband. You are still healing, and it is too dangerous, for the Whites and Bluecoats will remember you. They will remember you rode with Grattan to help the Indians against evil Whites; they will believe you are our friend and ally and will not trust you."

In a gentle tone, he refuted, "They will remember I helped expose and punish Whites who raided and killed Bluecoats and attacked the stage to do the same, so I will appear as their friend and ally. Do not forget I can act the part of a white man."

"One who took an Indian wife," she remarked.

"Only the shaman there knows of our joining, for others did not see us approach his dwelling or hear us speak those words."

"What of the trader who saw us together?" she reminded him.

"He told me many trappers and traders take Indian wives. If our paths cross, he will not doubt me, for he does not doubt them or refuse their trade. I must go, my beloved wife. Do not worry. I will be alert and safe."

Macha realized there was nothing she could do or say to change his mind, so she accepted the inevitable; yet, she pleaded, "If you must go, wait a few more suns so you will be stronger."

"I cannot wait, for our enemy grows stronger and slyer each sun. If they plan to challenge any or all Lakotas, we must know swiftly so we can prepare for battle and watch the direction from where danger will strike."

"Take a different companion to scout your back, not Bent Bow," she begged.

"Do not fear," Cloud Chaser coaxed as he read her skeptical expression, "for he will not show weakness and fear a second time. He is a good choice."

"I pray those words will remain true, my husband."

"Gather what I will need to take with me," he requested. "I must speak with others and will return soon to eat and sleep. I do not leave until the sun rises again," he hinted with a seductive grin.

Two Feathers sat with some of his friends and talked about the change in events which could return them to exhilarating lives as warriors. That was an existence to which they had been born and trained and which many missed, including himself. "It is strange trouble struck in the place where Cloud Chaser left not many suns past. The Bluecoat he rode with to expose the White tricksters was the one called Grattan. He did not tell us of that leader's great hatred for Lakotas. It is good Grattan's attack failed and he was slain. Perhaps Cloud Chaser sensed trouble was coming and that is why he thought he saw it in his vision. We must pray he does not allow his White half to be deceived by Evil Spirits. If they trick him into revealing the plan for a war council to the Bluecoats, they will attack the gathering and slay all who meet there."

"Do not worry, my friend," one said, "for your cousin has proven himself. He is strong, cunning, and brave; he will not fail us or betray us."

Two Feathers shrugged, sighed deeply, and muttered, "I pray your words are true, or great peril will come to us."

Chase met with Broken Lance at the river and asked his cousin to guard and hunt for Macha during his absence, as he had a brother to do the same for their parents. He observed the seventeen-year-old's elation and pride, but also noted a gleam of disappointment in the brave's eyes.

"I am honored you chose me, my cousin. But why did you choose Bent Bow to ride as your companion on your journey?"

"I did not ask you, Broken Lance, for I need you to stay here to protect Dawn for me and to provide for her. Your skills in such things are larger than his, and the one who rides with me is only needed to bring a message back to Father. I asked Bent Bow to do so, for he is in great need to prove himself. He will do this task and it will remove his father's sadness and shame, for Blue Owl must not have such things to distract him when he leads us into battle soon.

The same is true of me: with Dawn living under your skilled eyes and hands, I will not be distracted by worry over her." Chase witnessed how those words pleased and assuaged the young brave; and they were true, from all he had seen and heard.

"Upon my honor, I will protect her in all ways, my cousin."

Chase clasped wrists and exchanged smiles with a grinning Broken Lance before he headed to his tepee to spend time with his wife before their bittersweet parting . . .

CHAPTER FOURTEEN

As Macha lay down beside him and cuddled into his arms, Chase felt her tension. "Do not think of sad things, Sunshine of my heart," he coaxed. "Think only of good and happy ones this moon and on those while I am gone."

Macha touched the binding around his bare chest as she murmured, "It is hard to do so, my husband, when I fear for your safety and return to me. My Life-Circle will be dark and lonely without you to share it."

Chase grasped her chin and lifted her head so their gazes could fuse. "I will always share it, my cherished wife," he said in a tender voice.

Macha stroked his lips from side to side with the pad of her forefinger as she entreated, "Promise you will return to me."

Chase nestled her against his naked body and wrapped his arms around her shapely frame to offer her loving comfort. He swore as confidently as he could manage, "No matter how long it takes, I will do so, for we are as one. If our camp

245

is moved while I am away, I will find you, even if you and our people must hide from the Whites or other enemies. Wind Dancer, War Eagle, Swift Otter, River's Edge, and Red Feather have taught me many more skills since my return to the Red Shields. We have practiced many times with bow and arrows, with hands and feet, with eyes and ears, and with knives. I have learned to use my wits and . . . the strong feelings within me," he said, as he could think of no other words to explain "instinct."

"I have asked Broken Lance to hunt for you and to protect you from harm," he added. "Go to him for help if you need to."

"He is the brother of Two Feathers," she confirmed as she shifted her head and looked into his handsome face, confused by his choice.

Chase smiled and caressed her cheek as he replied in an assured tone, "That is true, but I trust him; we are cousins and friends."

"What if the trouble comes from his brother?"

Chase locked their gazes so she could read the honesty in his. "Even so, Broken Lance will honor his word to me."

Macha realized it would be hazardous and wrong to send him away worried and distracted, so she smiled and said, "You are sure, so I will obey."

Chase feigned a serious expression and tone as he asked, "Will you obey in all things and ways, my wife?"

Macha was unsure of his meaning. "You are my husband; that is my duty and training. Speak of what you want me to do or say," she asked.

Chase grinned. "If you are obedient, join your lips and body to mine."

Macha smiled and tickled his ribs. "That task is too easy. Do you not have a harder one for me?" she teased.

In a playful mood, Chase guided her captive hand to his groin and jested, "If that is not hard enough, make it so, my tempting wife."

"That is a task I will enjoy, my husband."

"As will I, for love beats swiftly within my heart for you."

"As it does in mine for you."

Their mouths met in a heady kiss, and soon they found and seized the sweet ecstasy they had been seeking with their entire beings.

At the edge of camp, Macha waved and smiled one last time before her husband shifted in his saddle and galloped away to join his companion to confront unknown perils and challenges. She was glad no one else had accompanied them this far so they could share a final moment alone before his departure; Bent Bow had ridden ahead to give them privacy. As she turned to walk to her tepee to fetch a water bag and sling for gathering scrubwood along the riverbank for smoking meat, she noticed Two Feathers standing near a friend's dwelling. He talked with the man, but his piercing gaze was locked on her. To be polite, she nodded a greeting to him and watched him—though his sharp gaze did not change—respond to her in like kind before turning his back to her.

After she left that location, Macha encountered Hanmani and asked her friend, "Will you do your chores with me this sun?" *So your cousin will avoid me,* she thought, for some reason not wanting to speak those dark words aloud.

"I was coming to seek you out, my friend, to do so.

Mother tends our chores this sun so I can do Grandmother's. Her hands and body no longer move swift and easy as they did long ago. It is sad Little Deer no longer lives in her parents' tepee to help them. But it is good she left no mate and children behind when she was summoned to the Great Spirit."

Macha reminded her, "When they can no longer live in their own dwelling, Nahemana and Little Turtle must move into the tepee of Strong Rock or Winona so their son or daughter can take care of them, for their seasons upon the face of Mother Earth number many."

"That is true, Dawn. My brothers and many Strong Hearts bring them meat and hides to use, and others give them things they need, for our shaman is much loved and respected. Even so, the sun will rise when they cannot be alone to tend themselves and each other."

"That is so, Hanmani, as it is with all people created by the Great Spirit; it is a part of each's Life-Circle. Come. Let us work so I will not think and worry about my husband."

Hanmani gave Macha's hand a light squeeze of encouragement. "No matter what we do, my friend, you will worry about him. But do not fear for his life, for Wakantanka guides and protects him."

Chase leaned against a stable post at Fort Laramie and asked the soldier with whom he had struck up a genial conversation, "I heard there was trouble here a couple of weeks ago. What happened?"

The private curried his horse as he related, "One of them Mormons passing through the area said some Indians stole his cow and he came here kicking up a fuss and wanting the

Army to go fetch it for him. Lieutenant Fleming figured if he didn't get it back and show the Indians they can't do such things, we'd have more incidents like that and somebody'd get killed and big trouble would break out. He told Grattan to handle it for him."

Chase didn't ask questions or make comments as the man glanced around as if to make certain no one was within hearing range. He noted the private's look and tone of disgust when he started talking again.

"Almost half of our garrison was out gathering wood and hay, but most of the men here volunteered to go with him. I guess they figured they'd get out of boring duties and maybe have a little fun teaching the Indians a lesson. Not me, you can bet your best boots; I ain't no fool and I smelled trouble brewing in that foul wind. It ain't smart to tangle with Indians if we don't have to, and surely not over some dumb cow that strayed away. Hellfire, we were left with only ten soldiers to guard the fort, so we're damn lucky we didn't get attacked. 'Course Fleming sent for the hay and wood cutters as soon as he learned about the fighting."

"So, there was fighting?" Chase asked when the man went silent.

"Yep. Grattan and his twenty-nine men took two howitzers with them to scare the Indians into obeying him. Seems he misjudged their reaction; they showed plenty of anger and courage."

"Did the Indians really steal that Mormon's cow? You said something about it just straying away from him. Is that what actually happened?"

"We don't really know the truth of it. They claimed it just walked into their camp, so they thought it was free for the taking, maybe one of them annuity cows that got loose, so it was all right for them to slaughter and eat it. Sounds like a reasonable mix-up to me, not something to go to blows over, but Grattan saw it otherwise and paid for his stupid mistake. He and his men rode into the camp, the one closest to where the Mormon claimed he was robbed. It didn't seem to make no never mind to Grattan it was a large one, filled with Brules, Minneconjous, and some Oglalas. I guess he figured them Indians would be cowered by such a show of the all-mighty force of the Army. That was another stupid mistake. It was like he didn't know or care them was skilled warriors he was about to tangle with. Word is the cow-shooter's name was High Forehead and he was just visiting there. Grattan demanded the shooter and everybody who had eaten the sorry cow surrender to him to be brought here and punished. 'Course the Indians refused, 'cause they didn't think they'd done anything wrong. Then some scared or hotheaded soldier opened fire, and some braves fired back with arrows. I guess that volley spooked Grattan, 'cause he opened fire with the howitzers and his men blazed away with their rifles. Brave Bear, he's the one Fitzpatrick and Mitchell appointed Head Chief for those treaty talks three years ago, he was killed; and that riled the Indians up even more."

"I'm sure it did," Chase concurred. "He was a well-respected leader."

"Spotted Tail was there, and he ain't no man to challenge. He's the one who probably ordered the retaliation and led the warriors into it. They took down Grattan and every soldier there in just a few minutes. Well, all except for Private Cuddy; he was wounded badly, but he was rescued by some

250

friendlies and hauled to Bordeau's Trading Post. Bordeau had him sent here and Cuddy told us what happened before he died, else we'd been ignorant of the whole matter, not that knowing the truth changes much."

"But Spotted Tail and the others didn't attack the fort, right?"

"Nope. Some other friendlies warned Fleming about the fighting and he recalled our other men pronto. I surely am glad I didn't volunteer to go with Grattan; he was too reckless and eager to make himself look good for a transfer; and he was too ignorant about the conditions out here. He shoulda never rode into a camp that size and got himself and his men swallowed up by so many Indians. And he shoulda never taken that Lucien Auguste with him as interpreter; Auguste was drunk, and the Indians hated him for how he treated them. Cuddy couldn't understand what he was saying to the Indians, but it made 'em pretty mad. If you askt me, what Grattan shoulda done was give that Mormon one of our cows or one from the annuity stock, and called it a good bargain for peace."

"But things have settled down since then, right?" Chase ventured. "I mean, I didn't encounter any hostiles or patrols on my way here."

"I wish I could say things are back to how they was before this mess sprung up, but they ain't. We're still on alert; hellfire, we hardly closed our eyes for days after that run-in. Afore it was over, a band of hostiles raided the quartermaster's corral and took off with thirty-six horses and cattle; they also stole the mules that pulled the wagons to the Indian camp. Some of them robbed the American Fur Company downriver, if you can call taking their own annuity

251

goods stealing. Some others raided Bordeau's Trading Post, but Chief Little Thunder—he's one of them Brules—he wouldn't let them kill Bordeau and his men. As soon as we were given the word from our scouts that area was clear, we went in and collected the bodies; weren't a pretty sight, I can tell you. We buried all of 'em except Grattan; his body was sent by wagon to Leavenworth—I guess 'cause he was an officer."

"Have you caught any of the Indians involved in the shootings?" Chase asked, and saw the private shrug and scowl.

"Nope, but they'll be captured and punished soon, mark my words."

"What do you mean?" Chase asked, worry filling him.

"Fleming sent for help, so more men should be arriving as soon as his report reaches the Government and they act on it. He sent word by special messenger, but the way things usually go around here, there's no telling when to expect a response. 'Course, he told 'em to hurry 'cause he's sitting on a hotbed of trouble. Fleming says they'll have to send a large force and heavy arms 'cause they can't risk a full-scale war breaking out here; this area's too important to the Army, settlers, and emigrants to let the Indians go taking it back and shoving us out. Clawing our way back in could take years and plenty of bloodshed on both sides."

"Has Lieutenant Fleming made any attempt to parley for peace with the Indians Grattan provoked into battle? Since he instigated the trouble and men were killed on both sides, it would be smart if the Army looked the other way this one time, or found a compromising way to settle the matter."

"That's what I think, but I ain't got no vote or say-so in

the matter. I wished I did, 'cause I'd search high and low for that compromise. It's a real shaky situation for both sides. If them Indians let our challenge ride, they lose face. Same's true with the Army; if they ignore a massacre, they lose face, and they're afraid more hostiles will think they can steal and kill and not be punished. Seems to me, we're all in a real tight bind."

"Maybe those bonds can be loosened or cut," Chase ventured, "if somebody can find a compromise acceptable to both sides."

"You seeking that job?" the private asked.

"I doubt I could pull off a stunt that big, but I hope somebody can. I surely would hate to give up trapping and traveling in this territory."

"Or losing your scalp and winding up as some buzzard's supper."

To dupe the soldier, Chase chuckled and quipped, "That, too."

In a secluded camp miles from the fort, Chase gave Bent Bow a full report on his findings there to carry back to his father and their people. Once more, the young brave thanked him for his confidence in him and for allowing him to partly redeem himself for failing in his Sun Dance ritual.

As they ate, Chase told the war chief's son, "I know how it felt when others viewed me as a weakling and outcast, so I understand your sadness and shame and your hunger to remove those stains on your face and honor. Do not fear, Bent Bow, for there will be more times in the suns ahead for you to earn coups from good deeds, ways to please your father and people and to make them happy and proud of you. Accept what happened at the Sun Dance pole as a way for the Great Spirit to teach you many things and to use it as a means to send you on challenging quests. There is a special purpose for all things in the Creator's plan for our lives, so the bad must be used to strengthen us and to urge us onward to do good and great deeds." *That's what Mama Martin taught me, and I believe her.*

"You are wise and generous, Cloud Chaser. It is good you were returned to us, for there are tasks only you can do. You have given me much courage and hope. I will never fail the Great Spirit or my people again, even if I must die proving myself to them. Will you sweat, walk, and whistle with me as my friend and companion at the next Sun Dance ceremony?"

"I will be honored to do so, Bent Bow, and you will find victory there."

They talked for a while longer before they went to sleep, as when they awakened, Bent Bow would head for the Red Shield camp and Chase would return to the fort to see what else he could discover.

During the next week, from chatting with soldiers and from keen observation, Chase learned that new officers and troops and more supplies and weapons were coming soon to replace those slain and lost in the "Grattan Massacre," and to have more men and arms on hand when the trouble worsened, which is what Lieutenant Fleming and the Army expected to happen. The soldiers already on duty there were kept busy. Many were put to work building more quarters, mostly of adobe, or were placed on additional hay- and wood-cutting chores so large amounts could be gathered and stored for emergencies during anticipated attacks. Others were posted as extra guards atop and below the bluff since the fort lacked a protective enclosure, or went riding on intensified patrols. Between those tasks, their regular daily assignments were being carried out as time allowed.

Late one afternoon, two covered wagons arrived to camp below the bluff near the river. As he wandered about nearby, Chase learned that the two families were returning East after having made it as far west as Mormon Ferry where the Sweetwater River flowed into the North Platte. The men had decided the going was too rough and long and they didn't have enough money and supplies to reach Oregon to take advantage of the government's Donation Land Claim Act, which provided a free "one square mile." 640 acres

Since he had lived in both territories and had attended school far away at Mrs. Martin's insistence, Chase understood why so many settlers yearned to come this far west and beyond. The land was beautiful and fertile, and people felt the soldiers would keep them safe. If it were learned, Chase fretted, that gold—and silver and other precious metals and ores—was available in the Black Hills and other nearby places, there would be no stopping a flood of prospectors, more traders to supply them, whiskey and female-flesh sellers to fill carnal needs, and more soldiers to handle the problems arising from such an onslaught of greedy men and women.

Was there, Chase pondered, a compromise that would work? Could two such different cultures coexist in peace and on equal terms? He doubted it, because the greed of the Whites outweighed simple needs, and too many of them were willing to do anything to fulfill their hungers. Since he had resolved to side with the Indians, he must be just as willing to do anything necessary to thwart the Whites' conquest. He hated to imagine what he would be called upon to do to his mother's and the Martins' people, but he had no choice since he felt the soldiers and settlers were wrong in their course of invasive action.

During that ensuing week, Chase encountered the sutler with whom he had traded many weeks ago. The man was curious about why he was still in the area and queried him about his Indian "squaw."

Chase shrugged, sighed deeply, and scowled. "I had to send her back to her family and people. At first, she was obedient and respectful, then she became sullen and defiant. She whined and cried about going away with me when she heard about the trouble with the Indians around here. I figured she'd just rob me and take off for home the minute my back was turned and I was off setting my traps, so I told her to git."

"That was smart of you, Martin; you don't want no Indian woman at your back who can't be trusted. And you surely don't want to get caught in the wilds without supplies if she stole yours and took off."

Chase nodded. "That's exactly how I saw the situation."

"So what you plannin' to do now?"

"If things keep going in this direction, I thought I'd speak to Fleming about working as a scout and translator. I figured he could use one if he tries to parley with them to get back on peaceful terms, and I surely didn't want to be off in the wilds alone if those Indians went on the warpath."

"I doubt there'll be any parleyin'. It seems to me as if the Army's gettin' prepared to handle things for good this time."

"You think the other tribes and bands will get riled up and form big alliances if Fleming goes after the Brules and Minneconjous for that Grattan mess? From how the Indians see it, Grattan and his troops fired first and spilled the first blood: leastwise, that's what I heard some of the soldiers saying. It seems to me it was foolish of Grattan to gun down Chief Brave Bear over a stray cow. I guess you learn plenty in your store from them."

"Yep, I hear plenty of talk, but some of it ain't nothin' but boastin'. I doubt half of them soldiers really know what they'll be up against if those Indians do ally together like you said. I was in the Army years ago and I know how fierce and powerful they can be, 'cause we had plenty of nasty run-ins with them, especially those Oglalas. 'Course they've been settled down for three years, so maybe they're rusty with fightin'."

Chase shook his head. "I wouldn't count on it; I bet those bucks still practice every day and I bet they've missed raiding and warring; I bet they're eager to fight again. Since you're ex-Army, you know what they think about retaliation and glory coups. If I was Fleming, I would be careful about challenging them."

The man glanced around to assure they were alone before he whispered, "If Flemin' was as smart as he should be for a post commander in a hot spot, he wouldna sent Grattan to handle that mess. 'Course he wouldna been much better at it since he had a run-in with Minneconjous last year. I'd be surprised if the Army don't hold him partly to blame for that fiasco."

"You could be right," Chase concurred. "I'll be hanging around for a while longer, so I'll come over to see you. If I hear anything important, I'll drop it in your ear. I hope you'll do the same for me. Who knows, if things get to looking too bad, we both might want to leave this area?"

"Not me, Martin, 'cause everythin' I have is tied up in my store. With more trouble brewin', nobody would want to buy her, least not for a decent price, and I ain't givin' her away. And I ain't handin' my stuff over to no Indian if they attack here. I'd burn my store to the ground first."

"I'd be sure to keep my eyes and ears open and my rifle loaded, 'cause Fort Laramie would have to be one of their main targets if they go on the warpath soon." As Chase glanced around, he said, "There's Fleming on his porch. I think I'll go have a little talk with him about my offer. I'll be seeing you around. Stay alert," he advised again before they parted.

After Chase joined Lieutenant Hugh Fleming—who was leaning against a post on his porch and gazing out over the fort's structures and his working troops—he related his request to sign on as a translator and scout, but the officer told him it was useless to speak with the Indians about the situation. As they conversed, Chase grew more and more pessimistic about the situation. Fleming was not even willing to have Indian Agent Thomas Twiss act as an intermediary—the lieutenant saw no point in negotiating at all.

What concerned Chase the most was that Fleming and the Government totally blamed the Indians—the Lakotas mainly—for the current hostilities and for what the Whites were calling the "Grattan Massacre." It sounded to Chase as if the Army was overlooking the crucial fact that *their* officer had initiated the conflict. Fleming told him repeatedly that the Army must regain control of the area and Indians fast by any means necessary.

On Thursday, September fourteenth, Chase learned it would not be Lieutenant Hugh Fleming who carried out that directive because he was replaced by Major William Hoffman, who arrived and took command, along with additional troops and weapons, and more were expected soon.

On the next day, as Chase observed the big change in leadership and tried to assess Hoffman's character and to learn his plans and strategies, shocking news came that Spotted Tail and his Brules and Oglalas had attacked a mail coach twenty-two miles from the fort, murdered three men aboard, injured another one, and robbed the stage of ten thousand dollars in gold.

Chase realized that was like a slap in the face to the new commander, who went after the "hostiles" immediately with a large and heavily armed unit of soldiers. The fort was placed on intense alert in case the robbery and slayings were bait to lure the forces away for an attack, one which didn't come, to the relief of those left behind and on guard. Chase reasoned it was unwise to shadow the unit or to offer to ride with them as a scout and interpreter until he discovered more about Hoffman. Yet, he was disappointed in Spotted Tail for calling down the wrath of the Army on the Lakotas, as holding up a stage and slaying nonmilitary men was hazardous to all Indians.

Chase waited until the soldiers returned from recovering the bodies before he rode to where the attack had occurred to scout it for signs of Spotted Tail's path of escape. It was obvious from ground clues and from how long the unit had been gone that Hoffman did not pursue the band, and Chase wondered why. He followed the Brules' trail for many miles until he realized the Indians were riding hard and fast and he probably couldn't catch up to them. Even if he did overtake the band, they might not believe who and what he was and might slay or injure him. It seemed best at that point to return to the fort to see what type of retaliation Hoffman was planning, upon whom, and when.

By midafternoon the following day, Chase had gleaned certain expected facts from soldiers and the amiable sutler: troops were assigned to escort and guard all stages, Army supply wagons, and wagon trains. New outposts—though small and crude and in constant jeopardy—were built along the road for protection and to provide horses so the teams would always be fresh enough to outrun any peril. His worst discovery was that word had arrived that Secretary of War Jefferson Davis wanted rapid reprisals for all attacks and wanted peace restored in the territory as soon as and in any way possible; Jefferson warned that if Major Hoffman and his replacements could not achieve those two goals and within a limited time span, he would send General William—"By God, I'm for battle, not peace"—Harney to the area to obtain them. The officials in Washington believed the "Grattan Massacre" was caused by the Sioux seeking to steal annuity goods, a belief that Chase knew was inaccurate and dangerous. But who would believe *him?* After all, the Army had an eyewitness account of the incident, although Private Cuddy was no longer alive to verify it. Since the Army knew who and what had precipitated the bloody event, why was it so determined to solely blame and fiercely punish the Indians involved? Was it, Chase worried, only an excuse to attack and subjugate all Indians since the peace treaty had failed to do so? Was the Government willing to slaughter any and all Indians—men, women, children—in order to confiscate this territory?

Since Hoffman did not want it on his military record that the Army had replaced him as they had his predecessor for failure to perform his duty, Chase concluded the officer would make any and every attempt to resolve the dispute and fast.

Before dusk settled across the land, Chase was en route to the war council site, where he was certain Spotted Tail and his own family were heading at that same time. He wished things had turned out differently at Fort Laramie, wished a new peace treaty was in the making, and wished he were heading home for a reunion with his beloved wife.

CHAPTER FIFTEEN

On September eighteenth, when Chase approached the White River site, which was located many miles northwest of the enormous span of the Sand Hills, two scouts from another Lakota band halted him. He had prepared himself for such an encounter by wearing the gift shirt from his wife's family, a breechclout, leggings, and moccasins. He also had ridden up at a slow pace and had given the *peace* and *friend* signals as soon as he saw the men coming toward him, their weapons at the ready. In Lakota, he identified himself as the son of Chief Rising Bear and said he was there to join his father and people for the war council meeting which was set to begin on the following day. The scouts eyed him with suspicion and doubt, as it was obvious he was half white and was using a *wasicun* saddle. As the alert men glanced all around him, he assured them he was alone. The encounter reminded him of a similar incident with War Eagle months ago. Though it was dismaying, he had to accept the fact his White heritage would always be conspicuous and questioned. Finally one motioned him onward to travel between them, their sharp lances pointing at him in warning.

The two braves rode with him the remainder of the distance until he found his father, War Eagle, River's Edge, and twenty Red Shields who were already there and awaiting the arrival of the rest of their allies, as were many other Oglala groups and various members of the other six tribes of the Lakota branch of the huge Dakota Nation. He was relieved his people were present to confirm his claims, else he might have been forced to spend the coming night in bonds until they were proven to be authentic. As soon as the scouts were satisfied he had spoken the truth, though Chase sensed lingering curiosity about his lineage, they returned to their lookout posts.

Chase dismounted and joined his family and friends near their campfire, as the Plains weather was chilling fast at dusk at that time of year. He was happy when his father stood and embraced him, his brother and wife's brother clasped wrists with him and smiled, and others greeted him with respect and affection, as he knew he was being observed by allies nearby. Even so, their campsite was secluded enough for private talk. He was told Wind Dancer and war chief Blue Owl had remained behind to protect their people and escort them from the grasslands to their wintering grounds in the sacred Black Hills. Nahemana also had stayed with them, as the journey was too long and arduous for the elderly shaman.

Chase was a little surprised and greatly disappointed to see Two Feathers among his group, as that meant—along with War Eagle—that two of their four Sacred Bow Carriers were far away from their band at the same time, and it also meant his cousin would probably seek sly means of harassing and shaming him before their allies. He also knew that Two Feathers would speak and vote for immediate war, and would attempt to persuade others in all bands to do the same. He was glad when his silent cousin sat on the fringe of their gathering, though it was obvious to him that Two Feathers was listening alertly to all Chase said.

As they ate, Chase related what he had learned since Bent Bow had carried his initial message to them. Most were astonished to hear of the many events taking place at or near Fort Laramie; in particular, the aggressive actions of Spotted Tail and the Army's heavy reinforcements worried them. When he was done speaking, many praised his deed, then asked questions or made comments about his findings. All the while, Chase furtively noticed, Two Feathers remained quiet and watchful.

Afterward, Chase walked and spoke with River's Edge

and War Eagle, as he wanted to check on his wife and to hear the camp news since his departure weeks ago. He was relieved to learn the summer buffalo hunt had been completed without any trouble and was a large success, so they had ample food, hides, and other needs for the winter season. Since the war parley was being held at that time, the annual gathering of the Seven Council Fires of the Lakota for their combined powwow had been canceled, a genial occasion which would have divulged his identity to other Lakota bands.

As soon as those and other facts were disclosed to him, as such matters must be covered before personal ones, Chase asked. "How is Dawn? Does Broken Lance act as her hunter and protector as he promised me?"

"Your cousin keeps his word to you, my brother and friend," River's Edge said. "Your wife works hard and well, but she also misses you and fears for your safety. Her heart will sing with joy to look upon your face again."

"As mine will sing loud and sweet to gaze upon your sister's."

"I do not know of such feelings to this moon," War Eagle jested, "but they must be powerful, for your eyes glow with flames like the fire's and your voice becomes soft as the rabbit's fur when you speak of her. If I had known Dawn possessed large magic, I would have looked her way before you took her as your mate. But even before she became my sister when she joined to you, she was as a sister to me, for she and Hanmani were as close as family."

Chase smiled and advised, "Allow Wakantanka to choose your mate for you as He did for me and Wind Dancer and you will find great happiness and victory in your joining."

"I hope that does not happen before we push all Whites and other enemies from our territory and these are Lakota lands once more," War Eagle said in a serious tone, then grew silent as he experienced a strange and potent chill racing over his body. It was as if he were being sent a portentous message which he could not grasp.

Chase witnessed his half-brother's reaction to his own words but did not comment on it. "If we allow the Great Spirit to guide our steps, War Eagle, we must be willing to walk the path He chooses for us and at His pace. I did not expect to meet Dawn and join to her this season, though she was shown to me in the sacred dream which summoned me home. It was the same with Wind Dancer; Dewdrops walked into his life and heart when he did not expect such a glorious event. Perhaps it will be the same for you. It is hard for me to be away from Dawn in times of great peril, but it must be so."

River's Edge regarded Chase's grave expression and tone and asked, "From what you have seen and heard, Cloud Chaser, do you believe the White-eyes will ride the warpath soon?"

"Yes, my friend and brother," Chase replied somberly, "for the Bluecoats and White leaders believe they must not lose face before the Indians and their people, and they prepare for battle. The raids of Spotted Tail and others will only provoke them to challenge us faster and fiercer, when we need many suns to prepare to confront and defeat them. Come. We must sleep, for the council meets on the next sun when those here will speak and vote for the journey to our destinies. May the Great Spirit watch over us when it rises and lead us to the right path to ride."

At dusk on the next day and after more Lakotas had arrived and all had eaten their evening meals, a considerable crowd of seasoned warriors and observant young braves gathered around a bright campfire. Each of the band chiefs present sat in a vast circle with his companions close behind him. War Eagle and Cloud Chaser were positioned slightly to the right and left behind Rising Bear, with the remaining Red Shields clustered nearby.

Eight Hunkpapas sat around a large kettle drum beyond the throng. They struck its taut surface with willow sticks, and sent forth melodic vocables with bowed heads; their moods and expressions indicated reverence instead of gaiety. Assorted warriors, some clad only in daily buckskin wear and others attired in ceremonial regalia, danced around the center blaze and stirred up dust and dead grass from the dry ground. Most moved around the flames in rhythmic patterns while others leapt and whirled and stamped their feet in a near frenzy. Some chanted; some sent forth whoops and yips; some remained silent; and some prayed in muffled voices. The loudest and most active dancers also waved hatchets or wooden clubs over their heads as if slaying invisible foes or evil spirits. The rest of the men sat cross-legged on folded hides or rush mats and observed the preparatory custom, which was followed by a Brule shaman's prayer to summon their Creator to witness the crucial meeting and to bless it and them in their endeavors.

Next, a sacred redstone pipe was smoked for the Making Of Brothers ritual to signify their friendship and unity in the grave matter that loomed before them. After the last man drew deeply upon its stem and exhaled a gray haze, the pipe was returned to Tatanka Yotanka—Sitting Bull—shaman of the Hunkpapas. A leather pouch was passed from chief to chief in the front circle to see who would speak first and be in charge of the parley. That temporary rank was earned by Mahpialuta—Red Cloud—of the Old Smoke Oglala band when he withdrew the only black stone from inside the bag.

Chase went on full alert to study and listen to the esteemed chief. Red Cloud, an impressive warrior with a wide mouth and broad chin, was strongly opposed to enemy intrusion. As with each man who would follow him, the older man stood in the center of the human enclosure and near the fire so he could be heard and seen by all.

"The Whites have not kept their promise to us in the treaty," Red Cloud said. "Broken Hand told us they would give us trade goods for fifty circles of the seasons, but they changed it to ten after our chiefs signed. Before he walked the Ghost Trail and the snows left our land, he told many about that change, and some agreed to it; my band refused, as did others. If they do not have to honor their treaty words, we do not have to honor ours."

As the light of a full moon beamed down on everyone, Chase's attention shifted to Little Thunder of the Brules, who had been embroiled in the "Grattan Massacre" and was known by Indians to harass settlers along the emigrant trail. It was also known that Little Thunder was cunning and deceitful where soldiers and traders were involved; the chief often pretended to be peaceful and friendly—as when he saved Bordeau's life and those of the trader's employees—but, in truth, he hated Whites, detested their encroachment, and wanted them gone from the territory. If that proved impossible, the man wanted to dupe and use the Whites to his benefit. Little Thunder was an odd-looking man: he had a large nose, droopy folds beneath his eyes, cropped-off bangs across his forehead and around his crown, and the rest of his long braids were wrapped in red trade cloth.

"Who gave the Army, Great White Chief, Broken Hand Fitzpatrick, and the one called Mitchell the power to part our land into territories and to order us not to fight our ene- mies?" Little Thunder asked in a sarcastic tone. "I say they did not and do not possess that power, so the treaty is no good."

Chase was surprised when Rising Bear said his second son would talk in his place—as that was his right—so Chase could tell what he knew of the *wasicun* from living among them, though Rising Bear did not explain that odd occurrence. As he wriggled his way into the clearing, Chase pondered how to explain the 1803 Louisiana Purchase. "Many of you know French trappers and traders," he began. "The French Nation believed they owned all lands in this territory and called it *Louisiana*. The Whites who lived beyond the Big Muddy River and their chief Jefferson gave much money to the French chief Napoleon to buy these lands." When Chase paused to choose his next words, Sinte Galeska made a few quick remarks.

"Land belongs to the Great Spirit; it cannot be owned or traded. In exchange for peace and trade goods, we gave the Bluecoats permission to place forts and trails upon it and we said Whites could cross it. But both abuse our generosity; they come; they take; they stay; they destroy; they insult us and shame us; they kill our loved ones and allies."

As many others nodded or murmured agreement, Chase focused on the Brule who always wore a raccoon tail as a medicine symbol. He knew the shrewd and aggressive chief had played a huge part in the lethal fiasco with Grattan and the ensuing episodes, which included the recent daring robbery on the ştage, and who would be largely responsible for the impending retaliations.

"Your words are true, Spotted Tail, but that is not what the Whites believe," Chase said. "As with our Sacred Bow race, many white men run a race with words instead of feet; they tell other Whites how they will lead them best. The Whites vote for one man to become their leader for the passing of many circles of the seasons, usually for four or eight fingers' count, and his rank is called *President*. While the chosen one is leader, he tells other Whites what to do, as the one called President Fillmore ordered Agent Fitzpatrick to make the Long Meadows Treaty. But the White leader does not remain chief for his life and his son does not take that rank after he leaves it or dies; another is chosen by the Whites to take his place. One called Pierce is now the Great White Chief, their President. He is the one who will order his people to go to war or to keep peace with us. Pierce, as with all Whites, believes this land belongs to their Nation, called *America,* as the Lakotas are part of the Dakota Nation. The Whites know we live in this land and know we are powerful; most do not want war with us; that is why they seek a truce by offering us peace and trade goods so we will share it and not battle them for it. As with the Crow and Pawnee and other enemies, some Whites are greedy and do many things to provoke war so the Bluecoats and President will be forced to battle us, to slay us or to push us from this land, so the bad Whites can take it."

Chase related the incident he had witnessed when the gang of white men murdered and robbed soldiers and tried to blame the Indians, and he revealed how they had been entrapped and slain with Grattan's help. He noted that last disclosure surprised many of the chiefs and their men. He returned to his previous point by cautioning, "If we refuse to make truce with the good Whites and we begin war with the Bluecoats and settlers, the President will order his forces to attack us, and a great and long war will come; many from both sides will die or suffer, our women, children, and old ones; and the face and heart of Mother Earth will be scarred forever."

Rising Bear disclosed that Chase had been scouting at Fort Laramie before he joined them. "Tell us what you learned while there, my son," he urged.

Chase—who was astonished and elated the others were allowing him, a half-breed, to speak for such a lengthy time—nodded to his father before he explained the Army's view of the Grattan massacre. "The Bluecoats believed the cow was stolen and they had the duty and right by the treaty to capture and punish those who committed the bad deed. While Grattan was speaking with Brave Bear, one of the Bluecoats became afraid, for he knew of the Lakotas' prowess and they were outnumbered and surrounded. He fired his weapon without being ordered to do so by Grattan, and other soldiers became afraid when warriors retaliated with a flight of arrows. Things turned out of hand, and all soldiers were slain. The Army is angry about the killings and the raids on the American Fur Company and Bordeau

Trading Post, the theft of the thunderstick-wagon mules, and the taking of the horses from the fort. The President and Bluecoat leaders fear if they do not retaliate for those slayings and raids, they will lose face and other bands will think they can do the same without risking punishment."

"Do the White leaders know of how the man they sent to speak for them insulted and threatened us, for his body was filled and fevered by their firewater?" Spotted Tail scoffed. "Do they know the soldiers attacked first? Do they know Brave Bear, the man they chose as the peace chief, was slain?"

Before Chase could respond, Little Thunder added, "Do they know I asked my people to spare the lives of trader Bordeau and his companions? Do they know High Forehead and his Minneconjous have ridden from this area and will cause no more trouble?"

"One soldier did not die in your camp, Little Thunder," Chase reminded him. "He told the Bluecoat leader Fleming of Auguste's bad words and deeds. He told Fleming the soldiers fired first. But Fleming was angry because all soldiers were slain and many places were raided. Fleming is no longer the Bluecoat leader; one called Hoffman came and took his place; he brought more men and weapons with him; and soon, more will come, many more. If Hoffman does not settle the conflict between our peoples, another Bluecoat—one more powerful and fierce called Harney— will be sent here to do so; and Harney will bring more men and weapons, many giant thundersticks. The soldiers at the fort make more lodges for them; they gather wood and grass; they ride on scouting journeys and many guard the fort. They prepare for war, for they believe we will attack again. Spotted Tail's raid on the big rolling travois proved their fears are right." Chase grew silent as Tatanka Yotanka spoke. He had heard much about the mystical powers of the young Hunkpapa, a revered and trusted shaman.

"Why do you provoke the Bluecoats and Whites against all Indians, Spotted Tail?" Sitting Bull asked. "Why did you not restrain your hunger to fight them when their leader did not give an attack order? Why did you not allow Grattan to punish his defiant and weakling warrior? If you had done so, the Bluecoats would be alive and the Army would not be angry at us."

A strong breeze wriggled his raccoon symbol as Spotted Tail refuted, "They came eager to battle and shame us, Sitting Bull; we attacked while we were strongest and before they could ready the giant thundersticks to roar. We raided the rolling travois to get the shiny yellow stone to pay for the damage Grattan did to Brave Bear and others and to our possessions. It is easy to find a greedy white man who will take gold for weapons and supplies, things we need for war. They are weaklings, for they did not pursue us. It will be the same when we challenge them for *our* lands."

Chase was cognizant of being watched by the young brave who sat slightly behind Spotted Tail: Tashunka Witco—Crazy Horse—the chief's nephew by his sister; although only in his teens, already the Oglala brave was known for his prowess and his fierce hatred of the Whites. It was evident to Chase—and probably to others—that Crazy Horse concurred with his uncle. He saw Red Leaf and Long Chin, brothers of the slain Chief Brave Bear, nod agreement before Chase said, "Hoffman and his men did not follow you because he believed your raid was a trick to lure them away from the fort so you or another band could attack there. When war comes, Spotted Tail, Bluecoats will pursue and challenge any band they encounter, even one that wants peace, for no Indian will be trusted after that dark sun rises. Bluecoats have been ordered to guide and protect stages, wagon trains, supply wagons, and their new outposts along the road. Davis, the war chief to President Pierce, is angry; he wants peace and punishment; he believes Grattan was attacked as a trick to steal the annuity goods and horses. He or others might use those deeds as a reason to attack and enslave all Indians and take all Indian lands. I asked Fleming and Hoffman to make me a scout and translator so I could watch and listen more, but both said peace talks were no good; they will not even send Agent Twiss to parley. Each time you or another band attack Whites, their mistrust, fear, and hatred grow. When it becomes too large to be contained, they will strike at us in great numbers and with powerful weapons."

"Were you cunning and wary while scouting at the fort so the soldiers did not learn who you are and why you were there?" Two Feathers asked. "Are you sure they did not trail you to this war council?"

I was wondering how long you'd stay silent! "I am sure, my cousin. Just as I am sure the Army will send out scouts, White and Indian, to learn what the Lakotas will do soon. If we are to defeat them, all bands and tribes must ride as one great force against them. To do so, each warrior must ready himself and his weapons, and must be willing to follow the chosen war party leaders. But we must not act in haste."

"Do you say we must not punish the Bluecoats and Whites for their bad deeds against us and our Lakota brothers?" Two Feathers asked.

Chase shook his head and struggled to appear calm. "No, my cousin. I say we must not strike the first blow and shed the first blood."

"The Bluecoats have already done so," Two Feathers sneered. "Do we sit on our mats and hold our hands while they do so again?"

Control your temper, Chase. Don't reveal your annoyance with him. "You hear my words, my cousin, but you do not understand them. Spotted Tail and his party have punished them for the attack on Brave Bear and their joint camp. If our united forces strike next, we will be doing so without being challenged. We must make it as clear as the waters in our streams that we try to honor the treaty and keep our promises and we fight only when we are attacked. Such actions will help to prevent the Army, their war chief, and their President from blaming us for the war which comes. We need more time to ready ourselves and our weapons, to choose party leaders, to make plans, to learn to think and ride as one. I have seen the white man's large number and powerful weapons. If we begin fighting and more soldiers and weapons are sent here, we cannot win."

"I say we do not act as cowards and weaklings," Two Feathers said. "I say we chase them away from our territory as the crow does with the hawk."

Chase reasoned, "Many crows attack one hawk to make him flee, my cousin. If we attack the Bluecoats, more of their hawks with sharper talons will come. We must defend ourselves with all of our prowess when we are attacked, but let the Bluecoats bring the war to us. If we carry it to them, we will appear as the provokers to the Great White Chief in Washington."

"Do not forget, my friends and allies," Sitting Bull reminded, "when Broken Hand Fitzpatrick took eleven of the chiefs who signed the Long Meadows Treaty long ago to Washington, many were frightened by what they saw; one chief was so afraid he sent himself to the Ghost Trail. Others told of large numbers of Whites, many powerful weapons, many strange things. That is what the son of Rising Bear of the Red Shields tells us this moon, and I believe his words are true. I do not fear the white man or Bluecoats, but this is not the season for our Hunkpapas to fight them. In my sacred vision, I saw us battling and defeating them many circles of the seasons from this one; and their leader had long yellow hair. Until that enemy comes to our lands and challenges us, we will honor the truce."

Chase was glad Sitting Bull spoke for peace, at least for the time being. Rising Bear voted in the same manner, despite Two Feathers' protest and scowl. After hearing all he had revealed to them, Red Cloud—as did some other chiefs—also voted for restraint, but recommended constant vigil and preparation. But Spotted Tail, Little Thunder, Red Leaf, Long Chin, and others voted for war.

Those on one side of the conflict continued to try to persuade the other to join their way of thinking. After all chiefs had their say and final vote, the result was split down the middle of the large group. Since it was not a band or tribal vote where all must be in agreement before action was taken or not taken, the bands were not obligated to go along with their allies' decisions, a point which Spotted Tail made clear to those in favor of restraint. Despite their vast differences of opinion after the meeting ended, most continued to sit around the fire to talk in a genial manner.

When Rising Bear and his group returned to their campsite, except for Two Feathers who stayed behind to prolong his visit with Spotted Tail and others, the chief rested a hand on his second son's shoulder, smiled, and said in an emotional tone, "I have great pride, love, and trust in you, Cloud Chaser, as I do for Wind Dancer and War Eagle. It is good we will watch and wait to see what the Bluecoats do before we ride against them. As we do so, our warriors will practice, make more weapons, and keep themselves strong and ready for what lies ahead. The cold season is a bad time for war; if food, tepees, and garments are destroyed by the enemy during the snows, our people would suffer and many would die, for those items could not be gathered or replaced then."

"That is why I spoke so strongly for peace, Father," Chase told him and the others. "Our people must be kept safe from all harm until the inevitable trouble strikes."

Rising Bear nodded. "On the next sun, we will return to them."

Chase was eager to see his wife who awaited him in their winter camp in the sacred Black Hills. He wanted to spend every moment he could with his beloved Macha before that grim day of war came . . .

CHAPTER SIXTEEN

"It is good to be together and to hold you again," Chase murmured into Macha's ear as she cuddled in his embrace on their sleeping mat. He was both aroused and calmed by the way her head rested on his shoulder and her fingertips drifted over his bare chest. It was elating and enchanting to be in her presence once more, to feel her flesh making contact with his, to hear her sweet voice, to inhale her special scent, and to know he meant as much to her as she did to him. "I have missed you, my cherished wife. When we rode into camp and I gazed upon you, my heart filled with great joy. I love you, Dawn, and needed our reunion."

The tenderness in his tone, the words he used, and the possessive way he held her thrilled Macha to her very core. She was the luckiest woman alive to have this unique man, and was blessed by his feelings for her. "As *I* needed it, my husband, for you filled my thoughts each sun and my dreams on every moon while you were gone. My heart sings with much happiness to be touching you once more. Will you leave again to scout?" she asked in dread.

"If so, not for the passings of many suns," he answered, not wanting to think or talk about war or other evils on this night. But if she needed to appease her fears, he would allow her to do so.

"My pride in your good deeds and prowess are large."

"As large as your love and desire for me?" he jested, attempting to guide them away from difficult and painful subjects.

"Nothing matches those feelings within me. I am glad your father, and others, voted for peace. I do not want our people to war with the Whites until it must be so to save our lives and lands. You have been in my Life-Circle for less than four full moons; that is not enough time to be with you in the ways I crave before fighting steals you from my arms and our tepee. Is it bad of me to be so selfish and greedy?"

Chase nestled her closer. "No, my beloved wife, for I feel the same way. Without you, I would not be the man I am now. I thank the Great Spirit for joining us as one."

Macha shifted her head and gazed into his handsome face. "Soon, we must travel to Bear Mountain to place prayer tokens on the trees growing there to show our thanks to Wakantanka for His many blessings. We must do so before a great snow blankets our land, as I told Him I would."

"We will go soon, my love," Chase promised, "for I must also give Him thanks for all He has done for me and given to me this season."

"We have each other, our families and people, and peace for a while. What more could we ask for?" she murmured dreamily as she caressed him.

"We could ask for this," he whispered as he nibbled at her earlobe and caused her to wriggle in amusement. "Or this," he added as his lips trailed over her face and one hand fondled her breast, its peak already taut with yearning. "Or this," he continued a few minutes later before his questing mouth fastened to hers and his fingers inched their way down her body to the center of her desire.

Unable to control their enormous cravings, they surrendered to a swift and urgent union the first time; then, after they rested for a while, they made slow and titillating love, which rewarded them with a second burst of glorious passion.

The following day, Chase halted at the ceremonial lodge and observed as the Story Catchers painted symbols on the band's history hide to record the recent events. His gaze trailed over past ones which depicted the many exploits of Wind Dancer and Chumani, which took place three years ago, including an awesome battle with a grizzly and victorious tricks against the Crow and Whites. He felt honored to have some of his own achievements portrayed there for all time.

When Chumani approached him, he asked her about the hawk she had raised and who had helped her and his brother accomplish some of their past feats. He listened with amazement as the lovely woman—once a warrior and hunter—related those stirring adventures. He wished he had been there in 1851 when they occurred and wished he could have been one of the five sacred vision-quest companions with the couple, War Eagle, Red Feather, and Zitkala. Their talk was interrupted when her son came running up to join them.

"How are you on this fine sun, Tokapa?" Chase asked with a grin as the small boy held out a rock in one hand and a pinecone in the other for Chase to study. "They are good, Tokapa. We must fetch a pouch to put your playthings in. I have one in my tepee."

"Me go?" the boy asked his mother.

As Chumani nodded permission, Chase put both objects in one hand and the child clasped the other. "I will fetch the pouch and return him soon, Dewdrops. I will guard him until he is in your arms once more."

Chumani watched the two walk away as Macha joined her and also observed the departing pair as the two males laughed and talked after Tokapa begged a ride on Chase's back. "He has much love for my husband's brother, as do I for saving my son's life. He will be a good father when you two are blessed with a child."

"I yearn to have one, Dewdrops. I also yearn to help save our people as you did at Wind Dancer's side long ago, but I cannot travel with Cloud Chaser and do such deeds, for I lack your prowess as a female warrior and hunter."

"You earned a large coup when you returned Cloud Chaser to life so he could help us during these dark suns," Chumani said, "and you make him happy as his reward from the Great Spirit for his good deeds. Do not forget, Dawn, you showed large prowess and generosity when you helped save Tokapa's life, the life of our future chief. Those things mean much to our family and people. We are fortunate you are a Red Shield, for Cloud Chaser's love for you held him here until we accepted him."

"Your words are kind, Dewdrops, and give me much joy. You are wise, for I am in the place and walk the path chosen for me by Wakantanka. Now I must go finish my chores before the sun sleeps."

After Macha left to do her work and Chase returned with a laughing Tokapa, who held a pouch with the rock and pinecone, Chumani took the boy to her tepee to finish her own daily tasks.

Chase joined his father's wife as she worked at a cookfire near Rising Bear's tepee. He smiled and greeted her. "*Hau, Winona, anpetu waste.*"

The woman stilled her busy hands and glanced at the sunny sky. "Yes, Cloud Chaser, it is a fine day. I am happy you returned to us unharmed. You do many good deeds for us, and I thank you."

"As you do many good deeds for us as our chief's wife, and as you did for me long ago when I was a child and my mother lived no more."

Winona put aside her task. "Walk with me in the forest while I gather wood and where we can speak away from the ears of others."

Chase followed her into the dense trees where she found a huge fallen pine and sat down upon it. After she motioned for him to sit beside her, he did so, then waited for her to speak. He saw her take a deep breath as if she were deciding what to say and how to say it. He was surprised when she clasped one of his large hands within her two smaller ones, then looked at him and began.

"It is past the time for truth to live between us, Cloud Chaser. Long ago I was attacked by evil jealousy toward your mother, though Omaste was a good and kind woman, and I hid such wicked feelings from everyone. I feared the feelings which had drawn my husband to her and feared the bond between them in their son, though I knew he did not love her as a man loves a woman or as he loves me. After she was lost to us, I was afraid to accept and love you as my child, for I believed your White blood would take you from us one sun, or the Great Spirit would do so as He had done with Omaste. I understood my husband's suffering and a man's needs on the sleeping mat, and I forgave him for his one weakness, but I have not revealed to you my own weakness and wrongs and asked your forgiveness for them. Hatred has never lived in my heart toward you, Cloud Chaser, for you carry the blood of my husband and the Red Shields. Now, greater love fills it for you. I am happy and proud you are of our family and were returned to us. I believe Wakantanka has planned and controlled your existence since He created you from my husband's seed. It is good you had the courage and prowess to return to us and to endure our tests and doubts before accepting you. Will you forgive my bad deeds and the sufferings I caused you?"

Chase gave her hand a gentle squeeze. He was touched deeply by her enlightening words. "I did so long ago, Winona, for I envisioned what troubled you deeply, as it would anyone who walked in such difficult moccasins following your return from the Pawnee. You are a good mother to your children, a good grandmother to Tokapa, and a superior wife for our chief. You bring great joy to my father's heart. The truth now lives between and within us. I am proud and happy to call you a second mother and a friend."

"As I am to call you my accepted son and a friend."

That night, Macha whispered to Chase, "I do not believe the union of Two Feathers and Robin is a happy one. After you rode away, she did not smile, laugh, talk, or work with other females, only with her mother and grandmother. After your cousin left our camp, she became as her past self again. Now that he has returned, she is once more the person she became after their joining."

"If she is unhappy, why does she not speak the parting words before their tepee flap and choose another before there is a child between them?"

"She does not do so out of false pride and great fear. I am certain of it, for I see such feelings in her eyes and movements."

"You believe she fears him?"

"That is so, my husband."

"But he would not dare harm her if she leaves him by

our custom."

"Have you forgotten from the bad and bold way your cousin treated you and still treats you in private that Two Feathers dares what he wills? And it would shame Robin and her family to speak against a member of our chief's family and to part with him unless he abuses her before others. If he harms her in their tepee, he leaves no marks upon her face and body which others could see. Perhaps he only wounds her with cutting words and deeds, for Two Feathers is a sly and cautious man."

"Your words are wise, my beloved wife. But if Robin lacks joy and finds courage, she will part with him. Let us think and speak of sad things no more. Let us find our own joy and courage in the journey before us."

Macha looked at him in confusion. "What journey, my husband? Do you speak of the one to Bear Mountain soon?"

"No, I speak of this one, Sunshine of my heart," Chase disclosed with a grin as his mouth sought and found hers, and he eagerly pulled her close.

When it was Chase's turn to scout the surrounding area for enemies and other perils, he chose Bent Bow to ride with him, which elated the young brave. They armed themselves, took food and water, and left camp early that morning, as their task would require all day.

As it had been peaceful since reaching that winter location, the two men didn't think they would encounter any threats; yet, both stayed alert for dangers.

It was shortly before midday when trouble struck.

Chase reined in his sorrel and told his companion, "Look there," as he motioned to fresh prints on the ground. "Iron shoes of a white man's horse."

"Two horses, and they ride into the sacred hills," Bent Bow deduced.

"We must track them to see where they go and what they do here."

Without further words or hesitation, the two men followed the trail a long way from their camp into the forested foothills and canyons. They halted when they heard gunfire and glanced at each other to signal caution. They dismounted and moved with great stealth toward the ominous noise, taking cover behind large boulders on an incline which overlooked a rushing stream.

Using fieldglasses, it did not take Chase long to assess the situation and locate their positions. He listened as the two White aggressors shouted back and forth between them.

"Don't waste no more ammo, Hank; he ain't got no more arrows, so let's rush 'im and kill 'im pronto." He referred to the one Indian concealed in a rocky area against the other side of the canyon wall. "We cain't have 'im escaping to bring down a bunch of redskins on us afore we stuff our pockets and saddlebags with plenty of gold. It's just laying there waiting fur us to pick it up, and my hands are itching to oblige it."

"You sure he ain't got no more arrows?"

"He'da done fired another one by now if'n he did. Good thing he's a bad shot and we saw 'im first, or we'd be in big trouble, probably dead."

"Let's give him a few more minutes before we charge him. You know these red devils are meaner than a snake and tricky as a fox. He ain't going nowhere stuck in them rocks with no way out; he can't make a run for it; we'd cut him down in the open."

"Well, we cain't waste much more time on 'im; it's acosting us plenty of nuggets and flakes. We gotta be outta here come morning."

"Hold your horses, Sam; we got plenty of daylight left. Nobody knows there's gold here excepting us, or these hills would be crawling with miners and prospectors, Injuns or no Injuns."

"We're sure lucky we wuz the ones who stumbled on to it whilst watering our horses. We're gonna be rich men soon."

"If we stay alive. We won't if he gits away."

"He won't. We'll just collect enough to last us until summer. After them Injuns head fur the Plains to hunt buffalo, we'll sneak back and git plenty more whilst it's safe."

Chase squatted and whispered to Bent Bow, "Two white men; they seek the yellow rocks to steal. Two Feathers is entrapped by them; he has used all of his arrows. They seek to slay him so he cannot flee and bring others to slay or capture them. We will sneak up on them and defeat them," he decided and revealed his bold and dangerous plan.

Using all of the prowess they possessed, Chase crept toward one man while Bent Bow did the same with the other. Though they knew Two Feathers' life was in jeopardy, they could not move fast, as dislodging a rock or stepping on a small branch would expose their presence; they had ample cover from boulders, trees, and bushes to conceal their advance. Soon, both were positioned to attack the enemies who were focused on Two Feathers to make sure he did not make a daring escape attempt; or if he did, to be sure they killed him, as their weapons were loaded and aimed in that direction.

Chase sneaked up behind his target and rendered the prospector unconscious with a blow to the head. He sent forth a certain bird call to let his companion know he had succeeded, then waited until it was answered to indicate Bent Bow had achieved his objective. After he heard that signal, Chase stood and shouted to his cousin, "We are here, Two Feathers, and our enemies are defeated! It is safe to show yourself!"

Chase watched his cousin come forward with a scowl on his face, dangling a bow in one hand and an empty quiver in the other. Chase grasped the prospector's arm and dragged the man to where the second gold-seeker lay on the ground with Bent Bow standing over him. He smiled. "You earned a large coup, my friend. You are brave, skilled, and cunning. Your father will be pleased with your victory."

Bent Bow grinned. "We make good companions, Cloud Chaser."

Two Feathers joined them, glanced, still frowning, at each in turn, and glared at the two disabled white men. "You stole my coups," he said angrily.

Chase shook his head. "You were trapped; we saved your life."

"I did not need your help to defeat only two foolish White-eyes," Two Feathers scoffed. "I would have found a way to trick them and survive."

"It did not look that way to us," Chase refuted.

"Your arrows are gone and you were ensnared," Bent Bow added.

"I have a knife, cunning, and strong hands. And the Great Spirit provides many weapons nearby—rocks, limbs for clubs, dirt for blinding."

"You could not reach your enemies with them," Bent Bow argued. "Soon, they would have charged you and slain you with their firesticks. Cloud Chaser heard their words and told them to me. Your peril was large."

Two Feathers glared and retorted, "If I could not have reached them with such weapons from Mother Earth, he who failed at the Sun Dance, I could have waited there and sneaked away beneath a blanket of darkness."

"You insult me with such words, Two Feathers; that is cruel."

"I speak only the truth, weakling son of our war chief."

"Your tongue is sharp and cutting on this sun, my cousin," Chase scolded the irate man, "so you must sheathe it and practice the Four Virtues and honor your Sacred Bow vows. I will fetch the felled prospectors' horses to transport them to our camp. Bind their wrists for loading them," he ordered and left to do so, as they should allow his father and their council to decide the men's fates.

When Chase returned with the animals, his tawny gaze widened in shock, then narrowed in anger; and Bent Bow was staring at Two Feathers with a similar expression on his own face. "Why did you slay them when that should be our chief and council's choice?" he demanded as he viewed the men's slit throats and the wet red blade in Two Feathers' hand. The wicked warrior casually wiped the victims' blood on dried grass and sheathed his knife.

"They are evil and had to die," he said flatly. "There was no need to take them to our camp and risk them being seen going there or being found there."

Chase quelled the urge to strike him. "The deed is done,

so we must hide their bodies and possessions and free their horses. It would be perilous to have such things found on our land and near our camp."

"Do as you wish, Cloud Chaser, but I ride for camp. They are unworthy of my touch. Let the forest and sky creatures devour them."

Chase and Bent Bow watched Two Feathers hurry to his horse, leap upon its back, and gallop away. Chase took a deep breath to calm himself. "We must cover the men and their belongings with rocks and brush, my friend, for no White-eyes or Bluecoats must find them in this condition."

"That is wise, Cloud Chaser, for our people's safety. Your cousin seeks to flee the place of his great shame and weakness and flee from the eyes of those who witnessed it and saved his life. He did not give us thanks for our good deed; that is bad."

"I do not know why, Bent Bow, but my cousin hates me," he repeated the sad observation. "It does not please him I was one of those who rescued him from certain death. He killed the Whites as revenge on me for my White blood."

"I could not halt him. When I turned to fetch my weapons where I had placed them to free my hands to strike the man, he drew his knife and took their lives. It is wrong for him to have such bad feelings for you. He shames himself with them and his actions."

"That is true, my friend." Sensing Bent Bow's dismay, he coaxed, "Do not blame yourself; you did not fail in your duty. My cousin is sly and quick, and you could not read his wicked thoughts before he carried them out."

The son of Blue Owl nodded his gratitude.

As Chase noticed the excellent condition of the two

breech-loaders, a Hall carbine and Sharp's '48 rifle, he said, "We will keep their weapons, and I will teach you how to use them on another sun." He also kept the ammunition, as it might be needed later. He noted that the two roans had telltale brands, so he decided to free their horses and hide their other possessions. "It would be dangerous for them to be discovered in our camp," he told Bent Bow. "Let us do our tasks now, return to our scouting duty, and then ride for our camp."

At dusk in the meeting lodge, the Red Shield chief and council sat in a group with Chase, Bent Bow, and Two Feathers positioned before them as they listened to the revealing episode and observed their demeanor.

After each had given his version of the incident, Rising Bear asked Two Feathers, "Why did you ride alone and hunt so far from camp?"

"That is what my restless spirit told me to do. When I saw the White-eyes, I tried to slay them to prevent them from gathering the yellow stones and stealing them. If they showed them to others, more would come here. They used their powerful firesticks against me," he reminded them.

"None of your arrows struck them?" an elder asked.

"That is true, for my enemies hid behind rocks."

"Why did you insult those who rescued you?" another elder asked.

"I did not need their help, so they stole my coups."

"Coups belong to the warriors who earn them, to the ones chosen by the Great Spirit to receive them for good deeds," Nahemana said.

"Since I was guided to our enemies, Wise One, does that

not mean I was chosen to earn them, but others intruded and stole them?"

Nahemana shook his head, but Blue Owl pointed out, "You were helpless when they arrived and were guided by generosity to save you. It is bad to use knifing words on companions and band members, and it is bad to slay the captives of another warrior and to defy a scout's orders."

Two Feathers repeated the things he had told Chase about how he could have defeated the prospectors if given the time, and he considered it *his* right to deal with *his* attackers in the manner in which *he* chose.

Bent Bow, delighted by his father's pride and defense of him and Chase, repeated his responses and actions—and those of Chase—at the scene.

Following more questions and remarks, the chief and council huddled to discuss the matter in whispers and reached their decision swiftly.

"It is good Cloud Chaser and Bent Bow rode the path shown to them by Wakantanka," Rising Bear said. "It is bad what Two Feathers said and did after his rescue. Two Feathers must enter the sweat lodge and purify himself of his weakness, shame, and wickedness. During these suns and moons, great danger surrounds us as a mist we cannot see through and battle. We must not slay Whites unless there is no other action to take, for all Lakotas are being watched for attacks and raids, and to do them will call down the Bluecoats' anger and big weapons upon us. We will tell the Shirt-Wearers to give our words to all warrior societies, who will tell their members. Until war is thrust upon us, we will not provoke it."

"But what if we are challenged to a fight, my chief and council?"

"If so, Two Feathers, we," Rising Bear said as he gestured to himself and the elders, "will decide what action must be taken on that sun. Do not forget, we voted for peace at the great war council." He did not think it was necessary to add, *If you seek out more Whites to slay, you will be punished, perhaps banished,* as their decision implied that grave warning.

Following the tense meeting and Two Feathers' hasty retreat, Blue Owl spoke to Chase outside the buffalo hide lodge. "I thank you for helping my son remove the stain on his face and against his honor; you have done many generous deeds for him. If war comes, my son will ride to my right and you will ride to my left when I lead our force against our enemies."

Chase was elated by that enormous honor. "I thank you, Blue Owl, for your kind words and generosity, but your son is a good warrior and the greatest deeds were his. I only gave him the chance to prove such things to himself and his people. All weakness and doubt have been driven from his body by the Creator. He has earned your pride in him."

They talked for a few more minutes, then went their separate ways.

Before he reached his tepee, Chase was stunned and suspicious when Two Feathers approached him and spoke unexpected words within the hearing of War Eagle, Wind Dancer, and a few others.

"I come to ask forgiveness for speaking and acting rashly and to thank you for saving my life, Cloud Chaser. I come to bury the hate knife between us. For the good of our people, we must have peace. Do you accept my gratitude and offer of truce and friendship?"

Chase was positive that Two Feathers was lying and being clever, was certain his cousin despised him even more for being the one to rescue him and for earning another coup at his cousin's expense. Even so, he had no choice except to clasp wrists with the man and pretend to believe him, as it would make himself look bad to refuse. "I accept your thanks, truce, and friendship," he said, faking a smile. "It is good you offer them to me."

"It will be a hard path for me to walk, Cloud Chaser, for evil still tries to place doubts within me about your loyalty to us in future suns. I will seek to defeat that evil and to trust you."

After his three cousins thanked him and told him his action was good and wise, Two Feathers watched them walk away together, talking about Chase's new victory, one which should have belonged to him; and one day, he vowed, his half-breed cousin would pay for dishonoring him.

That night, Chase told Macha, "I do not trust my cousin. His offers are false and sly, but I do not know how he will use them to harm me. But do not fear or worry, my beloved wife, for I will be on alert against his evil," he added before she could voice those he was sure she must be experiencing.

"You have won the hearts and respect of our people, so they will not let him harm you. But I will also stay on guard against his tricks, for they are sure to come, if not in this season, then in one beyond it. You are wise to doubt him. After his return and the news of his attack was revealed,

Robin did not look happy. I think it would please her if he was slain."

"Do not go near him," Chase cautioned, "for he knows if I ever lose you, it will cause me much suffering."

"As it would cause me much suffering to lose you. I suffer even now from hunger for you," she added, then sent him a provocative smile.

"That is a pain I will seek to end," he vowed, taking her in his arms.

Two days later, scouts galloped into camp with grim news. After the incident with the prospectors, more parties of two braves each had been assigned to search their surroundings for other encroachers.

As soon as their report was given and plans were made in haste, a large band with Wind Dancer as the leader rode away to handle the perilous matter. It included his best friend Red Feather, War Eagle, Cloud Chaser, Swift Otter, River's Edge, Bent Bow, and two other warriors.

Within two hours by Chase's reckoning of *wasicun* time and using his long-range fieldglasses to avoid getting too close and risk being seen, their target was sighted gradually crossing the rolling terrain: a box-bed wagon filled with various-sized crates and barrels. Two armed men rode on its wooden seat and an armed man on horseback traveled on either side of it, making the odds nine to four in the Red Shields' favor. The wagon was traveling in a direct path toward Bear Lodge Mountain, where Crow were camped for the winter, thirty miles northwest of the upper section of the Black Hills. Although the awesome site, called Devil's Tower by *wasicuns,* was beyond their treaty-assigned territory, the White "peddlers" were carrying suspected goods which they believed must not reach their Indian enemies, and they were crossing Lakota grounds to do so. As instructed, the scouts had not attacked and had returned to camp for orders.

Wind Dancer selected a location near the Wakpa-mni-sa that Chase and the others thought was perfect for the impending ambush. The band, their presence obstructed by the many and full trees and high grass, hurried to the Redwater River to conceal their horses and themselves amidst dense trees and bushes before their enemies' arrival.

The Red Shields prepared to respond to Wind Dancer's bird signals as the wagon jostled along on a trail well trodden by passing Indian bands. They heard its wheels squeaking, its leather harnesses creaking, the iron shoes on the team and mounts thudding against the hard ground, and the men laughing and talking. The day was sunny and mild, with a steady and light breeze blowing in their direction, taking their scents away from enemy horses.

When the wagon and riders were between them, Wind Dancer gave the signal to surround them—three cries of a local bird—and he was obeyed.

Chase, selected as speaker to prevent exposing his brothers' English skills, yelled, "Don't fire or you're dead! Keep calm and you're safe!"

The astonished driver jerked back on the harness reins and halted the team as the band of Indians seemingly appeared from nowhere and enclosed them with weapons at the ready, while theirs were lowered. He had reacted with caution, as had his three companions, to the shouts in their language.

When the four white men focused on him, Chase said, "We don't want to kill you or injure you, so drop those rifles and pistols to the ground, slow and easy. If you don't follow my orders perfectly, my friends will take any other kind of movement as a threat and will shoot you. Do as I say and you won't be harmed. I give you my word of honor."

Chase was relieved when they did as told.

"What do you want with us?" the driver asked. "Who are you?"

Chase responded with, "What's in the crates and barrels?"

"Just trade goods. We have a treaty and we ain't here to fight, so we figured we could pass unharmed. Why are you attacking us?"

Chase read the driver's tension and deceit and asked again, "What's in the crates and barrels, and where are you taking them?"

"If you harm us, soldiers will come swarming down on you."

"There are no soldiers in this area. Answer my questions."

"It's flour, blankets, and such. You'll be in big trouble if you rob us."

Chase was almost amused by the driver's false bravado. "You don't mind if I take a look in a few of them, do you?"

"Yep, I do, stranger. I done told you what I'm hauling. I ain't no liar."

"Hauling where?" Chase demanded.

"To trappers along the rivers ahead."

"There are no trappers anywhere near this territory and you can't reach their real locations and return to Pierre Post before the snows fall."

"Then we'll turn around and head back now."

"After you prove what you're carrying. I'm going to climb aboard the wagon and see for myself. If any of you make a suspicious move, my friends will cut you down with arrows. I should warn you, if you have any hidden weapons on you and go for them, they can fire six to eight arrows before you can fire one shot. I wouldn't challenge those odds."

"Let 'im see what's in 'em, Pete," one of the riders coaxed.

After the other two men nodded agreement and the driver exhaled loudly in annoyance, Chase leapt onto the wagon bed and pried open several barrels and crates. He locked gazes with the driver and scoffed, "Looks as if somebody gave you the wrong load; all I see is whiskey, cartridges, and guns. Don't you know it's illegal to sell or trade either one to the Crow?"

"I didn't say nothing about visiting no Crow."

"Well, your route was heading straight for their camp. I doubt they would have allowed you to pass by without relieving you of this load, or let you ride off alive. But that's exactly what I'm going to do."

"Do what?"

"Dump this whiskey, burn these rifles, and let you ride for Pierre."

"You can't do that! I got lots of money and time tied up in this haul."

"This *illegal* haul, you mean, one I can't allow to fall into the wrong hands. If those Crow get liquored up and have these guns, they'll start a big ruckus against other Indians and soldiers. If you want me to arrest you and take you to Fort Laramie to speak with Major Hoffman about our difference of opinion," Chase bluffed, "that suits me fine. Of course, if he doesn't believe you, either, you're talking broken laws and a long stay in jail. If you want to stay alive and free, I suggest you and your friend unhitch that team, climb on those horses, and all of you men get out of here as fast as you can."

"Let's go, Pete; he ain't fooling."

"Jim's right, Pete; let's get moving before they get antsy."

"Count me in on hightailing it fast," the fourth man agreed.

"Well, Pete," Chase asked. "What's it going to be? Do you vote smart with your friends there or challenge us alone?"

"We'll do as you say, mister, but I don't like it one bit, and I'm gonna report you and this robbery to the soldiers."

"I hope you do," Chase scoffed. "But if you forget, I'll be sure to do so very soon. If I'm right about my suspicions, the Army will be looking for you afterward. If I were you men, I would get out of this territory fast."

"Can we keep our guns in case we run into trouble?" Jim asked.

"Just your own personal weapons—you might need them with renegade Crow lurking about. Fetch and sheathe them, and no tricks."

While Chase related their talk in Lakota to the Red Shields, who kept their arrows aimed at the peddlers, the white men made their preparations to depart without the wagon. Without further talk or even a backward glance by any of the four, they left the scene with Pete grumbling about his men's cowardice and about being "scraped clean by a bunch of redskins."

As two braves stood guard to make sure the men did not attempt a sneaky return and surprise attack, Chase suggested they keep several long crates of rifles and ample smaller ones of cartridges. "We will hide them nearby until we can come for them with a travois. I will teach my brothers, friends, and other warriors how to use them. When trouble comes to our land, we can use those weapons to help defeat it. But we must not keep all of them; if the traders return with armed companions or soldiers, it will be suspicious if burned portions of many firesticks and whiskey holders are not found here. They will believe we only sought to raid them, not prevent trouble; that would look bad for us. The food which feeds the firesticks must be dumped into the river to destroy it, for burning it is dangerous."

"Your plan is cunning and wise, my brother," Wind Dancer concurred. "It is good you learned so much about our enemy and his weapons."

While the two guards watched for possible trouble, the rest of the band concealed the chosen crates amidst rocks and trees not far away, then brushed away their tracks. Afterward, they dumped the whiskey, piled broken boards around the crates, and used one of the "magic firesticks" from the match tin which Chase had purchased weeks ago at Fort Laramie to set the items ablaze. Smaller crates were forced open and their contents were dumped into the rushing water, their wood added to the roaring fire.

The men sat and talked as they waited for the blaze to consume the rifles and wagon and for the sated flames to die down. To make certain no ember sparked a wildfire on the dried grass nearby, two barrels had been saved to haul water from the river to extinguish and soak them.

After their tasks were finished, Wind Dancer smiled and said, "We have done a good and large deed, my brothers and friends. We destroyed these two evils and did not slay any Whites. Our chief and people will be pleased with us. Come. Let us return to our tepees and families before night blankets our land and slows our pace."

"It is not the approach of night which darkens the sky, my brother. Look there," War Eagle said as he pointed in that direction. "A large storm threatens to strike soon. We must find a safe place to stay before it reaches us."

Wind Dancer nodded. "War Eagle speaks wise and true. We must ride to the forest and find cover from the sky's fiery lances and heavy rain."

As they mounted quickly to gallop that lengthy distance, Chase was disappointed he would not be sleeping with his beloved wife that night. Surely she would realize the storm had delayed them and would not worry about him. Dreams of her would have to give him comfort and warmth on the wet and chilly night to come.

Near their camp at that same time and as she rushed to finish her chores before the ominous weather closed in on that area, Macha stumbled upon a lethal scene and quickly used her sharp wits to handle it . . .

CHAPTER SEVENTEEN

Macha stared at the horrible sight for a moment before she tossed aside the warming blanket from her torso and rushed into the stream. The cold water soaked her moccasins, chilled her feet and legs, and splashed upon the bottom of her dress. Her hands also were chilled to the bone and her garment fringe was drenched as she squatted near the motionless body and lifted the woman's head. The female's wet hair floated on the swift-moving surface and clung to her cheeks and shoulders. Sisoka's face was pale and the flesh was puckered, her lips a bluish-white color, her eyes frozen wide open in terror. A dark bruise was visible on her forehead, which had rested against a large rock, but any blood had washed away in the current.

Macha felt the woman's throat and one wrist for a pulse, and found none. She bent over and listened for a heartbeat, and heard none. Nor were there any signs of breath. It was obvious Sisoka was dead and had been so for a long while. Macha noticed something clutched in the woman's hand, and discovered it was a broken *wanapin*. Though the necklace implied her death was the result of an enemy's attack, Macha did not believe that was true, and what she suspected alarmed her.

She grasped Sisoka's icy hands, dragged her from the stream, and lay her body on the bank. She removed the *wanapin* from the female's hand and quickly hid it beneath a large rock near several bushes. She reasoned that if a Crow was lurking nearby, he would have been seen by their many scouts; and Sisoka either would have been captured or slain in a different manner. With the saturated fringe slapping at her ankles and her moccasins sloshing, she ran back to camp and alerted the first man she encountered to the grim incident: "Robin, daughter of Coyote and wife of Two Feathers, lies dead near the stream. Her body must be fetched before the storm comes."

Tall Elk, one of the Strong Hearts, asked what happened to her, dismay clear in his voice.

"I do not know. I found her facedown in the water," she began, and quickly related her shocking discovery, not telling him about the broken Crow *wanapin*. In the event she was mistaken in her speculations, she urged, "If enemies are responsible for this, the area should be searched before the rain washes away their marks upon the face of Mother Earth."

"I will summon others to help; you will take us to her body."

As soon as three other warriors were gathered from nearby, Macha guided the four men to the location. She listened and watched as Tall Elk revealed her previous disclosures to the others and they examined the scene and the lifeless woman. It was decided she tripped and fell, struck her forehead on the rock, and drowned while unconscious.

"What if this is the wicked deed of an enemy and was made to look like a terrible fall?" Macha reminded. "Do you not think her expression of fear is strange for someone who was knocked out by a sudden blow to her head?"

"You saw and heard nothing odd?" one of the men asked.

"That is so," Macha responded, though she hated to lie to them. Yet, if it was the malicious act of the one she suspected, she did not want an enemy blamed falsely, which would focus attention elsewhere. If Two Feathers was guilty of this cruel and cunning violence, the absence of the token he had planted might cast doubts upon him.

Tall Elk told one of his companions to alert Sisoka's husband and parents to her death and—in the event it was an attack—to send out scouting parties while he and the others used Macha's blanket to retrieve the body.

As they entered camp with the men bearing the burden in a blanket sling, Macha watched Two Feathers, Coyote and his wife, and others rush to meet them. The body was lowered to the ground and the new arrivals enclosed it. Macha observed as Sisoka's mother dropped to her knees, wailed in grief, and caressed her daughter's ashen cheek. Coyote sent forth a soulful cry of anguish and stood behind his wife, gazing downward.

"Who did this evil thing to my mate?" Two Feathers demanded.

"No one," Tall Elk said. "She fell and struck her head and drowned. We found no enemy signs nearby. Only Robin's and Dawn's tracks are there."

As soon as the details were related to him and the others, Macha saw Two Feathers stare at her in a curious manner. *He wonders if I know the evil truth and concealed his false sign, or if another force destroyed it.*

"Robin was not careless; she was pushed into the water upon the rock. It is the work of an enemy," he accused. "I will find and slay him."

"We saw nothing to point in that direction," Tall Elk told him again. "But I have sent word to Blue Owl to have scouting parties ride out to study the area for signs of any encroachers."

Two Feathers looked at Macha. "You saw and heard nothing strange when you found her this way?"

Macha kept her true feelings masked as she responded, "No, and Tall Elk and his companions searched the banks and stream for enemy signs. I could not help her, for her spirit had left her body when I found her. Robin is a big loss to your tepee and to the Life-Circles of her family. It is a sad day for our people. She must be prepared and placed on a death scaffold before the storm comes, for it is near and large."

Coyote glanced upward and nodded agreement. He looked at Two Feathers. "Bring Robin to our tepee so her mother can wash and dress her and wrap her body in a blanket and buffalo hide," he said. "While she does so, we will gather wood and make my child's resting place on the hill nearby. We must hurry; soon the rain, wind, and fiery lances will attack."

"Tall Elk and others will help you, Coyote," Two Feathers countered, "for I must go to the place where she was slain to search for enemy signs."

"We searched and found nothing there," Tall Elk stressed.

"Perhaps my eyes and ears will find things yours did not."

Coyote scowled. "If you must do so, go, but it is useless, for the skills and wits of Tall Elk and the others do not fail them."

Macha tensed, but concealed her reaction. What if, she fretted, Two Feathers found where she had hidden the Crow *wanapin* and pointed out her guilt to the others? Even if she revealed her motive, she would be in big trouble for her deception. As she prayed hard she had left no clues on the ground, it was as if the Great Spirit rescued her and displayed His anger at the wicked deed by calling down the storm's wrath upon the area. Large and heavy raindrops began to pound upon them. Wind yanked at garments, tepees, weapon and cook stands, trees, dry grasses, and dying wildflowers. Lightning flashed across the sky, and thunder roared in its wake. "We must take cover fast," she warned, hoping everyone would.

"Bring my daughter," Coyote almost ordered the sullen Two Feathers. "We will tend her body during the storm and place it on a scaffold later."

As Macha hurried toward her dwelling, she glanced back to see the annoyed warrior lifting his wife's body to obey the older man's stern request. She thanked Wakantanka for protecting her from exposure, assured now that she had done the right thing. Even if Two Feathers suspected her trickery, she reasoned, he could not be certain of it, as either the swift current or a displeased spirit or another person could have stolen the false hint which he had undoubtedly left behind to fool others. She wished Cloud Chaser were there to calm her and to assure her she had performed a good deed. She assumed he was safe and was only trapped somewhere by the fierce storm which was now raging overhead.

Macha removed her soaked garments and moccasins, dried herself and her hair, and donned another dress for warmth. She sat down near the small and cozy fire, cuddled in a blanket, and ate the soup and bread she had cooked earlier, a meal she had wanted to share with her husband, as well as a passionate night in his embrace. Soon, he would be with her again.

The menacing storm had passed and the weather was clear and mild when Chase and the other band members returned the next day and were greeted by their chief and council at the meeting lodge. Everyone in that group was shocked to learn of Sisoka's death and of Two Feathers' suspicion an enemy had slain his wife, though there had been no indication he was right. He faulted the rain for washing those signs away before he could find and follow them.

After that grim news was shared with those who had been absent, Wind Dancer related the incident which his band had handled, pleasing his father and the elders.

"Why did you not slay them?" Two Feathers asked. "They sought to give our enemies firewater and thundersticks to harm us and may try again."

"We obeyed the orders of our chief and council," Wind Dancer said. "Those Whites will run from our land forever, for what they tried to do breaks their laws and they will be punished if they are found."

"Why did you not bind them and send them to Fort Laramie? Cloud Chaser could do so, for he can pass as a white man; he carries their looks and blood and the Bluecoats know and trust him."

Wind Dancer wondered why his cousin was so moody today. And why had he spoken so harshly about Cloud Chaser when he had so recently offered his friendship and gratitude? He reasoned the first part was because of Two Feathers' anguish and shame over losing his wife. "We did not think it was safe to do so," Wind Dancer answered, "for the Bluecoats live in fear of all Lakotas during these suns and would distrust what he told them after the Whites revealed how they were captured with Indian help. That could endanger his life. There also was no need to ride so far from our camp since we drove the evil traders away with our words and threats. My heart is sad over your great loss, my cousin, and it clouds your thinking; we did what is best for our people and allies."

"In the suns ahead, we will see if your words are true.

Now I go to hunt."

"Who rides with you, my cousin?" War Eagle asked.

"I ride alone."

Wind Dancer advised, "That is not safe when you are in pain," and saw Two Feathers scowl before responding to him in a sullen tone.

"Have you forgotten our training and teachings? A true warrior cannot allow suffering and loss to weaken or distract him. I go now."

Wind Dancer and his brothers exchanged questioning glances after their cousin left. "Perhaps Two Feathers needs to mourn his loss in privacy, but he does not think clear or act wise. Swift Otter, tell his best friend or brother to ride behind him at a distance to guard him. If he encounters other Whites as he did four suns past, he might forget the orders of our council and cause trouble."

When Swift Otter looked askance at the chief, Rising Bear said, "Go, Swift Otter, for my son thinks as I do."

The Sacred Bow carrier nodded and departed to carry out that order, as the others talked for a while longer.

After the meeting was over and everyone left the lodge, Chase went to his tepee, where he found Macha waiting for him. After they shared many kisses and embraces, he leaned back and said, "It is good to be here."

"You have heard Robin lives no more on Mother Earth?" she said with sadness. "I must tell you what I did after I found her."

"That discovery was hard for you, my wife, so if you do not wish to speak of it again, I—"

Macha silenced him with fingers across his lips. In hushed tones, she related the entire incident and her suspicion. "Was I bad, my husband?"

"No, it was a brave and wise deed," he acknowledged. "You told me of her fears, but I truly did not believe he would harm her," Chase admitted in dismay.

"Am I wrong about him, my husband?"

Chase caressed her cheek and shook his head. "I do not think so. But we must not tell others about the Crow *wanapin,* for many trust him. It could return doubts in some minds about me if I speak against him when we have no proof he is guilty and not many suns past he offered me friendship. And others could hold angry feelings toward you for hiding the broken *wanapin,* thinking you sought to place the blame on him for his dislike of your husband. Do and say nothing to arouse his suspicions against you or he will seek to have you join Robin on the Ghost Trail. We must watch him carefully. If he harms you to spite me or to hide his evil deed from discovery," Chase swore, "I will slay him with my bare hands."

Macha hugged him and rested her cheek against his chest as she promised, "I will be cautious and alert, my husband, as must you."

"I do not understand why he would place a Crow *wanapin* in her hand but try to make her fall appear her fault. That is strange. Yet, I do not doubt no Crow was to blame. It is possible, my wife, we are wrong. Perhaps Robin found the *wanapin* from a past attack and had it in her hand when she fell and struck her head. Yet, I feel certain my cousin slayed her for some reason we do not know, and he still hates me."

"As do I, my husband."

He caressed her cheek and said, "We will forget such

troubling matters for now, but stay alert in the suns ahead."

Two sunrises later and a day after a band led by Wind Dancer went to retrieve the hidden crates, Chase and Macha sealed the flap to their tepee, loaded supplies, bid their families farewell, mounted, and headed for Paha Mato to honor their vows to the Great Spirit at that sacred site.

At dusk on the following day, they made a small camp at the base of Bear Butte, having traveled slowly to enjoy their privacy and the seasonal changes on the landscape. They gathered branches and erected a shelter, which they covered with several buffalo hides to ward off the night's chill.

After they ate, they snuggled together on their sleeping mat and shared tender and leisurely lovemaking.

At dawn, the happy couple stood on the hillside with faces pointed toward the rising sun, soaking up its generous warmth and offering prayers of gratitude to the Great Spirit for their many blessings and evoking His guidance and protection in the wintry season ahead. They clasped hands and smiled, love and serenity filling their hearts and minds, as well as reverence for the occasion.

They walked to a nearby location where many short trees and bushes were adorned with objects from past visitors—mainly beadworks, hairlocks, tiny pouches of stones and herbs, bits of cloth or leather, or parts of animals—all of which had been placed there for many reasons. They secured their prayer tokens to empty branches without speaking, as they believed their Creator knew the purpose for each one. After their task was completed, they returned to their shelter to spend time enjoying each other's company.

Shortly before the sun would set, Macha gathered scrubwood for a cozy fire while Chase walked to a stream to fetch drinking water for their last night there. After she finished, she headed to join him to enjoy the return stroll together. As she approached the stream, she froze in panic as she saw a strange coyote sneaking up on her husband, who was on his knees and bending over to fill his canteen. Although an attack by that normally shy creature was extremely rare, Macha sensed something different, violent, about that particular one, and it was evident he meant to strike at her beloved mate.

All she had with her was a knife in a beaded sheath, and she knew it would be perilous to her to attempt to slay the creature at close range. There was no time to fetch her husband's rifle from the shelter and she decided it was hazardous to shout a warning to Cloud Chaser, as the maddened animal might be provoked into attacking. Yet, she knew she had to do something. Anything!

Macha noticed a tree nearby with well-positioned limbs. She snatched up several large rocks, ran toward the stealthy creature, shouted at it, and threw the rocks when it whirled and growled. Those blows enraged the coyote, and, as she hoped, it began to run in her direction with amazing speed. She darted to the tree and scrambled upward, attaining safety from its snapping jaws as it leapt up and down trying to grab her foot.

Chase, who had heard the commotion and reeled to check it out, flung down the canteen and hurried to retrieve his rifle. Soon, he took aim and fired, slaying the creature with his first and only shot. He ran to the tree, assured himself the animal was dead, and helped a trembling Macha to the ground. He hugged her tightly in relief, as it was apparent the coyote was rabid. He cupped her face between his hands and gazed into her dark-brown eyes. "Are you injured, my love?" he asked as his heart thudded wildly, for he knew how lethal and painful such a disease was.

"No, he did not bite or scratch me. I saw him sneaking up on you and knew that was the only way to save you. He is dead?"

"Yes. A madness lived within him, so I was forced to take his life to protect us and other creatures. See his wounded leg. A sick creature gave it to him from a bite. He did not know what he was doing. You were brave to challenge him. You showed great courage, cunning, and skills, as Dewdrops did long ago when she challenged the grizzly to save my brother. I am proud of you, my wife, and you are a perfect match for me in all ways."

Macha smiled in delight at his sincere praise and hugged him tightly. "I love you, Cloud Chaser, and could not bear to lose you."

"You have proven your feelings for me many times, Sunshine of my heart. Now, I must drag his body away from this area and cover it with rocks so no other creature will devour his flesh and spread his sickness. Return to our camp and wait for me there; I will come soon."

As they lay nestled together on their sleeping mat, feverish passions which were partly fanned by their brush with danger heated their naked flesh more than the colorful flames nearby. Its smoke escaped through narrow openings left between the enclosing hides thrown over the branches; yet, its pleasant intermingled spruce and pine scent wafted around them. Except for their swift and shallow breathing, occasional words, the crackling of the fire, and the muffled songs of a few nocturnal birds, it was quiet inside the small abode. The thick buffalo hide upon which they lay was soft and comfortable, and only a thin blanket covered them from shoulders to feet. There was something about being secluded from others and cocooned in the warm and cozy shelter which heightened their awareness of each other and made them feel even freer to express their love.

Chase's mouth feasted on Macha's, and hers did the same with his. Their tongues often danced together as each caressed and stroked the other's body, giving and receiving pleasure with each touch. Their spiritual bond seemed to grow stronger each time they made love, which thrilled and enchanted them beyond measure.

Chase used his hands and lips up and down her pliant form to arouse Macha to squirming need, and she happily did the same to her virile husband. Soon, they could restrain themselves no longer. Macha pulled Chase close, and as he entered her, she could not hold back a moan of delight. They moved together in passion's ancient rhythm.

Just before they climaxed within minutes of each other, Chase gazed into her glowing eyes and vowed, "Our Life-Circles will always be joined, my beloved Dawn, for they were entwined by the Creator. We are truly meshed as one. I love you more than any words can tell."

"As I love you, Cloud Chaser, my husband," she replied. As her mouth fused with his, she surrendered to another splendid consummation of their commitment to each other, one which immersed her in sheer ecstasy for breathtaking moments, then encased her in tranquil contentment.

Afterward, Chase cuddled her against his sated and serene body as he told himself how lucky he was to have her and his current existence; and he tried not to imagine how their lives could soon alter drastically.

After they reached the Red Shield encampment and Chase revealed his wife's awesome deed at Bear Butte, Rising Bear embraced her, took a feather from his chief's bonnet, and handed it to her with a smile. "You saved my second son's life and have earned this coup feather. I am proud of you, Dawn, and I am blessed with the two daughters who joined my family when they became mates of my sons. I pray War Eagle will find a wife as brave, cunning, and skilled as Dawn and Dewdrops are; and I pray Hanmani will find a husband when that season comes who is matched to her. Place this feather in a beaded rosette and wear it in honor of your coup."

"I will do so, my chief and second father, and I thank you for it."

After others had praised Macha and genial talk was shared, Chase asked, "Did any trouble strike while we were gone, Father?"

"It has been quiet and safe, my son, and I pray it will remain so," Rising Bear told him. "At the war council, others said they would send us word if danger neared their camps. Surely no word is a good sign."

"I hope that is true, Father. If Spotted Tail and those who believe as he does will remain in their winter villages, perhaps the Bluecoats' anger and fear will grow smaller and die during the cold season." For once, Chase prayed for heavy and deep snow to blanket the territory, as that should prevent the Army from leaving their forts and challenging any Lakota band.

As many weeks passed in peace, it appeared to Chase as if Rising Bear's evocation was being answered, as only occasional light snow had dusted the landscape. Even so, Nahemana warned the chief and his three sons that trouble was brewing elsewhere which eventually would involve them; yet, when and how, he did not know, as the Great Spirit had not revealed such things to him.

On what Chase reckoned to be about November twenty-second by the white man's calendar, his worst dread was realized when Nahemana's warnings came true when two Oglala braves arrived from Mahpialuta's camp.

After the chief, council, and warrior societies were gathered in the meeting lodge around midday, one brave divulged, "Red Cloud sent us to our ally, Rising Bear and the Red Shields. Six suns past, Spotted Tail and his Brules stole mules from Fort Kearny; his sister's son—Crazy Horse—rides with him. Ten suns past, Red Leaf—brother of Brave Bear who was slain by Grattan—and Spotted Tail and his followers attacked the rolling travois on the large trail between Fort Laramie and Fort Kearny. They took its animals, killed many white men, and stole what Whites call *mail* and *gold*."

A worried Rising Bear asked, "Did Red Cloud or any Oglalas ride with Spotted Tail and the Brules who yearn for war?"

"No, for Red Cloud chose at the great council to honor the Long Meadows Treaty until the Bluecoats break it and ride against all Lakotas. Before the fight between the Brules and Grattan, our band often hunted on the Laramie Plains and Platte River grasslands. We were camped near Fort Laramie on that dark day when Grattan and his Bluecoats were attacked and slain, but Red Cloud and our people did not strike back. We had no alliance with the Brules on that sun, so their battle did not involve us. When more attacks came from the Brules, Red Cloud told us we must leave that area to avoid trouble; only Old Smoke—our past chief—and a few elders remained nearby. To this sun no harm has come to them, for the Bluecoats do not fear an old man and others like him who are too weak to challenge them."

As Chase listened and observed, he remembered seeing Crazy Horse at the war council in late September and hearing about the young warrior's daring exploits and fierce hatred of the Whites. Like Chase, the brave, once named "Curly," had light skin and wavy medium-brown hair, and it was said that he was often mistaken for a white man or a half-breed. But those who had known his mother, Spotted Tail's sister, vowed the boy was hers by birth and swore his father was not one of the enemy, but a full-blooded Indian. Chase reasoned those claims must be accurate, since Crazy Horse would not be accepted so fully by the aggressive Brules if he were a half-breed.

The Oglala brave continued. "Red Cloud asks if the Red Shields still choose peace until we are all forced to fight."

"We think, feel, and speak as Red Cloud does," Rising Bear replied.

The second Oglala brave asked, "When war comes, will you ally with us against the Whites?"

Rising Bear responded, "We will do so."

"We ride now, but we will bring word when trouble strikes."

Wind Dancer took a deep breath and asked, "What action do the Bluecoats take against Spotted Tail and the Brules for their new deeds?"

"We do not know, for it is dangerous to scout at the forts."

Wind Dancer looked at his half-brother. "Cloud Chaser has scouted at Fort Laramie and can do so again if he is willing to go."

Chase nodded. "It is wise to learn the thoughts, feelings, and plans of such a powerful force, so I will do as Father asks."

"I will send my second son to the fort again," Rising Bear said. "After his return, I will send word of his findings to Red Cloud."

"That is good. We go now, and we will tell Red Cloud of your deed."

After the Oglalas left, Rising Bear asked, "Will you take companions with you for protection, for we do not know what perils you will meet along the trail from Crow and Whites? They can hide nearby while you scout."

His father's concern over his safety and survival warmed Chase's heart. It also was evident that Rising Bear believed he could achieve his goal for a second time, and that confidence gave him great pride. "I cannot take those who are the hunters and protectors for their families, and I need War Eagle to do such things for my wife while I am gone. I will take Bent Bow and Broken Lance with me. We will ride on the next rising sun, for we must seek the truth fast."

"So be it, my son, and may Wakantanka guide and guard you three."

When Chase went to his tepee to prepare supplies for the journey, he found his anxious wife awaiting him.

"Did they bring bad news, my husband?"

"Yes," Chase replied. As he related the entire matter to her, her gaze widened, then narrowed before she gasped in dismay.

"Why must you place yourself in peril again when the Bluecoats are riled against all Indians?" she asked in a quavering voice. "Is there not someone else who can go this time?"

Chase shook his head. "You know, Sunshine of my heart, I can pass as a white man and I am already known there, which makes it safest for me to go. We must learn how the Army will handle these latest events. It is my duty to help my people, and to help our allies."

"Such words are true," she admitted with reluctance as her heart drummed in trepidation. "Let me go with you, my husband. I will stay hidden nearby. I cannot bear being parted from you again for so long."

Chase cupped her face between his hands, gazed into her misty eyes, and asked, "Do you forget what you told me only this morning? You must not endanger yourself and the child you think you're carrying. War Eagle will guard you and hunt for you while I am gone. I will return as fast as I can, my love."

Fearing this new separation, Macha pleaded, "Please, my husband. I will be safe at your side, for your prowess is large."

Chase gathered her in his arms and stroked her back. "Even great prowess could not protect you and our child if we encountered many Crow, Pawnee, white men, or Blue-coats and they attacked us. It would be dangerous for you to ride swiftly to flee them. And it would be dangerous for me, as I would be distracted by fears for you and our blessing."

Macha took a deep breath and closed her eyes tightly for a moment. "You are right, my husband." She lifted her chin and looked at him. "Promise you will return to me," she implored.

Chase embraced her. "I will return to you, my cherished wife, for we are destined to grow old together. After my preparations are completed, I will show you in many ways how much I love and need you."

CHAPTER EIGHTEEN

As Macha watched her husband smile and wave before he rode away with Bent Bow and Broken Lance, she recalled the exquisite passion and enormous pleasure they had shared the night before. As promised, he had told and shown her how much he loved, desired, and needed her; and she had done the same for him. She had never even imagined those sensations and emotions could be so powerful and rewarding. And she knew that would not be true with any other mate.

Why, Macha fretted, did many seasons of peace have to end when he returned and why did he have to be the one to endanger himself in order to delay, according to the grim opinions of their leaders and allies, the inevitable war. Perhaps, she mused, that grave probability was why the Great Spirit had summoned Cloud Chaser home at that particular time, as he was needed for those tasks, and such events had enabled him to earn his way back into their band. If he had returned sooner, she reasoned, perhaps he would still be an outsider or would have been rejected and banished. She must believe the Creator knew best and carried out His plans in His own way and at His own pace.

Macha lay one hand over her abdomen and thought of the baby whom she suspected was growing there, and her heart warmed with joy and pride. She wondered if it would be a boy or a girl, what name it would carry, and what experiences it would confront during its lifetime. She prayed for her beloved's safe and swift return, and for a new and better peace to blanket their territory. If not—

"Why do you stand here in the cold and wind, Dawn, when you can see him no longer?" Hanmani joined her and teased. "Surely you will not plant yourself to this place until he returns."

Macha turned and smiled in amusement as she adjusted the buffalo hide wrap around her chilly shoulders. "One season, my good friend, you will understand such emotions and fears for the man you love. It almost feels as if he takes my heart and spirit with him."

"Do not worry, for my brother has much prowess and will return."

"That is so. Come to my tepee, for there is a large secret I will tell you," Macha hinted with a merry grin, knowing how pleased and excited Hanmani would be about her pregnancy. She also knew her best friend would not tell others until she was certain it was true. As soon as she knew for sure, she would reveal the news to her mother and Winona, as there was much those two women could teach her and there were many preparations to be made before that blessed event arrived.

Over a week later and far from the northern section of the Black Hills, Chase—attired in his old garments, hat, and boots—reined in his horse at the sutler's store at Fort Laramie. He was astonished and dismayed by the changes—the awesome progress—he viewed: many new quarters had been built, more than he had seen under construction during his last visit, which implied many more troops were expected. Several new and old cannons were positioned for fast and efficient use, and no doubt as warnings to would-be attackers.

After leaving his two companions at a safe and secluded distance to make camp and await him there, he had encountered a large patrol scouting the area closest to the military post. Upon arriving, he had seen many guards on duty, their weapons also at the ready. Other units practiced on the parade ground, and scattered small groups did their daily chores. Below the bluff, only a few tepees of "loafers" remained in sight, telling him some had either recovered their pride and returned to their bands or had been run off like unwanted scavengers or had moved to another fort. In another area, the conical dwellings of the past Brule chief Old Smoke and his elderly friends were situated amidst trees near the river. Since no settlers' wagons could be seen, he assumed none had gotten stranded there for the winter, which gave him a cunning idea to explain his presence.

Chase dismounted, secured his sorrel's reins near a water

trough, and entered the sutler's store. He noticed two soldiers strolling around and looking at items, men who only glanced at him and nodded. He walked to the wooden counter and smiled. "How are things going, Ben?"

The man looked up from the supply list he was tallying. "Chase Martin, isn't it?"

"That's right; glad you remember me. Been a while since I left. How have things been in these parts?"

"Business is pretty good since those new soldiers got assigned here. From what I was told, more's comin' next spring; that suits me just fine."

Chase returned the genial man's smile. "I guess it does. I imagine winter's a fairly slow period for you."

"Yep. I usually have to make real good durin' the other seasons to keep me in business. I'm hopin' it'll be better this year with these new boys here. Leastwise not as dull as the last two winters."

"There was a heap of excitement when I was here in September," Chase remarked in a casual tone. "Been having any more Indian trouble?"

"Yep, here and there, mostly raids by them Brules. Where you been and what you been up to? I thought you was long gone by now."

Chase faked a frown. "After I left, I rode along a few rivers north and west of here, but the pickings didn't look good and too many Indians are free-roaming these days. Trapping isn't good in these parts anymore; the creeks, rivers, and streams are about trapped out for prime pelts, at least enough of them to make my time and efforts worthwhile. It's also mighty dangerous out there alone with things going crazy. I called it quits and sold my traps down

Kearny way. I hung around there for a while trying to find odd jobs to see me through the winter, but not much was being offered. I figured I'd look up this way in case some settlers got stranded and needed to hire a scout and guard to help them."

"Haven't seen any wagons lately and don't know of anybody who needs a hired hand. I ain't busy enough to need one. So what's your plan now?"

After the two soldiers left together without making purchases, Chase quipped, "I surely don't want to join the Army, not when things are heating up so fast in this area. I'd like to keep my scalp a few years longer. If I lose any hair, I want Mother Nature to be to blame."

"Me, too," Ben concurred with a chuckle, "so I'm glad we've gotten so many reinforcements here, and I'll be even happier when those others arrive come spring or early summer."

"You think war's a sure bet?" Chase asked.

"From where I stand, it is, especially with Spotted Tail and his braves kickin' up a fuss every few weeks or so. Army can't look the other way, even if most of them boys don't want to go challengin' the Sioux Nation."

"You think Spotted Tail's still mad about that Grattan mix-up and Brave Bear's death? From what I heard, Grattan and his men fired first."

"That's what I heard, too, but it ain't what's bein' reported."

"What do you mean?" Chase asked. He watched the man glance toward the door to make certain they were alone, then lean closer to speak in a near-whisper.

"I heard some of the folks near the fight scene said the

Brules attacked first, just outright massacred those soldiers without provocation. Add them raids and attacks afterward, and the Indians are takin' full blame. I know what Private Cuddy said after he was rescued, afore he died, but I don't think that's what's been reported to Washington."

Chase realized that if what he was being told was accurate, the President and Secretary of War didn't know the truth about the Grattan incident and would consider the Lakotas as the aggressors.

"Did you hear what happened last month?" Ben asked.

"I know some Brules stole mules down Kearny way. Anything else?" Chase queried, seeking details on the second episode.

"Yep, they attacked a stage on her way here on the thirteenth. They took the mail and twenty thousand dollars in gold bullion and killed just about everybody aboard and the Army guards. Major Hoffman sent out a unit to try to track 'em and recover the mail and gold, but those boys returned empty-handed. If you know much about Indians, at least those high-rankin' warriors, if they don't want to be seen, you can't find hide nor hair of 'em. They know how to hide their trail so it'll look as if the ground swallowed 'em up. And you can bet if you do sight 'em, you best watch out for a trap. If you ask me, most of the boys here don't know half what those Indians do about fightin' and strategy. If we didn't have better weapons and if we don't outnumber 'em when war comes acallin', we're in deep trouble.

"I have to admit, Chase," Ben continued in a gruff tone, "I have to respect 'em in some ways, and I understand some of their problems and feelings. A man can't stay here long without learnin' at least a little about 'em, or he's blind and deaf. 'Course, my opinions don't matter none to the Army. Hoffman's already sent out another report on last month's trouble, but he says mail to and from Washington is slow as a snail this time of year. He don't expect any action to result before spring. Then, I'd bet my store, it'll blow in with a vengeance when they retaliate."

Chase returned to a dismaying point. "Why would any White witnesses lie about the Grattan fight? Don't they realize that'll only provoke war?"

"I imagine so, but how else can they get the Indians shoved out of the area? I would guess that'd please them settlers so they can enlarge their farms. Please some traders along the road, too. If the Indian trouble is solved, more settlers will move in or pass through, so that'll give them plenty of business without dealin' with the locals. Like you said, good trappin' days are gone and the buffalo herds are thinnin' out and they've been ordered not to raid enemies for horses and hides, so they don't have much left to trade with. Makes me wonder why they'd break the treaty and lose them annuity goods they'll be needin' something desperate soon."

"I guess it has to do with pride and freedom and a way of life they've practiced for hundreds, maybe thousands, of years," Chase tried to explain. "You know what most folks—Whites and Indians—think of the 'loafers,' so you can guess what the Indians must think and feel about having to depend on Whites for survival. Either way, Ben, it isn't a hopeful situation for them. It's a shame, but a lot of people on both sides are going to get injured and killed."

"You're right. I guess we'd both be feelin' like they are if we were in their place, about to lose everything and—" Ben halted and glanced at the door. "Looks like I got a few customers comin'. Did you want some supplies today afore I get busy?"

"Yep," Chase answered and told the owner what he supposedly needed. As Ben gathered his requests, Chase thought it was good men like the sutler and innocent women and children who made Chase hate what was bound to happen to them when the destructive hostilities swung into full force. If only there was something he could say or do to delay them for a long time, he brooded, knowing there was no way he could prevent the inescapable. *If there is a peaceful path to follow, Great Spirit, lead me to it and help me walk it to save many lives and much suffering for my father's and my mother's peoples.*

"Did you ask for writing paper and sealers?" Ben questioned.

The man's voice pulled Chase from his intense thoughts. He hadn't requested such items and wondered why the sutler made such a mistake. Then an idea leapt into his head, and he realized the Great Spirit had answered his prayer in haste and with cunning. "Sure do, Ben. I'd like to write some friends back in St. Louis to let them know where I am and how I'm doing. Thanks." *And thank you, Great Spirit, for Your guidance.*

After Chase obtained permission to bed down later in the Army stable, he strolled around the fort making observations and talking with soldiers to learn all he could about the military's preparations and future plans.

By the time he was resting on his sleeping roll beneath a

blanket and a dark new moon, Chase felt assured the Army wouldn't provoke a war with the Lakotas until its additional reinforcements and weapons arrived next spring, unless it was issued a challenge it could not ignore. That, Chase concluded, was a decision which seemingly rested on Spotted Tail's broad shoulders, as the Brule chief was the one who was initiating most incidents and arousing the soldiers and settlers against all Indians. Surely his band had retaliated enough to avenge Brave Bear's murder and Grattan's attack. Was there any way, Chase pondered, that he could persuade that chief to halt his raids and killings to allow matters to settle down for at least a while? Since Spotted Tail's nephew—Crazy Horse—looked as White or as mixed-blooded as he himself did, his own appearance shouldn't cause hatred and suspicion to rise in Spotted Tail against him. Chase viewed the situation as a two-pronged problem: he didn't know where the Brules were camped or if they were moving about to keep their location a mystery to the Army, and he doubted Spotted Tail would heed his pleas for cessation since the chief was obtaining great coups.

On Sunday, Chase took a course of action which could help avoid or at least delay trouble if he was believed and his advice was followed. He wrote long and detailed letters to the President and Secretary of War of the United States of America and to Major Hoffman. In those missives, he related the facts concerning the Grattan battle and urged them to check Private Cuddy's report on the incident and to speak with trustworthy men like Bordeau and other honest traders. He revealed the Brules' motivation for raiding the businesses where the annual annuities had been stored and had been refused to them, items to which the Indians felt they had a right. He explained that the thefts of the horses and mules and robbings of stages were viewed as payments for the losses of Indian lives and possessions during Grattan's attack. He disclosed facts about the White gang which had tried to frame Indians for their evil actions; there was an Army report at Fort Laramie detailing that. He related news of the whiskey and gun peddlers and gave the names and descriptions of those four men.

Chase explained the Lakota way of life, their beliefs in one Creator and in closely knit family circles, customs, tribal differences, ways they were dissimilar from their Indian enemies, reasons for past warfare with foes, dependence upon the buffalo and grasslands. Then he related the Government's demands upon all Indians and how White infringement had drastically changed things for them. He included the pernicious effects of diseases and whiskey which had been brought to this land, how they were cheated by fur traders, and the eventual annihilation of life-sustaining buffalo herds and other animals. He disclosed facts about the greed and fraud concerning the annuity goods, their inferior condition and inaccurate amounts, and how Indians were forced to line up for hours and practically beg to receive them.

Chase wrote further that most Lakota tribes wanted a peaceful relationship to continue but their warriors would fight if provoked. He urged them not to allow false beliefs and lies and rash behavior on the Brules' part to provoke a Great Dakota War that would result in many years of bloodshed and loss on both sides. He also urged the President and

Secretary of War not to send General Harney there with numerous troops and awesome weapons that would be taken as an intimidating threat; for once a challenge was given, it would be accepted by discontented warriors and then respected and influential chiefs who recently had voted for peace during a multitribal war council would be uncontrollably drawn into a deadly and costly conflict.

In fact—Chase warned—the entire Dakota Nation, which you call the Sioux, will unite and ride as one powerful and determined force against the Army and white settlers. If you truly want peace in this territory, make sincere and swift efforts to negotiate it, to understand the Indians whose lives and futures have been greatly disturbed and altered by the White encroachment, who have been disillusioned and angered by deceptions and insults. I cannot sign this letter for various reasons, but I swear all I have recorded here is true, and in most instances, verifiable through honest sources. I urge you not to take military action in this territory, or the blood of many people—Indian and White—will be upon your hands forever. Peace can be achieved if you offer the Indians an honorable and honest treaty and you hire trustworthy men to carry out its terms and oversee its provisions.

After he finished his arduous and draining task, Chase read the letters several times to make certain he had included everything he could think of in his plea for understanding, compassion, and peace. He closed his eyes and prayed, *That's all I can do, Great Spirit; the rest is in Your hands.*

On Monday, Chase waited until the stage arrived about noon and was ready to depart again within the hour before he handed two of the letters to the driver, who stuffed them into a large leather pouch with *U.S. Mail* branded on its flap. Soon, his missives would be on their three-and-a-half-day trip to Fort Kearny, then onward to two influential men in Washington. Now, all he could do was pray those messages would arrive safely and be heeded.

Chase waited until it was almost dawn before he evaded the guards and crept to Major Hoffman's quarters, eased open the door, and left a similar letter inside for the officer. Afterward, he returned to the stable, saddled his sorrel, mounted, and quietly left Fort Laramie, probably for the last time. Soon, he would join his two companions, and he would head for home and his beloved wife.

Despite the trouble which loomed ahead for his people and their allies, he was a lucky and blessed man to have a cozy home, a beautiful and wonderful wife, a child on the way, a special place in his family and people's lives, and to have been used by the Creator as a tool for making peace. Only six months ago, he hadn't even imagined such changes in his life. With a little more good fortune—no, Divine guidance—these dark clouds of possible war looming overhead would dissipate.

On the third day after leaving Fort Laramie, Chase and his friends encountered Tatanka Yotanka and five of his Hunkpapa Lakotas. Both small parties halted and greeted each other. Chase, whom Sitting Bull recalled from the war council, introduced Bent Bow and Broken Lance and identified them: son of war chief Blue Owl and son of Pretty Meadow, sister to Rising Bear. After Sitting Bull spoke the names of his followers, everyone dismounted to talk, rest, and eat together.

When questioned about their presence in the area during winter, Chase disclosed where he had been, what he had observed, and what he had done. He was elated and pleased that his ally gave him praise, and offered gratitude for his sharing of information.

"We rode to the joint camp of Spotted Tail and Red Leaf to urge them to cease their attacks on the Bluecoats and Whites, to let things settle down on both sides," Sitting Bull revealed, "for war is difficult during the cold season when food and tepees are lost. Spotted Tail agreed to hold off on more raids and slayings until spring, unless he is challenged. If what you saw and heard is true, that challenge will not come for many full moons. That is what I saw in my last vision and what sent me to speak with Spotted Tail and Red Leaf."

"It is good the Great Spirit sent you that message and our allies agreed to honor it," Chase said. He was glad he had changed into his Oglala garments in his friends' camp before their departure and that he spoke Lakota fluently, since he was recognized by the shaman who—to him and others—was a true visionary. There was an undeniable aura of mystical power, wisdom, and keen intelligence about the young chief. He was a great man, one to be respected and admired, one whose counsel should be taken, one who had contact with the Great Being, one who would be fiercely loyal to his people and allies, and one for the enemy to fear and elude. Chase felt honored that Sitting Bull remembered him and appeared to respect him. He was certain his father also would be pleased.

Following more talk and eating, the two groups parted and rode in different directions, with Chase eager to reach home and Macha.

Six days later and just before dark, Chase dismounted at his tepee to tether his horse and to let his wife know he was back. Though weary from riding for days, what he wanted and needed most was to spend private time with his wife. He beamed with joy and excitement and chuckled softly in amusement as she fussed at and fumbled with the flap lacings in eagerness to respond to his call to her, as many people were already enclosed in their dwellings at that hour. She finally untied them, shoved the stubborn barrier aside, ducked, and rushed to join him. Even if every Red Shield was watching, he could not resist clasping his arms around her body, lifting her slightly, and swinging her around as he embraced her. "I have missed you, Sunshine of my heart," he whispered into her ear, "and I am happy to be home again. My life is cold and empty without you around to warm and fill it."

Macha laughed and hugged him, surprised and elated by his public greeting. She did not care who saw them behaving in this romantic manner. She leaned back and looked into his glowing tawny eyes. "You are unharmed and alive. I give thanks to the Great Spirit for protecting you and returning you to me. What of your journey, my husband? Was it good?"

To protect his beloved from a chill, Chase kept his arms wrapped around her shoulders and held her close to his passion-inflamed body. "Yes, it was a victory, but I will reveal all things to you later. First, I must speak with Father, and with the council if he wishes. When I return, we will eat and rest on our mat, for it calls loudly to me."

Macha surmised his true meaning for "rest." She nodded her head and gazed at his handsome face once more to be certain she was not dreaming, that he was truly standing before her. She smiled and said, "Go and talk. I will be waiting for you to come to me soon."

Chase hugged her once more and left for his father's tepee, glancing back and smiling after taking only a few steps.

War Eagle, Bent Bow, and Broken Lance made their way around the sprawling village to summon the council, Shirt-Wearers, and society leaders to the meeting lodge. Wind Dancer went on ahead to build a fire in a shelter made of tall pines and covered with buffalo hides. He ignited two torches already planted in the ground to give sufficient light.

After the men were gathered around the large fire, Chase gave a full report on his findings, on his actions afterward, and on their encounter with Sitting Bull and the Hunkpapas—news which the society leaders would share with their members the next day, as the lodge was not large enough for all Red Shield men to crowd inside it.

The chief and council nodded and murmured approval of his deeds before the discussion of his disclosures. After all questions were asked and answered, it was the opinion of most present that a conflict would be escaped during winter, and some even thought that perhaps a new peace treaty might result from the actions of Chase and Sitting Bull.

"I am proud of you, my son," Rising Bear said. "You have done much for your people's safety and survival, as Wind Dancer and his companions did three circles of the seasons past."

"As it was in my sacred dream long ago at Long Meadows when we met to speak of the first treaty, he was returned to us to chase away dark clouds during these two seasons," Nahemana said. "What the sacred owl messenger told me has come to pass. It is good. On the next sun, Cloud Chaser must be honored with a feast and his many coups must be chanted, for he has become a great Red Shield warrior. At the feast, we must give thanks to Wakantanka for His many blessings and for Cloud Chaser's return to us many full moons past."

Once more, the others nodded and murmured agreement.

"My brothers and companions must sit and dance with me, Father, Grandfather," Chase announced, "for they helped me grasp victory and earn those coups: Wind Dancer, War Eagle, River's Edge, Swift Otter, Red Feather, Bent Bow, and Broken Lance. They, too, must be honored."

"Your heart is generous and your mind is wise, my grandson," Nahemana replied in an emotional voice. "It will be so."

After learning there had been no trouble during his long absence and listening to genial talk of past hunts and victorious exploits, Chase left the lodge when the crowd began to disperse. As he did so, he saw Two Feathers from the corner of his eye; his cousin had been included as a Sacred Bow Carrier, as had War Eagle and Swift Otter. Two

Feathers' expression and behavior remained guarded during the meeting, as Two Feathers wouldn't dare to say or do anything harmful against him when he was held in such high esteem by their people. But one day, Chase mused, he would have to challenge the embittered man for the truth, as such knowledge was the only way to settle the lingering conflict between them. At least for now, they had a cautious truce. As for Robin's death, it had been accepted as a tragic accident, and Chase admitted that could be true.

For now, the thing foremost in his mind was to hurry home and into the arms of his cherished wife.

Twelve days later Chase and Macha cuddled together in their tepee. The sturdy dwelling was cozy with a glowing blaze and their aroused passions to warm their naked bodies as they kissed and caressed each other. Extra wood was piled at the entrance and a buffalo hide lay nearby for use during the chill of the night.

Outside, the hard ground and black boulders were concealed by thick snow under a half-moon and countless stars. Creeks and streams were frozen, leaving animals and birds to drink from waters of swift-moving rivers or in places where hot springs kept water too warm to freeze. Red Shield horses were grazing in safety and comfort in a sheltered canyon. The area's creatures must now depend upon stored supplies and evergreens and unlucky prey to feed them. Some were hibernating, and others were snug in burrows, caves, crevices, or nests. Butterflies, seasonal birds, and other insects were gone, as were wildflowers. The big snows and frigid weather had finally come to the Lakota's territory and would no doubt last all winter, providing an impediment to Army and Indian enemy travels. Winter was a huge obstacle to war.

Those circumstances suited Chase and Macha just fine, especially at that glorious moment when all they knew and felt was centered around each other and the sensations flowing over them.

Chase was lying on his side against her, looking into her eyes as he said in a husky voice, "Your beauty is as large as the rainbow's. You are gentle and strong, brave and wise. You give me great pleasure on our sleeping mat, and joy and pride as big as the mountain beneath every sun. You calmed my restless spirit; you returned laughter and smiles to my lips. I could have no better wife or match than you. I am fulfilled at last, and you are truly the Sunshine which warms my heart and mind. I love you."

Macha lifted one hand to trail her fingertips leisurely over his strong jawline from ear to ear, pausing at the dent in his chin, then roaming upward to his prominent cheekbones, and finalizing her journey at his full lips. As she did so, she murmured, "Your looks steal my breath and cause my body to burn as wood in a fire. Your prowess with warrior skills is large. You have great strength and tenderness. You give me more happiness and pleasure than I imagined could be real. No matter where I am or what I do, joy and pride surge through me to be your mate. I could have no better husband or match than you. I, too, am fulfilled and blessed. I love you, Cloud Chaser, and will belong to you forever."

Their mouths met in a slow and tranquil kiss, which they savored for a while before surrendering to their growing hunger for more. With questing hands, they stroked and caressed each other to new heights of desire, joining at last to seek passion's summit, which they reached in blissful splendor.

As they lay wrapped in contentment's embrace, Chase realized, in the *wasicun* world, it was Christmas Day. He could not help but remember past holiday seasons with Tom and Lucy Martin in Oregon. They had been good and loving adoptive parents, despite their small flaws and weaknesses and—yes, in a way selfish—deception. But at the end, truth had prevailed; and it had sent him back to where he belonged. He thought about his mother and felt as if she were smiling down on him.

Tonight, instead of the differences, he thought about the similarities between most Whites and Indians, especially concerning their beliefs in one Creator, love for and loyalty to family and people, and the human emotions—love, hate, joy, sadness—which filled their hearts and controlled their actions. Although he had discarded all ties to the *wasicun* world, he still gave thanks for the birth of the White Creator's son long ago and asked for His help in the dark days ahead for both sides. Who better, he reasoned, than two— perhaps only one in different forms—Creators to bring true and lasting harmony to this land?

At least for many months, he hoped and believed, peace would be a reality. That and great love and happiness for him and his wife. By the end of next June, he and Macha would have a son to play with Tokapa or a daughter to play with Cikala, the child of Red Feather and Zitkala.

Yes, Chase concluded, he was where he belonged; he was part of his true family and people. As his father and shaman had said, he had helped rid this land of many dark clouds, though it remained to be seen how many more would drift across their sky in years to come. But he would not worry over what might be in the future, not when the present was so gratifying.

Chase glanced over at his beautiful sleeping wife who was still cuddled in his arms. He smiled and pressed a light kiss to her forehead without awakening her. They were destined to share their lives, the good and the bad times. What more, he mused, except for peace, could he ask for than this exquisite and rewarding Lakota Dawn at his side and all she had brought into his life and heart? Nothing.

Center Point Publishing
600 Brooks Road ● PO Box 1
Thorndike ME 04986-0001 USA

(207) 568-3717

US & Canada:
1 800 929-9108